THIS
RIVER
AWAKENS

STEVEN ERIKSON

A TOM DOHERTY ASSOCIATES BOOK / NEW YORK

This is a work of fiction. All of the characters, organizations, and events portrayed in this novel are either products of the author's imagination or are used fictitiously.

THIS RIVER AWAKENS

Copyright © 1998, 2012 by Steven Erikson

Previously published in the UK by Bantam Press, an imprint of Transworld Publishers.

All rights reserved.

A Tor Book
Published by Tom Doherty Associates, LLC
175 Fifth Avenue
New York, NY 10010

www.tor-forge.com

Tor® is a registered trademark of Tom Doherty Associates, LLC.

ISBN 978-0-7653-7023-5

Tor books may be purchased for educational, business, or promotional use. For information on bulk purchases, please contact Macmillan Corporate and Premium Sales Department at 1-800-221-7945, extension 5442, or write specialmarkets@macmillan.com.

First Tor Edition: July 2013
First Tor Mass Market Edition: July 2014

Printed in the United States of America

0 9 8 7 6 5 4 3 2 1

To the memory of May-Britt Lundin
for all the ships that never sailed

PART ONE

Four and Twenty Blackbirds

CHAPTER ONE

I

FLY!

Two crows returning. The years sweep past under their wings. The clouds scud like motes before their eyes. Roll away these years. It is too late, too late to stop their driven flight.

The past is uncertain. It is a place filled with wishing, with invention. To look back is to see what was begun. To go back, however, is to begin again.

I have been down to the river – stay with me. I have my reasons. The crows sat on a branch overhead. Even now, as then, the season is spring, and the young buds on the trees are clenched like fists. I have sent a gift from now, sent it into my past. It is not an easy gift. I don't believe in easy gifts.

And now the crows take flight, from now to then. Back and back. They wheel in their sudden freedom,

*and look below to a steaming city, and onwards to
where it stumbles to an end in low, evenly laid suburban homes, and along the river factories persist, squatting like dark fortresses on foreign soil. They glide over
farmland caged in by roads. In the fields the black
earth lies rippled like a brown and muddy cloak. Grey
and leafless windrows stitch the scene forlorn and
frayed.*

*Over here the air is cool. It tastes of the rendered
earth. The breeze spreads the season's quickening
breath across the world.*

*The crows swoop low over a farm. Their shadows
flit over a muddy field and then frame four boys walking, walking for the river.*

Long ago, now. What I have done is unfair.

Forgive me.

II

Memory begins with a stirring. Spring had arrived.
There was life in the air, in the wind that turned the
cold into currents of muddy warmth. And life in the
ground as well – a loosening of the earth and its secrets, a rustling of spirits and the awakening of the
dead.

Like remembrance itself, it was a time when things
rose to the surface. Forces pushed up from the tomb
of wintry darkness, shattering the river's ice and spreading the fissures wide. Sunlight seeped down, softening
the river bottom's gelid grip. And things were let go.

What I look on now, after all these years, is a place

of myth. For this was a place that told us that there was more than just one world. Middlecross sat between the farmlands and the city, grasping fragments of each, the first with sad mockery, the last with diffidence. A land of suburban homes and fallow fields. Along the river crouched patches of forest, slowly being peeled back. The new money fashioned flat bungalows with impeccable lawns while the old money rose in shadowed mansions. Between them, overgrown lots hid the rubble of past ruin.

The year was 1971. Middlecross was my family's last stop in our migration from the city, from the ever smaller apartments out to rural sprawl. It was part of a struggle we'd always known, against something faceless, and we'd had our share of last, desperate gasps. Outwardly, my family seemed plain enough: a father, a mother, a sister in her teens, me on the edge at twelve, and toddler twins. Outwardly, the world holds no secrets. That was my family.

I continued my schooling in the city, and would do so until term's end. Each day I made a bus trip between two worlds, one tired and heavy with a vague, confused air of familial failure, the other new, unlike anything I'd ever known before.

It was a time and place of discord. This much my memory tells me. But memory is not enough . . .

III

Hodgson Fisk had giant hands, the kind of hands that forced bent nails into wood, that twisted wire, that broke fragile presents; the kind of hands that made fists in pockets and curled around the arms of a chair like roots gripping rock.

His knuckles were bloodless, scarred white by a lifetime of closed doors and encroaching walls. The nails, chipped and stained amber, protected flattened fingertips that had long since gone numb.

His muscles were like taut ropes now, as he sat rocking in his chair on the porch like he usually did in the late spring afternoon, when the chill returning to the air reminded him of death. Beneath the sure grip of his hands, the chair's arms reassured him with their smooth, warm familiarity.

Fisk listened to the crunching, grinding ice in the river beyond the row of trees. He stared at the black mud of the field before him. Tufts of yellow grass dotted it like human heads. Squinting, he thought he could see them sinking.

Slowly, his rocking stilled. A long, narrow shadow had crawled imperceptibly across the unkempt lawn, and now – at last – it reached for him. There wasn't any need to look up, no need to find its source. Marking the boundary between the lawn and the field was the maypole. It rose fifteen feet high, a galvanised pipe pitted with rust, unadorned for the last eleven years, since his wife's death.

Once it had heralded spring's birth with gaily coloured ribbons, with stringed popcorn and tiny brass bells. And covering the earthen mound at its base, there'd be freshly painted flowers – white, yellow, red and violet – he'd never known their names, it never seemed to matter back then. Didn't matter now.

The maypole's shadow was like a spear, edging up the porch steps. And the earthen mound was tangled with dead weeds and shredded nylon still bearing the memories of colour. It had been his wife's maypole, his wife's celebration of the new season. But that, Fisk told himself, was a memory he didn't want to revive. For her, spring – the turning over of the season – had marked some kind of victory. For him, spring was the turning over of the earth – the black mud – and nothing more. More daylight meant more hours of work. That was all.

He hated spring. The season that Dorry had celebrated had also been the season of her death.

The shadow climbed the steps. Fisk resumed rocking, his boots skidding on the dusty gravel that covered the wood planks. As he rocked he let his head roll forward and snap back in time, until the hot blood in his skull seemed to swish back and forth, numbing his cheeks and mouth and ears. Only his eyes felt alive, fixed like buoys in the storm inside his head, fixed on the field of mud.

Odd, he knew, that a sense of urgency could hold him rooted to his chair. Waiting for the darkness demanded patience, and he was a patient man. He'd waited eleven years, and was still waiting. Nothing was going anywhere, he told himself. Not the maypole, not the storm in his head, not the field of mud. *None of us is going anywhere.*

Fisk watched the four boys trudge across his field in the growing dusk. Their presence didn't surprise him. It had been their ritual since the snows melted. They crossed his field with impunity. His dark eyes followed their vague shapes, tracking them, fixing their gestures, memorising their every movement.

It was something he'd come to, an idea that had both excited him and terrified him. The terror made sense. The excitement didn't.

Stacked high around him, crowding his porch, rose wood and wire boxes. Walls of long, narrow cages to his left and right, cages where the flowerpots used to be, cages blocking out the living-room window and its faded lilac curtains, cages jammed against the railing. Others around here grew wheat when they grew any- thing at all, but Fisk didn't – not any more. For the last ten years he had raised mink. Over six hundred animals lived with him now.

At night he'd often stand at his kitchen window with all the lights turned off, and his back yard would glow with hundreds of unblinking, yellow eyes. Eyes like imprisoned moonlight, watching him.

In the crepuscular air the field had grown smooth in front of Fisk, like a pool of oil. The four boys had reached its far edge, their grey shapes disappearing like wraiths between the ash trees lining the river. The field looked deep in a way that Fisk found disturbing. The muscles in his chest trembled, as if he'd brushed feelings that had long since sunk into oblivion. He didn't want to dredge up those feelings. It frightened him to stand at the edge, as he did now, and gaze at the dark surface of his life, seeing ripples as something moved beneath it.

He sat still a moment longer, then he lurched to his feet, turned and entered the house. The screen door banged behind him, its spring humming in the darkness. The hallway that led to the kitchen door was narrow, the hardwood floor creaking beneath him. He felt his hands tremble and slid them into his pockets. The faded flowers of the wallpaper marched by on either side, a dead garden, the leaves of a sealed book. In the closet beside the kitchen entrance he collected his work gloves and put them on. At the back door he flicked on the yard lamps. Cages rattled under the sudden blue-white glare. Fisk's breath quickened.

He opened the door and descended the flatboard steps. He approached the rows. Eyes flared as small bullet-heads turned in his direction. He sucked air through his teeth and entered the first row.

Something he'd come to. Terror, and pleasure.

'Four,' he muttered, scanning the cages, 'I want four of you.'

IV

We crossed the field that day as usual, on our way to the river, and I could feel Old Man Fisk watching us long before we came close enough to see him sitting on his porch. There was light enough to see his face and it seemed it was made of cracked plaster and chicken wire. Something evil and viciously small slunk behind it. Watching him sitting there amidst his cages, I imagined that he had gone to a place beyond death, and now stared out at us from that unearthly realm.

Fisk's field lay between us and the river. Our steps slowed as we crossed it, boots burdened with straw-laced clumps of mud that climbed up around our ankles. We carried some of that gritty clay to the river and watched it dissolve in the current pushing past our shins.

Beside me Lynk pointed. 'Look! A fuckin' cow!'

Two crows stood on its bloated flank, watching us and laughing.

We threw stones, trying to dislodge them. *Fly!* we screamed. Our arms ached as we tried harder and harder. Digging rocks out of the mud, following with eager eyes their curved flight, swearing as they fell short.

In minutes the current pulled the cow and its raucous passengers away. We remained on the dock, ankle-deep in flowing water. We felt the current wrapping the cold rubber of our boots around our shins. It made us feel invincible, time itself parting around our feet.

Four boys, nothing more. But it was our world and our time, when the earth loosed its secrets, staining our hands, our knees. The river birthed our cruel laughter, as it did our pensive silences. It carried pieces of the city half submerged past us, a barbaric pageant, a legion burdened with loot. Dead dogs and tree branches, tricycles frozen in bobbing ice, a water-filled wooden boat with pieces of dock still trailing from nylon ropes, a television casing – showing endless scenes of flooding – and small, bedraggled clumps of feather. The booty of a strange war.

The scene remains vivid in my mind. Four boys, aged twelve one and all. What lay before us was the river, remorseless like thought itself, in its season of madness, burdened with chunks of brown ice and cryptic messengers. The air that rose from it was cold, wet and overripe.

There was a Sunday school teacher in the city, a tall, beaked and pinched woman with sad, hopeful eyes. She'd once told me that the soul is like a bird, flying from your body when you pass on. I spent that day and many others imagining those birds, shining and white-winged and full of music. The spring, she'd said, was a time for rebirth, the final proof of proper things under God's Heaven.

But as I stood there on the bank of the swollen river, I thought about the crows riding the bloated cow. Middlecross wasn't the city. It was something else. A place where the bird souls linger, picking at what hasn't *passed on*. Wings not white, but black and greasy. Not music, but dark laughter.

Crows. They were my rivals. This place was the rotting underside of the world, decay a slow revelation of truths. My rivals, because I'd screamed *Fly!*

Crack! Lynk had found a stick, attacking trees as we walked. 'Just wait till summer,' he said. *Crack!* The sound shivered in the air – Lynk beating his demons into submission. Summer was everything, it was All. A future time to be unleashed into, like a dog with a snapped chain. Bounding into the unfolding world of heat, lightning storms, games of war. Lynk wasn't alive yet, but he would be come summer, his season of bright, painful light.

Maybe his trees had faces. *Crack!* Frowning faces impeding his impatient nature. He'd made his march relentless, but his words gave him away. 'Just wait till summer.' A thin, reedy call to distant power. A birth-cry of someone not yet alive, not yet here in the world. His carnivore grin was a pup's, incomplete but still a warning worth noticing. Lynk was coming alive, soon, only a matter of time.

Flush with the river's pageant glory we'd left the bank, pushing inland through the bracken. Lynk's stick spoke for all of us in one way or another. Grim and determined like soldiers looking for an enemy, we were marauders, hunters, giants. Fearless, on the edge of calculated rage.

A game, I told myself. The forest wrapped us tight, hid all signs of civilisation. It played along, sharpening the sounds of twigs snapping underfoot, filling our moments of silence with significance. The dusk caressed us as it filled the forest, seeming to call to us, to urge us towards an unseen and unknown goal. We would sweep aside armies and kings, we would level mountains, we would topple gods.

Like Lynk, I dreamed of summer. Unlike him, I didn't know what to expect, nor did I much care. The day that school was over, my last tie to the city went under the knife. Cut loose, withdrawing from the crowded streets, the steamy buses – what I anticipated was clear in my mind. What came afterwards was left to Lynk, or so it seemed, since the eagerness I felt came from him alone. He carried the stick, and ahead waited the throne of summer. He was full of ascendant visions, and neither Roland nor Carl seemed mindful of opposing him.

Such were my initial readings of these three friends, which I still held on to, despite what my careful eyes caught, were catching even now. Lynk talked, he filled the air with his claim to dominance – but it was all for me, a challenge and a warning. He was telling me where I stood, as subtly as if he'd jammed his boot on my throat. Lynk talked, but the power, I had come to realise, was in the silence.

'Old Man Fisk,' Lynk said. 'Piles up all the mink guts and burns them. He lets us watch. Me and Roland and Carl. Might let you, too.'

Small and wiry, Lynk was like one of Fisk's cages bent and twisted into human form. His blue eyes shone with an eerie, hungered look, cold, hard eyes pinning a narrow, long nose. Greasy brown hair hung to his shoulders. His teeth curved inward. He moved furtively, making me think of escaped animals, promising a wildness that made me fear his freedom.

Here, deep in the woods with the smell of decay heavy on all sides, small patches of snow persisted, crusty and stroked with black dirt. As we pushed deeper into the wood the air grew cooler. On all sides shadows reached down through the tangled branches like swords. The colours drifted into grey, making the world flat, compressed under our feet. Past floods had reached this far, I realised as I stepped over the weathered planks of a broken dock. Booty tossed aside, here to rot into the earth, here to become part of our world.

'Burning mink guts,' Lynk said breathlessly.

Walking behind me, Carl added, 'Burns all night!'

'Must stink like shit,' I said to Lynk, ignoring Carl as he stumbled in my wake.

Lynk shrugged, *a tough world for city kids, huh?*, then said, 'He soaks the pile in kerosene. Massive clouds of black smoke.'

I'd never smelled burning kerosene. I'd never even used the word, though I knew about it from school. But I nodded. It was harder thinking about mink guts, trying to picture them. Pale and pink like balloons, maybe, or yellow lumpy ropes. Soaked in kerosene. Black clouds all through the night. I wasn't even sure what a mink looked like.

Carl started talking behind me. His face floated into my mind, spittle gathering at the corners of his mouth. 'He piles on other stuff, Old Man Fisk. Bone and stuff. You can see the sparks for miles around, Owen. Fuckin' right, Lynk?'

'Fuckin' right.'

An unexpected confirmation from Lynk, making me curious. Lynk with his stick, talking, talking. Me keeping my mouth shut most of the time, just like that powerful, other silence. Lynk felt a need for allies. Carl wasn't much, but he was the only choice, already under Lynk's eager heel.

Crack!

'You gotta watch out for Old Man Fisk some-times,' Lynk said, raspy voice falling deeper, seeking a tone to match a real, adult threat. 'He's nuts. Once he threw rocks at me, big fuckin' rocks. I was cross-ing his field, just like we did today. Getting dark, and out he comes, tearing down the porch and screaming at me. Something about the bloody mud – that's what he was screaming. "The bloody mud!" Fuckin' nutso, man.'

Lynk whapped at a branch, then continued, 'I called him a shithead. That's when he started throwing rocks.'

'Fuckin' nutso,' Carl said.

I scowled. 'What are you, a parrot?'

Carl shut up. Breath loud as he stumbled through the brush, trying to keep up, not catch up. Unwelcome in the front line. Small and weak. His teeth were yellow, his words thick like he talked through a wall of spit. Lots of Carls in the world, a life in the shadows, at least one in every classroom. What did they become? Where did they go?

On that fine, treacherous path I walked, the New Kid path I'd walked a half-dozen times before – already a wise, cautious veteran – Carl had his place. I despised him, openly, a statement to Lynk – to every Lynk I'd met in every school, every new neighbourhood. An old hand, I was convinced that there were no mysteries left – not in this fragmented sliver of the world. The niche I needed to carve depended on Carl staying what he was.

And yet, a mystery remained: the source of the powerful silence that seemed to tolerate Lynk as a patron would a devious whelp. A silence generous enough to encompass Carl in its benign wake. Open to me without challenge, without even a question. Roland strode ahead. Big for a boy of twelve, with wide shoulders and flat hands that made me envious of farm life and hard work. When he broke his silences, the words came out slow and thoughtful. Even Lynk shut up and listened. We all did. We didn't feel there was any choice, and we didn't want one in any case.

We travelled through the woods, each on our own paths, ranging like wolves. But for all our tracks of independence, Roland led the way. My gaze returned to him again and again.

Crack! Lynk whirled to face me. 'Could you believe that fuckin' cow?'

Grinning, I shook my head.

Lynk laughed harshly, turned away. 'It was nothing, man. Happens all the time. You don't know a fuckin' thing, man.'

I held my grin. Never reveal when a point's scored.

Lynk gave me an odd look, a second too long – showing me his doubt – before whirling a swing at the closest tree.

We were all unbalanced. But I was more unbalanced than the others. This was their world, not yet mine. My weakness, a temporary condition I did my best to disguise – an easy, casual stride, bored expression, trying to see this new world with old eyes. A tightrope, the oblivion of a misstep was a place I'd lived in before – no, living wasn't the word – a child's hell. If my family's stumbling moves held anything positive for me – anything at all – it was the chance to start again, scarred but wiser.

Emerging from the forest we came to the first borderline. The outer lands belonged to Fisk and men like him – distant, aloof, dangerous – farmland broken by ragged windrows and the winding river. The inner land before us was marked by a loop of residential properties.

An asphalt road came down from the highway, dipping then flattening out and coming around to return to the highway, making a 'U' shape with the bottom running parallel to the river. All of the lots on the inside of the 'U' had gardens in their large back yards, one kept distinct from the other by thin walkways of grass or raspberry-bush hedgerows. Sheds stood like the bastions of forts, woodpiles like ramparts. The men who owned those houses worked in the city. Grey- and blue-suited, they drove in their Furies and Customs, a daily march to the weekends, when the suits were shed and old polyester pants and t-shirts were donned. All through their weekends they manned their forts and ramparts; a peaceful détente of friendly competition. Hoes borrowed, rakes loaned.

Many of these families had children, but they were mostly younger than us. A few were older, too. Both groups seemed ghostly to me.

There were the four of us. Only the four of us, at least at first.

In the summer, I learned from Lynk, those gardens became our no-man's-land. Like shadows we would move down the rows of plunder – the raspberries, Nansing cherries, apples and crab-apples. We'd raid, moving silent through the heavy acrid smoke of refuse heaps.

Ringing the 'U' were older lots, with their tall houses hidden by giant oaks and elms. The newer homes – the flat bungalows with the Furies and the Customs parked in the driveways – marked the loop's inside. No trees blocked these homes from sight for those walking the road. Nothing but grass, cropped once a week barring rain.

A playground ran outside the first line of the 'U'. It began at the bend and ended where the road started its steep climb to the highway level. Separating the hill and the playground was Louper's lot.

From the forest we entered the playground, appearing along its south edge. At the far end, we could see Mrs Louper standing beneath one of her crab-apple trees. The sound of barking dogs came from beyond her.

Lynk pointed in that direction with a slight jut of

his chin. 'Old Lady Louper's got the best fuckin' crab-apples around. When we raid those we got to be real careful, 'cause of the dogs. We can't get at her garden. The fuckin' dogs would get us for sure.'

It was the end of our journey. Lynk and Carl moved on up the road on their way home. Their fathers worked in the city. Roland's farm was on the other side of the highway. He nodded to me before jumping the ditch and making his way across the playground. The dogs at the Loupers' set off wild barking from somewhere behind the house.

I walked a short distance along the bottom road of the loop, then turned into a shadowed driveway that wound between tall elms. It was dinner-time, and I was home, and this was the last border.

V

Sten Louper's hand groped under the bed for the bottle, but it had rolled too far. The thought amused him. As a child he'd believed that monsters lived under his bed. Something he would grow out of, his father had said. Amusement. Here he was, fifty-three, and monsters still prowled in that thick darkness beneath him.

Father's bed. Sten had inherited it, along with the house, and the trees and the grass and this orgasmic come-on with booze, this love/hate thing he loved to hate, this gift of genetic susceptibility – or so went the latest theory. *A beauty, a fucking beauty. Don't blame me, fellas, it's right here in these genes, my Levi's chromosomes excusing my weakness, isn't that sweet.*

Never mind the monsters down there. They knew

him well. They shared his taste for rye. They stole from his bottle sometimes, when he and it had rolled too far.

His father had lied. Sten knew he should have recognised the look in the old man's ravaged face. He'd had his own monsters, the same ones, the ones that never went away, the ones that dragged him into death – *dead liver, by God, let him go quietly.* No genetic weakness back then. No, just a simple moral failing. Self-pity right into the pit and that's all she wrote.

Sten knew all this. Flowing through the dizzy currents in his head was a river of vomit, piss and rye and secretly delicious awareness. He contemplated getting up, but all his will had drained away – thank bugger God. Drunk, hating himself with sweet vengeance, hating his surrendering of control, loving those sour notes in his double-helix of mercy.

Nope, can't get up.

But he could think, his brain weaving through *Scientific American, National Geographic, Popular Science, Psychology Today,* weaving random pages and notes and details into lovely excuses. Thought never took much energy, never taxed his lead limbs, never revealed his loss of control. It came easy. So easy. Came, conjured, then left. But really going nowhere. He never tired of the travail. All so easy, a whirling spiral, follow it up and down, down and up, no end and no beginning.

A man's brain shouldn't leave him helpless. Nosiree. Shouldn't. Nope.

A game he played. A battle between sobriety and surrender, the outcome always the same. Posture, strut, fall flat on his face. It'd been three months without a drop. Desire stayed under the sheets, at night, a soft hand on his cock. For a time (part of the game) he'd filled himself with long days of hard work. Stoke the furnace of his brain – read, read, read – keeping the cold fear at bay. Hammer and nails to keep the hands busy. Clean living. Living cleanly, mimicking health.

A talent for acting: could fool even himself sometimes. Posturing like his own king, strutting like his own lover, falling flat on his face – like his own clown.

I'm only human, he whispered to himself. *I don't like pain. Who does? Reasons – okay, excuses. I'm only human.* He giggled, sending creaks through the bed, a coded message for the monsters, can't be cracked, no point trying.

Bringing him around, like always, to Kaja and her sons. His dogs, pure-bred German shepherds. His obsession, a thin veil hiding his deeper obsession – the one with violence, but save that for later. He could see Kaja's face, brown eyes accusing – it had to be accusing. Sten's fault. The new kennel unfinished, the run's side door unlocked, the stray dog crossing the playground.

Kaja and her three sons, now two. Max – the youngest – was in a green garbage bag three feet under ground, body crushed and twisted, lips drawn back in a frozen snarl.

The road killed dogs all the time. The tyres grabbed them, chewed them up, spat them out. Children cried, the faces of men grew dark and stern, women spoke of fate and became older and sadder.

It's the way of things, he told himself. The way. Roads and tyres and garbage bags – that's all there was in the end.

He struggled against a roar of laughter. That manly grief was a killer. Hollow words pretending wisdom, sod-cropper backwoods tic-below-the-eye bullshit.

He wiped wet streaks from his cheeks and pressed his knuckles against his eyelids. Swirls of colour spun, blushing outward and fading into blackness. He thought about going mad.

It shocked him, cleared his head. Madness, the monsters' cipher, his father's double-recessive crap-shoot.

No, not this time. Sten rolled on the bed and reached under it as far as he could until his fingers closed on the bottle's cold glass. Not this time. He rolled back, holding the bottle against his chest, his sight fixing on the ceiling.

'Look at all those cracks,' he mumbled. They radiated outward from the corner above him. Cracks, stained yellow as if by thinned blood. Or rye. His father's house, right? The walls, the floor, the ceiling, all reeked of that insane bastard. Wood and plaster playing the old game – swallowing histories, whole lives. Listen to the echo of the old man's screams, the smashing dishes and crashing furniture. And the smell, of course, the smell. Booze and blood, piss and tears. Bile and canine fear. And faintly, so very faintly, the sweet, bruised-flower smell of his mother.

He barely remembered her face. The pictures had gone into the attic years back. But he remembered skin that had been innocent, almost translucent; he remembered arms holding him tightly, smotheringly, shielding him from the violence. He remembered her bouts of crying, and, once, the crack of her ribs and the gasp torn from her lungs.

Stupid woman. Should've run, taken him and run.

His father's house. The angry, maddened god. And dogs, always dogs, filling the house, cowering and licking the old man's hands. Dogs who stared at his father's back with eyes hot with murder, the glare of starved wolves.

Young Sten had found a way to hide from it all. He'd built his own house, inside his head, where he lived and kept all the doors barred. Safe, and alone. And even now, twenty-eight years after the old bastard turned yellow and died, the house inside Sten's head remained. But it had changed, almost imperceptibly.

He told himself that he knew every inch of it, every corner, every hidden room. All the while fumbling for door handles, falling down stairs, running into walls. His house – and this was the most cherished secret he kept from himself – his house had become a stranger's house. Monsters under the bed, in the closets, in all the rooms where ruled the shadows. A wonderful secret, wonderfully bitter, like *Psychology Today*'s secession of free will.

'So,' he slurred to the cracks in the ceiling, 'is this all there is?' But the house in his head had no answer. He was alone, the furnace a bed of cold ashes, cold fear everywhere. Nothing to do but wait for the monsters to come clambering into the light, talons bared. He knew all their faces – easy to know – they were all the same. Guffaw.

He shivered in his father's bed, the bed now his own. Clutched the bottle, frowning as a sickly-sweet stench filled his nostrils. A stench that didn't come from the air around him, but from inside his head. That house he'd built, the secret fortress he'd called his own, now came to him with a smell that made his heart pound. The monsters edged closer, their breath washing over him – the breath of his house. Booze and blood. Piss and bile.

VI

Elouise Louper worked in her garden. Behind her the window to the bedroom was open and she could hear her husband crying. The sound filled her ears as she overturned the muddy earth and broke it up with her trowel.

There were steps to follow, she reminded herself. There were patterns to repeat over the years, as certain as the seasons themselves. Soon she would plant the seeds and if she could keep the pests away, she'd have enough tomatoes and peas and wax beans to last through the winter. And with the raspberries and cherries she'd make jam.

A gardener, she told herself, has to be patient.

As she worked, she thought of her husband dying. She thought of their daughter leaving home. She thought of living on, and on, immortal in her garden as the rest of the world slowly sank beneath the horizon. Watching the years pull at Sten's face and body made her aware of the days dying behind them.

If she could drag her husband out of his bed. Away from his endless bottles. If she could pull him into the light of day. He'd see things differently, she was certain. It was when he was living the past that things went poorly; when he was feeling the weight of all those nights behind him – behind them – that look would come into his eyes. Skittish, like someone hunted.

Trying to talk about it never helped. She'd given that up a long time ago. His drinking had become a subject the family walked around, skirting its treacherous edge, a pit to be avoided at all costs. Still, they all circled it like the planets circled the sun.

Without words, she was left with what her eyes told her. Watchfulness had become an exhausting necessity.

The promise had been there, though. She'd seen her husband fight off the alcohol, strive through the shaking hands and bouts of stomach cramps and vomiting. She'd watched him find his way through it all, come out cautiously on the other side. She'd been ready to take a step towards him, then.

With promise comes hope. A small bud at first, then expanding like a blossom under the warm spring sun. Elouise had tied hope and love together, a long time ago, and together they seemed to wax and wane with fated rhythm.

She should have known. Deep down, she believed in fate. It kept her from expecting too much, from hoping too greatly. Fate blunted the edge of disappointment. It made hope wry and tolerable like a child's frail belief. And she could now smile at herself for a lesson never learned, and the pain and sadness could be taken as just punishment. Punishment for the crime of hope. After all, she should have known better.

She heard Sten's drunken words drift out from the bedroom. *So*, he said, *is this all there is?*

Elouise's face set like stone. She climbed stiffly to

her feet and wiped her hands. Well, she said to herself, it's time to check the crab-apple trees.

Tomatoes, peas and wax beans. And jam, jam for the winter.

She remembered breakfasts years ago. Mornings full of bright, clean sunlit air; of sizzling ham and fresh orange juice. Mornings without the sour smell of vomit and alcohol, without the broken dishes of the night before littering the floor and crunching beneath their feet.

It was a sickness, of course. Still, to see it, to smell it, to feel its fists. And the way it soured every remembrance, stained every memory of better times, these seemed dreadful prices to have to pay.

Hands on her hips, Elouise surveyed the budding branches of the crab-apple trees. Last autumn's cutting back had done its job, she saw. It always helped to see what was coming and plan ahead.

VII

The machine had appeared in our driveway one morning as if conjured from the earth itself. It was massive, fully six feet high and five feet wide, weighing perhaps three thousand pounds. A cowl of raw, rust-pitted metal covered most of its inner mechanisms, except for what I took to be the machine's back end, where a giant geared wheel was mounted on the machine's flank, and seized gear chains emerged from the insides to hang like clotted braids of hair.

As I walked in from the road that day I saw that

the cowl had been raised. A tarp lay on the driveway beside the machine and on it tools were scattered like discarded weapons. My father emerged from the garage with a mallet in his hands.

I approached. The rust had turned Father's blue coveralls dusty red. He dropped the mallet on to the tarp then turned his attention to a wrench he had locked on to a bolt. He grasped it with both hands and pulled down with all his weight and strength. Metal shrieked. I watched my father's thin face redden, the vein on his temple throb beneath a few stray locks of iron-grey hair.

'Looks a hundred years old,' I said.

Father grunted.

I glanced about the yard. Changes had come to it since we'd arrived. Most of the puddles in front of the garage had disappeared. The few that remained were now slick with oil. Alongside the winding driveway metal junk studded the ground like otherworldly plants, glinting with sharp, dangerous edges. Most of the yard remained new and fresh. The trees lining the front of the lot blocked our view of the road. Our yard lay in shadows, like an underworld.

I headed to the porch, then stopped and turned back to the machine, watching Father work. Behind me I heard the clash of cutlery and dishes from the kitchen window. Mother was angry. Father had promised he would leave the junk behind, leave it all back in the city, or in his new gas station on the highway. But the machinery followed him, as if of its own accord, like migrating beasts. Every day when I came home there would be more of it, encroaching deeper into the yard, hanging from hooks in the double garage, lining the driveway the way some people lined driveways with painted rocks.

I hesitated, then approached Father and the machine again. Sweat stained the underarms of his coveralls, and more glittered on his high forehead. He grunted and wrenched and poured solvent over the seized bolt.

'What kind of machine is this?' I asked, as I had asked a dozen times since it had first appeared a week ago. Once again, I didn't get an answer.

He glanced over at me, his brow knotted. 'Hand me that mallet.' He took it and turned back to the machine. 'You shouldn't ever hammer a wrench, remember that.' He swung the mallet and the bolt screamed.

'Then why are you doing it?'

'It's stuck,' he grunted, pausing to wipe his forehead. 'Got to get it off.'

The screen door squealed behind me, and I heard my sister Debbie's voice, 'Mom says supper's ready.'

Father glanced up. 'It's stuck. Tell her I'll be there in a minute.' He began hammering again.

I swung around to find Debbie staring down at me, still framed by the doorway. She was sixteen but looked older, especially with the make-up – she never used much of it, just enough to make her look somehow older.

'What're you staring at?' she asked.

'Nothing.' I headed up the steps. 'Move, I want to get by.'

Instead she turned around and walked inside. I had to catch the door before it closed in my face.

VIII

Somewhere in the attic was a photo of six-year-old Jennifer Louper. Wearing a bright flowery dress with white laced sleeves, she stood beside a grand piano, like a violet at the edge of a dark forest. On her face was an innocent smile, and her deep green eyes held the colour of summer. In her hands she held, awkwardly, a framed certificate.

Jennifer's mother had written on the back of the photo the date and the title, which read *Jennifer's first award*.

The six-year-old girl stood in a pose of uncertainty, frozen by the camera, and by the silent nods and hushed predictions of the future – of concerts and standing ovations, of a child's innocence played for the world.

The picture lay amidst countless others in a closed trunk that had not been opened in years. Its colours were still sharp.

Elouise had proudly written *Jennifer's first award*, yet she remembered a hesitation, a slight bewilderment, and maybe something of fear. The talent had seemed to come from nowhere.

Jennifer herself had been born less than a year before Elouise's fortieth birthday. A miracle in and of itself; she had made Elouise question her belief in fate, and she had made Sten happy to be alive.

It was a memory Elouise still believed in, though time and events since had badly faded it. She and her husband had suddenly found their dull world brighter, its blurred lines sharpened to breathtaking detail.

The grand piano that was and had always been

no more than an heirloom dominating the dining room, now became something more, coaxed by a child's hands. With a kind of fevered purpose, Elouise and Sten somehow found the money for teachers, who arrived and left as better teachers took their place. Not long after that the young girl had been made to stand beside a piano with a certificate in her hands.

But all along, Elouise had suspected the truth of things eventually to emerge, a tarnishing of this faith in gifts no one had thought to ask for in the first place. It wasn't long before the world's real colours, faded and worn, took the place of bright pictures.

Some things, she concluded as she staked down the last of the chicken wire in her garden, were just too big to believe in.

West St John's school stood between the highway and the railway. It had been there when the grain fields covered this part of the land, when the farmhouses wore healthy paint and all the children had rural faces and rural hands. Built of Tyndal stone – a golden limestone crowded with fossils – it was blockish and small, an edifice of stability.

And like all country schools, it was a communal teaching ground sown with virtues and morals rooted deep in the land. It had stood in this immovable obsti-nacy for fifty years before the highway was widened and houses crept out from the city and urban children crept out from the houses. In this new age the changes forced on the small country school proved too much for it to bear, and so an addition was built by city plan-ners and city builders. The edifice sank into the shadow of a tall, square concrete temple at its side.

Jennifer Louper sat with her friends behind the school, facing the railway track and the open sky above it.

The four boys had just passed beyond their view, making for the highway and the river beyond it.

'Who was that new boy?' Barb asked. 'I've never seen him before.'

Jennifer studied her friend from under lowered lids. 'Watching boys now?'

'Well, no—'

'Don't bother,' Jennifer continued. 'At least not with them.' She sat cross-legged, her lower back against the wall. 'None of those guys,' she said as she slowly leaned forward and began squeezing the tobacco from her cigarette, 'even know where their dicks are.'

Sandy giggled, her face hidden by black bangs. She sat leaning forward on Jennifer's right, crushing marijuana leaves between her fingers.

'Could be Lynk's cousin or something,' Barb said. 'They sort of looked like each other.'

'I don't know.' Sandy looked up. 'The new guy's bigger.'

Jennifer paused and eyed Barb. 'Oh yeah? What size is his underwear?'

Barb shrieked a laugh. 'Yeah, Sandy, why don't you ask him?'

'Fuck off both of you.' Sandy whipped her head back, tossing the hair from her eyes, and looked away. Then she said in a low tone, 'I was talking to Roland yesterday. He said the new guy's name is Owen, and he's got an older sister. They moved into the Masters' old place.'

Barb sneered. 'Talking to Roland, huh?'

'Shut up, Barb,' Jennifer said quietly, studying Sandy's face. 'How old's this sister?'

'Sixteen.'

'Give me the grass.'

Sandy slid the flattened paper bag with its small mound of marijuana to Jennifer.

Everyone fell silent as Jennifer began refilling the cigarette tube. She knew Barb and Sandy were watching her every move, and she could feel their tension. Chicken shit sucks, she thought. 'This way you got a filter, so I don't have to hear you coughing your lungs out. We'll roll the next one.'

Barb asked in a hushed voice, 'We're gonna smoke two?'

'Sure, maybe three. Maybe four.'

'I don't know,' Sandy said. 'My throat still gets sore from cigarettes.'

Jennifer exchanged a glance with Barb at this admission, but neither said anything.

The match flared like the beginning of an occult ritual. Jennifer slowly lit the cigarette, pulling even but hard. She handed it to Sandy, then leaned back, waiting to feel the now familiar loosening of her senses. She tilted her head upward and gazed at the dull grey sky, but it was not dullness that she saw. Mists swirled up there, heavy with rain. The clouds, rolling towards the setting sun, would soon swallow fire and somewhere, far off beyond the horizon, the rain would fall hot and steaming, and its rhythm as it fell on the slick steel and concrete buildings of a city, as it filled the streets and rushed into the sewers and tumbled down into the dark underworld – the rhythm of all this – came to her as music.

Now thirteen, she hadn't played the piano in two years. There'd be no songs of innocence coming from her. That had been their dream, not hers. And yet, down deep in her own underworld, the music played on. A promise of power, a promise of thunder and lightning.

'Jennifer?'

She blinked, then, smiling, reached for the cigarette.

IX

We tried to ignore the empty chair at the end of the table, while the clanging from the driveway continued. Mother served the food stiffly, letting the plates clunk as she set them down.

I sat between the twins so they wouldn't fight, but the gesture had little meaning these days. Meals passed in silence, with the placing at the table's end unoccupied more often than not. Tanya and William ate without protest, methodically, their gazes rarely leaving their plates. To me, they didn't act like normal six-year-olds. Opposite me, Debbie spent most of her time casting surreptitious glances at Mother.

It was all hard to understand. Before I'd become used to that absence, I would try to think of things to say. Normal, meaningless words. No one ever picked up on my efforts, leaving me feeling stupid.

Just one more scene we'd brought with us from the city. Within this, the last border, little had changed. I think we all felt the disappointment – even Tanya and William, with their occasional squalls and tantrums that acted out what they couldn't say. While this vague sense of failure persisted, I nevertheless held on to a sense of optimism. Some things had changed.

We'd left the cramped apartments behind in the city. For the first time, we lived in a house, and it was ours. In the city our yearly changes of address had somehow made our lives private, isolated. We seemed to live like ghosts, slipping through places unnoticed.

I'd pictured in my imagination the new world we'd be entering. Scenes of back-yard barbecues, rakes borrowed and then returned with handshakes, laughing faces and greetings tossed across wooden fences, living rooms full of people – scenes tightly framed, complete in themselves. They filled my mind and created a longing for a familiarity I'd never known.

This was the world of people who lived in houses. A world where I wasn't embarrassed by the thought of inviting a school friend home to dinner, or the Saturday night hockey game on television. It was a world where we were the same as everyone else, not different.

In the first couple of weeks I waited with growing impatience for the first of the neighbours to arrive. Meeting Roland, Lynk and Carl was something I took for granted; they didn't count in my expectations. What I wanted was to see my parents find friends, to play out the roles naturally, to enter those scenes I had created in my mind.

I'd thought we had left our unbroken isolation from others behind – in the city, in those anonymous apartment suites. But it turned out that I was wrong, and it was slowly dawning on me that being poor had little to do with where you lived; that maybe, after all, being poor was a state of mind.

I still felt it, clinging to us like musty cobwebs. I had begun to believe we would never escape that feeling.

Surrounded by tall trees in a giant shadowed yard, this house seemed perfectly designed for my family. It stood alone, hidden, wrapped in a cocoon of privacy.

We ate in silence for a long five minutes, then Debbie rose from her chair. She glanced at Mother. 'I'll go call him again.'

Mother shook her head. 'He'll come when he can,' she said.

'But—'

Mother's eyes hardened. 'No. Your father is in a hurry to finish rebuilding that engine. We all have to be patient.'

Debbie sat down.

I nodded. 'He's working on a bolt right now. It shouldn't take much longer,' he said.

'Can't he at least take a break?' Debbie demanded, her face reddening.

'He'll come in when he's finished!'

'No more arguing,' Mother ordered in a low voice.

Tanya stood and pointed. 'Look,' she said, 'a furry thing.'

As one we turned. In the hallway near the front door, I saw a flash of movement.

'Good God.' Mother lurched up from her chair, sending it toppling backwards. 'A rat.'

Grey and round, the rat paused to look up at us, lifting one paw. I sat in my chair, staring at it. Its smooth fur looked soft, and its black eyes glistened like tiny marbles. Then it moved down the hall.

Her face pale, Mother jerked a step forward, then shouted: 'Jim! There's a rat!'

Outside, the clanging stopped. Then heavy boots thumped up the porch steps and the screen door flew open. Father stood in the doorway, seeming to fill it. In one hand was the mallet. His gaze fixed on something down the hallway, beyond our line of sight. Expressionless, he strode forward.

I leapt from my chair. Three fast steps carried me into the hallway. Near the basement door stood Father, his arm raised, the mallet high in the air above him. There was a sudden scampering at his feet, then the rat leapt past him, half climbing the wall as it ran. I froze. It had been so fat, it had looked so slow. Now it moved, and it was fast, coming straight down the hallway and darting past me before I could even react.

I whirled around just as Mother, still in the dining room, let out a scream.

Father wheeled and came lumbering towards me. Stepping to one side to let him pass, I said, 'In the dining room.'

Mother stood beside the dinner table. Up on their chairs, Tanya and William stared into the living room, their eyes wide and faces flushed. Debbie leaned against a wall, her arms crossed, her expression closed and her face white.

'It went into the living room, Jim,' Mother said, her voice taut. 'Under the couch.'

He pushed past her and entered the living room, walking slowly, the mallet ready in his hand.

When the rat made its dash across the centre of the floor, Father was ready. With a quickness that surprised me, he whirled and swung down. The floor shook, and then there was silence.

I gaped. A new colour had come to the living room,

startlingly bright. It stood out in tiny spots on the couch and the chairs, on the lampshade and the curtains. It spattered my father's forearms, his coveralls, his face.

The rat's mangled body twitched in the centre of the room, intestines lying pink and wet beside it. All on the new rug.

Behind me, Mother bolted for the kitchen, where she threw up in the sink.

'Yuck,' Debbie said.

I stared at Father until he looked at me. 'Where did all that blood come from?'

His answering grin was strange. He slowly straightened, the mallet hanging limp and glistening in his hand.

Debbie laughed. 'Where d'you think, dummy?'

I shook my head. There was too much of it. There had to be. It was just a rat. 'But it was just a rat. Rats don't have . . .'

Father walked past me, holding his arms out to either side. 'You'd be surprised,' he said as he walked into the kitchen.

I crouched down beside the rat. 'It's still alive,' I whispered.

Debbie glanced at it, then away. 'Nerves,' she said.

'No way. It's blinking at me.'

My sister came close, kneeling down. I heard her gasp. 'What's that coming out of its mouth?'

I bent closer. 'Huh?'

'That!' Debbie pointed. 'Crawling out of its mouth!'

'Oh, that's its tongue.'

Gagging, Debbie ran into the kitchen.

I looked back at the eyes, but they had already glazed over. The excitement I had felt now faded. I stared hard into those eyes, wondering what it would be like to watch the darkness closing in from all sides, and the light glittering inside dimming, winking fitfully, then vanishing. I felt like crying.

CHAPTER TWO

I

IT WAS SATURDAY, and the sun beat down with a force that made the ice flowing down the river crack and shatter like buried thunder. I left the house and strode the gloomy length of the driveway. The machinery squatting along the edges seemed almost threatening, as if the shadowy darkness had leaked from their blackened, seized insides.

I emerged into sunlight at the driveway's end. My three friends were waiting.

'You bring the tools?' I asked Roland.

He nodded, lifting an old tattered backpack.

'I brought a hammer,' Lynk said, stepping forward. He raised the tool and swung it through the air between us.

I scowled. 'What do we need a hammer for?'

He bared his teeth. 'In case it's all rusted up.'

'You never hammer seized bolts,' I said. 'Besides, they'd hear us for sure.'

Lynk's grin broadened. 'Maybe I'll bust some windows.'

'Let's go,' said Roland.

As we walked, I once again felt the urge to tell them about the rat. Again, however, something held me back. The rat hadn't been outside. It hadn't been in the garage. It had been in the house, and that made a difference. But it was more than that. I was afraid if I told the story I'd start crying. I still remembered vividly those black eyes, though they had changed, and now when I resurrected the scene I saw intelligence in them, an awareness. The creature, I was now convinced, had known the difference between life and death.

We continued down the road until it began its sharp bend back up to the highway. Branching off from the corner was a narrow paved track crowded on either side by gnarled oaks. It led to the grounds of the Yacht Club. We slipped into the track, which opened out after a dozen paces. The driveway divided here, turning to the right and forming a broad circle that ran up to the red-and-white house that was the club proper. Straight ahead, beyond the ringed road and beyond the gravel parking lot, lay the yards, our destination.

We crossed the gravel lot at a lithe run that took us over its milky-white puddles in soft bounds. Apart from the potholes, the lot was empty.

The Yacht Club's dry-docks and hangars waited like a graveyard. Reeking of rancid grease, its ground was mostly packed clay and crushed limestone, glittering with broken window panes and pieces of metal.

Here and there twisted yellow grass lay pasted to the ground like oily hair.

In three ragged rows the yachts stood high in their scaffolding like corpses laid out on pitched wooden pyres. The newer ones had locked doors and shaded windows. The old ones had been looted long ago.

Between the yards and the main house rose a screen of red-needled pine trees and rampant elm and dogwood thickets. There was a watchman who lived in a cottage just beyond the last of the boats. Once in the yards, we had only him to worry about. Roland said the old man's name was Gribbs, but I'd yet to see him. By late afternoon, and from our secret vantage point, we'd see a dim yellow light burning steadily behind the dusty window of the cottage, but he never seemed to venture outside.

Crows roosted in the tall oaks that ran in a line behind the hangars, cawing endlessly at the barn swallows flitting like bats around the gaping hangar doorways. We came to the first line of boats and stopped. Roland moved a few yards forward, slipping into the shadow of a huge yacht. He cautiously edged around the boat for a clear view of Gribbs's cottage, then he waved us forward.

I darted in front of Lynk. Heart thumping, I passed Roland. Thick rusted cables were stretched tight over the uneven ground. I stepped high to clear them. Rail tracks ran the length of the yards, all the way down into the river. Black-cowled winches flanked the rusty rails. I jumped the tracks and made my way between two hangars. The grey, riveted walls were high, blocking out most of the morning's light and leaving the air chill.

At the back of the buildings a narrow trail ran down the length of the yards. To my right the trunks of the oaks crowded close. Somewhere in the branches above me the crows still complained, clattering their way through the leafless maze like monkeys. Beyond the trees I could see the black mud of a ploughed field, and the dark grey fringe of a forest following the river's edge.

The sixth boat I came to was called *Mistress Flight*. It was old, the blue trim and white hull chipped and stained. Hadn't been in the water in years. A forgotten member of the rich men's fleet.

I laid my hand against its stern and gazed up at it, wondering who owned it, wondering why he'd left it here, neglected, like a dead dream.

'See anyone?' a voice beside me asked.

I glanced at Lynk, shook my head.

He pushed his long, dark hair away from his forehead. 'That was fucking stupid, Owen. Roland leads the way.' He had his hammer hanging in his belt. 'Gribbs might've seen you.'

'Nobody saw me.'

'How do you know? He might be calling the cops right now.'

'There's no phone line going to that shack,' I said.

'How do you know, asshole?' Lynk pushed past me and quickly climbed the scaffold's ribs.

I watched him scramble into the aft deck as Roland and Carl joined me.

'Anyone see you?' Roland asked.

'No.'

He grinned. 'You go next.'

This was our second visit to *Mistress Flight*. The

first time, a week past, we had boarded the boat on a whim, bored with our wanderings along the riverbank. Assailing the scaffolding and gaining the rail had made it seem like a capture, but I think now it was the other way around. Like us, *Mistress Flight* seemed lost here, a presence unremarked, a promise unheeded.

We'd claimed each other, then, and in this our second visit the four of us arrived with a mission. The idea had been mine, to make *Mistress Flight* ours, to merge something of our futures. I'd thought of a clubhouse, secret and forbidden – an idea to snare the imaginations of the others – but for some reason the image that rose in the back of my mind had nothing to do with a clubhouse. In fact, it had nothing to do with my friends. The image had been, inexplicably to me, that of my father's machine in the driveway.

I slipped over the rail and crouched on the aft deck. Roland and then Carl climbed aboard, Carl licking his lips and breathing heavily through his mouth. Lynk had gone ahead, down into the cabin. I moved to the narrow doorway and leaned into the cabin's dusty gloom. 'This place stinks,' I said over my shoulder to Roland. 'Smells rotten. Let's open the ports.'

Roland shrugged. 'Smells like my father's truck.'

'It's just old,' Lynk said, emerging from the forward cabin.

I unlatched the nearest port and opened the small round window. The hinges were stiff. 'We'll need to oil these,' I said.

We opened the rest of the cabin's ports, letting in the cool breeze.

'There's fuckin' beds up front,' Lynk said. He swung

to Carl. 'I'd love to see your old man try sleeping in one of those!'

Roland set his backpack down and loosened the flap. He rummaged inside and withdrew a crescent wrench and a screwdriver with extra bits in its hollow handle.

'I brought the soap and rags,' Carl said.

I stared at his yellow-coated grin. 'Why don't you use them on your teeth?' I pushed past him to return to the aft deck. Lynk's laugh rattled behind me. I reached down and lifted the hatches covering the big engine. 'If we clean this up and put in new plugs we might even get it started.' I went down on my knees beside the opening.

'What for?' Lynk asked, dropping down beside me. 'You plan to drive it over the ground and back into the river?' He sneered. 'We can throw confetti and cheer you on, and if the rich guys say so the cops will beat the shit out of you.'

Ignoring Carl's snort, I reached down into the engine hold and tested the spring on the carburettor. 'Yeah, right. If this boat's going to be our secret fort, it's gotta be in good shape. Besides, if we get caught we can show them all the good stuff we've done to it.' As I stared down into the dark hold, I thought of rats. 'You don't want to live in a dump, do you?'

Roland said, 'That's a good idea.' He looked at each of us and added in his usual measured pace, 'I mean, about showing them all the work we done. So maybe they wouldn't call the cops.'

'Hand me that wrench,' I said. I began removing the valve cover nuts.

Lynk said, 'How the fuck do you know what you're doing?'

'My dad is a professional mechanic, jerk. Remember? I've helped him lots of times.'

'Can you get parts?' Roland asked, pausing to look over at Gribbs's cabin, which was just visible behind another yacht.

'Maybe.' With a grunt I lifted one of the valve covers. 'Look at that!' Everyone bent close. 'No rust! Still got oil in it, that's fucking great.'

The others cleaned the cabin while I continued working on the engine. Bringing it back from the dead. They'd probably thank us if they ever found out. I made a list in my head of what I'd need: new gaskets, plugs, oil, a battery. As I worked I saw the oil staining my hands and forearms. *Perfect. Just like Dad, and I'll have to use that jelly soap to clean up, only I'll have to do that in the garage, before anyone sees me.*

'Wait till school's over,' Lynk said from the cabin. 'Then we'll have tons of time. Sand these cupboards, get some marine paint.'

I smiled to myself.

II

The old tea kettle whistled a song of steam. Walter Gribbs rose from his chair and crossed the musty dimness of the room. The nightmares of the previous night remained only as the faintest residue in his mind. Now, the sunlight's warmth coming in through the cabin's single window suffused him, soothing his bones, calming his thoughts.

The black iron stove filled one corner of the room. The kitchen counter consisted of three warped six-by-two boards; a single shelf above it held his metal plates and cutlery. The sink was a galvanised washtub with a hole punched through its bottom, a rubber hose providing drainage to a sinkhole under the outhouse. His food came from cans, since he had no refrigerator. His furniture consisted of a narrow cot with squeaking springs, a wooden Coca-Cola box for a table where he ate and played Solitaire, two kerosene lanterns, and an adjustable russet-brown easy chair.

It was enough. Most of the time Gribbs believed in his own contentment. They'd put him here to watch the yards, and he'd been doing just that for twenty years. His grocery lists were always filled and there was a bank account in his name. When the time came to launch the yachts or haul them up, he showed his employers a benign smile and they were pleased at just how contented he was.

He placed two used tea bags into a chipped ceramic pot, then poured water from the kettle. The air was tinted grey with woodsmoke, stinging his eyes. He would have to do something about the stovepipe. He placed the teapot and a chipped china cup on the old STP Oil sign he used for a tray. He carried the tray back to his chair, set it down on the table and then resumed his seat.

The window fronting the shack was on his left: he faced the wall, which was covered with calendars. The most recent year was 1962. Some went back to the thirties. All the photographs and illustrations were of sailing ships, and he knew their every line.

Walter poured the tea. He raised the cup to his lips,

blew gently, then sipped once and set the cup back down. He squinted at the ships on the wall, trying to clear the blur from his gaze. It was that damned smoke, he told himself, that made things so hard to see. He would have to do something about that. For now, he simply moved his chair closer to the wall.

For a moment he thought he heard voices outside. He listened, but there was nothing but the cawing of crows from the garbage dump. Walter leaned back and rubbed his large, veined nose, then sighed.

They had put him here to watch the yards. *To mark the waxing tide grow, wave by wave.* He smiled as the lines rolled through his thoughts. But that wasn't why he stayed. He had his own reasons. While he knew and loved every yacht that wintered in his dry-docks, it had become a difficult thing to watch over them. Years of neglect had led to years of decay for some of the old boats. Some, like *Mistress Flight,* hadn't been in the water for years. Watching meant seeing, and seeing meant feeling. That's what made it difficult, these twenty years of standing guard. No, it wasn't a sense of loyalty that kept him here. Nothing so noble.

Still and all, he mused, sipping his tea, not all beached whales die. To see the grand old yachts returning to the river each spring, to see them proudly ply the swirling currents on their way to the lake fifteen miles to the north – such moments were a true salute to those boats left behind.

Walter listened to the ice marching in disordered ranks down the river. The wall in front of him dimmed and blurred; it seemed that clouds filled the room now, obscuring everything, drawing darkness in from the edges. He shook his head, muttering.

Seventy-three years is a long life, he told himself. And most of those years had been hard ones, days of struggle, nights of restless undefined yearnings. Wave by wave, a ceaseless weariness. But a storm was building, somewhere ahead, some time in the future, and it was not a natural storm. The cracking of the ice was only the beginning. There were the nightmares that came night after night, leaving him feeling battered and somehow twisted inside his body upon awakening. He found it hard to recall the details; he knew only their aftermath in the chill mornings when he curled tight beneath his woollen blankets, waiting for the sun to dispel the night's wintry air.

Walter let out a slow breath, wiped at his eyes. 'The tide grows,' he said to the wall in front of him, 'and I'm still waiting.' He closed his eyes, swung his face to the window and let the sunlight warm it. 'Where are you, my lady?' he whispered. 'I need to talk to someone, you understand. And it's always been you. So, where are you?'

III

Inland, the boat yards came to an end with a ragged windbreak and the Yacht Club's garbage dump. The blackened mound of kitchen refuse and soot-stained broken machinery smudged my view of the tree trunks beyond. Oily smoke rose from the dump continuously, as if its fires were fuelled by the earth itself.

The mound disturbed me, conjured frightening images in my mind. It might have been a boat once, burned on its pyre in some unholy rite. Among the garbage were beams of wood, black and dusted grey with ash. Some rose from the heap, curving like ribs.

'Hey, Owen! What the fuck are you doing?'

The voice – Lynk's – came from below. I realised that I had stopped halfway through the forward hatch. The prow of *Mistress Flight* was pointed at the garbage dump.

'Want somebody to see you, man?'

I felt a push from below, and began climbing down. The boat lurched. I careened to one side, hitting my ribs against the hatch edge. 'Christ!' I gasped. 'What the fuck?'

Lynk pulled me back down into the cabin. In the shadows his eyes looked slick. 'Just Roland,' he said. 'He slipped.'

Behind Lynk, Carl and Roland crouched low on the aft deck, both looking panicky.

I swore again, then drew a deep breath. The boat's motion had been forward, as if *Mistress Flight* had come alive, as if it had set a course for the dump's smouldering mound.

I pushed past Lynk, leaving the cabin, and went to the port side.

'I don't think anybody heard,' I said quietly, looking out over the yards.

'Maybe we should go,' Carl said.

I sneered at him. 'Scared?'

Mouth hanging open, Carl shook his head. But his eyes were wide.

'Maybe Gribbs is calling the cops right now,' I pressed, grinning. 'They're probably on their way. What would we do? Run in every direction, right? But what about you, Carl? Can you run fast? You'll have to.'

His eyes were filling with tears, but he didn't move from his crouch in Roland's shadow. Glancing at the faces of Lynk and Roland, I saw frozen expressions and felt within me an eager flush.

'Well, Carl?' I asked in a hushed voice. 'What'll you do when they catch you? Give them our names?' Tears rolled down his face, but again he shook his head. 'They'll call your dad to come get you. What'll he do—'

Carl lunged, fists swinging. I caught a single, momentary flash of his face – the spit in the corner of his mouth spinning away as if on a thread – and then he was on me. We fell back, rolling down the three steps to the cabin deck. Fists pounded against my chest. A finger clawed across my jaw.

He was small. He was weak. Even enraged he struck poorly, and it was only moments before I had both of his wrists in my hands, pulling him to one side then pushing him down and straddling him. I grinned, gripping harder to still his wild thrashing, but I couldn't think of anything to say. The shock was fading, and in its place came a wave of panic. I didn't know what to do next, so I just held him until he stopped struggling. We were both gasping. I stared at the tears that streaked dirty trails from his eyes.

I'd been cruel. The realisation made me hate Carl all the more. I raised my right hand, closing it into a fist.

'No,' Roland said behind me.

He knelt at the top of the steps, his broad face – half in shadow – staring down at me. I hesitated, then laughed and moved off Carl.

Carl scrambled to his feet, pushed past Roland and rushed to the starboard rail. He disappeared over the edge.

Roland said, 'You shouldn't have done that.'

I studied his face, the steady gaze, the heavy frown.

'You shouldn't have said anything about his dad,' Roland admonished in his quiet, measured voice.

I straightened my shirt, then looked away.

Lynk was at the rail. 'Aw, fuck,' he muttered. 'He's run off into the brush.' He turned and exchanged a look with Roland. Whatever it was that passed between them made me feel empty inside.

My voice cracked when I said, 'He's run off?'

Lynk shrugged, a loose jumping of his narrow shoulders. 'That's what I said, isn't it?'

I rose. 'Well,' I said quietly, 'let's go find him, then.'

Roland rubbed the back of his neck, a slow, strained gesture. Then he nodded.

In silence we pushed our way through the brush. Every now and then the river appeared in patches through the trees off to our right, its islands of ice keeping pace.

This was my first time downriver from the Yacht Club. The forest was deeper here, wilder. At times we skirted its edge; muddy fields stretched away on our left, broken only by section roads and narrow windrows. We had passed beyond the influences of the city. Here, the flat country was motionless, as if waiting for something.

Roland led us, sure and confident, as if he knew where Carl had fled. I thought to ask him but I couldn't break the silence. My thoughts ran in a jumble, pieces and fragments caught in a swirling current.

From the forest's edge we entered a trail leading back to the river. Thin, clawed branches wove a net four feet above the path. Hunched over, we broke

into a loping jog – half human, half something else, I
imagined as I focused on Lynk's back a few feet in
front of me.

Carl sat on a log at the river's edge, his back to us,
a muddy stick in his hands with its end reaching down
into the red-brown water. The log under him was
gnawed blunt at one end; the other end disappeared
under a mound of intertwined branches and dead saplings. It was a moment before I recognised the hump
of sticks: a beaver lodge.

Roland slowly strode forward, stepping over the
log and sitting down beside Carl. He began speaking
to him in a low tone. I made a move to join them but
Lynk gripped my arm and pulled me back. I twisted
his hand from my arm and swung to study the beaver
lodge. Most of it was under water, but the flood had
been higher; tangled swamp-grass and mud hung in
clumps from the highest sticks in the mound. I wondered if beavers could drown.

I moved closer and tried to pull a branch from the
knotted pile. After a moment I stopped. 'Any beavers
left here?' I asked Lynk, who'd followed behind me.

He shrugged. 'Sure. Probably hibernating or something.'

There was no wind. The air smelled faintly of
smoke, reminding me of bus exhaust. Looking down
on the lodge, I wondered at the sudden reverence I felt
for it, and for the animals inside. Still asleep, while the
world melted around them, thick-furred and curled
up and lying in the warm darkness, huddled together
beneath the season that buried their home in snow.
Waiting, easily waiting.

'Everything's waiting,' I said.

'What?'

I gazed at Lynk, met eyes that might have been a mirror of mine when I had baited Carl. I scowled against a sudden chill in the pit of my stomach. *We're all waiting*.

After a few moments, Lynk turned away. He crouched down and scooped up a handful of mud. He rolled it into a ball.

Roland and Carl were standing now, looking out over the river. On the far bank squatted a factory of some kind. Towering smokestacks bled greasy smoke that drifted down over the river.

'What kind of place is that?'

Lynk said, 'Oil refinery.'

The smoke I'd smelled earlier had come from there – the bus exhaust that for me was the city. Finding it out here was disappointing. The factory was an intruder, crouching there in its own foul breath.

Carl had left his stick standing upright in the mud at the water's edge. Its dull grey shaft threw a worm-like shadow up the bank; already the current had wrapped swamp-grass around it. Slowly, the stick toppled.

'What're we waiting for?' I asked, the words coming out harsh.

The look I turned on Roland must have been a glare, but he only ran one of his thick hands through his straw-coloured hair. 'Nothing,' he said.

I nodded sharply, his answer striking me as profound.

Lynk threw his mud ball into the river. 'Wait till summer,' he grinned. 'I'll bring my pellet rifle out here and we'll shoot beavers. Hah! Fuckin' drill them!'

'Leave them alone,' I said.

His grin got wider.

'We'll shoot at the yachts,' I continued, 'unless you're chicken shit, Lynk.'

Another jump of Lynk's shoulders was his only immediate reply.

'We'd get in trouble,' Roland said, frowning at me.

'Hey,' I laughed. 'What're they going to do, beach their yachts and chase us on foot? Forget it.'

'Fuckin' right I'll shoot the pricks,' Lynk said, clearing his throat and spitting.

We swung away from the river and made our way inland once again. 'Let's head over to the school,' Roland said. 'You ain't seen it yet close up, right, Owen?'

Lynk laughed. 'I know why you want to go there, Roland.' He turned to me. 'Jennifer and her friends usually hang out there, smoking cigarettes.' He raised his hands as if cupping breasts. 'Sandy'll be there, right, Roland?'

The farmboy just smiled and pushed ahead of us on the trail.

'Who's Sandy?' I asked.

Lynk nodded at Roland's back. 'He's in love with her.'

Roland drawled, 'In the bag, Lynk.'

'Hah!'

'Up your ass.'

Lynk and I shared a grin, even though inside I struggled against a surge of envy. For a brief moment I hated Roland. For his height, his looks. Then the feeling faded, leaving me with nothing but a fierce, desperate yearning.

Carl walked behind us. He hadn't said a word since we'd left the river. I ignored him, though the scene in the boat cycled through my mind, shifting from comical to macabre then back again as I replayed it in detail – the rage on Carl's face, the spinning thread of spit, the large, thick yellow teeth bared by lips pulled back. It was as if Carl had cast off a mask, revealed his true self. A creature springing from its corner, lashing out with weakly thrown fists and blunt fangs.

We came to the boat yards once again, passing between two hangars and then crossing the rail tracks. Grey smoke rose from Gribbs's soot-stained aluminium chimney and the curtains had been pulled back. As we passed in front of the small house, I tried to look through the dusty, cracked glass. But all I saw was my own reflection: an intense face beneath tangled brown hair, eyes the colour of deep ice, an expression drawn and serious. It was a face I barely recognised, as if a sudden strangeness had come to it. I quickly looked away.

In the air hung the smell of woodsmoke and burnt garbage. The afternoon sun was losing its heat, and the shadows seemed confused and uncertain, as if with the fleeing warmth all meaning, all sense of purpose, had fled as well.

The small winding driveway took us away from the Yacht Club and brought us to the lower right-hand corner of the 'U' road. We walked up the narrow asphalt street, stepping around the puddled potholes. The road climbed the hill; from the summit we could see, and hear, the highway. Beyond it was the school.

'Jennifer's got big tits,' Lynk said to me. 'Maybe she'll show them to us.'

'You wish,' I said.

'How the fuck would you know, Owen?' Lynk demanded. 'You don't know Jennifer. You don't know anybody.'

I thought of the face looking back at me in the window pane, and for some reason I thought of the animals sleeping inside their mound of sticks. 'Soon,' I said to Lynk.

IV

The cellar, long, dark and low, smelled of madness. Fisk hesitated at the top of the stairs, staring down at his own shadow running the length of the worn steps – it ended at the shoulders, the shadow of his head lost in the cellar's own gloom.

His hands twisted around the cattle prod's shaft. He sucked a breath in between his teeth, then reached up and flicked on the light. Skittering sounds – claws and metal – came from below. *A dance? A dance for me?* 'I'm coming, don't be impatient now.' His words felt thick in his mouth.

He'd bought the cattle prod years ago, for no special reason. It was too messy for killing mink, and besides, its electrical charge burned the fur. Sometimes he carried it around like a baton. Sometimes he called it his own, special maypole.

But now, with the selection of his four pets, the prod had found a new function, one more suited to its original purpose – excitement tightened his throat at the thought. He paused at the foot of the stairs and let his gaze travel down the cellar's length. To the right ran a long workbench, cluttered with mason jars and rusting garden tools. Along the left wall, on a second

workbench, waited four cages. He'd named his new
friends: Moon, Rat, Gold and Bruise.

'Hello, kids,' Fisk said as he stepped forward. At his
words the panicked skittering from the cages stopped.
The only sound left was Fisk's own raspy breath, which
began to quicken. 'Yeah, it's me. Just me.'

He walked up to the first cage, where Bruise crouched
against the back wall. Fisk peered inside. 'Well, you've
stopped dancing. Shame. Your friends look up to you,
you know.' He ran one hand down the length of the
cattle prod until he found the switch. 'The least you
can do is sing for me.' He set the switch, pushed the
prod through the wire, taking care not to touch it with
the charged tip. 'Here we go, Bruise.' Fisk stabbed the
prod into the mink, pinning it against the wall.

The animal's scream was shrill. In the dim light Fisk
saw Bruise's mouth stretch wide open. Then it leapt
high, rebounding off the cage's ceiling. It stilled, lying
huddled along one wall – stilled, he saw, except for the
twitching, the jumping limbs, the snapping jaws.

The convulsions lasted for a few minutes, after
which Bruise crawled away from the piss and shit it
had spilled.

Fisk let out a long breath. 'Not dead. Good.' He
withdrew the cattle prod. 'Now you know, don't you,
Bruise. No one mocks me. Tell that to your friends.'

He climbed the steps; at the top he turned off the
light and strode into the hallway. *A dead garden,
pressed between the leaves* . . . He shut the door behind him.

As the sounds of Fisk trailed away, the mink in the
third cage scampered forward and resumed gnawing
at the wires of the latch. Its mouth was bloody. More

blood stained the wires. The animal worked freneti-
cally, unceasingly.

The living room had gone grey. Fisk checked the lamps
to make sure that no bulbs had blown. Frowning, he
shook his head, walked over to the sofa and lay down.

He felt hot and itchy. The beat of his heart was loud
in his head. 'Christ,' he muttered. He had an erection.
He'd felt its beginnings down in the cellar, though at
first he couldn't believe it was happening. After all, it'd
been eleven years.

But there it was, a pressure both familiar and alien.
In his mind Fisk resurrected the image of Dorry's face,
decades stripped from it, eyes bright and young, soft
lips slightly parted, her halo of blonde hair touched by
the sun.

The erection died. 'Goddamn,' Fisk moaned, rolling
over on to his stomach. He stared down at the carpet:
dingy green, worn down to the stiff weave in places.
Slowly, almost lazily, his eyes travelled up the leg of the
low, long table, and came to rest on the cattle prod.

Replaying the events of the cellar in his mind, he felt
once again the mounting pressure in his loins. With it
came a savage excitement, fraught with perversion and
sin, which only seemed to make it more pleasurable,
more visceral.

'Bloody goddamn,' he whispered.

V

Jennifer lit a cigarette once her mother had cleared the
dinner dishes from the table. She felt her father's bleary

eyes on her as she flicked ash into the ashtray. She took a deep drag, slowly exhaled, then swung a sweet smile on her father.

Sten said nothing. His hands were wrapped tightly around a coffee cup; his blotchy face held an unreadable expression. She smelled the alcohol exuding from him, and wondered at the cold absence of feeling within her. Of course, he'd been drinking for years. Even disgust goes numb sooner or later. She remembered once, when she'd been seven, seeing her father come stumbling into the house, reeling against the wall before making his way into the kitchen. He re-emerged, holding a slice of white bread, then disappeared into the basement. It was her first memory of seeing him drunk.

She never understood what had happened, what had caused it all. Questions like that weren't asked. He'd been injured on the job, *an industrial accident,* they called it, so he didn't have to work, ever again. But she didn't know what was wrong with him. He didn't limp, wasn't blind, had both his hands. *Injured, industrial accident. Who the fuck cares any more? He drank before the accident; he drank more after it, was probably drunk when it happened and that's why it happened.*

There wasn't any point thinking about it any more. *Better if he'd died.*

She blew smoke rings across the table, watched them whirl up then dissipate.

Her mother returned from the kitchen with the coffee pot. 'More coffee, Sten?' she asked quietly.

He nodded without looking up, pushed his cup to the centre of the table.

Elouise refilled it, then sat down. Sighing, she placed

the pot down then rubbed her eyes. 'I wish you wouldn't do that, Jennifer,' she said wearily.

'Do what?'

'Smoke.'

'I do what I want,' Jennifer snapped. 'Nobody can stop me.'

'I know,' her mother replied.

'Right. Daddy smokes, doesn't he.'

Sten looked up at the sarcastic *Daddy,* then shook his head. 'Shouldn't take after me,' he said, his gaze falling to his hands and staying there.

Jennifer laughed harshly. 'You can count on that, Daddy.' She stood, the movement abrupt enough to startle both her parents. 'I'm going out tonight.'

Her father said, 'Don't be too late.'

'Sure thing. I wouldn't want to miss the fights, would I?' She took down her faded jean jacket from a peg beside the back door. *'With a bag of goodies and a bottle of wine,'* she sang, then turned back to her parents. 'Know what that song's about?'

Neither replied.

With a smile and a wave Jennifer left the house. As she walked across the yard Sten's dogs barked at her. She ignored them.

Halfway up the block Jennifer met Sandy and Barb, who had been coming down to call on her. As always, it was important to meet them away from the house. 'Hi,' she said. 'You ready?'

Barb grinned behind her hand.

'Ready for what?' Sandy asked.

'Didn't Barb tell you? We're going into town.'

Barb giggled and said, 'Jenny knows some Grade Nine guys. We're meeting them at the McDonald's.'

'Come on,' Jennifer said, draping her arms around her friends and pulling them forward. 'We're going to hitch in.'

'Hitch-hike?' Sandy asked.

'Yep.'

Sandy pulled back.

Jennifer reached out and took Sandy by an arm. 'Don't worry. If some perve tries anything I'll rip his nuts off.'

Barb screamed her laughter. Halfway back down the block, the shriek set off Sten's dogs again.

The three girls walked towards the highway.

VI

We arrived at the traffic lights. Across the highway stood the school. Along the playing field rose a high chain-link fence that stretched around to include the now empty parking lot.

'We're Patrols,' Lynk said. 'We get keys to work the lights, and we take all the little kids across. You got Patrols in your school?'

'Sure.'

'You a Patrol?'

I shook my head. 'I take the bus home, right?'

'But when you lived close,' Lynk persisted.

Again I shook my head.

Lynk swaggered as he walked up to the highway's gravel shoulder. The traffic lights blinked green for the cars, blinked red at us. Cars and trucks rolled past us at high speeds. We waited for a lull.

Lynk said, 'The Boorman kid got killed here last

year. That's why they put up the lights, and put us in charge. He was six. Had big ears and a runny nose.'

Roland, hands in pockets, said, 'He was the third kid killed around here in the last ten years.'

'Happens all the time,' Lynk said.

'A girl in an apartment block we lived in fell from the third floor, right over the balcony rail on to the grass.'

Lynk looked at me. 'You lived in an apartment?'

'For a little while,' I said, turning to watch the traffic. 'She broke both her legs.'

Roland put a booted foot in a puddle and swirled it until the water turned grey. 'That's a long drop. Good thing she didn't die.'

I nodded. 'We lived on the fifth floor. I went out on our balcony when I heard this screaming. The mother was on her balcony, screaming and screaming. Everybody came out to look, all of us leaning over the rails – the whole side of the apartment, twelve storeys, all these people leaning over and watching her scream. We couldn't see the girl, but we watched her mother scream.' I glanced to see that they were all watching me. 'They took the mother away. The police did. There was talk that she pushed her daughter over.'

Lynk's eyes went wide. Roland scowled. Carl licked his lips.

I shrugged and kicked at some gravel. 'In the city you get accidents, sure,' I said, scanning the blacktop. 'But lots of times they aren't accidents. They just look like accidents.'

The lull came, not a long one, but long enough. My three friends ran hard across the highway; I followed at a slower, slightly daring pace. The last bit of my story, about the mother, had been a lie of sorts. *That* mother did live in the apartment, and had been taken away because she beat her kids, but it was a different mother from the one whose daughter fell from the balcony. And it had happened years earlier.

I didn't think there was anything wrong in putting two truths together to make a lie, especially since it was a good story. No, not just a good story. It had been ugly enough to take the swagger out of Lynk, to make Roland study me carefully, as if he saw something he hadn't seen before. It had been enough to make all three of them run hard across the highway.

We walked down the short driveway leading into the parking lot. My thoughts had moved on, flipping through scenes in my mind. The Boorman kid, his mother screaming and running up the highway to where he lay in the muddy ditch. The stopped cars, the flashing lights on the police cars and the ambulance's wild wail. I ran it all through my mind, then checked myself for whatever feeling came from it.

When the screaming goes away, that's when it gets bad. That's the way it seemed, anyhow. Because the quiet kind of sadness doesn't go away – it stayed with every new scene I conjured up: the family at home, the little boy's room, his empty bed.

Next year I'll become a Patrol.

We approached the school's glass front doors, the four of us looming large in the reflective, smoky panes.

Lynk gave Roland a light push, then said to me with a grin, 'The girls usually hang out back.'

'What do they do?' Even as I asked I remembered: *They smoke cigarettes.*

But Lynk laughed. 'What the fuck do you think, Owen? They sit in a circle and show off their tits.'

With a smile, Roland said, 'Problem is, only Jennifer's got any.'

'Only one in Grade Six,' Lynk said, nodding.

The area around the school was paved. Hopscotch lines stood out in bright yellow contrast on the dark asphalt. Back of the school the pavement gave way to gravel, where there were monkey-bars and concrete tubes big enough to walk through. Beyond them rose a wire fence, and beyond that ran railway tracks on a raised bank.

We came to the school's back wall – high, windowless and made of dark brown brick. Two recessed metal doors without handles marked the only variation down its length. Just past the new construction, the high wall ended abruptly at the juncture with the old school, with its own low span of pitted, crumbling limestone. The fence was closest here, only ten feet away as it followed a drainage ditch from the railway tracks back to the highway. On the other side of the ditch ran a narrow dirt road that turned before reaching the tracks and encircled a massive, blockish building made of Tyndal stone. It was at least four storeys tall and looked abandoned.

Lynk looked around, then leaned his back against the old school's wall. 'No one's here,' he said.

Carl bent and picked up a stone, which he threw over the fence.

I pointed. 'What's that old building there?'

'Candle factory,' Roland answered. 'All closed up now.'

'Looks old.'

Roland nodded and said, 'My dad says it was built in 1900. There wasn't even a school here back then, and the highway was just a gravel road.'

Lynk joined Carl in throwing stones. He flung one hard at the building, but it fell short.

Roland's eyes remained on the factory. 'Making candles used to be big business, I guess.'

'Ever been inside it?' I asked.

He shook his head. 'It's all boarded up.'

'There's piles of candles out back,' Lynk said. 'Little brown ones. Thick.'

Roland said, 'We got a whole box of them in the barn.'

I turned back and looked at the school. In a few months I'd be inside it. New teachers, faces I wouldn't recognise. I'd get into fights. I always did. If I won them, things would be okay. If I didn't . . .

'What's the matter with you?'

I glanced over at Lynk's question. He stood with a large stone in his hand, chest thrust out, feet planted wide. Our eyes met. 'Nothing,' I answered, forcing myself to relax.

'Yeah,' Lynk drawled. 'Fuckin' right, Owen.'

Something was happening. I wasn't sure what. Roland and Carl were both watching. I hesitated, then sauntered up to the limestone wall. I unzipped my fly and moments later was peeing against the wall.

'What the fuck are you doing?' Lynk demanded.

I looked over at him. He was fidgeting, his head turning this way and that.

'What's it look like?'

'Jennifer and Sandy and Barb could walk up any minute,' Lynk said. He stared at me, then laughed. 'I don't fucking believe it.'

I finished.

Lynk swung to Roland. 'He's a fucking idiot! Did you see that?'

Roland frowned at Lynk, then shrugged. 'So?'

I was wondering the same thing, though a part of me was quietly satisfied. I'd rattled Lynk, somehow, as if I'd answered a challenge with contempt. Even as I thought that, I knew that it was right, though I had no idea what the challenge had been. 'Hell, Lynk,' I said casually, 'it's not as if I pissed on your shoes, is it?'

His face reddened, then he spun and threw the rock hard. It fell short of the candle factory.

I glanced over at Roland, and was surprised to see his expression animated – more than I'd ever seen it before. There was something in his eyes as he stared at Lynk's back, and the look he finally turned on me was sharp, intense. *He knows what just happened. He understands it completely. How come I don't?*

VII

'Aren't you girls a little young to be going into the city all alone?' the bearded man asked as he pulled his car back on to the highway.

'Not as young as you think,' Jennifer answered, leaning back in the seat beside him and stretching her legs. Barb and Sandy, sitting in the back, remained silent.

At her response the man shot her a quick look, then returned his attention to the road. 'Maybe you got relatives there?'

'Nope. You can drop us off at the McDonald's across from P. E. High.'

'All right.'

Jennifer watched the city take shape alongside the highway. The gas stations came first, then the streets with their square houses and small gardens. The movie drive-in went by, and then the cloverleaf bypass. More houses, smaller lots, then under the old railway bridge, and suddenly there was a cemetery on the left, a used car lot on the right. People on the sidewalks, cars and trucks crowding the lanes.

'Next light is fine,' she said.

'Somebody driving you back?' the man asked.

'Of course,' Jennifer replied.

He pulled into the parking lane in front of the high school. The back door opened and Barb and Sandy hurried out. Jennifer smiled at the man. 'Thanks. You've been sweet.' She opened the door and stepped out, then leaned back in. 'Drive carefully.'

'Yeah, sure.'

'That was cool,' Barb said as the car drove off. Her round face was flushed as she gazed at the restaurant across the street.

'You told him we had a ride back,' Sandy said, frowning. 'Do we?'

'Sure. Some guy just like him, heading the other way.'

The light changed and they crossed the street. The restaurant was crowded, most of the booths filled with high-school students, and a few from Junior High.

Voices and smoke filled the air. Jennifer stationed herself in a line. 'Let's get some shakes,' she said. 'And remember,' she added in a lower tone, 'when we meet Dave and his friends, we're all fourteen, right?'

'Hey, Jenny!' a boy's voice called out. She turned to see Dave edge his way through the crowd. He grinned at her. 'We got a table,' he said. He was wearing a faded, torn jean jacket with peace symbols drawn on it in black ink, and rust-coloured bell-bottom pants held up by a wide black leather belt with a brass buckle. A pack of Export 'A' jutted from the jacket's breast pocket. Dave stepped up to Jennifer, placed a hand behind her head and then kissed her.

Jennifer pulled him close, laughing when their lips parted even though she felt a moment's revulsion at seeing a half-dozen new pimples on his shiny forehead. He must have followed her glance, for he stepped back, ducking his head to bring his long blond hair forward.

'Hi, Dave,' Jennifer said. 'These are my two friends I was telling you about. Barb and Sandy.'

Dave nodded at them. 'Hi.'

Jennifer ordered the three milkshakes and paid. She and her two friends then followed Dave back to a table where a half-dozen boys and girls sat. Spaces were made for them, Dave sitting on one side of Jennifer, Barb on the other, with Sandy opposite.

Dave nudged Jennifer. 'Guess what?'

'What?'

He ducked his head again. 'We got some hash. We're going over to Mark's place. His old man's not home.' Dave took out his cigarettes. 'We'll have to keep all the windows open,' he said.

'Mark's old man is a cop,' Jennifer explained to Sandy and Barb.

'He'd bust us all if he ever got the chance,' Dave said.

Jennifer leaned back in the crook of Dave's arm. Whenever Dave laughed she joined in, though she wasn't really listening to him. A girl sitting at the far end of the table drew her attention. She was pretty, and seemed to have snared the attention of Jim and Mike – two boys who, like Dave, were in Grade Nine. A nudge from Barb brought Jennifer's attention back to her end of the table.

A boy had turned to Sandy. 'Hi,' he said after a moment. 'I'm Mark.'

Sandy looked down at the table and smiled. 'Hi.'

'You from Middlecross, too?'

She nodded.

'Going with anybody?'

Barb giggled and Sandy shot her a glare before glancing up at Mark. 'Not really,' she said.

Barb sneered. 'She's hot for a farmboy,' she said, shakily lighting her cigarette. 'Big and dumb.'

'Roland's not dumb,' Sandy snapped.

'His name's Roland?' Mark asked. 'Roland?' He rocked back and laughed loudly.

'That name sounds familiar,' a new voice cut in.

Mark said, 'This is Debbie Brand. A transfer.'

Something cold clenched Jennifer's stomach as she slowly looked over at the girl at the far end of the table. Their eyes met, and the girl smiled, then winked. Jennifer swung a glare on Sandy. 'Roland's got hairless balls and a limp prick,' Jennifer said, smiling coldly as the colour left Sandy's face.

Debbie said, 'Poor kid.'

Their eyes met again, and again Jennifer looked away first. Around her the conversation stumbled off in a new direction, but it had become faint and distant as a storm thundered through Jennifer's thoughts. *The bitch, she knows! Fuck!* A year's difference in age meant everything. Being in the seventh grade was a whole lifetime away from being in Grade Six. *If Mark and Dave find out . . . fuck it!*

The new girl knew the truth, only she wasn't telling. *Why? Why not carve us up right now and get it done with? What the hell did that wink mean, anyway?* Jennifer scowled. *We got to talk, Debbie Brand. You and me. I got to know what kind of game you're playing.* Once she knew that – Jennifer smiled to herself. *I don't lose games. Ever.*

CHAPTER THREE

I

It was Sunday, the day we declared war on the rats in the house. We began by rolling up the carpet in the living room. I helped Father carry it out to the service pick-up truck he had driven in from the gas station. While he took the carpet to the garage – where he'd clean it with a high-pressure water hose and heavy-duty soap – I was to place the traps and poison.

'Figure you can match wits with rats?' Father asked.

I grinned up at him. 'Nobody better than me.'

He drove away, and I turned to face the house. Twenty traps to lay out; the poison would go into the crawlspace under the basement stairs, and into the attic. The traps, baited with Cheddar cheese, would go everywhere else.

Mother kept the twins in the kitchen, her two helpers in some baking venture. Debbie was visiting friends in the city. The rest of the house was mine.

The basement seemed the obvious place to start. As I descended the stairs, I listened for sounds from below. But there was nothing. I came to the bottom of the steps and paused, looking around.

A thousand places for rats to hide. Behind the washer, the dryer, the water heater, the furnace, all of our cardboard boxes from the move – some of them still packed.

After a moment I moved quietly forward, around the large freezer and into the laundry room. A basket of dirty clothes caught my eye and I thought of rat nests. A tingling feeling crept over me. Suddenly certain that pairs of black marble eyes watched me, I removed the first of the traps from my backpack. *Pull back on the stiff bar, set the catch, place the cheese on the pan. Simple, but be careful, Father said, 'cause these aren't mouse-traps. These can break your fingers.*

The concrete floor was cold under my hands and knees. I slid a trap down between the washer and dryer, reaching until it was against the back wall. A second one went behind the furnace, then I left the room and approached the small plywood door under the stairs.

If rats could build secret cities, they'd build them in the crawlspace. I crouched down and slowly opened the door. The basement's light exposed only a few feet into the crawlspace. On the concrete floor was a scatter of bits of cotton-like material that I thought might be insulation, clots of hair and dust, and rat pellets.

Gotcha.

The image of the dying rat in the living room came back once again. Its death had left me feeling dulled inside, and now the sensation returned. Something older than pain, older than hurt. Something like those parents might be feeling even now about the son who'd been killed on the highway. A dullness that wouldn't go away. And yet, here I was, armed with traps and poison. I had been given the job of killing rats.

Father would be checking on them. I wouldn't have to see the results. Somehow, that made things easier. I removed the plastic bag containing the poisoned cheese from my backpack and opened it. A strong, bitter smell wafted up, burning the back of my throat – Father had said *don't touch, just spill a few out*. I tilted the bag on its side and dumped out on to the crawlspace floor a clump of powdery cubes. With the corner of one of the traps I broke up the pile and flicked pieces into the darkness. Then I shut the door.

For the main floor, I was only supposed to set traps in the closet and the storage room. Once I had done this I ascended the stairs to the second floor. There were five rooms, each with a closet; and a hallway with a linen closet. I was to ignore the twins' room.

For some reason, I felt certain that there weren't any rats above the main floor. Though I hadn't yet explored the attic, I envisioned a single, large empty room with an arched roof. A room with no hiding places.

At the top of the stairs, I gazed down the hallway. Ahead and to my right was the door to the guest room. We'd never lived in a place that had a guest room before now. The thought of having guests seemed strange. *Who? Nobody ever comes to visit us. Mother's rela-*

tives live in the old country. Father's relatives never even write him – they might be all dead, the way nobody ever talked about them. I'd had sleep-overs when we'd lived in the city, and Debbie had done the same, but at those times everyone slept in the same room. Maybe guest rooms were just rooms that happened to be empty.

I walked into the guest room. No furniture, of course. We barely had enough to fill our own rooms. It seemed vast, too large to be a part of the house. Opposite me were two windows. I went over and looked out of the one on my right. Below ran the garage's sloped roof, its green tiles battered and the gutter full of rotting leaves. Beyond the garage the driveway wound its way into and through the line of firs that marked the yard's boundary. Through the branches was another yard, and another house. I had no idea who lived there.

A third window, to my left, looked out on the front yard. In the city I'd never imagined that someone could own so much land – except for farmers, but that was different. I counted seven trees, all thick-limbed and tall and widely spaced. This wasn't a farm, just a house, on a lot that in the city would hold three or four houses.

Recalling my duty, I went to the closet and opened it. Dusty and empty. I set a single trap.

Past the guest room the hallway turned left and ran the length of the house. I walked past the first door, which was my own room – I planned to leave it for last since the attic's trapdoor was in there. The next door led into Debbie's room.

The Forbidden Zone, she called it. *Sorry, ma'am,*

but it's my job. Blacklight posters covered the walls. I recognised most of them: Jimi Hendrix, Led Zeppelin, Frank Zappa sitting òn a toilet; but others were more obscure. There were scenes of bridges over deep chasms, towering, jagged mountains beneath alien skies filled with moons, winged horses with single spiralling horns on their heads, and still other abstract designs that hurt my eyes.

There were no clothes on the floor. A record player sat on a stand, a large speaker to either side. Records waited in a neat stack beneath the stand. The Guess Who, Grand Funk, Janis Joplin, Jefferson Airplane, Melanie. I recalled the only record I owned, a present from last Christmas, the Partridge Family, and I realised that I had never even played it yet. Debbie said it would destroy her record player. Unlikely. *Damage it, maybe, but not destroy it.* Music didn't mean that much to me, though some songs from the radio had a way of haunting me, like 'A Dog Named Boo'. All Debbie ever did these days was listen to records. Every night I'd lie in bed in the dark and listen to the bass notes thrum through the walls, deep like the beat of an exhausted heart. Those sounds carried me into sleep, eventually, but sometimes I'd stay awake, trying to guess which record she'd put on next. I usually guessed right, and that led me to certain theories about Debbie, especially the way the music changed from angry to depressing as the hours dragged on.

I opened the closet door. Her clothes smelled of perfume, a pungent, urgent smell. On the floor inside lay a half-dozen pairs of shoes – sneakers, high-heels, sandals. I pushed them aside and set a trap, wondering if Debbie took her shoes out of the closet before putting them on, or did she simply step into them?

Even with the authority of my mission, I was glad to leave Debbie's room. Something about being in there made me feel guilty, as if everything in there was fragile, and that even the touch of my glance might shatter the world she'd made. I could already picture her outrage at discovering my intrusion.

The master bedroom was the next stop. It was hard to imagine there being rats in my parents' room. The shelves in the double closet were precisely ordered, the clothes neatly folded. My father's clothes occupied the left side of the closet, my mother's the right. A fainter perfume mixed with cigarette smoke wafted from my mother's dresses, more subtle than Debbie's. From Father's side the cologne was mixed with garage oil.

I set a trap down behind Father's dress shoes, which he never wore anyway, then closed the door and swung around. At first the face staring at me was startling, but it was just the mirror. The face was my own, but as I studied it, I saw again a strangeness to it, echoing the reflection I had seen in the window of Gribbs's shack. An expression all too serious stared back at me, the wide mouth drawn into an almost bloodless line, and on the forehead a growing frown. Abruptly I looked away, down at the double bed. There were no creases on the bedspread, just smooth perfection.

I left the room, quietly closing the door behind me.

Mother always called my room 'frightening'. Her refusal to clean it was always voiced as a threat, though for me it was a personal victory – a view I kept to myself. I stood at the threshold, studying the mess. Piles of dirty clothes hid the floor, toppled stacks of comic books surrounded the unmade bed. Smudges and streaks relieved the plain white walls. On my desk waited a model '55 Chevy, not yet finished, and on a shelf above it sat a '32 Deuce, a 326 Hemi Model-A, and a Model-T roadster.

This room could easily hide rats. Warrens beneath the piled clothes, nests among the dustballs under the bed, baby rats in the back seat of the Chevy. I looked up at the B-27 bomber hanging from the ceiling, my eyes narrowing on the cockpit, but the plastic glass remained impenetrable.

The closet door was jammed open by socks snagged under the frame. Inside, stacked cardboard boxes containing old models leaned against one wall. Dozens of wire hangers hung bare and vaguely accusatory. I sniffed. The air was musty, reminding me of the crawl-space. I scanned the few areas of visible hardwood floor, hunting for rat pellets. None. This wasn't very reassuring. Here on the second floor – I was suddenly convinced that there were rats here – they'd be smarter than their comrades in the basement. They'd take their pellets with them.

I went to work. Three traps under the bed, one beside the radiator, another beneath my desk. Three more in the closet. Within the biggest mound of clothing I fashioned a cave in the centre and a corridor leading out. I set a trap and pushed it down the corridor until it was inside the cave.

Satisfied, I turned my attention to the trapdoor in the ceiling. No handle was visible, so I assumed it would push upward. From my equipment bag I took out a flashlight. I pulled the desk chair over and stepped on to it. I paused. Through the window I could see the river between the trees. There was less ice now – the red-brown water was flat, unmarred for long stretches. Watching the inexorable current, I felt a moment of dizziness and put a hand against the wall for balance. Over the river two crows wheeled in low circles above something riding the current. Whatever it was bobbed once, then slipped beneath the surface again, leaving spinning eddies in its wake. The crows stayed above it.

I swung my attention to the trapdoor above me. It was beyond reach, so I stepped up on to the window sill. Father had said to use the stepladder if I had to, but from the sill I found I could push the door upward. Woodchips and sawdust drifted down. I pushed harder and it cleared the attic floor and slid to one side.

I hefted my knapsack and tossed it up through the opening. It disappeared into the darkness and I heard a thump. Then I gripped the edges and swung away from the sill, hanging a moment before pulling myself up.

The attic's floor wasn't flat, as I'd thought it would be. A grid-work of boards lay set on end about thirty inches apart, the spaces filled with woodchips. I flicked on the flashlight and directed the beam forward.

A narrow corridor ran no more than ten feet ahead, opening out into a larger space. An attic with tunnels. Tense with sudden excitement, I crawled forward.

I I

In 1962, while towing an Iberian oil tanker into Halifax Harbour, a Samson cable snapped ten feet under

water. The first indication Walter Gribbs, able-bodied
seaman on the tug *Lifeliner,* had had of danger as he
stood near the winch amidships was the growing shriek
behind him. He awoke two days later in the Halifax
General Hospital, suffering from a severe concussion
and a partial loss of hearing in his left ear.

Suddenly freed from the tension created by the
tanker's weight, the cable had recoiled back to the tug.
It swept three men from the deck in less than a second.
Walter was the only one still breathing. One had gone
down into the water, wrapped in the cable, where he
drowned before anyone could get to him. The other
man had been decapitated.

Nineteen sixty-two was also Walter's last year at sea.
After the accident he found it difficult to keep his balance on a sidewalk, much less a pitching deck. For him
it was over. He soon realised that living close to the sea
was like sleeping night after night beside a woman he
couldn't touch. He boarded a train bound for the centre of the continent, and eventually found a job at the
Yacht Club. Once a seaman, now a grounds keeper.

Gribbs had always been a solitary man. Even among
a crew months out at sea he remained a loner – it was
never an obvious thing; it never led to discomfort or
resentment. He was there when needed, ready with a
smile, and somehow able to mend arguments as a
healer mends broken bones, and though he didn't say
much, when he spoke he was listened to.

And yet there had always been a distance between
him and everyone else. Not a wall – nothing so deliberately constructed – but a span of nothingness that no
one could cross, and that distance had grown steadily

for as long as he could remember. It had never left him feeling lonely, for inside his head there lived a rhythm, a slow music that gave every thought, every memory, the cadence of a poem, or a song. He'd heard stories told for most of his life, stories recounting the tragic lives of women in ports, stories told by old men in ship's cabins and staterooms, who'd seen their share and more. He'd heard poems that lodged in his memory and stayed with him, and he'd seen things with his own eyes that were of themselves poetry.

The music in his mind cushioned him, made him an observer of the outside world. Gribbs had never spent much effort trying to understand that world, but he did strain endlessly to catch its every note.

It had been at sea that Gribbs found his lover. He'd feel her coming in the air; he'd be the first on board to see her smudge on the horizon; and when she arrived – the old Witch, the wild-haired lover who lifted high the seas and brought the squalling sky down with howling winds and curtains of rain – Gribbs would be the first to greet her, and he'd talk to her, his words gently reproachful, and he'd sing her lullabies and roll out poems and stories that his mates would swear calmed her, easing her rage, and so saving their lives.

You being nice to the lady today, Gribbs? they'd ask, the question its own refrain, from ship to ship, wherever Gribbs signed on. *How's her mood, Gribbs?* They knew he'd be there when she came, singing for their lives.

His second night on the prairies, he'd awoken in his hotel room to the fury of a summer storm. He'd thought he'd left her behind, but he realised, that night as he stood at the window and watched the storm, that she had followed him. And she was giving him an earful.

It was still spring. The witch had yet to stalk the skies. Gribbs knew that it wouldn't be until the sultry heat of summer that she'd start blowing off steam.

Under his breath, Gribbs murmured soft words. Maybe, he thought, maybe she was near enough to hear him. He told her about his dreams, describing in detail those frightening images that remained with him. He spoke of the flames sweeping the world, the skies splitting open, the rains pouring down like blood; he spoke, in low tones, of the crags of ice exploding skyward, and of the things that flew down from the darkness with swords of flame. He told her of the weeping children.

The wind whispered against his face. After a time it dried his tears, which had come suddenly, inexplicably. He rose from his chair and closed the window.

III

Caesar lay on his back in the dirt, his legs in the air as Kaja and Shane padded up to him and took turns sniffing his anus. Less than sober but not quite drunk, Sten watched his dogs bemusedly from where he sat on the back porch steps.

The sun, high overhead, had bathed him in sweat. He sat very still, concentrating on every trickle running down his body.

I'll just let it suck every drop from me. Cool, clear streams of poison soaking my clothes. They won't need washing, my sweat will kill the germs. All of them. Hah.

With a growl, Caesar rolled upright, then began strutting back and forth along one side of the kennel.

'Christ,' Sten muttered, 'you're one helluva bastard, Caesar.' The big male had a good ten pounds on his brother Shane, and more on Kaja, his mother. 'And yet you play the suck, eh?' Sten shook his head. 'Max had you all beat, you know that? And he never played the suck.'

Damn but I'm thirsty. Hell, just one beer. Just one? No, sweat it out. Just like that.

Kaja whined as she poked her nose at the cage door. Her tail half wagged, then dipped and went still as her deep brown eyes met Sten's gaze. A moment later she turned and walked to the far corner where she lay down in the shade.

'I'm not letting you out,' Sten told them. He wiped sweat from his face with a sleeve. 'It's simple, you see.' He giggled. 'We're all out of garbage bags.'

He could hear the vacuum cleaner moving from room to room in the house behind him. Every now and then came a skittering clatter as the machine picked up some more broken glass. From room to room, a methodical beast removing evidence. He smiled. *I like machines.*

'All out of garbage bags.'

He stiffened in sudden fear as the door swung open behind him. A moment later, Jennifer walked past, ignoring him. Sten watched her. Her golden hair reached down to the small of her back, just above the patched, faded and embroidered jeans. *She's going to be a tall one. Just like my old man. Damn, she's some looker, though*. He gazed at the deliberate sway of her hips, and frowned.

'Hey, what're you doing that for?' he blurted.

She stopped and slowly faced him. 'Doing what, *Daddy?*'

Sten's gaze fell. He stared at his hands for a moment, then down to his stockinged feet. He scowled – he didn't like looking at his hands. Not now. 'Where you going?'

'Why?'

Sten glanced up at her, then at the dogs in the kennel. 'I just want t'know, tha'sall.'

'Oh well, in that case. I'm going to meet someone. He's going to sell me some drugs. There, how's that?'

Sten closed his hands, wrapping one hand over the other. 'Oh,' he managed. His heart hammered painfully against his ribs. He felt like he was sweating from every pore now, and it sent a shiver through him.

'Bye, *Daddy*,' Jennifer said over her shoulder as she walked away.

Shane leapt against the kennel's wire wall as she passed, snapping and growling. Sten jerked to his feet. Jennifer laughed. Sten's anger became rage. He charged the kennel.

'Shut up!' he roared, driving his fists against the cage.

Yelping, Shane scurried away, stopping every two or three steps to cast a cowering glance at Sten.

His fingers twisting the wires, Sten stared down at the dog. 'Just shut up!' he hissed. *That's my daughter!* He wanted to scream those words, knowing that she'd hear him. But it was impossible. His throat closed up at the very thought – she'd only laugh again.

Sten's eyes slowly focused. All three dogs now crawled towards him, whimpering, their tails wagging fitfully. 'I'll do it,' he whispered. 'I will. Garbage bags, for all fucking three of ya.' He released his grip on the wires and stumbled back to the porch steps. In the house the vacuum cleaner stopped abruptly. Sten sat down on the rough boards again, and held his head in his hands.

All the glass is gone. So what's she doing now? His hands throbbed. He dragged them down his cheeks and let them fall into the shadow of his crotch. *I'll sweat it all out, and the poison'll be gone. But what's she doing now?*

Inexorably, Sten felt his gaze travel down to his hands. Even in the shadows he could see the lumps, bruises and cuts on them. The cuts had a regular pattern. 'Those,' he muttered, 'those were her teeth. Her teeth done those.'

He wanted to cry, but the sun had baked him and there wasn't anything left inside. 'God!' he hissed. 'But I'm thirsty!'

IV

The attic room wasn't as large as I'd thought it would be. Windowless, it was about the same size as the master bedroom. On one wall a wide, square projection rose up past the angled roof. Packed with insulation, with red bricks peeking out from tears in the fibreglass padding, it took me a moment to realise I was looking at the chimney.

I walked over to it, then swung around and played

the light across the room. The far wall split into three corridors. The one on my right was the aisle I'd come from, leading back to the trapdoor. The middle aisle ran lengthways down the mid-line of the house, while the corridor on the left ran parallel to the outer wall.

Clumps of cotton and tissue – rat nests – lay here and there amidst the woodchips, but my flashlight detected no movement, and the only sound I heard was my own breathing.

I chose the middle corridor. It ended at about thirty feet with a blank wall. The third corridor was the same. I returned to the large room and sat down on one of the boards.

The wall at the end of all three aisles couldn't be the house's outer, north wall. When I'd come through the trapdoor from my room I'd appeared at the corridor's far end, and yet I knew that, north of my room, there was a hallway and then the staircase, and beside the staircase was the guest room. So, where was the rest of the attic?

'Owen!' The voice was faint, coming up from below. I hurried over to the trapdoor.

'Owen!'

I knelt, stuck my head down into the opening. 'Up here!'

'Aren't you finished yet?' my mother asked.

I pictured her standing there at the foot of the stairs, her head tilted up, seeing nothing but walls and carpeted steps. Below me the chaos of my room seemed almost orderly. 'Just about!' I called down.

'Your father's home, and he wants you out in the garage!'

'Okay!'

Enough fooling around, I told myself. Time for traps and poison.

It was raining. I watched my father draping a paint-spotted tarp over the machine in the driveway. Water ran down my face like oily sweat. Like Father, I didn't wipe it away.

'You do the whole house?' he asked.

I nodded. 'Didn't see any, but they're there, all right.'

'Rat shit?'

Again I nodded. 'And nests, I think.'

He placed his hands on his hips. 'Where?'

'In the crawlspace. That's where I put the poison.'

He grunted. 'Good. You've done enough. I'll handle the garage myself. Got the traps?'

I handed him the equipment bag. He opened it and looked inside, then nodded and walked into the garage.

I felt reluctant to leave, regretting the end of this conversation. It'd seemed so grown up, curt and professional. The light rain felt good on my face. It had been a good day. My gaze found the roof and lingered there. I hadn't told Father about the rat nests in the attic, because I didn't want him going up there. I'd found a secret, and the secret was behind the small window just under the roof's edge. It was a half-circle, flat end down, with dark panes set in a web of black iron. Figures of coloured glass filled the spaces. I'd found no windows when I'd been up in the attic, so I knew that behind it was a hidden room, beyond the walls at the end of the three corridors – the final third of the attic.

The slope of the shingled roof stopped short of the window, and a squat construction projected out around it, neatly framing it. The construction had its own roof, steeply sloped and brown-shingled. At the pinnacle rose a lightning rod.

Amazed that I had never noticed it before, I walked around to the back of the house. As I passed the living-room window I saw Mother standing beside the fire-place, lighting a cigarette. The sight of her made me think about the girls Lynk and Roland had talked about, smoking behind the school. I wondered if my mother had started the same way. I wondered if it was something girls did. Of course, men smoked, too, but that was different, somehow. Less grown up.

There wasn't much of a back yard, just a slope of muddy grass leading down to an undercut bank and then the river. I faced the house, and there it was – an-other window, this one smaller, round like a porthole. It gleamed milky silver, reflecting the sky. With my back to the river, I studied the window, my imagina-tion running wild. Whatever was in that secret room, it was mine. No one else would know, not even Lynk, Roland and Carl. No one.

V

It had taken a third of a tube of Orajel to blunt the pain. Elouise stood at the kitchen window and silently gazed down at her husband's back. In one hand she clutched a wad of tissue, which she periodically brought to her mouth to wipe away bloody drool.

But the numbness was welcome, though her neck

remained sore and the swelling made her jaw feel heavy. And despite the effect of the Orajel she could feel, deep in the bones, Sten's knuckles. She wondered if that feeling would ever go away.

He hadn't remembered any of it, he'd told her in the morning, voicing his claim as if it were a worthy defence, excusing what he'd done. Elouise wondered. She thought of the look in his eyes, the moment when he threw his fist at her face. She imagined he'd seen the same look in her own eyes – hatred.

Even now the thought shocked her. She'd always believed, no matter what happened, that the love they held for each other would survive. But now that conviction was gone, and she wondered if that hatred had been there all along, buried deep inside.

Silent, Elouise stared down at her husband's hunched back. He hadn't moved since his last words. Still, she could almost feel the war that was even now raging inside him. He wanted a drink, and the only things stopping him were the cut and bruised hands in his lap. She felt no pity. In fact, she felt nothing at all. She had become as numb as her torn, bruised mouth.

And that's for the better. I need to keep from feeling anything, and I especially need to keep from panicking. I mustn't do that. Not now. She had come close to it every now and then through the morning hours, and it always began with the question: *what do I do now?*

She brought the wad of tissue to her mouth. The effects of the Orajel were wearing off. The pain was coming back, behind a cool itch tingling along her jaw. The tissue in her hand had soaked through. Saliva trickled down her chin. *More Kleenex.*

'Elouise!' Sten's voice snapped from out on the porch. 'Bring me a beer. There's one in the freezer.'

In the freezer. Of course. She wiped her chin with a sleeve, then turned from the window and approached the refrigerator. 'Cubbin,' she said.

VI

The puddles alongside the highway lay sheathed in the night's ice. As I stood waiting for the 7:45 bus to take me into the city I could see my breath. The winter came back each night, and in the early morning, with the sun a cold white disc on the horizon, the frost clung to the air. Like a passing beast, winter had licked the yellow spikes of grass around the fence-posts; it had lain down here and there, leaving ochre pools of shard-strewn water, and its breath had left a melting dazzle of silver on the highway's blacktop.

I waited, watching the cars and trucks hiss past. The bus was late, and I feared that I'd miss my connection. It was Monday, the beginning of a long day and a long week. Up at 6:30, home at 6:00. I longed for school's end, I longed to escape the city's hold on me.

Twin shadows crossed the highway a little to one side of my position at the bus stop, dipping down into the ditch. I heard the flap of wings and didn't bother looking up.

My thoughts remained with the city. Though the old classroom and the faces were familiar, I now felt like a stranger, and the old world had lost its drama, becoming small, confined, crowded with meaningless gestures.

The bus arrived, and the driver greeted me with the

now familiar refrain. 'Morning, Mr Gloom.' I nodded in his direction as I clambered up the steps, dropped my ticket into the change-holder, then headed down the aisle to my usual seat at the very back. I leaned against the side and stared out at the scene sweeping past, squinting to make out details through the green-tinted glass. Heat gusted up into my face, smelling of oil and metal and dust.

Mr Gloom. Yeah, well, who wouldn't be gloomy? It's too early in the morning for sane people.

Through the window the city took form, encroaching on my thoughts – buildings, stores, cars, people, colours. It all seemed washed out, as if mere moments from crumbling away completely – everything into piles of dust, even the people.

The bus edged its way into the city's concrete heart. The buildings reached skyward, leaving the sidewalks in shadow. Monotoned clumps of people moved here and there, seeming less than human, more like cloaked creatures bent on harried tasks for some unseen overlord. They hurried from one dark hole to the next. I imagined them clutching rough black iron tools beneath their coats, and within the skyscrapers I pictured grey mazes carpeted with clumps of cotton and littered with rat pellets.

Mr Gloom.

The bus swung ponderously into the station. Pulled from my imaginings by the need for haste, I quickly left the station, crossed the street, and took position among the crowd at the bus stop. I hadn't missed my connection – the crowd told me that much. It felt like the only kind of victory I was allowed to have.

At the end of this ride was Montrose Elementary

School, a low flat-topped building painted white and cream-yellow. I'd known it since Grade Four. Before that there had been Lincoln Ness School, Doncaster School, and South Grosvenor School.

The bus arrived, and I joined the line filing into it, my head at chest level with nearly everyone else. I worked my way down the aisle and saw a familiar face, middle-aged and round, the eyes small and blue, all of it framed by short wavy blonde hair. It smiled at me.

'Good morning, Owen.'

'Morning, Miss Shevrin,' I replied. The seat beside my teacher was vacant. I tried not to notice it.

'Sit down, won't you?' She pulled the edge of her coat away to give me more room. Just a gesture, of course. I wasn't big enough to spread all over the seat. Even so, as my teacher she was used to telling me what to do. I sat down.

'Do you take this bus every day?' she asked.

Her perfume swirled all around me, along with the sharp tang of menthol cigarettes. 'Yes.'

'You come to school pretty early, then.'

'Yes.'

'My car's in the shop.'

'What's wrong with it?'

My question seemed to startle her. 'Well, it's something to do with the transmission.'

'My dad doesn't do transmission work,' I said.

'Oh.'

'Though he could if he wanted to.'

'Mmhmm.'

The silence stretched a little too long, then she said, 'So tell me, how do you like your new home?'

'I like it.'

'What's good about it?'

'It's not in the city.'

'You don't like living in the city?'

'It smells. I hate the smell.'

'The pollution?'

'Mmhmm.'

A minute passed. Miss Shevrin fidgeted in her seat. The school was getting mercifully close. She looked down at the books on my lap. 'What's that you're reading?'

'*Jason and the Argonauts*. It's an abridged version. For young readers.'

'Oh! Are you enjoying it?'

'It's too much like the abridged version of *The Odyssey*.'

Miss Shevrin stared down at me for a moment. 'I had no idea you read so much.'

Suddenly feeling nervous, I looked away. 'Mostly I read comics,' I said. 'And horror magazines.' I wasn't sure why I felt the need to lie – I read everything I could get my hands on. I'd read all of Debbie's English class books before she did. The only book I couldn't finish was *Lord of the Rings*. The magic was fun, but I'd found it impossible to get excited about a hero who was two feet tall. For some reason, the sharp interest I'd seen in my teacher's face had made me wary, almost skittish.

'Do you think those comic books are well written, Owen?'

'Sure. Some of them are great.'

We were nearing our stop. Miss Shevrin sighed and said, 'Well, at least you're not fighting all the time this year. I suppose that's something.'

'Yeah.'

'Have you thought of why that might be the case?'

'Sure,' I smiled up at her. 'I fight dirty.'

VII

Throughout the winter, bereft of heat in the shelters, the mink's fur thickened and took on an oily shimmer. After especially large orders had been filled, the remaining mink fed well on what was left of their less fortunate kin. There still were times, however, when there was simply too much flesh and guts, and then Fisk piled them into a mound beside the maypole. Doused with kerosene, the remains burned all night.

Fisk had just filled a large order.

A breeze had sprung up from the west, taking away the afternoon sun's heat. Fisk rested, leaning on his pitchfork. The wind also carried away most of the stench from the rotting meat, though he'd gotten used to the smell a long time ago. Still, he admitted to a measure of gratitude for the breeze.

This would be the last load.

After a moment Fisk resumed shovelling entrails into the wheelbarrow. The shaft of the pitchfork felt slick in his large hands. Blood and intestinal fluids covered his hairy forearms. It was still too early in the season for flies. *Thank God.*

When he'd shovelled the last of the mink remains into the wheelbarrow he dropped the pitchfork and pushed the load around the house to the front. The mound beside the maypole was already three feet high and six feet across. Grunting, Fisk heaved on the handles and dumped the load.

He'd have to wait until nightfall before lighting it. Even out here there were ordinances regarding the burning of refuse. From a pile such as this one the cloud that would billow forth would be black, thick and greasy. It would rise up for a short distance, then fall back earthward, gathering like floating shrouds in the low areas.

There'd been complaints, every now and then, from neighbours. And once the RCMP and a health inspector had come out to his farm to look the place over. But he'd already buried the evidence, and so there was nothing they could do.

Now, he was mostly left alone. Except for the orders, which came over the phone, and the occasional trip into the city for supplies, Fisk avoided making any ties. His local legion had sent information his way, but he never responded. He didn't want company. He didn't want friends.

When he heard and then saw the brown Fargo pickup truck driving up the section road, heading for his farm, Fisk scowled. As he stood beside the mound, he watched the truck pull into the driveway and then stop. Through the window was a vaguely familiar face, much older than the last time he'd seen it – which was before Dorry's death, when neighbours weren't just bitter reminders – older, and thinner.

The door opened and the man stepped out. Although of average height, he looked shrunken, thin to the point of emaciation, his hunched shoulders making his head jut forward. The man's clothes hung on him like shedding skin, tattered brown and black. Greasy brown hair fell in strands over his face, which he pushed to one side in a habitual gesture that was to Fisk pathetic.

'Goo'affernoon, Hodgson.' The man's words came out in a slurred croak.

Fisk nodded. 'Sten, ain't it?'

'Tha's right. 'Sbeen a few years, eh? Sten. Sten Louper.' He approached, a little unsteadily.

Fisk realised that Sten was drunk, and it disgusted him. If there was one thing he hated, it was men who drank. 'What can I do for you?' he asked, wanting to get this meeting over with – he had no interest in small talk with a drunk.

Sten's gaze fell on the mound beside Fisk. 'Came t'talk 'bout that,' he said.

'What about it?'

'I wanna make a deal,' Sten said.

Fisk frowned. He'd been expecting a complaint. 'What kind of deal?'

The wind shifted around and Sten stepped back. 'Whoo, tha's some smell.'

Fisk grunted.

'You get lotsa stuff left over, eh?'

'Two, three times a season. Why?'

Pushing his hair back, Sten nodded as if Fisk's answer had confirmed a suspicion. 'I might like t'buy some, tha's why. If th'price's right.'

Fisk pocketed his hands and shook his head. 'Buy it? What in hell for?'

'I got three dogs. Dog food's 'spensive.'

'I doubt they'd eat it,' Fisk said. 'Maybe just roll in it, or something.'

'I gotta grinder in the g'rage. I'd mix it up with reg'lar stuff.'

Fisk grunted again. 'It might do. Give me your phone number. I'll let you know when I get some fresh stuff.' He turned and headed towards the porch. 'Thing is, you don't want it to go high. Might sicken your dogs.'

Sten laughed, as if at some private joke. 'No problem there. Got lotsa jars. Fulla jam now, but I can empty 'em out.'

Fisk walked past him. 'I'll get a pen and paper.'

'Wait!'

Stopping, Fisk turned. 'What?'

'Well, we ain't 'greed on th'price, eh?'

'Jesus Christ, Sten.' Fisk shook his head. 'I'm not asking a price for something I'd just burn anyway. You just come and pick it up when I call you. Hell, saves me the trouble.'

Sten blinked, then he nodded. 'You call and I'll come right over.'

Fisk turned back to the house. 'I'll get a pen and paper.'

'Right.'

After he'd gotten Sten's phone number and the man had driven away, Fisk made some coffee and retired to his rocking chair on the porch to await sunset.

'Bloody drunk,' he muttered. *That's what happens when you don't work*. He remembered hearing some story about Sten having an accident on the job – was working for the railroad or something. Living the last ten years on an injury compensation cheque. The man was probably a drunk even back then, and that was what caused the accident. 'Once a drunk, always a drunk.'

He leaned back in his chair, watching the shadows crawl towards him. 'All you need is a purpose. That's all you need.'

VIII

The city falling behind me, I edged forward in my seat, feeling the anticipation growing inside. The day was over, but with the coming of dusk a new day would begin. And there'd be chill winds to sweep away the city's residue from my clothes, from my thoughts. And there'd be the fields of sweet mud and the bounty carried in the swirling currents of the brown river.

I saw them waiting there on the side of the highway when we were still a quarter-mile distant. I pulled the cord, stepped out into the aisle. As I made my way to the front, I continued watching them through the windshield. Lynk still had his stick. He stood on the ditch's other side, tossing stones into the air and taking wild swings. Carl stood next to Roland, who faced the bus.

With a hissing of air-brakes, we came to a stop and the driver opened the door. Grinning, I descended.

Roland nodded at the books under my arm. 'Homework, eh?'

'Yeah, my teacher's a real bitch.'

Carl following, we jumped the water-filled ditch and joined Lynk. He swung his improvised bat, striking a stone, and the flat cracking sound was echoed a second later as the stone struck a wooden sign a few yards away. The sign stood at the corner point of two fence lines, its red-painted words faded to a dull pink.

Maypole Mink Farm Half-Mile.

On the sign a mink had been painted, running, its brown coat chipped and faded.

Lynk gave me a tight smile and said, 'I hit that fuckin' mink five fuckin' times in a row!'

'You guys play baseball?' I asked Roland.

'Of course!' Lynk snapped. 'Can't ya see?'

Roland nodded.

'I'm first base on my school team,' I said. 'I got a Cooper glove.'

'Fuck that,' Lynk said. 'We play 500. None of that fuckin' team shit. Playing first base is piss-ass!'

I laughed.

'Let's go,' said Roland.

Without another word, he climbed over Fisk's fence and began crossing his field.

CHAPTER FOUR

I

THREE LOTS NORTH of the Yacht Club, at the top of the hill, there was a stand of trees shot through with bracken. In its centre lay the crumbling foundations of an old house. When it had stood, perhaps fifty years ago, it had not been large; the pitted limestone walls, now only knee-high, showed only four rooms. If there had been a cellar or basement, it had long since been filled in and no sign of it remained.

The driveway that led into the decayed homestead was mostly overgrown; only a careful exploration would reveal it. Because it was a place of antiquity, because it was a place where something had ended and nothing had risen in its place, Jennifer thought it perfect.

The trees and brush fashioned a grey-and-black barrier, like a thickly woven web, on all sides. Jennifer led the way into the clearing, Barb and Sandy behind her. No one spoke as they entered the ruins and sat down on the foundation walls.

Jennifer studied her two friends. Absently twisting the curls of her short brown hair, Barb kept her gaze fixed on the path that had brought her here, to this place. Jennifer glanced at her other friend. Expressionless, Sandy's face was turned in the direction opposite Barb's.

'Did you bring it?'

Jennifer turned to Barb, met her uneasy gaze with a smile. 'Of course,' she answered. 'Three hits, just like I said.'

Sandy stood up and looked around. 'Is this the right kind of place, though?' she asked.

'It's perfect,' Jennifer replied, reaching into the breast pocket of her jean jacket. 'There's just us. No one knows we're here. There couldn't be any place better.'

'I have to pee,' Sandy said suddenly.

Barb's laugh came as a shriek.

'Over at that tree there, then,' Jennifer suggested. The tree stood at the edge of the homestead's foundation. It was an old ash that had probably been planted when the house was first built.

'Is that stuff going to make us go crazy?' Barb asked.

'Maybe a little,' Jennifer admitted. She looked down at the three small squares of gelatin in her hands. She had taken acid twice before, yet both times it had been indoors. This time, she knew, it would be different.

Sandy had returned from the tree and now stood in front of her. 'So that's acid, huh?'

'Yep. Windowpane.' She distributed the squares to her friends. 'Cough drops,' she laughed.

An indeterminate time later, Barb muttered, 'I smell olives.'

'The snake's stopped moving,' Sandy replied.

'I hear flapping wings.' Barb sat down on the ground and looked skyward. 'Fluttering leaves.'

'There are no leaves,' Jennifer said. 'Just little fists.' Leaning back, she watched the currents of air moving back and forth, carrying scents and sounds attached to their threads like notes. *I'm watching music.* 'Little fists pounding. Hear them.' Suddenly she felt omniscient. She began to see visions not her own; she began to see with Barb's eyes, Sandy's eyes. 'Early begun.'

'Further spun.' Barb smiled.

'One day done,' Sandy finished.

They sat in wondrous silence.

I I

'Me and Roland saw an eagle today,' Lynk said, pausing to kick at a clump of mud.

I snorted. 'There aren't any eagles around here. Just hawks, and owls.'

'How the fuck would you know?' Lynk demanded hotly.

'There just aren't,' I replied, at a loss at how to explain my certainty, but feeling stubborn anyway.

'Pretty sure it was an eagle,' Roland said slowly, frowning. 'White head. Real big, gliding back and forth.'

I grunted. 'Maybe it was heading north or something.'

The field was still muddy after yesterday's rain. Heavy globules of mud clung to our boots as we walked. Up ahead stood Fisk's farm. From our approach the three long rows of cages created a wall in front of the house itself. As we neared, an old brown pick-up truck pulled on to the section road from Fisk's driveway. Moments later it clunked past us, heading for the highway.

'Who was that?' I turned to follow the truck. It seemed to sway from side to side, like a foundering boat.

'Old Man Louper,' Lynk said.

'The guy with the dogs?'

'Yeah. Fuckin' meanest dogs you ever saw. Just like Louper himself. The guy's half nutso.'

'Wonder what he was doing at Fisk's?' Roland mumbled.

I glanced at him. He seemed distracted for some reason. I had sensed it as soon as I got off the bus. He walked slowly now, almost aimlessly, as if he had lost interest in his destination.

I took a deep breath, then said, 'This is boring. There's gotta be something else we can do.'

Lynk swung his cudgel at a clod of mud. 'Like what, asshole?'

Something in me snapped. 'I'm getting fucking tired of you calling me an asshole, Lynk.'

Everyone stopped. Turning to face me, Lynk raised his stick. He grinned. 'And what the fuck're you gonna do about it, asshole?'

'Drop that toy pecker of yours and I'll show you,' I said slowly, anger curling my hands into fists.

Our gazes locked. Lynk's grin appeared frozen on

his narrow face. The stick moved up between us. 'I'll fuckin' bash your head in,' he rasped.

'Well, before you do,' Roland drawled, 'let me go home and get my bat.' He turned to me, but did not smile. 'You wanta borrow my bat, Owen?'

'Yeah,' I said, grinning at Lynk. 'Either that or we do it now, Lynk. With our fists.'

We stood there for another minute, then Roland walked between us. 'C'mon, we're wasting time.'

No one spoke until we were past Fisk's farm, and then Lynk, trailing the rest of us by a few yards, called out. 'Hey, look! Old Man Fisk's gonna burn some mink guts!' He pointed.

We saw the man standing there at the edge of his field. Beside him was a black mound and a tall, barren metal pole.

'That guy gives me the creeps,' Roland said.

I nodded.

'Aw, fuck that,' Lynk said, though without his usual bluster. 'He's just a fuckin' weirdo.'

'He can probably hear you,' I hissed. There was no more than fifty yards separating us from Fisk. 'So shut the fuck up, asshole.'

'What's he holding?' Carl asked in a small voice.

'Kerosene can,' Roland muttered. 'He's gonna douse the pile.'

'Maybe he already has,' I said, as if the distinction were somehow important.

'Can you smell it?' Roland asked, glancing at me.

'What? The kerosene?'

'No. Mink guts.'

With his words I became conscious of the odour, sweet and faint on the wind.

'And he's standing there.' Roland shook his head. 'Right beside it.'

'A fuckin' weirdo, man.'

Fisk took a sudden step forward, raising one arm. 'Get outa here!' he roared.

We stepped back.

'Get outa here! You goddamn vultures!'

As one we turned and ran. I could think of nothing but escape. My legs pumped wildly, flinging clumps of mud high into the air. Though on the edge of panic, something in the back of my head remained calm, and it sent out a stream of clarity that made the world around me seem all at once brighter, sharper. Lynk moved past on my right, his stick gone – left behind. That detail stayed with me, and I clung to it the way my eyes clung to Lynk's back as he pulled farther away. *He's panicked,* I gasped to myself. *Look at him go!* With that thought I began to slow, my fear dissolving, laughter overtaking me.

Roland stopped a few paces ahead and turned. Seeing his sudden wide grin, I whooped with laughter. All along I had been carrying my school books under one arm. Now they toppled forward, falling at my feet. Papers skirring out in all directions and then settling down on the mud suddenly seemed to me to be the funniest thing in the world. Tears coursing down my cheeks, I fell to my knees.

Roland did the same a few feet away. I glanced up at him. He pointed. Lynk had almost reached the edge of the forest lining the river. Carl caught up with us then, a broad smile on his face.

Fisk, I saw when I turned, was still standing there at the edge of his field. After a moment he walked over to the mound and began dousing it with kerosene.

'Lynk's coming back,' Roland announced, wiping at his face.

He must have stopped at the treeline; he must have seen us way back here. As he approached I saw the deliberate and not-quite-successful swagger he had assumed. I giggled again, only slightly more subdued than earlier.

'What're you guys laughing about?' Lynk asked as he came up to us. He saw the spilled books and paper and grinned.

We said nothing as we climbed to our feet. Roland helped me gather my muddy homework, and then we resumed our leisurely pace towards the river. We came to the edge of the forest, and as we entered the trail I heard a scuffle behind me and I turned. Carl had been following in my immediate wake when we had crossed the field. But at the trail's edge Lynk pushed in front of him. I caught only its aftermath, and yet it was at that moment that I was witness to a most surprising display: in one brief flash I saw Carl's hatred unveiled and directed at Lynk's back.

'I told you he was fuckin' nutso,' Lynk said behind me.

I shook my head. 'So what do you want, a gold medal?'

'Looks like all the ice is gone,' Roland said.

Over his shoulder I saw the swirling brown surface of the river. The pageantry was over, the spoils gone. It lost much of its magic for me, then.

'Maybe we should sneak back to Fisk's farm,' I ventured, an idea coming to me.

'What for?' Lynk demanded.

'To see if he lights the fire,' I replied.

'Yeah.' Roland nodded thoughtfully. 'It's almost dark. We could sneak in.'

'Exactly,' I said. 'It's barely six o'clock. We still got a half-hour before dinner, right?'

'We don't eat till seven,' Roland said.

'Great. Let's go.'

When the two of us headed back up the trail, it didn't surprise me that Lynk and Carl followed. They were both probably going to miss their suppers – as was I – but the challenge had been made, and it had to be accepted.

III

The barking dogs announced Sten's return. Taking a seat on the piano bench, Elouise began wiping dust from the instrument's polished surface. The wood was cool beneath her hands; she thought of tilting back the key-cover and playing a few notes.

She wondered where Jennifer had gone to now – dinner was only a half-hour away. The thought of eating with only Sten for company filled her with dread. She and her husband had exchanged no more than a dozen words in the last two days. With the seeds freshly planted and the first weeding still a week or so away, Elouise had no reason to leave the house, and Sten seemed to have planted roots on the back porch. When he had climbed into his truck and driven off a short while ago Elouise had rushed to the living-room window, imagining for a brief, terrifying moment that she was seeing the last of him. After a few minutes, however, she realised that the fear was a foolish one. Like her, Sten had nowhere to go.

And now he was back. She continued cleaning the piano, hoping that he would stay outside – at least until dinner. Reaching up, she touched her face as she had already done countless times since morning. Misshapen and oddly smooth – it had now become a mask.

Sten had shattered her dentures with his fist, he had driven the plate to the back of her throat, and she had almost choked to death. It was hard to eat; she could manage only soup and, of course, jam. But already the swelling had passed; its colour had deepened from red to blue and greenish-black, and the pain was only a dull throb now, though her neck was, if anything, stiffer.

The prospect of going to the doctor terrified Elouise. There was no disguising what had happened – the imprint of Sten's fist was all too evident. Nevertheless, those few times when she had attempted to move her jaw to any great extent had brought excruciating pain, and the sound it made was of two stones grinding against each other. She was fairly certain that Sten had broken her jaw.

She would need to get it looked at sooner or later, she knew. Thoughts of that time terrified her.

'Dinner ready?'

Sten's voice behind her snapped her upright on the bench. She took a rattling breath. 'Thoon,' she said, not turning around.

'Good,' Sten grunted.

Elouise listened to him walk away. Sten had been drinking on and off ever since the accident, but he had never struck her until now; he'd saved his violence for walls, doors, dishes and furniture.

Sten had gone into the kitchen. She heard the hissing snap of a bottle-cap, and sighed. She had hoped that he would have been shaken out of it. If anything, Sten was drinking even more, although only beer – it had been liquor, rye, that had triggered his rage. And he had poured his remaining supply down the sink.

Sten returned to the living room. 'Leave my supper in the oven, Elly. I'm going out to get some more beer.'

She nodded. Thank God, she muttered to herself. *Now I can eat alone.*

IV

We moved through the shadowed ditch like raiders. The pewter clouds had pooled just above the western horizon and the setting sun created a streak of orange and red beneath them. Long before we came near enough to Fisk's farm to see the burning mound we smelled its smoke. And now like shredded black wings the smoke curled down into the ditch around us.

Roland glanced at me from over his shoulder. 'Hear it?'

I nodded. The fire crackled, hissed, sizzled – combined, it sounded like endless chattering, as if living mink were being burned – burned, but not dying.

'Let's get closer,' I whispered.

We slithered along the inside slope of the ditch, parting the dead grass with our bodies. And then, up ahead, we saw the fire's glow. We edged up the slope and pulled ourselves over the ridge.

Fifty feet away stood the mound, lit up with white heat from within. The maypole glowed like a spear of fire beside it. Of Fisk there was no sign.

'That's not possible,' Roland rasped.

'What?'

'Meat and bones don't burn that hot,' he said, his face pink in the reflected glow.

'Must've put something else in it,' Lynk whispered. 'Birch logs or something.'

Slowly, Roland nodded. 'Yeah, you can sort of see them through all the bones and stuff.'

Even at this distance the heat brushed our faces. Within the mound I could make out leg bones and skulls. On one side I saw a hunched spine burst in a shower of sparks that lifted skyward as if flung by an invisible hand. 'I'm going closer,' I said.

'Are you fuckin' nutso, man?' Lynk demanded.

'Chicken shit.' I took a moment to sneer at him, then I dragged myself up from the ridge and began creeping towards the mound. There were lights on inside Fisk's house, but I figured even if he was watching, the fire from the mound would turn the rest of the world black.

At about thirty feet I stopped. It was too hot to crawl any closer. Still, from this distance, I could make out one individual skull, its eye sockets filled with red flames.

I lay there until Roland's hand closed on my ankle. The skull had long since burned to white ash. Together, we crawled back to where the others waited.

'The sun's gone down,' Roland said. 'I gotta get home.'

V

Sitting on the concrete pier where gas and diesel were pumped for the yachts, Walter Gribbs watched the sun set. The river had its origin far to the south, but its course here was set on a south-west–north-east axis. This early in the season, the sun – from this vantage point – sank directly behind the river's waterline, and this was what Walter had come to watch.

It reminded him of sunsets on the sea. The water turned into liquid gold trimmed with red fire; it spread the sun's gilded coat like a warm blanket, and even the darkness that claimed the rest of the sky seemed somehow benign and salutary.

An old chant he had once heard a mate singing – off the Portuguese coast, he recalled – came back to him. His voice drooping to a growl, Walter sang:

> *Grume goes the sun,*
> *Heal goes the wound.*
> *Bloom goes the sun,*
> *Bright goes the wound.*

He had never asked that mate what it meant. He had never heard of 'grume' and so he figured it was just there to rhyme with 'bloom'. Old wounds, he thought, that was what it was about, old wounds and the way hey could come alive years after they had healed.

He had signed up on the trawler *Helmquist* out of Copenhagen to do a North Sea run then hand the ship over to her new owners in Lisbon. *Helmquist*'s captain and crew were mostly Danish and they told tales

of the sea that seemed to go back to the days of the
Vikings. And when they had cleared the English Chan-
nel and plunged straight into an unexpected bank of
fog, one of the Danes told him about the Ship of Nails.
The day it came up from the south, from a spanse of
endless fog, would mark the end of the world. Nails
pared from all the men who had died the 'straw death'
– a bloodless death – would be constructed into a ship
by the prince of Hell, and it would lead the legions of
the damned to the battle at the end of the world.

The sun sank lower. Fire and ice, and blinding
clouds. Walter wondered if one day those clouds would
part, revealing the Ship of Nails, and at its prow, the
prince of Hell.

The sun was gone, the pool of gold turning a deep
crimson. A wind sprang up from the south, luffing the
surface of the river. Suddenly shivering, Walter climbed
to his feet. He stood for a moment, watching the water,
his hands on his hips. Then, sighing, he turned about
and made his way back up the bank towards his shack.

VI

We hurried through the deepening shadows of the
strip of woods separating Fisk's land from the playground. No one spoke as we emerged on to the playing
field. To our left, beyond the swings, stood Louper's
house and kennel, both cast in dull yellow from the
lone porch light. Within the kennel the dogs were visible as four black shapes, three gathered around one.

My gaze remained on them as we crossed the playground. There was something odd about one of the

dogs, I realised. Then I stopped. The dog in the centre had just risen on its back legs, and it stood there, watching us.

'Jesus Christ!' I whispered.

At my words Roland stopped and turned, followed my gaze. 'Weird,' he muttered. 'That's Old Man Louper in there.'

'With the dogs,' Lynk said beside me.

I shook my head. 'What's he doin' inside that cage?'

'Maybe he's feeding them,' Roland suggested.

Lynk pushed past me. 'Who cares? I gotta get home.'

We began moving again, but I felt shaken. I could've sworn I'd seen four dogs in there, not three and a man.

Reaching the road Lynk laughed suddenly. 'He probably lives in there.'

'Wonder what he was doing out at Fisk's?' I said.

'Probably ordering a fur coat.' Lynk turned to grin at me. 'Dog fur.'

I realised that he was making overtures, but I didn't trust him. So I didn't return his grin. I held his gaze for a moment, then turned my attention back to the road.

'I'll see you guys later,' Roland said.

'Did ya get the homework?' Lynk asked.

'Yeah. See ya.'

We nodded and he began making his way up the street. We continued on in the opposite direction.

I glanced at Lynk. 'What was that about home-work?'

'Roland missed the morning.' Lynk shrugged. 'Doctor's appointment.' He paused, then: 'Man, that was some fire!'

I grunted. 'I've seen bigger ones.'

'Oh yeah? Where?'

'In the city. I saw a whole apartment block burn down, once.'

'Anyone get killed?'

'Yeah,' I lied. 'Lots.'

'Did you see the bodies?'

I nodded.

'What'd they look like?'

I sneered at him. 'Bodies. What else would they look like?'

'All black and crisp, eh?'

''Course.'

'Just like those mink.'

I suddenly felt sick. They would've looked just like those mink. Bones bursting and veins popping, skulls with eyes of fire.

'Did somebody start it?'

I glanced at him. 'Start what?'

'The fire. Did somebody light it on purpose?'

I shrugged. 'Don't know.'

Lynk grinned. 'I once started a forest fire,' he said. 'Down near the beaver lodge. But it rained, and the firemen came and put it out. I bet if they hadn't come and it hadn't rained, it would've burned for miles.'

I stared at him briefly, then looked away. 'You're a fucking idiot, Lynk.' We had reached my driveway and so without another word I turned into it and left them.

VII

When the world had ceased its wild, warped dance, returning to more familiar rhythms, and when the

trees surrounding the ruins had retracted their claws,
Jennifer led her two friends out of the homestead
clearing.

No one spoke; their throats were tight and dry. The
occasional hallucination still flashed through Jennifer,
normalcy twisting and sliding into something else: for
a moment it seemed that the shadows scattered in all
directions and that the road beneath her feet dissolved
into black mud, but, smiling, she rode it out. There was
a sea within her, but the waves that had tossed her high
into the air, that had run her through cavorting chan-
nels for what seemed an eternity, were now growing
calm. She felt their tranquillity flowing down her arms
and legs, felt a sudden, deep conviction that she was
able to fly, the next moment sadly dismissed it.

'You look weird, Jenny,' Barb said, giggling.

Jennifer sighed, then glanced at her two friends.
'You two feel able to walk home?'

'Sure,' Barb said, reaching up to twist her curls but
missing. She groped for a second, then dropped her
hand and shrugged. 'It's not far.'

'Sandy?' Jennifer asked.

'Huh?' Sandy turned, a slightly wild look in her eyes.
'Home? Oh yeah, sure.'

Jennifer nodded. 'Okay, see ya later, then.'

She stood for a moment, watching them walk up
the road, then turned and made her way towards her
house. The sky was still playfully spinning threads of
colour before her eyes. It had been an incredible trip.
For a time there she had been seeing through Barb's
eyes, and Sandy's; and she was pretty certain that they
had shared thoughts – she remembered poems, full of
strange rhymes and odd inflections, lines they had each

spoken in turn, often using words they had never heard before.

The road seemed to be getting narrower as she approached the first of the two sharp bends that would bring her around to her house. She held out her arms on either side for balance, slowing her pace.

Shadows crept close on all sides, and Jennifer felt a tremor of fear. As she reached the bend she looked up and gasped. Ahead, at the very edge of darkness, stood three figures. It was a moment before she recognised two of them. Lynk and Carl. Both were facing the third boy. The new kid, a disembodied voice informed her. She nodded. He spoke a reply to something Lynk said, then turned and entered the driveway. He hadn't seen her.

Jennifer gasped again, then blinked and shook her head. For a brief moment she had seen large black wings on the shoulders of all three of them. But now they were gone, and so was the new boy.

Lynk and Carl approached. She watched as the sky above them reached down threads of colour and brushed the tops of their heads. Green for Carl, red for Lynk. The threads withdrew and suddenly the two boys were walking past her.

'Hi,' she said uncertainly.

Lynk nodded and Carl mumbled, 'Hi, Jennifer.'

'Was that the new kid?' she asked.

'Yeah,' Lynk muttered, not stopping.

'What's his name, Carl?'

'Owen Brand,' Carl replied, hurrying after Lynk.

'A third thread went down the driveway,' Jennifer said.

Lynk and Carl stopped and looked at her. 'What?' they asked in unison.

'A third thread,' she explained. 'It went in after him. It was white.'

'How come you're holding your arms out like that?' Lynk asked.

'Balance.'

'What thread?' Carl asked, a strange look on his face.

Without replying Jennifer began walking again, leaving them standing behind her. As she reached the second bend she saw Roland making his way up the road's hill. And above him, stretching from north to south, Jennifer saw a black thread. She shivered as a cold wave passed through her. A moment later the sky was once again normal, dark and colourless.

Leaving the road, Jennifer hurried across the playground. Barking dogs greeted her as she entered the yard and ascended the back porch steps. She kicked her runners off just inside the door, walked down the hallway and entered the dining room.

Her father sat at the table, eating dinner. A bottle of beer waited beside the plate. Stopping, Jennifer sneered. 'Down to drinking them one at a time, eh?' She walked past him. 'Well, good for you, Daddy. Where's Mom? Let me guess. You beat her to a pulp and threw her in the kennel, right?'

'Jennifer, don't,' her father croaked.

'Go to hell, Daddy,' she replied sweetly as she went to the doorway that led to the kitchen.

'Have you eaten?' he asked behind her.

'Just one little tab of gelatin since lunch,' Jennifer

said. 'But I'm not hungry so you just go ahead and finish it all off. It'll give you something to throw up later.' At the refrigerator she decided on an apple – it was true: she wasn't very hungry, but she knew she'd need something or else she'd wake up with a headache.

Without another word to her father she left the kitchen and made her way up the stairs to her room. Outside, the dogs continued barking. Entering her room, yet another shiver passed through her. Jennifer drew a deep breath. 'Fuck,' she hissed.

CHAPTER FIVE

I

HE'D TAKEN A bullet below the stomach, and now
crouched with his back against the crumbled limestone
ruin of a Roman temple. The wind, hot and dusty, carried taints of the Mediterranean to him like the smell
of corruption. Inland, the sounds of gunfire and shell-
ing continued, but it now seemed a million miles away.

Corporal Hodgson Fisk was the last member of the
squad left alive. All around him, baking in the Sicilian
sun, lay his friends – the men he had known since the
very beginning. Most were missing limbs: the shell that
had landed in the midst of the firefight had taken out
everyone who hadn't already been brought down by
gunfire. Scattered among Fisk's friends were the rem-
nants of strangers. Germans. Not that it mattered, he
told himself. The flies covered everyone, so that apart

from the uniforms there was almost no way of distinguishing friend from foe.

And now rats and mice had crept out from the tumbled limestone wreckage to join the carrion fray. They explored empty sleeves; they licked blackened blood and scurried among spilled entrails. They fought with the flies and maggots.

'Lots of little wars,' Fisk mumbled through cracked lips. He watched a mouse crawl from the mouth of one of his friends. 'Little wars.' The bleeding from the hole in his mid-section had stopped. A cool numbness had pooled around it. He kept his hand over it to keep the flies away.

Had it been hours, or days? Maybe years. He remembered the landing – he remembered all the landings. Dunkirk, El Alamein, and now Sicily. 'Madness, then death,' Fisk whispered, then coughed as a wave of pain crashed through him. 'Madness.'

He gasped. Something was coming up. Something was pushing through his throat. Gagging, he leaned forward. It was coming up. Madness. He felt it tear against the sides of his throat, and his stomach convulsed. It crawled into his mouth, clawed his tongue, gripped his teeth and pushed outward.

Fisk screamed. Wet fur wriggled against his lips. And then it fell into his lap. Eyes wide, he watched the mouse scurry away.

Choking, Fisk bolted upright in his bed. He reached out and found the lamp switch. Blood covered his chest, red-yellow streaks trickling around the beads of sweat. He had bitten his tongue, and his mouth was filled with bitter, warm fluid. Pushing the tangled sheets away with his feet, Fisk rolled on to his stomach. His head over the bed's edge, he opened his mouth and spat out the blood.

Slowly, the trembling faded from his muscles. The roar inside his skull lessened. Taking deep breaths, he blinked the brine from his eyes. After a moment, he rolled on to his back and then sat up.

His room and all its furnishings had become a mass of grey uncertainty; though he squinted, he could make out no details. *I might as well be sleeping in a cave.* Memories of the nightmare returned to him. He shivered. It had been years since he'd had that dream. Decades. Why had it come back? Why now?

Fisk pushed himself off the bed. He crossed through the grainy fuzz of his room, opened the door and entered the hallway. It seemed to lengthen as he walked down it to the bathroom, as if he had somehow found himself in an endless tunnel of half-darkness. In the bathroom he flicked on the light, then stood at the threshold, staring at his face in the mirror. Blood and spittle had smeared his lips and jaw, giving the lower half of his face a glossy sheen. The veins seemed prominent all across his face, blue-green branches that throbbed. On his creased neck he saw the pulse of his jugular.

Fisk went to the sink, watching the face in the mirror getting closer, and turned on the hot water tap. He waited until the steam obscured it, then he shut the tap off and sank his hands into the water. Though most of his fingers had nerve damage, he could still feel the scalding heat sinking into them. Swirling the water, he cupped his hands and then splashed his face.

It had been a splash in the face that had pulled him from unconsciousness that day almost thirty years ago in Sicily. An English medical officer and a squad of Gurkhas had found him in shock and almost dead. Back in Evac, it had been a source of astonishment that Fisk had survived to see proper treatment and a hospital bed. And the day he had been carried aboard a ship that would take him home, there were those who spoke of the departure of a miracle.

A small miracle, Fisk smiled to himself as he dried his face with a towel. *You sit there in your own blood, watching the flies and the maggots and the rats eating your friends, and it comes to you that you don't really give a damn. Because they're dead, and you're alive. And you've got a choice. You can live – for years, for ever – or you can join your buddies.*

So I left them there, and they're still there, waiting for me. Waiting for the mouse to crawl out of my mouth. Fisk spat into the sink.

He left the bathroom and made his way down the hall towards the back door. He could hear a wind outside, rattling the cages, moaning against the sides of the house, joining the chattering chorus. He walked out on to the porch.

The moon cast a pallid glow on the earth and a glimmer on the pools of water in the field, throwing shadows against him as he strode to the steps. The cold wind shifted and he could hear the bare branches of the trees at the far edge of the field crackling and rattling. Beside the maypole the mound of mink remains was a smeared, faintly luminescent pile of white ash. Three days of rain in the last week had diminished it.

Although it was late, Saturday's dawn was still hours away. *How long will I have to wait?* Fisk frowned at the maypole. Sometimes, especially after all these years, it was easy to lose sight of the purpose, of the goal. *Dying should be easy, shouldn't it?* He shook his head – *look at that man, Louper – he's dying. Makes it look simple, effortless.*

Fisk couldn't drink alcohol – the bullet in his gut had taken care of that. He'd bring up anything he swallowed. But he knew that, even if he could drink, dying that way would be wrong; it would be a coward's act. 'It's gotta be natural,' he said aloud. *I've given up a long time ago – I'm ready for the flies and the maggots. So why is it taking so long?*

The wind shifted, came swirling around the house, carrying with it the stench of the mink in their cages. Fisk smiled. *It doesn't smell so bad, does it? Just half-eaten meat, shit and piss.* He laughed as a thought came to him. 'We're all waiting to die here, aren't we?'

He turned to re-enter the house. 'All waiting for the hand of God, eh? His, and mine – makes no difference to you, makes all the difference to me.' He opened the door and strode into the darkness.

II

There would be no sleep for him this night, Sten realised. Grimacing, he sat up on the couch. The wind outside was howling, and so were his dogs. But neither was so unusual. The old season was reluctant to yield its grip on the earth, and the dogs had howled every night since Max's death.

I need a beer, Sten told himself. He climbed to his feet, tottered a moment before regaining his balance, then shambled into the kitchen. The curtains hadn't been drawn, so the moon's light was sufficient for Sten to find the refrigerator. Taking a bottle from the case inside, he turned and walked into the dining room. At its edge he stopped.

The far end of the dining room had been the only place to put the piano, since anywhere else would block a window. Jennifer was now sitting on the bench. Sten was certain that she hadn't heard him.

She's just sitting there. Sten frowned at the realisation. *She's not moving.* He took a soft step forward, wondering what to do. Jennifer was dressed in a pale pink nightgown, her hair tied up behind her head. Both of her hands lay on the covered keyboard, unmoving.

Sten hesitated, then whispered, 'Shouldn't you be asleep?'

Jennifer's head snapped around. 'What do you want?' she hissed.

He shrugged. 'I was just looking for the bottle opener.'

She gazed at him for a moment, most of her face hidden by shadows, then she said, 'You disgust me.'

Sten winced, stepped back. He looked down at the bottle in his hands. 'I know,' he mumbled.

Jennifer rose and stepped around the bench. 'Oh, you know, do you? And that makes it all right, does it?'

He shook his head, watched his hands trying to hide the bottle.

'Nothing to say?' Jennifer sneered. 'Nothing to say for the fucking mess you've made – the fucking hell you've dragged us all into? Oh yes, I forgot: you know. Well, now we're all saved, aren't we?'

Sten gazed at her. She stood in front of the piano,

her small hands balled into fists at her sides, her face twisted with hatred – it had to be hatred. He opened his mouth, but no words came forth. She glared at him, then, with something like a snarl, she whirled away and hurried from the room. He heard a torn gasp come from the stairs, and then nothing until the slam of the door to her room.

Sten stood rooted for a moment longer, then his eyes caught the glint of the bottle opener lying on the table. He walked towards it, then stopped.

'Yes, I know,' he whispered.

Outside the dogs continued howling. Sten set the bottle down. It was hopeless, he knew. He would have to return to it sooner or later; it was all that lay between him and madness. *All around me is hatred. My daughter. My wife. And that leaves only one place of escape.* He listened to the plaintive moaning outside.

The wind hissed through the torn screen of the back door. Sten opened it and stepped on to the porch, the wood creaking beneath him. The dogs fell silent, and he watched their black shapes pad up to the front wall of the kennel. Descending the steps, he strode towards them. He heard a soft whine.

'Cut it out, Caesar,' he muttered, unlatching the gate. 'Get back, damn you,' he snarled, pushing the dogs back as he entered the kennel and closed the gate behind him. 'Get back. Don't crowd me, and stop your bloody whining, you bastards.'

Tail wagging, Kaja pushed against him, and he staggered back. 'Fuckin' bitch!' he shouted, raising his fist. Kaja cowered at his feet. He struck her across the shoulders and she yelped, sinking lower.

Sten heard a low growl behind him and he turned

to see Caesar moving forward, ears back and teeth bared. Their eyes locked. Sten stepped backward and tripped over the still-prostrate Kaja. Falling heavily, he had the breath knocked from his lungs, leaving him lying helpless, unable to move, unable to scream. Through the stunned rush of blood in his ears he heard snapping and growling. A body slammed sideways against him and he felt claws gouge into his thigh. The body moved away.

And then sweet, cold air filled Sten's lungs. Gasping, he rolled over on to his hands and knees. It was an effort to lift his head and look around. His three dogs stood off to one side. Shane was between Kaja and Caesar, his black tail lowered and waving fitfully and his head turning from mother to brother and back again. Kaja watched Sten. Caesar watched Kaja. Only the wind made any noise at all apart from Sten's ragged breath.

He climbed to his feet. 'Bastards,' he hissed, wiping the muddy sweat from his face. Suddenly racked with chills, he staggered over to the gate. The dogs backed away, all three watching him now. He ignored them, fumbling with the latch. Moments later he was outside, locking the gate with shaking hands.

Back inside the house, Sten hurried to the dining room. He leaned against the edge of the table, opened the bottle of beer and quickly brought it to his lips. He let the beer pour down through his mouth and throat and into his stomach without pause. In seconds the bottle was empty, and the bitter burning along his throat fell away to numbness.

Suddenly dizzy, he pulled out the chair and sat down. Elbows on the table, he held his head in his hands.

'The bastards,' he whispered. 'They wanted to—' He shook his head. No, it was just an accident – it was dark. Caesar got spooked. Frightened. 'Oh, Christ,' he mumbled. 'My dogs—' They were terrified of him. Somewhere inside his head he heard the chuckling of monsters. 'Their master, all right. Master, yeah, right! Tyrant.' *Oh, God. It's hopeless.* 'No fuckin' point to anything.' The monsters concurred, applauded. 'It's you and me, Dad,' he mumbled. 'Claw your way back up, Dad. Come on, come out of the grave. It's only a garbage bag and some dirt. It's you and me, now.' *And us,* chittered the monsters. 'And them.' *And the booze, too,* they added.

Sten slowly pushed himself to his feet. He reeled, then made his way into the kitchen. 'Yeah,' he said. 'Yeah, sure.'

Outside, the wind and the dogs howled.

III

Elouise pulled the sheets up against her chin as the slamming back door indicated Sten's return to the house. She heard him moving around in the rooms below. Heart hammering, she stared up into the darkness, certain that in moments she would hear his footfalls on the stairs.

The wind in the branches outside the window cast a keening dance of shadows across the far wall, like cavorting figures. Elouise sucked air in through the wreckage of her mouth, the cool, dry breath soothing the throb of pain. It had become impossible to move her jaw at all now. Any question of choice had disappeared – she knew she would have to visit a doctor in the morning

And without a driver's licence, her only means of making the trip to the clinic in Riverview was the bus. Sten might drive her, but the thought of that turned her stomach to ice. She knew that, should she ask him, he might hit her again. He might kill her. Even if, by some bizarre twist of his mind, he agreed to take her, there was still the highway drive – Sten hadn't been sober in weeks: he wouldn't be sober tomorrow. And if they somehow managed to arrive, there awaited the questions, the looks, the whispers and the suspicions. No, it would be better all around if she went alone; if Sten didn't know anything about it.

With a big enough bandage, the nature of her injury wouldn't be noticeable to anyone on the bus, or in the clinic's hallways and waiting room. And that just left the doctor, and maybe a nurse or two. She would have to think of a story to tell them, even though she knew that they'd be unconvinced. *So long as they don't cause trouble. Then I don't care what they think.*

The house had fallen silent. *Maybe he's fallen asleep.* She hoped he had. There was a patter of rain against the window. The dogs had stopped their moaning – the shriek of the wind seemed to fill the world. Its cry echoed in her skull. The shadows no longer danced – she stared at them – they writhed against the wall as if nailed there. Unable to escape – voiceless, they couldn't even plead.

Pulling the sheets closer, Elouise closed her eyes. Silence was a good thing. Above the howl of the wind there was no way to hear her own inner screams, and it was this, more than anything else, that made her feel safe, insulated.

So long as he slept.

Like a faint whisper from beyond the walls came music – from Jennifer's room. Holding her breath, Elouise listened. Brahms. Piano concerto No. 2. She remembered buying that record for Jennifer's tenth birthday, along with a half-dozen others.

The music was cut off abruptly. Elouise began to wonder if she'd imagined it. Like an old echo lost in the house for years, only now reaching her. She became aware of all the silent rooms surrounding her, of the silent chambers familiar with darkness and regret. It had become, she realised, a house whose rooms sighed the breath of memories, and all the memories were painful ones. The house bled silence – but no, she could hear a voice, and it was Sten's, coming up from below as if from a pit.

'Master, yeah, right!' Muttering followed the exclamation, and then she heard: 'It's you and me, Dad. Claw your way back up . . .' The words dropped off again.

Elouise moaned. Dad. The old man's face took on blurry definition in her mind's eyes. She saw, once again, the snarl twisting his lips, the feral rage flaring in his red-shot eyes. She watched his battered fists bludgeoning his son, Sten, rocking the young man's head – the son, whose ears bled and whose eyes were glazed with dull incomprehension, whose cut and split mouth hung open, a red rose glossed with saliva. The son, who had made no attempt to defend himself, who had said nothing, not once crying out – who had just stood there, taking it.

And now . . . *It's you and me, Dad.*

So simple, after all. So logical.

Another moan escaped her bruised lips. Elouise rolled over and gently rested her aching head on the pillow. He wouldn't be coming up. She was safe; there was no more need to fight off her exhaustion. She would let her room join the others. Bleeding silence, breathing memories.

IV

Outside, the morning air was crisp and bright. I stood on the steps and watched my father working on the machine. It was half disassembled; rusted parts lay everywhere. Its inner workings, now revealed, reminded me of Fisk's mound – a massive jumble of intestines draped around a crumbling skeleton. I had hoped that seeing its insides would have given me some idea of the machine's function, but, if anything, they had made me even more confused. Countless gears of all sizes crowded the works; oil-blackened, oddly shaped parts filled the spaces; in all, the exposing of the machine's internal organs left me with the vague sense that with it I was witness to the workings of another world; a world of shadowed mystery frozen by the sun's light.

Father disappeared into the garage. I walked out into the yard. Beneath the trees the air was cooler, smelling of dead grass and mud. From somewhere in the branches high overhead came the chatter of a squirrel, and the answering cry of a robin. I wandered through the shadows, imagining myself a lone sentinel on patrol. There were secrets to protect – the work on *Mistress Flight,* the room in the attic, and a thousand hidden hatreds and desires.

Standing in the shadows, I was a soldier, guarding shadows of my own. There was the darkness inside me, and all the secret gears and silent pistons and blackened thoughts worked motives even I could not comprehend. Still, I stood guard, protecting an unknown purpose with fanatic heat.

Today, there would be explorations – I would discover the hidden room in the attic. And work on *Mistress Flight* would continue. And tomorrow, there would be the forests and the river and the beaver lodge.

I turned to face the house, gazed up at the small half-circle window set under the roof. The sun was striking it obliquely, casting an impenetrable mirror sheen over it. Standing up there, behind it looking outward, what would I see? Would that glass alter the world? Somehow, I was certain that it would, though I couldn't imagine in what way.

A tree off to my right had grown at a sloping angle – an easy climb. I walked over to it and laid my hands on the ridged bark. A sentinel needs a lookout, doesn't he. There might be enemies on the horizon; they might be crossing the fields *en masse,* they might be coming down the river, or they might be swirling down from the sky on wings of flame. I began to climb. When I had come to the end of branches that would hold my weight, I looked down. From here, I realised, I could mark the arrival of dragons and ogres moving through the shadows. They would never think of looking up – children are never looked for over one's head. They're to be leered down on, crushed underfoot. They're to be swept aside by the marching figures of adulthood. Trapped in dwarfdom, they're to be ignored in the great battle.

But not me. I had surprises in store for them. Here, on the shoulders of an unsuspecting giant, the strength that flowed through me was unassailable, it was—

'OWEN!'

Turning on my perch, I looked at the house. Mother was standing on the porch. I watched her cup her hands around her mouth.

'OWEN!'

I sighed. 'Up here!' I called.

'Come here this minute!'

Uh-oh, she was angry. I began descending the tree, horrible images of brutal punishments filling my head. I had never faced a brutal punishment before, but I imagined that there was a first time for everything, including torture.

I hurried across the lawn, came up to the driveway. Father had appeared and Mother was explaining something to him in exasperation. I saw him chuckle, and relief flooded through me. Still, delivery was everything. 'What did I do now?' I complained as I walked up to Mother.

She glared at me, but I could see that it was mostly acting. 'What's the meaning of setting traps all over your room, Owen? I nearly lost my fingers a dozen times!'

'Rats,' I explained. 'Our house is fulla them, right?'

'Looks like it,' Father said, grinning at Mother.

'See?' I said.

When Father grinned, Mother could not help smiling herself. I had seen this before, and I had often wondered if maybe they were sharing some secret joke, with me always the butt. Shaking her head, she turned back to the door, then said to me over her shoulder, 'Try informing me of such things in the future, Owen.'

'But I thought you said – just last week – that you would never clean my room ever again. That's what you said—'

'You're pushing it, son,' Father said, wiping rust and grease from his hands.

With another shake of her head, Mother went inside, headed down into the basement to do the laundry. I sauntered after her but stayed on the main floor. Debbie was sitting on the living-room sofa, reading a book. She saw me, scowled, and turned her back to me. Shrugging, I continued down the hall and then ran up the stairs. The time was ripe for exploration.

All my clothes were gone, making my room seem empty, abandoned. The rat traps had all been sprung, and sat in a pile on my desk. The cheese was gone, and so was that musty pervasive odour that had been filling my room for the last week or so. I closed the door and went to the window sill. On the floor beneath it was my knapsack of essential items: candles, matches, the flashlight, an old hammer with a ripped rubber grip, a heavy long-shafted screwdriver, kangaroo-leather work-gloves, and my father's binoculars. Picking the knapsack up, I slung it over my shoulders, spat on my hands, then climbed up on to the window sill.

To repeat the efforts of last week only took a few moments. Once again I crouched, looking down on my room. A wasteland: everything interesting had been removed or scrubbed away. Saddened, I carefully replaced the trapdoor. When it slid into its moorings, darkness closed in around me. I took off the knapsack, untied its flap and pulled out the flashlight. Flicking it on, I played the light down the passage. Nothing had changed. Somehow I had expected, with my new knowledge, that it would have undergone some kind of transformation; that now there might be spiders' webs hanging down from the angled ceiling; that glowing red eyes would burn malevolently in the shadows, that the sounds of heavy shuffling might be heard around every corner. But the musty air was still and empty, and the only sound I could hear was my own breathing. Slowly, I moved up the passage.

I checked the rat-traps as soon as I arrived in the attic's main room. None had been sprung. Vaguely disappointed, I walked back to the wall, entered the middle passageway. I reached its end, set the flashlight down and ran my hands along the press-board barrier. Beyond this wall, I told myself, lay the secret room with the windows. Was there some kind of hidden latch? All I could feel along the wall's edges were the heads of nails, one every five inches or so. I retrieved the flashlight and made my way back to the large room, then went down the third aisle. The wall at the end of this one was also studded with nails, but not as many, maybe one every foot. I took the hammer out of the knapsack and quickly set to work removing them.

The press-board was thin and soft, and I found I had to gouge it with the claw of the hammer in order to reach the nails. I moved from one to the next without pause, images of what lay beyond running through my head. A crypt, a laboratory (the lightning rod gave me that idea), or maybe a wizard's chamber. There were skulls on the shelves, mummy-hands nailed to the window sill, a pentagram etched in black wax on the floor, flasks and vials full of potions. And then the last nail was removed, carefully placed with the others in a small pile between my knees. I gripped the edges of the partition and pulled. It wouldn't budge.

Frowning, I leaned back to see if I had missed any nails. I hadn't. With the flashlight in my left hand, I raised the hammer in my right and levered the claw between the wall and its frame. I pushed the hammer upward. With a loud snap the board broke free, flying forward and striking me. I went down beneath it, swearing. In moments pushed it to one side. Then I scrambled back to my knees and shone the light into the pale darkness beyond.

Caught dead centre in the flashlight's beam, was a rat. We stared at each other. Behind it I saw another, and then heard some scurrying sounds crossing the wooden floor.

I bolted backward, scrambled wildly amidst the woodchips, trying to pick up the press-board even though I still held the flashlight and hammer. I heard even more skittering noises. Somehow, I managed to get the partition on to its edge. As fast as I could, I pushed it back into position, then leaned against it, gasping.

Rats. Thousands of them. I had found their city!

I used four nails, one for each corner of the wall, hammering them in as hard as I could.

So much for skulls, I mused, returning the hammer to the knapsack. And there hadn't been thousands of rats; maybe a half-dozen or so. And I had caught a glimpse of other things in that room; things that suggested to me that it wasn't as empty as was the rest of the attic. Angry with myself, I made my way back to the trapdoor. Rats. Just rats. When it came right down to it, I was a suck. Owen, the suck.

Next time, I vowed, it would be war.

V

The wolf pack moved beneath them, treading the murky darkness, among glowing ropes with diamond eyes. Their grey lean shapes parting flashing schools, their senses seeking the echoes of destruction. Beneath the pounding of the North Atlantic waves against the hull, Walter Gribbs imagined he could hear their abyssal growls. His gloved hands, gripping the depth-charge launch-handle, were frozen. He could feel nothing from his elbows down, and yet he knew that, given the word, they would move – like machines, they would obey.

As the destroyer-class HMS *Hector* sloughed yet another barrage of water and climbed high on to a swell, Gribbs could see flames on the horizon. The wolves had penetrated a flank of the convoy; they had struck, and they had drawn blood. With the first explosion to throw the world into red-lit relief, *Hector*'s engines had roared, and she and two other destroyers voiced the hunter's horn, and the pursuit was on.

There was nothing to see of the quarry; no betraying flashes in the darkness. There were only the fires of the victim as it wallowed in its own oil. But the hunt continued – *Hector*'s course corrections told Gribbs that much. Still, he glared at the seas, the muscles of his face feeling like bruised clay, and the world seemed shredded and beyond its frail fabric was the blackness of Armageddon. He crouched, leaning against the catapult housing, waiting.

The signal came. Gribbs's arms – the machine's limbs – jerked downward and, their function completed, froze into immobility once again. The canisters rolled down the racks, were immediately lost in the darkness. And then, thrumming through the wind and waves, came the first concussive thump. The seas in their wake bulged upward into a white-maned leviathan that appeared again and again as if in pursuit.

Teeth bared, Walter Gribbs snarled curses at the explosions in their wake. 'Come on, you bastard! Come on, you bloody snake!' Oh yes, he laughed to himself, they had drawn her up, thrashing and tossing on the foam-laden main. And maybe – just maybe – she'd bring the wolves with her. 'Come on, you bitch! Let's get the goddamn fuck on with this war!'

But, though she rose up in her wrath, after all the canisters had been expended and she fell away again into the deep, the wolves did not appear – not this time. Still, one of them might have burst apart down there, struggled briefly towards the surface, then sank in failure. Gods, Walter breathed to himself, shaking his head, to die unseen – to die down there with the only witnesses mindless eels that glowed in the darkness – nothing could be more hellish.

'But we're good at that,' muttered Walter as he pulled the catapult lever back up to its set position. 'Making hells to die in.' Turning, he saw that they had come close to the sinking freighter. Spotlights played across the churning waves, travelled the length of the hull, and there were drowning men everywhere. Ships moved among them like trawlers sweeping schools of fish. But the nets were all too few – so many slipped away.

The roar of *Hector*'s engines grew muted. The hunt was over, for now. A hand closed over Walter's shoulder and he turned. A familiar face leaned towards his.

'They figure we got one, Walt!' the seaman shouted, grinning.

Walter nodded. He raised his arms to relieve the ache in his shoulders.

'Walter? You in there?'

'Yep.' Sighing, he pushed himself out of the easy chair, blinked to clear his vision, then walked over to the door and opened it. A short, stocky man wearing a wool sweater and brown flannel pants stood beyond the porch, pudgy hands anchored on round hips. Squinting, Walter stared at the smiling face. Cheshire, he thought. *Cheshire, yes, that's it*. 'G'afternoon, Mr Dallow.' Walter smiled. 'What can I do for you?'

'Call me Chester, please.' Pivoting on his hips, the man turned and waved a hand at the yachts in the dry-dock. 'When do you figure you'll have the equipment ready to start launching?'

Walter rubbed his jaw. 'Well, I'd say by next weekend, Chester.'

'Great. I'll get a hold of the boys.' He sighed loudly. 'Well, another season, eh, Walter?' He grinned.

'Yep, and maybe the last.'

Chester glanced up at him sharply. 'You thinking of retiring, then?'

Walter smiled. 'No, I'm thinking of dying.'

Chester's smile fell away abruptly. 'Jesus Christ, Walter, what in hell's got you talking like that?'

Walter leaned against the door jamb and crossed his arms. 'Oh, I suppose it's those noises I keep hearing at night,' he said casually.

Chester frowned. 'Is it your ticker?'

Laughing, Walter shook his head. 'No, not that.'

'What noises, then?'

Walter let his smile fade. 'Chains breaking. All the links are parting. Used to be they just rattled, but now . . .' He pushed himself upright and stepped back into the house. 'I'll have everything ready for next weekend, then.'

'Uh, right. Thanks, Walter.'

'Sure.' Walter smiled as he began closing the door. 'See you then, Chester.'

CHAPTER SIX

I

THEY WERE WAITING for me at the end of the drive-way.

Lynk was scowling. 'Where'd all that junk come from?' he asked.

I shrugged, turned to Roland. 'We heading to the boat?'

'Yeah. I brought window cleaner and rags.'

'Good,' I grunted. We began to walk.

The morning was still, the stagnant air hot from the bright sun overhead. Birds wheeled in the sky; men in white t-shirts mowed their front lawns or washed their cars; squealing children played in the back yards and dogs barked. The world was settling into the season, with the weekdays long and hot and silent and the weekends a domestic travail.

As I walked I wondered if this would be the world

for me when I grew up. Hours in an office leading to hours pulling weeds and cutting grass. Blue and grey suits and pear-shaped white t-shirts stained with sweat and lawnmower oil – was this my future? Looking at my friends, I found it hard to imagine them in that kind of role, and yet, what else was there for us?

I did not imagine the future to be in any way different from the present. There would still be station wagons for the kids, washers and dryers in the basement, double beds and dens cluttered with the efforts of haphazard hobbies. And there would still be summers stained with motor oil and sweat. Nor did I think that we'd be any different: Lynk's quick grin and the stick in his hands; Carl fumbling behind us and wiping his nose on his sleeve; and Roland, silent and full of life, with dirt under his nails and calluses on his palms. And somewhere, there in the future, I'd still be the unknown with the darting eyes, his face an unreadable mask.

'Think Old Man Gribbs will be around?' I asked Roland.

He shrugged. 'Could be.'

'Might be getting ready to start launching the boats,' Lynk added.

Roland shook his head. 'Not yet. The water's still too high.'

I frowned. 'What difference would that make?'

'The docks are still under water,' Roland explained. 'Nowhere to tie up.'

'So you figure the place will be empty, eh?'

'Yeah.'

We entered the shadowed, winding driveway that led into the Yacht Club. Staying to the left, we edged along the treeline, the driveway's loop and the old white clubhouse off to our right. There were few cars in the parking lot – a good sign. Mostly, the members were rich people who liked to come out here to drink in the bar. Not all of them, Lynk had explained to me, even owned boats, and the ones that did hardly used them at all.

But since all the members came from the city, and so had I, I wasn't very impressed with those few that I'd seen walking around. That there were people with whom we shared the four acres – the Yacht Club's tree-hidden world – was at best a challenge to our skills in secrecy, at worst an inconvenient reminder of the ever-watchful eyes of adults. What made the club so interesting was its land – the trees and the hangars, scaffolds, and grease-laden rail tracks leading down to the water, the perpetual smoulder of the garbage dump, the twisted wire cables and the yachts. In the Yacht Club there were a thousand places to hide from the rest of the world. I had no idea what the rich people did when they came here, and I really didn't care.

'Look.' Lynk pointed at Gribbs's shack. 'There's smoke coming from the chimney.'

Roland grunted. 'Good. That means he's probably making tea, which means he doesn't plan on coming out for hours.'

I glanced at him. 'How do you know all that?'

'My dad knows Gribbs, from the war.'

'World War Two?'

Lynk snorted. 'What else, dummy?'

'Well, Lynk, there's the Korean War, and Canadians fought in it. You should watch who you're calling a dummy, next time.'

'World War Two,' Roland answered, a frown on his face. 'How come you know so much about the Korean War?'

'I don't know much. My dad's brother was killed there, though.'

'Your uncle, huh?'

'Well, I don't know – I mean, I wasn't born yet, right? I suppose I could call him my dead uncle, eh?'

Roland nodded solemnly.

We came to the edge of the boat yards, paused beneath a large oak. 'So your dad fought with Gribbs, then?'

'Not really. He met him over in England. They were both volunteers. My dad went in under-age, in the infantry. Gribbs was in the Navy. The way Dad talks about him he was old even back then.'

My gaze on the keeper's small shack, I said, 'Does he ever come out of there?'

'Not much,' Roland replied, his voice low. 'But Gribbs is good with engines and stuff. Sometimes Dad goes to him to get something fixed.'

We entered the yards cautiously, but all was silent and there was nobody in sight. On the other side waited *Mistress Flight,* tucked in between the treeline and another boat. We hurried towards it.

I I

Walter poured his tea then leaned back. It was coming, whatever it was, it was coming. And all he could do was wait. There was no questioning his certainty; in his dreams he had heard the chains snap. A maelstrom had come into his sea of thoughts, a storm unlike the witch's familiar brew – this one couldn't be talked to. It was mindless, dark and old and full of ancient fury. Walter could hear its approaching roar, and he knew that this was one storm he wouldn't ride out.

And yet he no longer felt any fear: the dreams had become visions of the future that were clear and simple and final. So he sat back in the easy chair and sipped steaming tea. He heard the four boys enter the yards, their mutterings indistinct but audible. Smiling, he added a small amount of honey to his tea.

Ah yes, the old lady's found little hands to smooth her wrinkled hide. Gentle, innocent hands, tentative yet eager – as if touching a new and fragile present. *Dear* Mistress Flight *will return to the living this summer.* The thought brought a grin to Walter's lips.

He'd checked her hull about five years ago, before the sight of the yard's continual decay had finally broken his heart, and he knew she was sound. There were some dry-rot patches near the screws, but they weren't deep – glass or even putty would do them right. She was well built, mahogany and maple, with solid brass fittings and keel. And the old Sea Horse – well, it was a Sea Horse, wasn't it? Those damn things would run with half their parts seized up.

It was better to think about stuff like that, he mused, than to brood over the coming darkness. Better to listen to the kids working on *Mistress Flight* than to follow the rumblings of destruction. Fire and ice, ice and fire – the recurring themes in his dreams.

His tea had gone tepid, and the smoke was making his eyes water. *Damn wood stove.* Anyway, it was time for lunch. Setting the cup down, he rose to his feet. The kids had been working on the lady the last three weekends running; he reminded himself that he'd have to check on their progress soon. Maybe tomorrow.

III

'My dad's in real estate,' Lynk said as he lounged on the aft deck. 'We own two cars, and I'm getting a mini-bike for my birthday.'

'They also got a Ski-doo racer,' Carl added.

'And I can drive it.' Lynk's gaze narrowed on me. 'You know how to drive a Ski-doo?'

'Yeah, we use them all the time in the city,' I said, rolling my eyes at Roland, who grinned.

'What kind of bike you got?' Lynk pressed. 'I got a three-speed.'

'Didn't know you could count that high, Lynk.'

'What kind of bike you got?'

'A Mustang.'

'Does it got a banana seat?'

I nodded.

'Can you pull wheelies?'

Again I nodded.

'For how far?'

I stopped my polishing of the tachometer and turned to him. 'Farther than you, that's for sure.'

Lynk barked a laugh. 'Prove it.'

'I will.' I hesitated. 'As soon as it gets fixed.'

Lynk leaned forward. 'It's busted? Hah, must be a piece of crap!'

'Has it got a flat or something?' Roland asked from where he was cleaning the starboard ports.

I shook my head. 'My dad said he was going to do something to it. Fix it up. He took it to the gas station.'

Roland smiled. 'What's he going to do to it?'

'I don't know. Make it faster, or something, I guess.'

'I got a slick on mine,' Lynk said. 'I can peel out better than you.'

'How d'you know?' I retorted hotly. 'You ever see me peel out?'

Lacing his fingers behind his head, Lynk sneered, but said nothing.

Roland sat down and glanced up at me. 'You find out what kind of parts you'll need for the engine?'

'Just gaskets, mostly. I'm gonna bring some solvent to get rid of most of the guck. And the battery needs charging.'

'This is stupid,' Lynk pronounced suddenly. 'What's the point? It's a good enough clubhouse as it is. Christ, I don't want to fuckin' have to work here. You're fuckin' nutso, Owen.'

I felt my face turn red. 'I may be nutso, you prick, but I'm not sitting around picking my ass like you're doing. You can jerk off all you want, but you're still useless.'

'Fuck off, you motherfucker!'

I laughed, turned away.

Through the port I could see branches full of buds, and small brown birds flitting around them. A matte of grey and brown filled the background, seeming to have knitted the world tight – there were so many shadows that the sun would never reach. And we lived in those shadows. Sighing, I turned and stepped out on to the aft deck. 'Let's go. There's nothing else we can do here, today.'

'Yeah.' Roland came to stand beside me. The forest held an impenetrable wall up before us, and we stared at it in silence.

After a minute Roland said, 'Ever seen a bear?'

'Only at the zoo,' I replied. Somehow, when I confessed my ignorance to Roland, it was all right, though I didn't know why. Roland didn't get my back up like Lynk did. It was a nice feeling, and talking to the tall farmboy with the grave eyes was easy. 'Have you?'

Roland nodded. 'Yeah. They come down from the north in the spring and fall, when they're hungriest. My dad took me with him when he went out to shoot one, last year.'

I glanced at him. 'Did you get him?'

He shook his head. 'We chased it across the highway and then down to the river. It was a big male. He crossed the ice floes. We watched him jumping from one to the next. He didn't even get wet.'

I grinned, trying to picture the scene in my mind. Then I frowned. 'But your dad could've shot him out on the ice, couldn't he?'

'Sure, it would've been easy. He just didn't want to.'

'How come?'

Roland shrugged, a strange look on his face. 'I don't know. He never told me. He just didn't.'

I gazed at the trees. 'I'd sure like to see a bear, someday.'

'Maybe today, eh?' Smiling, Roland nudged me,

then turned to where Lynk and Carl sat. 'Let's head over to the beaver lodge.'

'Fuckin' right, man.' Lynk climbed to his feet, Carl following suit.

I smiled at Roland. 'Bear-hunting, eh?'

He smiled back.

IV

'Where's your mother gone?'

Jennifer shrugged, not looking at her father. 'Don't know. She left before I got up.'

He stood there, his hands gripping the back of the chair, for a moment longer, then left the dining room, entering the kitchen. She heard him open the refrigerator door, heard him snap the beer bottle's cap, heard the door shut, then the sound of his footsteps on the buckled linoleum floor, and a moment later the grate of the back door's spring.

She reached across the table for her Player's Filter cigarettes, wondering why she was bothering – she hated the damn things. But she lit one anyway, exhaled a stream of blue smoke towards the ceiling.

It was going to be a strange day. Last night had been another night in the city. And she and Mark had had a fight; even Dave, when he drove her home, had been cool towards her. They'd made her feel like a little kid, and it was all because of that new girl, the one that Mark and Dave took turns drooling over. The new girl – Debbie Brand. The one whose first words to Jennifer last night were: 'You wear too much eye make-up. Makes you look like a hooker.'

Jennifer took a defiant drag on her cigarette. 'The bitch.' Still, she mused, it would've been worse had she taken Sandy and Barb with her – in a lot of ways those two were little kids. And worse yet, they would've witnessed her being made to look like a fool.

And, to top things off, she woke up this morning to find her bedsheets stained with sticky blood. Even her periods were coming in haphazard fashion. She thought those damn things were supposed to be predictable. 'Christ,' she muttered. 'What a lousy way to start the weekend.'

Stubbing out the cigarette, she climbed to her feet and walked, her limbs feeling leaden, into the bathroom. It stank of beer and vomit and she felt a tremor of nausea rise up inside her. 'Hah, sympathetic barfing.'

Well, one thing was for certain. She wasn't about to spend her day in the house – not with *him* for company. And where had Mom gone, anyway? A wave of fear ran through her suddenly. *Maybe she's taken off. Maybe she's left me – here, alone with that madman–*

Jennifer rushed from the bathroom, ran down the hall and then up the stairs. Breathing hard, she entered the master bedroom, hurried to the closet door and flung it open. All her mother's clothes were there, and so were the suitcases. 'Oh, thank you, thank you.'

No, Mother wouldn't have run away. It was stupid to even think that. *Hell, if anyone's going to run away it'll be me. And I'll tell her first. I'll tell her. I'll invite her, for Christ's sake.*

In any case, Jennifer wasn't planning to stay in the house today. With Barb sick with the flu and Sandy visiting relatives in the city, she'd be on her own, and in a

way that was good. It would give her time to think of
what to do about the bitch – about Debbie Brand.

'Jennifer?'

She whirled. Her father was standing on the bedroom's threshold, his face flushed, his eyes red. She
suddenly felt trapped.

He ran a hand through his greasy hair. 'You sure
Mom didn't tell you where she was going?'

'No.' She stepped towards him. 'I'm going out.'

He moved to one side. 'Where you going?'

Pushing past him, she crossed the hallway and entered her room. Without turning around she replied,
'Out,' then slammed the door in her father's face.

V

Somewhere above us crows laughed. We moved through
the bracken like hunters, eyes hungry for movement,
ears eager for sound. In our hands we gripped stout
clubs of water-worn wood, and they made us feel like
killers.

The afternoon had clouded over, bringing with it a
chill, as if the old winter was reluctant to surrender.
The shadows spread a cool blanket down on the world.
In the gloom it seemed the forest breathed an awareness; unseen eyes followed us – every knot in every
tree trunk was a dwarf's gnarled glower; the humus
seemed alive, as if churning with worms just beneath
the surface. The cold, damp air brushed our faces,
smelling of earthy sweat.

'Maybe we should head back.'

The three of us stopped and turned to look at Carl.

He was carrying a stick far too heavy for him, and it now lay on the mulched ground at his side. He drove his hands into his pockets, shrugged, then glanced at Roland. 'Maybe we should go back,' he said again.

'What the fuck for?' Lynk demanded.

'Well, it might rain.'

'So what?' I retorted. 'A little piss going to make you cry?'

Carl's face flushed and he looked down at the ground. 'No,' he mumbled. Then, taking a deep breath, he raised his head and met my gaze. 'It's close to dinnertime. And I think we should go back.'

Suddenly, I realised that Carl was frightened. I smiled. 'Okay, you go back, then. And if you run into that bear, just yell. Maybe we'll come running.'

'And maybe we won't,' Lynk finished, grinning.

Carl looked at Roland. 'Is there a bear around here?' he asked.

'Didn't you hear?' Lynk said, his eyes wide.

'Roland?' Carl's gaze did not waver from the boy's face.

Roland shrugged. 'Can't say. Don't know. Might be.'

Lynk and I grinned at each other. We knew we'd won. Turning about, we continued on our way to the beaver lodge. And Carl followed. Moving past us, Roland took the lead. After a few minutes he stopped. As I came up to him he glanced at me, frowning.

'You smell that?' he said.

I sniffed. 'Yeah. Something rotten.'

'Something dead.'

I stared at him. 'At the beaver lodge?'

'Maybe.'

'Fuckin' dead beaver,' Lynk said.

'Let's go back.'

Ignoring Carl, the three of us crept forward, our clubs raised. The lodge was just ahead, beyond some thickets. As we approached the stench grew worse. From overhead came once again the laughter of crows.

'Mink guts,' I muttered.

'Only worse,' Roland said.

Off to our right I caught glimpses of the river through the branches. We came to the edge of the thickets. There were no trees here, only gnawed stumps and deadfall. There were trails running through the brambles, but they were only knee-high.

'We'll have to crawl,' Roland said, dropping to his knees.

'We can go around like last time,' I said.

Roland looked up at me, his face pale and expression stern. 'What for?' And then he crawled into the trail.

I had to push Lynk to one side to follow the farmboy.

'Asshole,' Lynk muttered behind me as I crawled after Roland. The branches wove a net of brown and grey on all sides, making the trail feel like a tunnel. The bare mud under my hands was slick, cool and strangely yielding to my weight. It felt like flesh. Up ahead all I could see was the bottom of Roland's sneakers and his jean-clad behind.

A moment later he cleared the trail and, with a grunt, climbed to his feet. I quickly did the same. Roland glanced at me and nodded. 'It's coming from the beaver lodge.'

The uneven mound squatted against the riverbank about twenty yards upstream from us. The stench was overpowering in the still air. Side by side, Roland and I walked towards it. Behind us, at the mouth of the trail, Lynk had snagged his jacket on some thorns and, swearing, he stopped to extricate himself. Still inside the tunnel, Carl whimpered.

The water was making an odd sucking sound at the lodge, and there was also a faint clicking sound. We stepped up on to a muddy ridge that marked the side nearest to us, and looked down.

A dead man was lying in the mud, one arm snagged in the beaver lodge's branches. His lower half was submerged in shallow water which seemed to be gently boiling. But no, the man's lower half was crawling with brown crayfish, and there was hardly any flesh left; every now and then a flash of pallid bone appeared.

He was naked, his skin a dull white. His head was tilted back, hiding his features. Long blond hair – almost white – lay fanned out on the mud all around his head. And he was a giant.

I managed a dry swallow, but I could not pull my eyes away. Somewhere, far away inside my head, someone was screaming. While I just stood there, numb and silent.

'Holy fuck,' Lynk said beside me.

'Where's Carl?' Roland asked.

'He's barfing in the bush,' Lynk replied in a dull voice. 'Bawling his eyes out. Holy fuck, holy fuckin' Christ.'

I opened my mouth, closed it, then opened it again, determined to speak. 'He's, uh, he's too big.'

'Yeah,' Lynk rasped. 'A fuckin' giant.'

'Big as a bear,' Roland said.

I glanced at him, a torrent of undefined thoughts filling my head. He met my gaze, and it was as if I was staring at a blank wall. 'Think we should go and tell someone?'

He didn't reply.

'What the fuck for?' Lynk demanded.

With an effort I pulled my eyes away from Roland's and glared at Lynk. 'What do you mean, what for?'

Lynk's sudden grin shocked me. 'It'll just bring all these fuckin' people out here – pigs and stuff. And what'll we get out of it? Eh? Just a bunch of fuckin' kids. I say fuck 'em all.'

'So what the hell are we going to do with him, then?' I barked a laugh. 'Take him home?'

Lynk placed his hands on his hips, looked down on the body. 'All I'm saying is, we just leave him here. Don't tell anyone. Pretty soon he'll be nothing but bones, right? Besides, he was probably murdered—' He stopped, a wild light coming into his eyes. 'And maybe, if we go to the pigs, the murderer will come after us!'

'Holy shit,' I breathed, suddenly terrified.

'We keep it a secret.' He looked at each one of us. 'Anybody finks, and we're all dead.'

My gaze returned to the body. 'Ever seen anybody so big? Christ, must've been eight feet tall.'

Roland grunted, then turned around. 'Carl? You all right?'

I followed his gaze, saw Carl on his hands and knees, facing the river. There was a muffled reply that Roland seemed to take for 'yes', for he nodded and turned to me.

'Let's look at the guy's face.'

'Yeah,' Lynk added breathlessly. 'Who knows, maybe we know him.'

In spite of our voiced eagerness, we walked slowly, giving the body wide berth. When we were on the other side we approached cautiously.

The three of us screamed and leapt back. On the bank on the other side Carl jumped to his feet and shrieked. And then we were running, clawing our way through the thicket, then whirling past trees, weaving between the boles as if their branches were making grabs for us. There was no time for more screams; the world had closed in to the ground at our feet.

And in my mind, four words pounded with my heart over and over again, each utterance bringing on yet another wave of horror – *He had no face. He had no face.*

VI

Jennifer emerged from the old lot's narrow track and stepped on to the asphalt road. She had just spent the last two hours sitting on the crumbling foundation wall of the ruined house, smoking one cigarette after another, and thinking. And all that had come from it was a greater feeling of hopelessness and a sore throat.

Both Dave and Mark were sixteen years old. And so was Debbie Brand. 'And I'm only thirteen,' Jennifer muttered as she walked down the street. It was as simple as that. It was a fact, a bitter fact, and there was nothing she could do about it. Obviously the make-up didn't help her look older. She glanced down at the front of her t-shirt, casting an appraising eye at her breasts. They were bigger than Debbie's, weren't they? And Mark liked her breasts, didn't he? Hell, he'd played with them often enough.

It felt good when she let the boys hold her breasts, knead her ass, and French-kiss. But though she sometimes liked her reputation – she knew most people considered her loose – she knew it was for the most part exaggerated. She never went all the way. But maybe Debbie Brand did. Maybe that was the difference.

And that just made everything worse, since she had led Mark and Dave to believe that she wasn't a virgin: thus far, her excuses that she didn't want to get pregnant had kept them from pressing their attentions, though she knew that they were beginning to distrust her continual 'bad timing'. So, if she was to lose her virginity, it couldn't be with either of them.

Goddammit, what a mess. And even if I start screwing, I'm still thirteen years old, and Debbie's still sixteen. That problem doesn't change. Shit, how do I get rid of her?

Jennifer was halfway down the street's hill when she saw, coming from the treed entrance to the Yacht Club, first Lynk, then Roland, and then the Brand kid and Carl – all running like madmen. She stopped, watching them, her gaze narrowing on the third runner. They'd probably broken a window or something, she mused. And there was the Brand kid, Debbie's younger brother – what was his name? Owen. Owen Brand.

He was running on Roland's heels, his stride long and sure. From the looks of it, he could've overtaken both the farmboy and Lynk easily. Owen, who was twelve years old, who didn't look half bad, who was Debbie's little brother . . .

Jennifer smiled. 'Well, well. Two birds with one stone, maybe.'

She watched them running down the street, not stopping once to look behind, to find out if they were even being pursued. 'Chicken shits,' Jennifer chuckled. All running full tilt, except for Owen.

After they passed beyond her range of vision, she continued on her way, pausing once to light a cigarette. Suddenly she was feeling much better. 'Two birds,' she whispered. 'All fucking right!'

PART TWO

Ship of Nails

CHAPTER SEVEN

I

A CHILD WITH a sprained wrist sat with his mother across from Elouise. There was no one else in the waiting room this Saturday morning.

The bus trip to Riverview had not been as traumatic as she had feared. Like the clinic's waiting room, the bus had been almost empty; she had found a seat up front and thus did not come under any sort of scrutiny from the few passengers – at least, not that she was aware of. When she came to the reception desk the nurse had given her some forms to fill out and had asked if it was an emergency. Elouise had shaken her head 'no'. There had been no more questions, which was a relief, since she couldn't open her mouth to talk.

Under the bandages her face felt hot, and the world had acquired a painful clarity to her eyes. She was certain that she had a fever.

160   STEVEN ERIKSON

Since she had taken her seat the child – a young boy – had not taken his eyes off her. And they were such strange eyes, Elouise thought. That kind of glittering blue that seemed to carve sharp edges on all that they touched on. And though his sprained arm must have been painful, his expression was one of cool control. The child had a man's face, Elouise realised. Why?

The door to the examination room opened and a nurse stepped out and read a name from her list: 'Arnold Fraser?'

'Let's go, Arnie,' the mother said to her child. They both stood, the mother offering an apologetic smile to Elouise. 'A farming accident,' she whispered. Elouise nodded.

After the door closed behind them, Elouise leaned back and shut her eyes. Even her hands, folded together in her lap, felt hot. It was as if her blood was boiling in her veins. She wanted to cry out, to give voice to this pain, which went so much deeper than just bone and flesh, but she couldn't. If she screamed now, it would be a scream that would last for ever. And so she turned her thoughts to that other stranger living in their house, the one who walked with endless anger. Poor Jennifer. What a terrible world the young girl with the music in her eyes had found waiting for her. It came as no surprise that she had raised walls of rage around herself – it was a protective measure. Still, there were times when Elouise could not bear to see what those walls were doing to her daughter.

It all made her feel so helpless. Somehow, she had to find a way through to Jennifer. Somehow.

'Mrs Louper?'

Her eyes snapped open, and she saw the nurse standing in front of her. Elouise nodded and rose unsteadily to her feet. She followed the nurse into the examination room.

The nurse indicated a paper-covered bench. 'Please sit up here.' She was an older woman with silver hair and smile-lines around her grey eyes. But she didn't smile when she unwrapped the swath of bandages covering Elouise's face, and her voice had assumed a stiff tone when she asked, 'When did this happen?'

Elouise tried to say 'a week' but the words came out unintelligibly. She held up seven fingers. Their eyes met briefly, then Elouise looked down.

'A week?'

She nodded.

'Why didn't you come in earlier?'

She shrugged without raising her head.

The nurse looked at Elouise's forms on her clipboard, then said, 'The doctor will be with you in a minute,' and walked out of the room, closing the door behind her.

Elouise was still staring at her hands when the doctor entered, the nurse following.

'Good morning, Mrs Louper, I'm Dr Roulston.'

She glanced up at the young man, tried to smile but failed. She nodded.

'Don't try to talk, Mrs Louper.' Wheeling out a chair from the desk, Dr Roulston sat down facing Elouise.

'She writes here,' the nurse said, 'that she tripped and fell and hit her jaw against the corner of the stove.' She paused, then added, 'Seven days ago.'

Nodding, Elouise glanced at Roulston. He was just sitting there, watching her. After a moment he sighed and rose to his feet. He leaned close, examining her face, then reached up and touched her swollen jaw. Wincing, Elouise pulled back. He straightened and said to the nurse, 'Set her up for X-rays at General.' He turned back to Elouise and gazed at her for a moment before saying, 'Now, we both know you've been beaten. You've got an infection and probably a broken jaw. I'm having you admitted into Riverview General—'

Elouise stood up quickly, shaking her head, but the doctor held up a hand and continued.

'Look, either you go into the hospital to get this properly treated, Mrs Louper, or I phone the police on this matter. And if I do that, well, this will get very messy. Your choice, Mrs Louper.'

It was hopeless, she realised. There wasn't any choice. She nodded.

'The hospital? Good. Now, Nurse Stevens will take care of the details. Do you wish to stop off at your house to get some personal effects?'

She shook her head, then thought: *Jennifer*. She indicated her desire for pen and paper, and received them. She wrote: *Let my daughter, Jennifer, know where I am. Just my daughter, please.* Then she handed the notepad to Roulston.

He read it, then nodded. 'Can she be contacted through her school?'

Elouise nodded.

'West St John's?'

Again she nodded.

'I take it your husband hit you, then.'

She looked down at the floor.

'Has he ever hit you before?'

She shook her head.

'Was he drunk?'

Yes.

'Does he have a drinking problem?'

Yes.

'Is he getting treatment?'

No.

Roulston turned away and slowly pushed the chair back to the desk. 'You'll be in the hospital for at least two weeks. After that,' he faced her, smiled, 'we'll see what we can do.'

II

His wife was outside planting flowers around the maypole. Rolling a cigarette, Hodgson Fisk paused to watch her for a moment before setting the paper to his tongue.

God, she was still so beautiful. So graceful. She was on her knees, concentrating on her task, carefully removing the flowers from their pots – they had spent the winter indoors, and were now only days away from full bloom – and gently lowering them into holes she had dug in the rich black earth.

Beyond her the field lay black and overturned, ready for seeding. He would be working a whole quarter-section this summer; if he didn't lose any to hail he'd be hiring a couple of hands to help him with the harvesting. Fisk never knew whether it was him or her that was sterile – he told himself that it didn't really matter, that it was something you couldn't blame someone about. They'd talked, years ago, about adoption, but nothing ever came of it, and even that didn't seem to matter. He had a woman he loved, and she loved him, and that was all that counted. Come the harvest, it was easy enough to hire hands.

Full of contentment, Fisk lit his cigarette. It was a beautiful spring, wasn't it. Just enough rain, no flooding from the river, and at the very least a break-even harvest ahead.

'Hodgson?'

Fisk grinned at his wife. 'Yeah?'

'Could you mix me up some Alka Seltzer?'

He frowned. 'Heartburn again?'

Walking towards him, she nodded.

He rose to his feet, flung away the cigarette. 'Bad?'

She nodded. 'Getting there.'

'I'll bring it right out.' Fisk entered the house, walked to the kitchen, vaguely worried. He filled a glass with cold water, dropped two tablets in it then returned to the back porch.

His wife lay on the ground, and the only part of her that was moving was her hair and apron, fluttering in the warm spring wind.

Sitting in his chair on the porch, Fisk stared at the weeds crowding the base of the maypole. Those weeds, he knew, were a kind of defamation. And yet, he did nothing, he felt nothing. She had been gone eleven years to this day – he had waited a long time to die. It seemed he was going to have to wait for ever.

And all the while he would be sharing this world with the weeds, the black field, and a sea of glittering eyes watching his every move.

They're all waiting for me to break, but I won't. If I have to wait for ever, I will. If that is my punishment, so be it. I can just sit here and stare at the growing shadows. I can wait for the darkness that's coming, I can watch this world go to hell. I can watch those little punks walking across my field, I can keep them locked up in my cellar and those cold little black eyes can stare at me all they want – we'll see who blinks first.

His hands twitched. It had been some time since he had made his captives sing. Just staring at them had been enough to bring his loins alive, and he exulted in the luxury of taking his time, of letting the temptation pull him taut. And he loved to watch them eating the intestines he fed them – they were so avid when they tore into the rotting guts of their kin – the way they licked their muzzles and forelegs afterwards – it was beautiful.

The little punks, with their twisted little brains full of brave thoughts, all the while sucking my blood dry. Sure, we handed them everything on a fucking silver platter – we fought for those snivelling bastards, and what's the first thing they do? Spit on our feet, and shake their fists in our faces – hell, it's all there on the news, isn't it? Peaceniks. As if peace is free.

Bastards. But now, oh, now, I've got 'em where I want 'em. And I can do what I want with them, that's the clincher. I can lock 'em up, feed 'em guts, and I can make 'em sing. That's the clincher.

Nobody spits in my face and gets away with it. This is my land and on it I'm king. And I can line them up in rows and I won't be the one who blinks first. Their eyes aren't the only ones that glow at night. Not here. Not on my land.

Fisk began rocking in his chair, and he watched his

hands slowly wrap themselves around its arms. They waited for him down there, in that black cellar. They waited for him. But he wasn't in any hurry. He would just sit here in the shadows, rocking, staring at the weeds and at the black field – they couldn't reach him now.

With darkness came a cold wind, the last sigh of slumbering winter. It slipped through his clothes, plucked the sweat from his flesh, and slowly stole the gleam from his bared teeth.

III

It was as if she had just left every room he entered. Sten could swear he saw the swirling air of her wake, the telltale currents of her imminent presence, but he knew he was just fooling himself. Another game, cynically cheered on by the thousand monsters mobbing his thoughts. But where was she?

Outside, his dogs were whining. They were hungry, and he'd run out of food for them. He entered the kitchen and stood by the window, trying to force a decision through the cacophony in his head. The dogs were hungry. She was gone. And he was thirsty. Statements, nothing but statements. They didn't go anywhere, just went on over and over again through his brain, a child's rhyme. And all the while the monsters laughed – oh, how they loved his helplessness; they laid suffocating deadness in his inner rooms like carpets, absorbing the echoes of his screams, his rants, his pounding fists.

Sten rubbed his hands on his thighs, but it was

hopeless – the sweat just kept oozing out, and every-thing kept slipping from his grasp, and it didn't help him decide what to do. He knew he was trapped, that there was no way out, now. Just that endless spiral down into the seething darkness – but God! how thirsty he was!

And yet the dogs whined, and she was gone, and he didn't know what to do.

Sten frowned, then shook his head. The dogs were hungry. He'd have to phone Fisk. Anything to make them stop their whining. He'd get them food, all right. He stumbled from the kitchen. Holding his arms out to either side, he negotiated the hallway and then pushed open the back door. He paused on the steps, reeling slightly.

She was gone. *Listen to them whine!*

Rage poured outward from his skull, filling his limbs with fire. The back yard dissolved into a swirling haze as he staggered down the steps. He saw the three dogs lined up in an expectant row with their noses pressed against the wire, watching him. And their tails – *oh yes, so bloody hopeful, weren't they?*

Sten roared when he collided with the cage, a word-less explosion of sound that sent all three dogs bolting for the far end of the kennel. His fingers curling sav-agely around the chain links, he pressed his face into the wire.

'Shut the fuck up!' he screamed. 'Shut your fucking whining! She's gone! Don't you fucking get it yet?'

IV

It was supper-time, but Jennifer wasn't hungry. The playground was empty, as usual, when she entered it and approached the swing. It wasn't much of a playground, actually. Just a swing, a slide, and an open field. But it had been there all her life, in all its mundane familiarity. She sat down on the swing, gripping the cold chains on either side, but did not rock herself into motion. She faced the open field, her house a mere twenty yards behind her.

Dimly, she remembered her father's hands at her back, strong yet gentle. And she remembered her own childish laughter, as she flew higher and higher into the air, and it seemed it would go on for ever – she'd never imagined that those hands could get tired, she'd never dreamed that they'd eventually turn away and leave her suspended there, clutching at chains that would only pull her back down. She'd never known what it was to be betrayed.

Times had changed, she told herself. The foolishness was over, no more senseless laughter. The times of asking Mommy and Daddy 'why don't I have any brothers and sisters?' were gone. That question had been answered a thousand times since then, in the silences and murmured evasions, in glances exchanged over her head, in sheets tucked up to her chin and swift, empty darkness.

Jennifer knew about accidents, now. Unwanted pregnancies – the little girl nobody wanted, sitting there on the swing wanting to be pushed higher, higher,

higher. Wanting wings, wanting to soar into the world, forever demanding strong, gentle, supporting hands.

She jumped when her father roared behind her. Pushing herself to her feet, she whirled and faced the house. He was nowhere to be seen. And then came his screams. At the dogs – it had to be at the dogs. A sickening chill pooled in her stomach. *He's gone insane.*

The slamming of a car door turned her attention to the road. A car had stopped at the edge of their driveway, and a man was now standing beside it, facing the house.

Slowly, she walked towards him. She didn't know who he was but she didn't want him to go to the house. He began walking around the car, noticed her and stopped.

Jennifer studied his face. His broad forehead was clenched in a troubled frown, and he ran a long-fingered hand through his thinning blond hair. For some reason this deepened her fear. She opened her mouth to speak but he was quicker.

'Are you Jennifer Louper?' he asked, his voice deep and soft.

Her breath caught. She nodded.

'I'm Dr Roulston.' He stepped forward, smiling.

Jennifer did not return the smile. 'What do you want?' she demanded stiffly.

Roulston seemed unperturbed by her attitude as he continued walking towards her, his smile still in place. 'Perhaps we could go inside? I'd like to speak with you.'

Jennifer shook her head. 'No. Not inside.' She hesitated, a part of her mind noting with some satisfaction that his smile was becoming fixed. She said, 'Where's my mother?'

Stopping a few feet in front of her, Roulston looked away, sighed, then returned his gaze to her. 'In Riverview General Hospital.' His blue eyes narrowed. 'She has a broken jaw and it's infected.'

Somehow Jennifer managed to clamp a hold on her emotions. Without inflection she asked, 'How long will she be in there?'

Roulston's frown deepened. 'Two, three weeks,' he replied. 'Depends on how well the antibiotics work.'

Detached, she watched the doctor's growing discomfort while his words slowly sank into the numbness inside her. She blinked. 'Could she die?'

His eyes widened briefly. Then he shook his head. 'It's not likely, but the chance does exist.' He looked away. 'I mean . . . uh, no, I don't think she'll die.' His gaze returned to hers, and it had suddenly hardened. 'Look, is your father in the house? I'd like to speak to him.'

Jennifer could feel the blood drain from her face. 'No. He's not home, I mean.' Her shoulders jerked a shrug. 'He's gone out.'

Roulston stared at her for a long moment, then he nodded. 'I see.' He turned back to his car, then paused and faced her again. When he spoke his tone was cool. 'In case you're interested, visiting hours are between one and three tomorrow afternoon. Maybe you might bring your mother some flowers, or something . . .' His voice trailed away, and once again he stared at Jennifer.

'Yes,' she said, 'she'd probably like that. Flowers.'

A flash of anger showed in Roulston's eyes for a brief moment. Then he spun around and quickly en-

tered his car. He started it, released the brake, dropped
it into gear and drove away without once looking at
Jennifer.

She returned to the swing and resumed her seat. It
was a struggle to keep pushing the feelings, the
thoughts, away, but at last she succeeded. She told herself she'd think about it tomorrow. Maybe she'd even
visit Mother. And as for telling her father, well, let him
rot a little longer – it might do some good, couldn't
hurt.

Footsteps scraped on the road's gravel shoulder.
Swinging in her seat, Jennifer turned, thinking for a
moment that the doctor had returned. But no, it wasn't
the doctor.

'Hey!' she called out. 'Hey, you!'

The boy stopped, faced her.

'C'mere!'

He didn't move for a few seconds, then slowly
walked towards her.

The first thing about him that Jennifer noticed was
his eyes. They were a cold, impassive blue, unwaver-
ing in their gaze. A small gasp escaped her lips – he
was, openly and deliberately, appraising her. Suddenly
she felt a lot less sure of herself, and so said nothing
until he stopped in front of her and asked: 'What?'

His tone took her aback. It had sounded angry, almost affronted. After a moment she recovered, and
slowly looked him up and down. He was long-limbed,
though barely her height. His hands hung at his sides
as if he had forgotten they existed. For some reason
this struck her as meaningful. Most boys she knew always hid their hands in their pockets, or hung them
from their thumbs on the belt loops of their jeans – but

whatever the means, the gesture was always self-conscious. But not this boy. Not the new kid.

Her eyes returned to his face, and she smiled sardonically. But even this seemed to leave him unimpressed. His long face remained expressionless, his eyes flat and cold. She realised then something about the way he stood that was strange, somehow off kilter. *He's tense! He's tense as hell!* Her smile broadened with this realisation – *he's scared of me, and I've got him now.* 'You're the new kid, aren't you?' She began casually twisting on the swing. 'What's your name?'

'Owen Brand. Who're you?'

'Jennifer.'

His nod told her he knew about her.

She said, 'You've got an older sister, don't you?'

'Yes. Older than you.'

'So what?' Jennifer snapped. This wasn't going the way it was supposed to at all.

Owen shrugged, said nothing.

She took out her cigarettes. 'Want one?'

'No.'

Pulling one out she laughed. 'Chicken shit, eh?'

He turned and began walking away.

Jennifer gaped at his back. 'Hey! Where you going?'

'Nowhere,' he answered without turning around.

'Creep!' she shrilled at him, but to no visible effect. She leapt from the swing. 'You little shit! Just fuck right off!' He continued walking across the field, stiffly, as if driven.

She lit the cigarette and walked to her house. Out back she heard the dogs whining, but it was the only sound to break the deathlike silence. She entered through the front door, then stopped in the hallway.

Her father was standing in front of her. He held a bottle of rye by the neck in one hand, and steadied himself against the wall with the other. His red eyes seemed to burn right through her, and she felt a flutter of fear.

'Where is she?' he rasped.

'Go to hell,' Jennifer replied, turning to enter the living room.

He lurched forward suddenly, grabbed at her neck and got a handful of t-shirt as she jerked back. With a snarl he pulled her close. 'You fucking slut! I asked you a question, dammit! Now, where is she?'

Unable to move, Jennifer stared into her father's enraged eyes. Oh God, she said to herself, he's going to kill me. His breath washed over her, and its reek made her nauseous. 'She's gone to the hospital,' she gasped.

Abruptly, the fires in his eyes died. His expression went slack, his mouth dropping open. 'What?' he whispered.

Jennifer pulled herself free of his now-lifeless grasp, then pushed past him. 'The hospital, you prick. With a busted jaw and an infection! She's gone there to die!' She walked to the stairs, forcing calm into her stride. At the banister she whirled to him. 'Satisfied?'

There was a loud knock on the door.

Still staring at Jennifer, her father said in a quiet voice, 'Come in.'

She heard the door open, but could not see who it was from where she stood. Not that it mattered – she knew the voice.

'Mr Louper? I'm Dr Roulston.'

Before Jennifer turned to run up the stairs, she saw the expression that crossed her father's face at the doctor's introduction, and it found an echo inside her, roaring upward into her skull as if from a deep, black cavern in her soul. And when he turned to her and their gazes met, she felt a sudden closeness to him that made her heart jump.

Then she was running up the stairs, down the hall, and into her room. She slammed the door behind her and leaned against it, gasping. Tears filled her eyes, but she ignored them.

Yes, they'd looked at each other, and they'd both realised what they'd seen in each other's eyes. Terror, raw and exposed, welling upward from that open wound they both shared.

'Oh, please no, please no . . .' But the pleading had lost its power, and denial was a place she could no longer run to – even now every wall was being battered down, one by one, by the soft, deep voice coming up from below, and by the silence of her father.

CHAPTER EIGHT

I

AND THINGS WERE let go.

II

The giant lay there even now, I knew, a faceless lord with gummed slits for eyes, impassive to the world, impassive to the crayfish with their pincers clicking, snipping, clacking. The lord on his throne of gnawed sticks, his loins alive with maggots, reclined with one thick, white arm across his blank brow, and thought of nothing.

I had wandered through those thoughts, lost in the empty blackness. My hands groped outward, but the skull – the walls – were as unreachable as the sky – a sky barren of stars.

Scratching flakes of faded white paint with a fingernail, I realised, with a vague detachment, that I was aboard *Mistress Flight*. I had no memory of ever coming to this place, and of my final parting words with my friends I recalled only an agreement to meet again – tomorrow. But within all this there were visions heady with terror – the faces of my friends blurred and became the giant's face – the mouth a round black hole, the eyes pinched slashes across swollen white flesh, the nose eaten away, pink and gaping – a face round and smooth as a ball, the cheeks stretched and shining, the eyebrows plucked away – Roland's face, Lynk's face, Carl's face. My own.

III

The setting sun was turning the sky crimson. I sat on the aft deck of *Mistress Flight* and watched the stain spread outward. So relentless, that seepage, and though I drew my knees in tight against my chest, I could not move, and so it flowed over and around me. The flaking paint was no longer dull white, but washed-out red; like the laces of my sneakers, the fabric of my socks, the flecks under my nails.

Through the haze I gradually recalled another encounter – with a girl. Where? The playground. Jennifer Louper, whose nipples creased her t-shirt, whose green eyes even now brought a tremor to my stomach. We'd talked. About what? I couldn't remember.

Had there been anyone else? No.

The smell of rot clung to the air, but I realised that

it might just be my imagination. Slowly, it came to me that I was coming out of a kind of shock – details began pressing on to my consciousness. I reached down with one hand and touched the weathered wood of the deck; the wrinkled surface was cool and familiar. And from the cabin came mild wafts of the Windex cleaner we'd used on the windows this morning. Behind me branches shivered as a cool wind drifted in from the river. And the day darkened.

It was late, well past supper-time. I wasn't hungry – the taste on my tongue was that of rancid meat. Still, they would be wondering where I was – and I'd catch hell when I went home. The thought immediately struck me as silly. I grinned. So what if I got into trouble? It didn't matter – who cares?

Nothing seemed to matter much, any more – but no, that wasn't exactly true. What mattered now – more than anything else – was the feel of solid wood beneath me, the wind on my face, the rattling branches and the thickening air. And the giant.

Already, he seemed to have become something more than just a man. The giant. I let the word roll through my mind – Giant. Once a man, now a giant who had swallowed the river, a lord come to visit the wild-lands.

The grin on my face broadened even though I felt a touch of renewed terror. Yes, he'd come from the river, the river from the city; he'd come and the river had made of him a giant. Spring, the season of growth. Ha. The throb of my heart drummed in my ears, and I squeezed shut my eyes. *Only human still – yes? Yes? Maybe.*

I began to shake, as other things were let go . . .

* * *

A toaster, dismantled, covered the dining-room table. Pigeons cooed and skittered out on the apartment's balcony.

Father had been working on it all morning. It was the day after something happened, and there was more still to happen. But this is when the memory starts. He'd been working on it for hours, looking for why it wasn't working, looking but not finding.

I remember climbing on to the chair to watch him. Mother was in the kitchen, and the kitchen was silent. Debbie – it was as if Debbie didn't exist.

Father set down a part with one hand, a screwdriver with the other. And the hands rested there, on the table, and he stared at them.

'Dad?'

He made no reply; instead, he brought his hands up to his face, and began crying.

'Dad?'

How old was I? I don't know. A boy, and the boy's own personal giant, a god, master of all things, sat with his shoulders heaving, his face covered by his massive hands, and wept.

Between the apartment buildings crouched a block of shattered wood and stone. Two little boys threaded their way between the construction equipment and strode into the shattered world. They're giants, astride a dead city. Full of grim thoughts, they survey the ruin from behind slitted eyes. And they are faceless. Of course, being memories.

With iron bars they prise loose square concrete blocks and explore dark, dusty holes with pudgy fingers. Hunting survivors, broken-limbed GI Joe dolls, one blond with a scar (German), the other black-haired and angle-eyed (Japanese).

Dismemberment now is part of the ritual – the right of giants, the privilege of gods and victors in war. They hunt for the losers.

Reaching, groping down into the darkness, one of the boys feels sharp teeth pierce his palm, and he screams. He runs home, the other boy, white-faced, following. They are quickly parted, and the bitten boy is carried by strong arms down to the car. He's rushed to a hospital.

The doctor murmurs – a conference of tall people – and the boy watches, frightened and bewildered. The bite of a mouse, they tell him later, as he withdraws into the cover of his mother's arms while the tray of needles is being readied by a blond, scarred nurse. He is given a strange word to play with: rabies, hydro-something – he prefers the word 'rabies'. He likes its sound, and it rhymes with babies.

The boy faints after the sixth needle is plunged into his abdomen – and yet a part of him still remembers to this day. A part of him recalls every needle in the three weeks that followed, every session presaged with the nurse explaining: 'This is only a precaution.' The boy learns the meaning of the word 'precaution'.

Towards the end, through the endless pain, he voices to his father the question that had been haunting him for days. All that clear liquid being pumped into him, day after day . . . 'Daddy, has this made me different? Has this changed me for ever?' What do you mean, son? 'Daddy, can you see through me, now?'

Just a child, but maybe something more.

Still, the child harbours a secret: all along he has known that they'd all been mistaken. It hadn't been a mouse. No, there in the darkness of that hole – perhaps even to this day – there waits a broken-limbed doll (German or Japanese?), and if you look very carefully, he tells himself, you will see his tiny sharp teeth, and you will recognise his grin.

When it comes to children, there is no mercy. When it comes to children, there are only 'precautions'. And so the transparent boy continues his hunt for losers – he has earned the right of giants.

They are yelling at each other again. Something's happened. A dream has died. The boy is uncertain of the details, but the talk of a bright new world has ended, and now the voices are loud and angry. In the morning, Father cried. In the morning, Debbie didn't exist, but now she did.

Walking from the kitchen, he leaves the argument behind. Something has disgusted him; only he's uncertain what – but the memory whispers a single word: matches. The smell of burning matches. He hates that smell. They've promised to stop, but he has his doubts.

In the living room his sister sits on the couch, watching TV. She has the volume turned up loud: the whole apartment seems to be filled with people, voices clamouring from all directions. The boy sits down on the floor, stares at the record player. He wants to play one of his sister's record albums. The title has no meaning for him, though he knows it: Sounds of Silence. His sense of irony is still years away.

But he wants to sing along with the singers on the

*record: the words he doesn't know he tries to match
with sounds that he thinks are similar.*

*But it's the wrong time: he only sings when he's
alone; he only listens when he's alone.*

*Something's happened. A dream has died. The boy
feels guilty, and he wants to sing. He realises that, once
again, the future has changed, but the thought does not
distress him. It always changes. He's already known
three schools, three sets of faces, strange, familiar,
strange again. He doesn't miss any of them. He likes
being alone, like he is now, amidst this roar of voices
in this crowded apartment, singing wordless songs in
his head in the wake of yet another dead dream. And
years later all he will remember of those times will be
the smell of burning matches.*

I blinked, shook my head as a wave of dizziness welled
up inside and then slowly faded away, and along with
it the last of the memories.

Only human still.

Wings flapped close over my head, and I looked up.
Two crows were climbing into the sky above me, silent and ghost-like. In moments they were like flecks
of black ash carried high by the wind. They circled
once and then headed out over the river.

The sun had almost set, the red glint on the edges
of the world had deepened to muddy magenta. Once
again the faces of my friends returned to me: childish,
small and familiar – not the giant's face. Still, something had changed, as if every detail of their features
had shifted in some odd, uncertain way. And I began
to sense in them things I had not seen before, but even

still, the nature of that twisting remained obscure. I had realised that there existed a difference, but I could not recognise its meaning.

Well, time to go home. Slowly, reluctantly, I climbed to my feet, crossed the boat's deck and leaned against the rail. Ten feet below lay a shadowed realm of dead-fall and rotting leaves. I shivered as a chill ran through me, then hitched my leg up over the rail and began my descent. Dropping the last three feet, I landed in the soft humus and fell into a crouch, looking around to see if I'd been discovered. But no, the yards seemed empty. I padded down the length of *Mistress Flight* to her stern, checked the area once again, then quickly scampered across the open ground, my eyes on the softly glowing front window of Gribbs's shack.

I reached the edge of the shadowed treeline and plunged into the darkness to find myself face to face with an old man. I froze, suddenly terrified. Gribbs – the name flashed through my mind. This must be Gribbs.

'Hello there, son,' he rumbled. 'Out for a walk with us old folk, eh?'

His easy laugh made me relax. He hadn't seen anything. 'Yeah, I guess,' I replied.

Gribbs stepped forward, his eyes on the ground. 'Yep,' he sighed, 'quite a night for it, that's true.' He stopped in front of me and asked, 'See anything you like in the yards?'

'Huh?'

Chuckling again, Gribbs placed his hands on his hips and gazed up at the branches overhead. 'Well, I just figured you was looking for a boat to buy.' He glanced down at me, smiled. 'Get lots of buyers this time of year. 'Course, nothing comes of most of 'em. What about you? Are you a serious buyer, son?'

I shrugged and smiled. I realised he was having fun with me, but for some reason it didn't anger me – usually, I hated it when adults did that – with their faked fascination and stupid questions just to show how nice they could be. They had always left me wondering what it was they wanted. This time, however, there was no rise of the usual suspicion in me, and I could feel my smile broadening. 'Nah,' I said, 'they're all too small.'

Gribbs tilted his head back and roared with laughter, and birds leapt from the branches above us and fluttered away into the growing darkness. He laid a hand on my shoulder. 'You got good eyes, son. Good eyes.' Pausing, he cocked his head. 'I got tea brewing in the house. Care to join me?'

I hesitated, then shook my head. 'I can't. I got to get home.'

Nodding, he patted my shoulder. 'Nothing to be done for it, then. Well, a good night to you, son.' He began walking away.

I turned to watch him. Then a thought came to me. 'How about some other time?'

Stopping, he faced me again. 'Some other time it is.'

'My name's Owen.'

He nodded. 'And mine's Walter. Well, see you soon, then, eh?'

'You bet,' I replied, then turned about and resumed my hurried walk home.

It was only as I came to the road beyond the Yacht Club's grounds that I realised that, for a time there, I had forgotten about the horrors of this day, about the panic and the terror, the helplessness and the broken memories, and most of all, I had forgotten about the giant. And the world had seemed normal, unchanged; the night air fresh and cool, the stars appearing over-head, the sound of laughter and the touch of a warm hand.

'I was just about to go out and look for you,' Father said from the top of the porch, still buttoning the front of his jacket.

'Yeah,' I said, deciding that the time was right for telling the story I'd made up. 'I ate at Roland's.'

'You should have phoned to let us know.'

I ascended the steps, glanced up at him then down again. I nodded. 'I would have, except . . . except I forgot our phone number.'

Opening the door, he grunted. 'You do that, too, eh?'

I sighed in relief. 'Yeah. We should write it down or something, huh?'

Together, we entered the house and paused at the hallway to pull our shoes off. Mother appeared from the living room, her arms crossed and her face stern. I shrugged sheepishly. She turned her gaze to Father and raised an eyebrow.

'Ate at Roland's,' he said. 'Forgot our phone number.'

'It won't happen again,' I promised, walking over to the telephone and making a show of studying the number.

'Tomorrow morning you do chores,' Mother said.

'But—'

'And tonight – no TV. You go straight to your room and you stay there. Understand?'

I glanced an appeal to Father, who shook his head.

Debbie came out of the kitchen and grinned wickedly at me. Slumping my shoulders in dejection, I slowly went up the stairs. Despite the act, I knew I was getting off easily.

I closed my room's door behind me, crossed the cluttered floor and collapsed down on the bed. I stared at the model airplane dangling from the light fixture. If I stood on the bed, I reasoned, I could pluck it out of the sky. Like King Kong. Like a giant.

Yes, there had been a brief time of normalcy since then, but what of the afternoon, the hours of which I even now had trouble recalling? What had I done? Where had I gone? And what of the lost conversation with that girl, Jennifer? What had I said to her, what had she said to me? The thought of those blank hours frightened me. What if they happened again?

He appeared once again in my mind: the flesh so white, so shiny – like plastic. A giant plastic doll – but no, he'd been real. And faceless. There was fear in this recollection, but also, and in growing degrees, fascination. There he was, the giant. Murdered? Murdered. I pictured strong hands holding that faceless face down under the water, pushing it into the oily mud. Had he struggled? No, he'd known it was useless; he'd known he was helpless. Killed by a bigger giant, a stronger giant.

And then he'd come down the river, leaving the city behind, to finally wash up against the beaver lodge, to finally be found. By us. By me, and Roland, and Lynk and Carl. We'd found him, and it was our secret.

Tomorrow, we'd make our plans; tomorrow, we'd decide what to do. As my thoughts lingered on this my meeting with Gribbs came back to me. He hadn't been what I'd imagined him to be; for some reason I had pictured him as some kind of ogre, with a wizened face and a greedy glint in his eyes; a creature who lived in shadows and plotted evil deeds inside his broken-down shack.

The echo of his laugh returned to me. It had been so loud, so full; it had brought a flock of birds into the air above us – was that even possible? Maybe I had just imagined it. And yet, that laugh had seemed to come from the earth itself – a rumbling of continents. Or the laugh of a giant.

CHAPTER NINE

I

CARS STARTED ROLLING in at seven, and by nine the parking lot was full. The boat yard was crowded with people. Just like every spring, Walter Gribbs smiled to himself as he continued priming the track winch. There were children running everywhere, staining their hands and knees with thick grease the colour of gold; men walked around their boats and exchanged loud laughter.

Women made the occasional foray into the yards, walking here and there in groups; but when the morning lengthened and the heat rose, they retreated into the clubhouse to be served cool drinks on the veranda.

It's a fact, Walter told himself: we've all got our rituals, and when enough people can agree on them you've got a society. Could be high, could be low – the rituals met the same needs, and they stayed in place for the same reasons.

Things hadn't changed much in his lifetime, he realised wryly. Got people running around nowadays making all these demands: the rituals gotta go, break down the system, buck the establishment; and they're all acting like they were the first ones to have ever yelled about those things, like they were the first generation born with open eyes. Still, he couldn't blame them. When those open eyes start getting wider, it's just plain healthy to let off some steam.

Just like I did back in the twenties, he mused, grinning to himself as he moved on to the next winch.

'Hey, Walter! When do you figure?'

He looked up to see Chester Dallow standing beside his boat. ''Bout an hour,' he replied, wiping the sweat from his brow. He smiled. 'In a hurry?'

'Damn right I am,' Chester growled. After a moment the yachtsman wandered off, leaving Walter to man the winch.

Matched in mouth like bells, first the rattling of broken chains, now the hounds at my heels. He grunted angrily. There were times when his inner world became more bitter and sour than he'd care to admit. There were so many sunsets in his memories, so many long nights, the moments came when he forgot the sigh of cool wind on his brow, the birth of dawn and the cry of gulls – the moments of peace lost in the echoing clamour of war.

Hell, he muttered to himself, it's been a long life, and like day and night over the years the time balances out. *Just step back, old man, and take a good look.* Walter sighed. If only the good times left scars like the bad ones. *Not just goblins hiding in the shadows in my skull, but angels bursting with light as well.*

He stood beside the winch, watching the men checking the rails for sufficient grease, the tarred blocks for balance, watching them run smooth-palmed hands over hulls, listening to them laugh and joke. And he waited for them to tell him the time had come; he waited for his arm to move of its own accord, an extension of the winch handle and the oil-smeared gears and wheels trapped in the darkness of the machine's shell.

I've been here before. Haven't I? How many times reduced to this single reflex. So many years – a long life – and this is what's expected of me. This, and nothing more.

The hell with worrying about balances, Walter, can you pull the lever? Can you move that arm? Can you hear when we tell you it's time? Sure, a lotta years on you, Walter, so long as you've learned how to pay attention. We haven't got all day, have we, now?

We haven't got all day. We haven't got all night. Christ, what have we got, then?

'Hey, Walter! You sleeping at the wheel?'

Blinking, he looked up, saw Bill Smith's face grinning at him. 'Best place t'sleep,' he replied. 'You all ready to move?'

'Any time.'

Walter looked down, watched his left arm move, heard the gears engage and the cables spring taut. There it is, he told himself. You've done it. Just unplug everything now – your epitaph's written: *Here lies Walter M. Gribbs, who lived his life to the words: Can You Pull That Lever?* He could. He did. He never stopped.

Slowly, the yacht on its blocks moved off one set of

rails and on to another. Cables were redeployed; Walter manned another winch, and the boat crawled towards the water.

II

Walking down the aisle, Jennifer slowly met the eyes of every face turned to her. The bus pulled back on to the highway and began to growl its way through the gears. Jennifer took her time making her way to the back seat.

It was Sunday, and she was dressed to kill. *Dressed to kill* – her favourite phrase. She felt the eyes of every man clinging to her flesh like greedy fingers, felt their caress as she passed each row of seats. Women were watching her as well, she knew, young and old, with hatred, envy and disgust. Jennifer smiled to herself, wishing that the aisle was a mile long.

She didn't care what the women thought when they looked at her; it was the men who mattered. Still inwardly smiling, she took her seat on the last bench of the bus, carefully crossed her legs. The men – young men, men with their wives, their daughters; men with sons who watched Daddy to learn the ways of the world – the men, with their razor-blade eyes slicing her tight t-shirt into strips, peeling away her miniskirt one-half to each side; the men, licking their lips – at her, Jennifer. Thirteen years old. Thirteen, the age of taunting.

Full-grown men – they'd beg me, oh yes they would. I'd make them beg. Fucking right I would. Why not? One grovels and they all grovel – by the thousands.

Follow the leader, men are like that. And their eyes are all the same, glued there to the nipples pushing against the t-shirt – looking into them you can't tell the difference between one pair and the next. Robots. Robots looking around for a wall socket. Animals. Burrowing animals. Jennifer struggled against a burst of laughter, bit her lip until the wave of hysteria passed.

She held her gaze straight ahead, straight up the aisle to the front window. She saw the bus driver's face in the rear-view mirror, saw the man's eyes flick to her. She smiled.

Imagine all the male thoughts pouring out of all those heads in front of me. Personalised penises for sure, but there I am, in fifty different beds, in bathtubs, in shower stalls, in back seats, in the woods. I'm everywhere, ready, willing and able to fuck their brains out. And I'll look into their eyes – personalised eyes, of course – so they'll believe they're the only ones.

And all those women up there – all those wives and mothers – they know exactly what's going on. The silence tells them everything. And they hurt deep inside – they want to be me, even though I disgust them. And they want to be me for one reason and one reason alone – they want to see their men grovel – they want to see every man grovel.

The outer-lying houses of Riverview appeared through the front window; and people were getting ready to leave the bus. There were murmurs now, mindless questions bowing to the need to speak, to prove personal bonds, to hint at shared secrets. Jennifer felt like sneering, but decided it would be wasted on everyone, even the bus driver who kept looking at her in his mirror.

The machine growled down through its gears; the bus slowed and turned on to another street and then rolled into the terminal's parking lot. People rose to their feet, shuffled forward. Jennifer remained seated, watching them. Little lives and wasted motions. Lives empty but for daydreams and forbidden lust. *After all, it's Sunday.*

'Ma'am?'

The bus driver stood on the first step, looking back at her.

'Last stop,' he explained.

'Damn right it is,' she replied, rising to her feet.

Riverview General Hospital was the largest building in the community, a bastion of civic pride half filled with a dying generation. Passing through the glass front doors, Jennifer sauntered up to the reception desk.

'What room is Mrs Louper in?' she asked.

The nurse looked up from her phone conversation. 'In a minute,' she told Jennifer.

She turned her back on the nurse and leaned against the counter. *The place is full of old people. It smells of old people – even disinfectant can't hide that smell. Like dusty flesh, closed-in spaces, overcrowded chambers. The reek of history nobody will let go of –* the thought annoyed her. She wanted to yell at them: *Forget it! Forget it all. Let it go!*

The past didn't mean a fucking thing – everything important would happen in the next minute, the next hour, the next year.

'Now, you had a question?'

Slowly, Jennifer turned around. She smiled and said in a low voice, 'What room is Mrs Louper in?'

The nurse stared at her for a moment, then walked over to a clipboard hanging from a nail on the far wall. She lifted pages. 'Are you her daughter?' she asked, not turning around.

'Yes. Why?'

'Your name?'

'Jennifer. Why?'

The nurse turned to face her, glanced over Jennifer's shoulder. 'Is your father with you?'

They knew. Everyone knew. A cold deadness filled Jennifer's stomach. 'No,' she whispered.

The nurse's eyes seemed to soften. 'Room 216. Follow the yellow line from the elevator, or ask a nurse on the floor.'

Jennifer nodded, turned and walked over to the elevator. She pressed the UP button. Everyone knew. The bastards. She felt the nurse's eyes on her back, felt them like needles pinning a bug to cardboard. She wanted to whirl and scream: *Stop staring at me!* But the elevator doors opened. A doctor and an orderly walked out, and she walked in and pressed the button to the second floor. She faced a side wall until the doors shut.

The voice went on for ever, filling the house with a dull, toneless drone. In her room, Jennifer sat on her bed, not bothering to wipe the tears from her face. Her father spoke once or twice, breaking into the drone of Dr Roulston's endless accusation, and his voice came through in a broken whine – she knew he was crying, too, and she hated him for it. The coward.

The criminal, nailed to his crime, no sympathy for the bleeding, no mercy for his phoney martyrdom, and no, especially no, sanctity granted his secret. She pictured Roulston's face. How dare he! But there was no point in thinking about that – Roulston was downstairs, pushing his way into their world like a white knight full of raging purity.

And then the doctor's voice was gone. The front door closed shut and she heard the footsteps of her father crossing the living room, entering the kitchen. Anger boiled up inside her. The bastard. He was at the fridge, he was getting out another beer. He'd seen the good doctor out and then he'd gone for another drink.

Jennifer stood, reached for the doorknob with a shaking hand, walked out into the hallway and then down the stairs, through the shadows of the hallway, and into the kitchen. And there he was, sitting at the table, both hands encircling a bottle in front of him. Jennifer stopped at the kitchen's threshold, staring at him. He wasn't moving, he was just sitting there, his eyes fixed on the bottle.

'You fucking bastard,' she hissed.

He didn't look up. 'Get out,' he croaked.

'What did he say?'

'Get out.'

'What's he going to do?'

Looking up at her face, her father grinned crazily. 'Didn't I tell you to get out?'

I'm staring into the eyes of a madman, Jennifer told herself. *He could kill me. Easily. Right now.* She stepped back, shook her head once, then whirled and ran from the room.

The next morning she'd found him passed out at the table, the bottle – two-thirds empty – standing beside his head. Outside the dogs barked and whined.

They were starving, and though she spent a few minutes looking, she could find no food for them.

Eventually, the unconscious man collapsed in his chair at the table drove Jennifer out of the house. She didn't want to be there when he woke up. In her room, she selected her tightest white t-shirt and her favourite red miniskirt. Today, I'll visit Mother.

And as for the bastard – she hoped he was dead.

The elevator door opened, and she stepped into the hallway. On the floor were three painted lines: red, green and yellow. The yellow line went down the hallway to her right. She followed it, a strange numbness tingling in her hands.

Room 210, 211, 212 . . . 216. The door was shut. Jennifer opened it and stepped inside. The window at the far end of the room was open, and a fresh breeze lifted the curtains. There were two beds, the nearer one unoccupied, its sheets and blanket neatly folded and stacked on its smooth, white surface. In the other bed lay a woman with her head turned away. A tube full of clear liquid ran into one of her arms.

Am I in the wrong room? Jennifer wondered. But no, the woman's hair was the right colour – an almost-black brown with streaks of grey in it – even though there didn't seem to be enough of it. The head looked too small, with her hair flattened that way. Jennifer took a step forward. Yes, it was her mother – there were the bandages covering the lower half of her face, and also an odd-looking metal-and-plastic frame with straps that went around the head. Jennifer recalled Dr Roulston's words: *She has a broken jaw . . .*

'Mother?'

The head turned, and their eyes met.

Jennifer tried to smile, failed. She walked quickly forward, came to the side of the bed. Her eyes filled with tears. 'Hi,' she managed.

Her mother's eyes clung to hers, and tears had appeared in them as well. The woman reached up her free hand and Jennifer grasped it.

Jennifer sat down on the bed and they sat in silence for some time. It finally came to Jennifer that her mother couldn't talk. 'You okay?' With difficulty her mother nodded. Looking away, Jennifer tried to think of something to say. 'I'll bring you some of your stuff next time.' It suddenly struck her that there would be a next time. She met her mother's gaze again, was silent for a moment, then said, 'The doctor came by. Roulston. He – he talked with Father.' Mother's eyes had widened, filling with fear, and then with hope. Jennifer understood. She shook her head. 'No, it didn't help.'

III

The black field simmered, the black field boiled. Fisk watched in horror. It was coming alive. Its surface, once smooth and impenetrable, was now rolling, chopping, broken with writhing ribbons that lifted faces, blunt, pink and blind, skyward. The worm-heads jerked, flopped, they opened black maws and screamed soundlessly.

Mink guts, a sea of mink guts. His hands gripping the arms of the chair, Fisk stared, unable to move. They weren't going to wait any longer. They were coming for him and they were coming now.

'Down!' His roar made his whole body jerk. Wood cracked. 'Get down!' Wood splintered. The rocking chair slewed sideways beneath him. Snarling, he pulled on the arms, gained his feet. The chair collapsed, and he tottered, his hands balled into fists, glaring out at the black nightmare beyond the porch.

A gust of wind brought to him the stench from the freshly piled mound of intestines beside the maypole – not rot, not yet, but the smell of faeces, stomach acids, fluids and blood. Fisk's head snapped around, fixed on the pale pink and yellow pile.

'My barrow,' he breathed, then giggled. His eyes narrowed. He wiped his mouth with one forearm. He knew that the field was still boiling with life even though he did not look at it. Horror was giving way to cunning. 'They want to bury me. They want vengeance – those dead mink, all those dead mink.' He giggled again, then turned to face the field. Worm-heads swung around and stretched towards him. Fisk grinned. 'You think you got me, don't you. You think the time's come.' Slowly, he shook his head, then hissed, 'You're wrong!'

Fisk stepped over the ruin of the rocking chair and flung open the screen door. The shadows inside seemed to swirl. He plunged into them, then stopped. It took a long time for his eyes to adjust, and even then everything seemed smudged. But he couldn't wait any longer. Pushing forward, he raised both hands in front of him and entered the living room. *It's the middle of the day, but look at the darkness breathe.* He sat down on the edge of the worn sofa, took the telephone from the table beside him and began leafing through the attached notepad.

After a moment he found the number he wanted. He dialled shakily, listened to the click and then the first ring. 'Come on,' he breathed. The second ring. The field was a cauldron, ready to explode, ready to engulf him. Third ring. Ready to swallow him whole. He could almost feel that vertiginous plummet. Fourth ring. Down through the blackness, clawing at the stomach walls, choking on the acid filling his mouth. *Down, down, down. For ever.* Fifth ring.

'Hello?'

Fisk's breath caught. 'Sten? Sten Louper?'

'Yes,' the voice croaked.

'It's Hodgson Fisk calling. You still in the hunt for dog food?'

There was a pause, then, 'Yes. Yes I am. You've got some?'

Fisk scowled. The bastard was drunk. 'As much as you need. Bring a shovel and some garbage bags.'

'A – a shovel? But I thought—'

'Do you want it or not?' Fisk snapped.

'Uh, yeah. Okay. I'll come by th'saft.'

Fisk's scowl deepened. 'Don't wait too long. It's out under the sun right now.' He paused, listened to the ragged breathing on the line, then said, 'Wouldn't want your dogs to get sick, would you, now?'

'No,' Sten mumbled.

'See you soon, then.'

'Yeah.'

Fisk hung up, returned the telephone to the table, then leaned back on the sofa and sighed. 'Can't bury

me when it's not there,' he whispered. 'And I'll hold
you off till then. I will.' He took a deep breath, wiped
his mouth, then closed his eyes. It was just a matter of
holding out, of waiting and staying alive until then.
That's all.

IV

I killed the engine and walked the lawn mower down
the driveway and into the garage. The chores were
done.

The machine in the driveway seemed to be decom-
posing all on its own: every time I looked it was smaller,
as if, now that its soul had been exposed, it was crumbling under the sun. Father had removed most of the
larger parts and had carried them into the garage,
where each part was placed in its own bucket of gasoline, like organs in jars. A pool of black oil had spread
out from the machine – a tar pit collecting plant stuff,
insects – I grinned at the thought – woolly rhinocer-
oses, mastodons . . .

The pool's placid surface showed nothing – it might
be miles deep – there was just no way to tell. Somewhere under that surface might hide the history of
mankind, of the whole world. And, somewhere down
in the thick, congealing blackness, there might lie giants, suspended for all time.

But when I picked up a stone and dropped it into
the pool it was, of course, less than half an inch deep.
And the machine was not the body of some god, exposed and bleeding out Creation like an afterthought.
It had no soul, only parts, and none of those parts

worked. And it was not as massive and imposing as it had once been. Still, since I as yet had no idea of what its function might be, there was an air of mystery around it; a secret with all the clues laid out, yet still a secret.

I left the garage and walked to the front porch. The door opened and Father stepped out, dressed as usual in his blue coveralls. Placing his hands on his hips, he glared at the machine, then sighed.

'Think you'll get it to work?' I asked.

He didn't seem to hear me.

I studied him. He was a tall man, thin but with wide shoulders and thick arms. In my mind I compared him with the giant, then frowned. No, he wasn't big enough for the giant – I could find no echoes between them.

'Got something to say, buster?'

I blinked, realised that he had noticed me studying him. I felt my face flush, shook my head.

His stern expression softened, and he winked. 'Mom says lunch is ready. Don't forget to wash your hands.'

'Great,' I said as I ran up the steps and past him. 'I'm starving!'

Everyone else had already assembled at the dining-room table. The twins were silent, and the only greeting I received from Debbie was a brief glower. Mother came in from the kitchen with a tray of salmon salad sandwiches.

'Again?' I complained.

'It was tuna last time, idiot,' Debbie snapped.

'Tuna, salmon, there's no difference but food colouring,' I pronounced, grabbing one from the tray once it was on the table.

'What a jerk,' Debbie said, shaking her head.

I eyed her. 'Shouldn't you be studying or something? Hell, you're fat enough—'

'Owen!' Mother admonished. 'Don't ever say that word again, and don't call your sister fat. She isn't. Now, apologise to her this instant.'

'Okay,' I replied around a mouthful of sandwich, 'I'm sorry you're not fat. Still, I heard you were doing lousy in class, so I was just trying to be helpful.'

Mother remained standing over me. 'Where did you hear that?' she demanded.

'The walls have ears,' I answered nonchalantly. Then, grinning at Debbie, I said, 'I heard you were gonna flunk.'

'I am not!' Debbie retorted, her face reddening. For a second I thought that she was going to throw her sandwich at me, but then Mother spoke.

'Stop it, Owen, or you'll spend the rest of the day in your room. And you won't be sitting down, either.'

You won't be sitting down, either – that was code for a spanking. I quickly subsided, studying the bites I had taken out of my sandwich and trimming the edges with nibbles here and there until Mother returned to the kitchen. Once she was gone I looked up, waited until I caught Debbie's eye, then gave her a silent sneer.

Her eyes narrowed. 'God, you're mean, Owen,' she said quietly.

My sneer vanished. Memories of baiting Carl came back to me. *Am I? Am I mean?* The thought shocked me, then I smiled inwardly. *Yeah, mean. A mean bastard,*

*that's me. People will go around and say: yeah, that
guy's mean, all right. One mean bastard.*

It's easy to be mean, I told myself, when you've got
secrets, when you know things nobody else knows,
when you've seen a dead giant. I met Debbie's gaze.
'Mean? I'm not mean.' I paused, smiled. 'Just honest.'

Debbie paled. In a low, threatening voice, she said,
'I'm not going to flunk. My grades won't be so
good. That's true. But I'm not stupid. And I won't fail.
Now, that's honesty, Owen. Sound strange to you?'

I considered her answer carefully, then replied,
'Coming from you it does.' Reaching out, I gathered in
another sandwich, took a bite.

'What's happened to you, Owen?' Debbie asked
quietly, a frown on her face. 'We used to be such
good friends . . .'

'It's not me,' I retorted. 'It's you! All those stupid
phone calls, and that idiot David – it's always David
did this and David did that – I'm sick of it!'

With a shocked expression, Debbie sat back in
her chair, stared at me while I struggled to regain my
breath. My outburst had taken me by surprise as
much as it had her. The silence between us lengthened.
The twins had not yet spoken a single word, and they
now sat with open mouths, their heads turning from
one of us to the other. From the kitchen came the clank
of dishes in the sink, and I knew that Mother hadn't
heard.

Debbie continued staring at me, then she let out her
breath between pursed lips, her frown fading on her
brow. 'I get it, now,' she said. 'It's okay, Owen.' I gaped
at her.

Leaning forward, Debbie said, 'Let's talk tonight,

okay? We'll listen to some records – you haven't heard my latest ones, have you?'

I shook my head as a flood of emotion filled me. For a moment I feared I was going to start crying, but somehow I held it back. I took another bite from my sandwich, shrugged. 'Sure,' I mumbled.

'Owen?' William piped up.

I glanced down at him. 'What?'

He and Tanya exchanged looks, then William turned back to me. 'You're eating my sandwich, Owen. What am I gonna eat?'

When I stepped out on to the porch, I saw Father's bum and legs – the rest of him was inside the machine. The missing half – the words burst into my head like a comet. But no, it was just Father working on the machine. Shaking my head, I descended the steps, walked past him and down the driveway. I looked up.

They were waiting for me, three figures at the edge of the road, Roland in the middle, Lynk to his right and Carl to his left. I felt a surge of excitement. They were just standing there, silent and unmoving. Looking mean, I hissed to myself. There, beneath the shadow of a giant oak, their forms were a dim, swimming grey – grim, deadly.

I could feel my walk becoming a swagger as I approached them. *Mean, vicious, like wolves, or killers.* Giants, waiting to grow. When I came close enough to see their faces those thoughts vanished. *Look at you!* I wanted to scream. *You're all terrified! You're all sucks!*

My swagger died. Their fear was too palpable; I could feel its echoes rising within me. I met Roland's eyes, and he looked away.

'Hi,' I said uncertainly.

'We gotta make plans,' Lynk said, stepping forward. His face looked somehow dried out, old. I stared at him.

'I know,' I replied. 'Where should we go?'

'The boat's out,' Lynk answered. 'There's fuckers crawling all over that place.'

'Launching,' Roland said.

Nodding, I turned and glanced up the road. 'Who're they?'

Everyone turned, and Lynk sneered, 'Barb and Sandy. They're in our class.'

The girls were walking towards us, not speaking. In moments they had reached us. 'Hi, Roland,' the one with black bangs said, offering a slight smile.

Roland looked down at the ground. 'Hi, Sandy,' he mumbled.

Lynk picked up a rock. He sent it flying down the road with a grunt.

'Any of you seen Jennifer?' the brown-haired girl asked – must be Barb, I thought – her eyes brushing mine briefly before turning to Roland.

Roland, Lynk and Carl shook their heads. I frowned. 'Saw her yesterday,' I said. As one my friends turned to me, and I shook my head and said, 'After.'

Sandy and Barb exchanged glances.

'You talk to her?' Lynk asked tightly.

'No – yes, sort of.' I shrugged.

Seconds passed, and no one spoke. I felt the suspicious gazes of my friends on me, thought desperately for a way to alleviate their fears.

Sandy spoke: 'You guys are weird. Well, seeya later.' They began walking away.

'She was in the playground,' I explained quietly. 'I
was wandering around. She just said, "Hi." We hardly
talked at all.' At least, I added to myself, I don't think
we did. But there was one thing I was certain of – 'I
didn't say anything about the, uh, what we found.'

After a moment, Roland nodded. 'Let's head down
to the river,' he said. 'Behind Old Man Fisk's place.'

I let out my breath, nodded. 'But let's make sure
that they' – I jerked my head in the girls' direction –
'don't see where we go.'

'Fuckin' right,' Lynk responded.

Walking slowly, we kept our distance from the girls
ahead of us, and at the bend where the road turned
right we continued straight on the gravel track that
led to the windbreak, and the east edge of Fisk's field.
The girls had kept to the asphalt road, heading for the
highway. We skirted the south end of the playground
and moments later lost sight of them as we entered
the windbreak.

Once inside the windrow we turned left and followed its length down to the thicker woods edging the
river. Leaves were starting to sprout on the branches
above and around us, and we did not see the river until
we were almost upon it. The water level had dropped
dramatically in the last week; the banks were steep
and caked with mud.

'Shit,' I said as I stood looking down on the waterline six feet below me, 'we can't even reach the water
any more.'

Roland grunted. 'Back to normal,' he said, shrugging.

I found a dry patch of earth and sat down. In moments everyone had followed suit. I grinned wryly.
'Anybody sleep good last night?'

Lynk had been staring out over the river. At my words his head snapped around and he glared at me. 'Sure. Why the hell not?'

Sighing, I shook my head, turned my attention to Roland, who was sitting cross-legged and carefully stripping the bark from a twig. 'So, what do we do now?' I asked.

Roland met my gaze, was silent for a moment, then said, 'I didn't.'

I frowned. 'You didn't what?'

He studied the bare twig in his hands. 'Sleep good.'

'Me neither,' Carl mumbled.

I ignored him, remained gazing at Roland. 'I kept seeing his face,' I said softly.

He nodded. 'The one he didn't have.'

I blinked. 'Yeah, his faceless face.'

Sticking the twig into the earth, Roland shook his head. 'No, I kept seeing his face.' He glanced up at me again. 'The one he would've had. When, when he was alive.'

I looked away quickly, frightened by what I had seen in Roland's eyes. My mouth suddenly dry, I croaked, 'How?'

Roland found another twig, began peeling bark. 'Don't know,' he mumbled, his wide forehead creasing in a frown. 'Kinda looked familiar, his face.' He placed the second twig beside the first one, began working on a third.

'Familiar?' I breathed.

He shrugged.

'No fuckin' way!' Lynk snapped suddenly, his voice sounding thin and brittle. We turned to stare at him, but he averted his gaze. 'No way,' he repeated. 'Nobody could fuckin' figure out his face.' His fingers clawed gouges out of the mud before him, and his face worked strangely for a moment. 'It was gone.' He glared up at Roland. 'His face was gone, you couldn't tell fuckin' nothin' from it!'

'I could in my dream,' Roland retorted, his voice rising slightly.

'Just a fuckin' dream, man.' Abruptly, Lynk jumped to his feet, faced the river. Over his shoulder he said, 'He came from the city. Somebody fuckin' murdered him and threw him in the river. He must've been frozen in the ice all winter, came down with the thaw.' He turned to us, sneering. 'Just some fuckin' loser, some guy nobody's ever seen before, and he's got all of you shitting bricks.' He tossed his head back and barked a laugh. 'Now you got him feeling important – fuck, some shitface who's so stupid he ends up rotting in a beaver lodge. But now he's important for the first time in his life – only he's dead!' With another laugh Lynk turned back to the river. In a lower tone he added, 'You guys make me want to puke.'

Roland had continued peeling the bark from twigs and planting them in the earth around him all through Lynk's bizarre outburst, but now he looked up, met my bewildered gaze and said, 'Not sure. Might've been me.'

I frowned. 'What?'

'The face. Me, but older. I think.'

'He might've been somebody important,' Carl said. 'How'd we know?'

I glanced at him. Carl had also found a twig, and was studiously picking the mud from the treads of his laceless sneakers. He seemed determined not to look up, even as he continued speaking: 'And how'd we know he was murdered? Maybe he just drowned—'

'Fuck off, Carl,' Lynk snapped. 'The guy was murdered.' He turned and glared down at him. 'I know what you're fuckin' thinking, man. Go tell the cops. Go say: Hey, look, we found this drowned guy and we think he's somebody important, so here, take him. And then they pat our heads and off we go. Little Carlie's got a big silver halo and a gold star beside his name, and maybe Daddy won't—'

'Shut up!' Roland shouted, suddenly on his feet and facing Lynk. His hands were balled into fists and he was shaking. 'Shut up, Lynk, or I'll pound the shit out of you.'

Slowly, I got to my feet, stepped back to watch.

To my amazement, Lynk seemed unfrightened by Roland's threat. 'Like to see you try.' His eyes narrowed. 'Yeah, Roland, I know all about you. My old man's friends with your old man's insurance agent.' Lynk smiled, then turned his back on Roland, who had suddenly gone pale.

Baffled, I looked at Carl, but it seemed that he was as confused as I was. Insurance agent? So what? And yet Roland looked deeply shaken. Slowly, he returned to his seat on the mud, sat hunched over with his head lowered on his chest, and resumed building his wall of twigs.

'Betcha that shitface is laughing,' Lynk said into the silence.

'Looked like me,' Roland mumbled.

'He hasn't got a face,' I said in exasperation.

Glancing over his shoulder at me, Lynk grinned. 'Roland's right. He's got a face, all right, and it's laughing. Laughing at all of you sucks. Laughing his face off, hah!'

'He's not,' Carl asserted. 'He's dead.'

Lynk whirled, took a threatening step towards Carl. 'You sure about that?' he asked softly. 'Maybe he's just faking it. Maybe he's coming after you, eh, Carl? He'll get you when you're sleeping, Carlie—'

'Stop calling me that!' Carl shouted, his face reddening.

'Carlie Carlie Carlie – he'll come when you're sleeping, Carlie. And what're you gonna do? Sit up and say: You're dead. Go away? When he's reaching for your throat?'

'He's shitting you,' I told Carl. 'The guy's dead.'

Lynk swung his burning gaze on me, grinned. 'Fuckin' Mr Cool talks, fuckin' whoopty shit. Poor Mr Cool can't sleep nights, poor boyyy! Bet he just crawls in bed with Mommy and Daddy, I bet. Sucks Mommy's tits—'

'Keep it up, Lynk.' I took a step towards him, a strange calm flowing through me. 'I'll bash your face in—'

Lynk's mouth curled into its usual sneer. 'Sure, motherfucker.'

I grinned in reply. 'And I haven't got an insurance agent to stop me.' I moved another step closer. 'Care to try me, Lynk?' I asked softly.

'Maybe I will.'

Slowly, I dropped into a crouch, then waited.

Lynk's gaze flicked to Roland, and then to Carl. 'The city boy wants to take us on,' he said. 'He thinks he can take us—'

'Not "us",' Roland said. 'Just you.'

There was a flash of anger in Lynk's eyes. 'Sure thing, old buddies. Just what I figured.'

'Lynk thinks he needs help.'

He glared at me. 'Fuck you, Owen. Just fuck you.' Again he turned his back, faced the river.

Laughing, I relaxed my stance and stepped away, carefully watching Lynk's back for any sudden movement, but after a moment it was clear that he didn't want a fight. Still, I remained standing.

'We don't tell anyone a fuckin' thing,' Lynk said.

I met Roland's gaze, then nodded. He hesitated, then returned it and looked to Carl.

'Okay,' Carl mumbled.

'School's over in three weeks.' Lynk slowly turned around.

I waited, then asked, 'So?'

Looking away, Lynk shrugged. 'So nothing.' He swung a glare on me. 'All I was saying was that school's over in three weeks, for fuck's sake.'

Roland rose to his feet. 'His face was mine,' he repeated slowly, meeting my eyes. 'Only I wasn't laughing.'

'He had a different face,' Carl said. 'A stranger's face, but it doesn't matter, 'cause he's dead, and now his face is gone.' Rising as well, Carl gazed steadily at Roland. 'Gone.'

Roland seemed unconvinced. With a shrug he turned away and began walking inland. 'I'm going home,' he said over his shoulder.

'Yeah,' I said, falling into step behind him, and in moments Lynk and Carl followed. We threaded through the shadows, not speaking.

V

Fisk stood behind the screen door and watched Sten's truck pull into the driveway. He laughed. 'I told you,' he whispered. 'I knew I'd hold you back.' He flicked his gaze to the field, then grinned. *Yes* – the worm-heads were sinking back into the black mire.

Hearing the truck door open, Fisk turned his attention to the man clumsily climbing out from behind the wheel. He scowled. 'Bloody drunk,' he muttered. *Look at him, already dead. Just doesn't know it yet. A dead man, stumbling around looking for a hole in the ground – look, he's even got his shovel, hah.* Fisk pushed open the door and stepped on to the porch. 'G'afternoon, Sten,' he said. 'You bring some garbage bags?'

Sten stopped, ran a hand through his greasy hair. 'Forgot,' he mumbled.

Fisk shook his head, inwardly gleeful. 'Well,' he said, descending the porch steps. 'Guess you'll just have to use the flatbed, wash it out later.'

Looking lost, Sten nodded.

'Pile's over here.' Fisk pointed.

Hefting the shovel, Sten walked over to it. He stared down at it, did not move.

'Don't smell bad yet,' Fisk said. 'Should be safe enough.' *Christ, the guy's already sweating a river. Wait till he's been at it half an hour.* 'Tell you what,' Fisk said, walking over to the truck. 'Just drop the back. I'll get a plank and my wheelbarrow.'

Slowly, Sten turned to gaze at him. 'Thanks,' he said, 'I 'preciate it.'

Fisk lowered the gate. 'Nothing to it,' he said.

Though sure as hell you wouldn't've thought of it. Mush for brains – nothing left in that skull. Dead man. Hope he knows how to use that shovel. 'Course, if you're dead, that's one thing you'd better know. 'I'll go get the wheelbarrow and plank.'

''Preciate it,' Sten repeated, wiping his brow.

Fisk walked to the back of the house. 'With luck,' he said under his breath, 'he'll roll his truck on the highway and bury himself. They'd find him and wonder, "What in hell was he doin' with five hundred pounds of mink guts?" And I'd walk up and say: "He thought they were sausages, Officer."' Fisk laughed. '"Was gonna have a barbecue, Officer. Was gonna invite everyone!"'

He righted the wheelbarrow and found an old weathered board that would serve as a plank, laid it sideways across the wheelbarrow and then walked it back. Sten was still standing beside the mound, his face white as he stared down at it.

'You all right?' Fisk asked as he came up beside him.

After a moment, Sten nodded, glanced at the wheelbarrow, then lifted the shovel. 'Well—' He turned a yellow grin on Fisk. 'Here goes.'

Not trusting himself to speak, Fisk took the plank and brought it around to the back of the truck, where he propped it against the tailgate. He turned to find that Sten had begun. Grunting, he dumped a shovelful of entrails into the wheelbarrow, which promptly fell over, the intestines flopping out to rest against the truck's front tyre. Sten stopped, stared at it for a moment, then laid down the shovel and righted the wheelbarrow. He then picked up the shovel and worked its blade under the slippery ropes until the iron edge abutted the tyre. Slowly, he lifted the load, stepped back and dumped it in the centre of the wheelbarrow.

Fascinated, Fisk continued watching as Sten returned to the mound, filled a second shovelful. The air was filling with the buzz of flies – Fisk hadn't noticed them before, but now he saw the black clouds rising up around Sten, who had fallen into a slightly arrhythmic pattern of inserting the shovel, straightening, swinging, then flipping the entrails into the wheelbarrow. Already, Fisk saw, the man's clothes were soaked in sweat.

'Christ,' Fisk said with a shake of his head. 'You'll be here for ever. I'll get out my shovel, give ya a hand.'

' 'Preciate it,' Sten gasped.

It had been on his mind all through the hour he'd spent helping Sten load the truck, and now, as he watched the man drive away, it rose up like a black-headed serpent in his thoughts. His loins stirred and he drew a sudden breath. Maybe, he thought. Maybe this time.

He walked the wheelbarrow around to the back of the house, then turned on the water hose and washed it out. The cage rows were alive with sounds: scratching, skittering, gnawing – eternal music, echoing the rush of his own blood in his veins, animal whisperings that, at times like these, seemed to caress his soul. Such beautiful music, he thought, as he walked over to the water tap and shut it off. He turned, placing his hands on his hips, and gazed, with satisfaction, at the three rows of cages arrayed before him.

'Maybe this time,' he repeated softly. After a moment he turned back to the house and ascended the steps. 'Make you sing one last time, eh, Bruise?' He entered the house, strode down the narrow hallway to the cellar door. His hand closing on the latch, Fisk paused, glanced back down the hallway.

Flowers. The word seemed to burst in his mind. His eyes narrowing, he stared at the wallpaper lining the hall. Flowers, faded now, the paper yellowed at the edges and peeling away. Wrinkles and blisters, smudged with dirt. Dorry's wallpaper, once as bright as her smile the day she'd picked it out. Fisk's breath caught as he heard a sound from the kitchen. She's back, he thought, his heart pounding. *She's gonna walk into the hallway and see me standing here, one hand on the door latch, the other gripping my crotch. She's gonna see me, and her smile will die, and she'll fade away – fade away like the flowers.*

He opened his suddenly dry mouth, then shut it again. No, he couldn't call her now, he couldn't let her see him. *But she is still there – I can hear her. She's laughing now, that soft warm laugh she saves for me.* He frowned. *But no, she's not saving it for me – she's laughing. Now. In there.* He lurched forward, reached hands out to either side for support. *She's with someone!* A snarl curled Fisk's lip, and he pushed himself forward.

The laugh deepened, and it was the voice of sex. *Someone's in there, and he's having her!* His hands bunched into fists and they travelled the walls on either side as he strode forward, his steps jerky and mechanical. I'll kill them, he hissed to himself. *I'll kill them both.*

Vision blurring, Fisk reached the end of the hallway and staggered into the kitchen. 'God!' he croaked.

There she was, her smiling face resting on a strange shoulder, arms wrapped around a strange body. Their eyes met, and her smile widened. Tears filled Fisk's eyes, and he reeled to one side, his shoulder striking the wall. 'No,' he cried softly.

Dorry stepped back, and the man turned at Fisk's words.

With a wordless bellow, Fisk stumbled backward into the hall. He spun around, stared wildly down its shadowed length. The flowers seemed to be falling from the walls – bleached and ragged, they fluttered down like a swarm of dying butterflies. At the far end the cellar door was open, and white light poured from it. Fisk's gaze fixed on that light. A gasp breaking his lips, he staggered forward.

Blossoms pelted him, each touch like the sting of a wasp. Flinching, bunching his shoulders and ducking his head, Fisk ran towards the glowing white light. He ran on and on, hands out before him, his eyes squeezed shut. But the hall seemed to go on for ever, and he was now wading through flowers hip deep. Fingers groping, he wailed, flung himself forward with all his strength.

He struck the wall, his hands and arms unable to stop his momentum. An explosion of colour filled his head and a loud crack sounded in his ears. Head snapping back, Fisk crumpled. Pain radiated in waves from the bridge of his nose, from his forehead, and, as if from a great distance, he followed the sudden warm flow of blood down through his nose until it issued from his nostrils. Numbly, he licked his upper lip, drew into his mouth the bitter blood. His eyes snapped open, and he looked back down the hall.

Empty, dark.

The stings prickling his flesh began to fade, leaving no mark. Drawing in ragged breaths, Fisk leaned his back against the wall, glanced at the closed cellar door. No white light. Nothing. His head was buzzing. He reached up and pinched his nose, winced at the stab of pain. 'Christ,' he mumbled, 'I ran into the bloody wall.'

Shivering, he closed his eyes and tilted his head back. No one's in the kitchen, he told himself. Some kind of hallucination. She's gone – she was never there. And that man – his face – it had been Fisk's own, years younger, smiling, eyes afire with lust. 'For Dorry. For my wife.' He shook his head. 'But that's all right, isn't it?' He nodded, wiping at his eyes.

The tears wouldn't stop, nor would the shivering, and soon he was bawling uncontrollably, his whole body heaving.

Hours might have passed – Fisk wasn't sure, but when the crying stopped and he uncurled himself from the corner he had crawled into, his joints cracked painfully and his feet were asleep. Exhausted, feeling washed out, Fisk slowly climbed to his feet, leaned against the wall. 'Dorry?'

He glanced at the cellar door, then, with a gasp, he pushed himself down the hall. 'Dorry? I can explain.' He staggered into the living room and sat down in the chair, drew his legs up against his chest. 'Please, Dorry,' he mumbled. 'I can explain.' As he spoke the blood that had dried around his mouth and in his nostrils cracked, making him wince as it plucked whiskers. 'Please.' He sucked in a lungful of musty, cool air, then croaked, 'I'm scared, Dorry. I'm scared. That's all.'

He waited – for her soothing words, for her calming touch, but the house remained empty, the air touching his flesh with cold, careless hands. Fisk rubbed his eyes. 'I'm scared,' he said stiffly, opening his eyes and looking around, his eyes fixing on the dull details of the room. 'Does anybody give a damn?' he asked, his voice lowering to a rough growl. 'That's all I wanna know, now. Anybody?'

Faintly he heard the muted madness of the mink in the back yard. He nodded. 'Somebody, eh? No, just nobodies, lots of nobodies.' He leaned his head back and closed his eyes. 'One thousand, six hundred no-bodies – all singing. Listen to them.' His eyes flicked open, his lips peeled back. 'Listen to them!' he hissed. 'So satisfied! Sure, won't be long now, they figure. Bunchin' together, now, ready to crawl.' He barked a savage laugh. 'Crawl outa this mouth.' He pushed his swollen tongue against the back of his teeth, trying to remember what it felt like the first time.

VI

In the shed, Sten giggled. He looked down into the stained ceramic sink, watched the last of Elouise's jam swirl down the drain, then turned off the water tap. On the table-top all around him sat empty jars. 'Fifty,' he said aloud, filled with glee. Fifty jars, twenty filled with jam and preserves, thirty waiting – waiting for this year. 'Not any more,' he laughed.

Sten turned and walked to the back of the room. He bent down and gripped one handle of the alumin-ium washtub. He paused to let a moment of dizziness pass, his eyes fixing on the ground meat that filled the tub, then, grunting, he began to pull the tub across the earthen floor. He rested three times before finally managing to drag the tub close enough to the jars and the table. Straightening, he frowned. 'Suppose it would've been easier to carry the jars over,' he mumbled, then shrugged. 'No matter. Next load.'

From the table-top he took one of the jars and Elouise's hand shovel. 'Tools of the trade.' Sten giggled again. He began filling the jars one by one, muttering between harsh breaths. The room reeked of blood and bile, and the hot air seemed laden with steam. Laughter filled Sten's skull – the monsters. And yet, suspended somewhere in the haze of his thoughts, remained a detached awareness – a small piece of sanity looking outward into the maelstrom, offering comments every now and then with a voice cold and sardonic. Of course they're laughing, the voice told him now – *look around you, Sten, smell the air, taste your lips. It's reality that's all around you now, Sten, and it's no different from this pleasant little house that's in here – right inside your head. You've done it, Sten. You've achieved the dream of a million philosophers. You've shaped reality to fit your ideal, to a tee. Aren't you proud? You should be.* Sten's breath caught, then he shrugged. 'Tools of the trade,' he mumbled again.

Grind the meat, fill the jars. 'It's my house,' he said, grimacing. 'I can do what I want.' He continued filling jars, his motions becoming mechanical. 'Sweat it out, who cares what she thinks? Who cares? Grind the meat, fill the jars, who cares?' He noticed that blood had dried on his hands, turning them black – he thought of lepers, he thought of flesh rotting and falling away, revealing twisted, stained bones. 'It's my house, smells fine. I can do what I want. I can sleep during the day, I can make my eyes glow at night. Grind the meat. I can drink all I need. Fill the jars. I can feed my dogs. Who needs garbage bags?' *Stained bones, go crunch crunch in the grinder, and what about her? Wearing those t-shirts. No bra, no, never a bra. Strutting it, pushing it, shoving it in my face, what's she trying to prove?*

'And what about the other one? Hiding there, nice white room, nobody sending flowers. Think I'd send flowers? Hah. Fuck, I put her there, hah. Tyres grab dogs, didn't grab her, no, she's not six feet under in some rotting garbage bag – she didn't even care, just a dog, eh. Fuck. More than just a dog, but what does she know?' The voice in his head spoke up: *right, more than just a dog – we know that, don't we?* Sten nodded. 'Damn right. The dog's a – a . . .' He frowned, then the voice finished it for him: *an excuse, Sten, the dog's an excuse.*

That's right, Sten, the voice continued. *Not all monsters are laughing. After all, there's me.*

Sten shook his head. *Six feet under, frozen snarl in the dirt. It's all black down there, black as my hands. My hands, what does she care? Hate me, they hate me. Grinding me, always. Over and over again. Making jam, filling jars. I'd never fit in a garbage bag. Besides, they want to preserve me, hah. Fifty jars, almost all filled. I don't care. They can't touch me. They can't touch me because I don't care, hah.*

Sten stopped suddenly, straightened and stared out of the smeared window, the white light making him squint. Nausea was building inside him – but it wasn't the smell, he realised – it was the sound of his own voice, and the laughing monsters, and the careening shadows, and the dizzying spaces on all sides. It was the taste of poison in his mouth, dry and bitter, and the hot gusts of his breath. 'I've caught a cold,' he muttered. 'That's what's happened. I've got a fever, too, I can feel it.' He clapped a hand to his forehead. 'Hot. I'd better go to bed.'

Glancing around, he realised that he couldn't leave things as they were. The jars had to be sealed. He'd leave the rest of the guts for now – the dogs had already been fed some. They'd eaten it like starved wolves. There was enough in the jars to last a month.

Reeling slightly, Sten began sealing the jars. He could feel the fever coursing through him, and it seemed that his own flesh was becoming too small for him, tightening and tightening until he wanted to scream and strike outward, claw and tear his way out from his own body. 'It's the flu,' he croaked. 'A white room, no visitors, but send me flowers, okay?'

After what seemed like hours, he finished with the jars. He staggered out of the shed and hurried across the driveway and entered the back of the house. He half ran down the hallway and then up the stairs. He entered the bathroom and stood in front of the sink, staring at the reflection in the mirror.

He almost shrieked. Spanning his forehead was a black, flaking imprint of a hand. Runnels of sweat had streaked through it, tracing brownish-red trails into his eyebrows and down on to his cheeks. Inside his head, the monsters roared with laughter.

In sudden terror, Sten whirled and plunged through the doorway. He ran down the hallway and entered the bedroom. Then he stopped. The bed – he'd been sleeping down on the living-room sofa, even after Elouise had left. He stared at it, dull pain churning through

his body. The bed was made, the sheets crisply folded –
not a single wrinkle. 'I hear you,' he whispered. 'Under
there. Just waiting. You know what you want, you
know what I want.' Sten took a step forward, reached
down and pulled back the bed's cover sheet. He began
removing his clothes, not once shifting his eyes from
the clean white sheets.

A minute later, he was naked. The cold air plucked
the sweat from his skin, and he shivered. Then he
crawled into the bed, pulled the blankets up and rolled
on to his back.

He stared up at the cracks in the ceiling. 'I've got the
flu.' One hand reached down and gripped his penis.
'Grind the meat, hah.' Savagely, he pulled down with
his hand. 'But no, never a bra. Never.'

VII

Leaning back, I kicked out with my legs, swinging
higher and higher. Flight, the only way I could achieve
it, and even then the feeling was momentary; an illusion. The chains squeaked and squealed, pinched my
palms, pulled me back towards the ground.

Below, the playground seemed to shrink into nothingness, then explode beneath me – flying, falling, flying, falling; I played games with my shadow, I tossed
the horizon up then pushed it away on all sides. I
reached higher, only to be once again plucked out of
the sky. Blinking, I would see the lines of forest, the red-
brown river snaking through the underbrush, overturned
black earth, rooftops and ribbon roads. Blinking again,
I faced the earth below, flattened and grey, the edge of

the playground's grass field, yellow and lifeless – and there, blackness seeming to pour into an invisible hole: my shadow.

I swung on, my breath coming in gasps, the world cavorting, pulsing, spinning. I was unstoppable – I would go on for ever.

'Hey!'

The power coursing through me died suddenly; my legs dangled and I let them drag the earth as I swung backward. I looked around.

Standing at the foot of the slide was a girl; it took a moment before I recalled meeting her here once before. *What's her name? Jennifer.* 'What?' I asked, coming to a stop.

She took a step towards me. 'We've been through this before,' she said.

I frowned. 'Through what?'

She shrugged, then walked over and sat down in the swing beside me. Warily, I watched her. There was a strange expression on her pale face, and her eyes were red. She sat staring straight ahead.

I hesitated, then asked, 'Something wrong?'

Looking startled, she faced me. 'No,' she snapped. 'Something wrong with you?'

Yes, I wanted to reply. Instead I just shrugged, looked away. *Jesus, she's worse than Debbie. What does she want?* Suddenly angry, I glared at her, found her staring at me quizzically. The anger disappeared, replaced by exasperation. 'What is it with you?' I demanded.

Her face went white, her eyes glassing over. Then she turned away from me.

'You're crying!' I exclaimed, pulling myself up from

the swing. 'Let's see,' I said, running around to look at her face.

'Fuck off,' she mumbled, swinging her head around so that her long blonde hair covered her face. She began wiping her eyes with the back of one hand.

'What are you crying for? I didn't say nothing to make you cry.' I paused. 'Did I?'

She shook her head. 'No.'

Staring down at her, my eyes seemed to acquire a will of their own, noting the reddish glint in her hair, the beginning of a tan on her smooth arms, the funny way she made a fist with the one hand gripping the swing's chain, the crazy red of her skirt, the tiny gold hairs on her thighs. I scowled.

'Then what are you crying for?'

'Nothing.' She looked up diffidently. 'It's over with, now.'

Our gazes locked for a moment, then I turned away, resumed my seat in the swing. 'You've got weird eyes,' I said.

'What's wrong with them?' she demanded.

I shrugged. 'They're green.'

'So?'

'So, that's weird.'

'No it isn't. You're the one with weird eyes.'

I had no reply to that, since I agreed with her. 'Well, at least I'm not cross-eyed.'

'I'm not cross-eyed!'

'Never said you were.'

'You did so.'

Sighing, I pushed back with my legs, began swinging. 'What're you wearing that dress for?' I asked between grunts. *Higher and higher.*

'It's not a dress, it's a skirt. A miniskirt.' Jennifer had twisted in her seat to face me.

The wind swept against me as I pumped harder, watching her watching me. 'So?' I asked as I swept by. 'What're you wearing that for?'

'Because I like it, that's why.'

Flying, falling, flying – she was becoming a blur. 'Were you ever Lynk's girlfriend?'

Jennifer stood up. 'No – look, would you stop doing that!'

I slowed. 'Doing what?'

'What are you, a retard? Swinging, that's what.'

She had folded her arms beneath her breasts, which was what Debbie always did when she was mad at me. I stopped swinging, began twisting the chains. 'Lynk said you once let him cop a feel,' I said.

Jennifer laughed harshly. 'With Lynk? No fucking way! He's a liar.' She paused, then said, 'I necked with Roland, once.'

I stopped twisting the chains, stared at her, dumbfounded. 'Roland?'

She shrugged nonchalantly. 'Sure, about a year ago. Behind the school.'

I looked away. 'Roland,' I muttered.

'He wasn't bad,' Jennifer continued, 'though I think it was his first time.'

'He lied!'

'Who? Lynk?' She laughed again. 'He always lies. About everything.'

I hadn't meant Lynk. It was Roland who'd lied. But no, I realised suddenly, that wasn't true. He'd just never said anything about it. He'd held out. 'Some friend,' I mumbled.

'What?'

I glanced at Jennifer. 'Nothing. Look, how come you were crying before?'

Her gaze fell to the ground in front of her. 'My mom's in the hospital.' Then she quickly looked up, her eyes wild.

I frowned, then realised that she hadn't planned on saying that – there was panic and fear in her gaze; for some reason I could feel my face blushing. Looking away, I groped for something to say. 'I was in the hospital once.'

I heard her let out a long breath. 'Weren't we all, once.'

'Huh?' Glancing at her, I saw that she had recovered, and there was now an odd grin on her lips.

'Well,' she challenged, 'you were born in a hospital, weren't you?'

I returned the grin. 'Okay, twice, then.'

'Were you in an accident or something?'

I fidgeted. 'Nah. I got bit by a mou . . . a rat.'

Jennifer cocked an eyebrow. 'They put you in the hospital 'cause a rat bit you? What'd it do, bite off your pecker?'

My face felt on fire, and I scowled at her. 'No, dummy. It was because of rabies. You get bit by a rat you get rabies. Your mouth froths and you go crazy and attack people and they end up having to shoot you, like Old Yeller.'

Leaning towards me, Jennifer said, 'Funny, you don't look shot.'

'I wasn't,' I snapped, drawing back from her sudden closeness. 'The doctors reached me just in the nick of time.'

'Before or after you started frothing?'

I sighed. 'Before, of course. Once you start frothing it's too late.'

'Oh. So how did they cure you, then?'

'Needles.'

'Uck, I hate needles. Was it a big one?'

The memory of that time had seemed far away up until then; now it rushed close and I felt a moment of queasiness. Taking a deep breath, I replied, 'Yeah, big ones.'

'They gave you more than one?'

I nodded.

'How many?'

'Don't know,' I answered, shrugging. 'I sort of, uh, lost count.' When no more questions seemed forthcoming, I looked up at her. Though I couldn't read the expression on her face, something about it made my heart jump. Instinctively, my gaze shied from hers. 'Mostly, it was all just a precaution. That's what they told me.'

A door slammed at Jennifer's house. She seemed to jump. 'I've got to go,' she said.

I shrugged, watched as she hurried off. *Too bad. I liked talking.*

CHAPTER TEN

I

FISK WONDERED WHAT was left. He reached up and scratched through the bandage bridging his nose. From his seat on the steps of the porch the maypole rose from the mound of ashes, black against the cool blue sky. It seemed almost insubstantial, like a slit of darkness behind a door left slightly ajar.

As if the world was opening. Showing me what's behind this pastoral scene. Nothing. Oblivion. The door's opening for me. Nothing to do but wait it out.

Dorry lived only in his mind. Everything else was dust. The pictures of her in the house behind him had cut paper-thin layers from her soul. Almost painless, her smiles in them, frozen for all time, were only faintly pinched. A pinprick of pain, but there every time the camera caught her lively face. As if she'd looked into the camera's eye and seen only what would be left of her in the years to come.

His wife had been a simple woman, in some ways too simple. Seamlessly happy, but sidestepping a thousand superstitions in her seasonal dances. *Plant around the maypole, such bright flowers, and skip your circle. Straw dolls tacked to the door frames, salt over the shoulder and knock on wood. Did you ever know how much you amused me, my darling? I looked like a farmer back then, didn't I? But I was just fooling, dear. I lost my soul in the dry white dust of a Mediterranean island, years and years ago. Crawled right out of my mouth, I guess. I didn't even say goodbye.*

Fisk wiped at the tears on his lined cheeks. *Damned nose so busted up I can barely breathe.* He wanted to die. At times he imagined Dorry waiting there on the other side. Such images let him look forward to the last beat of his heart. *But I know better, really. I'm looking at the crack and at the darkness beyond, and that's all there is.* These days, he had begun to look forward to even that.

Fisk climbed weakly to his feet. He didn't feel well. He felt sick. He turned and reached for the handrail, but the sight of his dark, silent house changed his mind, and instead he walked around the house and entered the cage rows.

Some of the panic from the last order still hung in the air. The piss and shit stank fouler than usual. He strode slowly down the first aisle, feeling their eyes tracking him from each cage. For some reason their attention steadied his stomach. His mink had been fed, and fed well. Hearts and liver and lungs and muscle. A feast of kin.

I like that. Makes you no different from us, and that's the way it should be. Us humans rule everything under the moon, everything under the sun. Our will to live just swallows you up, and that's what it means to rule. Remember that. Don't ever forget that.

He stopped and scanned the cages nearest him. Eyes glittered back at him. *Nothing but fear. I like that.* 'Almost time,' he told them softly, 'to start breeding again. People don't like you much. They just like your skins. I'll need more of you. Another generation just like you, not knowing any different. Just my cages.' He smiled. 'Nobody says the world's perfect, eh?'

What's left, then, for Old Man Fisk? His smile broadened. 'Just pain, my friends.' He continued on his way, up and down the rows, until he came to the house's back door.

'The little shits,' he said as he went inside. 'We made it too easy for them. We said we didn't want them to have to struggle like we did. Then we told them that you have to work hard to get anywhere.' He descended the stairs to the cellar. 'Which is it, eh? If I'd had a boy I wouldn't't've made it easier for him. I'd tell him comfort's overrated, then I'd hand him a shovel and tell him to get to work.'

The cattle prod was in his hands, charged. He stood in front of Bruise's cage, eyeing the trembling mink inside. 'Get to work, you little shit. Stop fucking around on my land like you owned it. We all made it too soft for you, and now you spit on a soldier's uniform. Then laugh at the camera, there in your beads and long hair. What you were born to, eh? Don't know any different, eh? Well, I'm here to give you the hard lessons.'

He pinned Bruise against the back of the cage, watching as the charges jolted the animal's body, listening to the mink's snapping pain, its scrabbling claws, smelling the scorched fur and the piss. Bruise had clamped his jaws on the cattle prod's sheathed shaft, biting uselessly.

Fisk held it there a moment longer, then he gasped and backed away. He'd come in his pants. 'Holy shit,' he hissed, leaning against the workbench behind him, feeling the honey-like trickle down the inside of his leg.

Breathless and shaking, Fisk headed back upstairs. He entered the living room and fell down prone on the sofa. The air whistled through his broken nose. He licked the salt from his swollen lips. *I'm alive again. Christ, I'm alive again, aren't I? That's what all this is, isn't it. The season's almost done. I've survived another, what's left to do now? Come alive again. Again, and again, and again and again.*

He rolled over, feeling sticky and messy in his crotch, no better than an adolescent, no better than some pimple-faced scrawny kid. Dreaming wet dreams in some classroom, or on a bus. Those agonising embarrassment dreams that go on and on until you just let go and the mess is there and that's that. *God, I'd forgotten those. So long ago, and all the guilt and shame. If Dorry saw me like this, if she walked in right now . . .*

Fisk groaned and sat up. 'The lesson was pain, wasn't it. The rest is just distractions.' He rose, collecting the cattle prod, and made his way back to the cellar.

He thought he heard a clatter of claws from the top of the stairs, but as he turned on the light and descended, there was nothing but silence from below. 'Didn't expect me so soon again, my friends? Too bad for you.'

Fisk stopped again in front of Bruise's cage. He crouched and looked in on the mink. It wasn't moving. He inserted the prod and gave the animal a poke. The charge sounded, but that was all. Bruise, he realised, was dead.

'Well,' he said, straightening. 'That was too easy. Too easy by far.'

II

The dogs had grown quiet. Jennifer lay on her bed, barely able to catch the soft clack of claws on the kennel's concrete walkway. They paced, bellies round and hanging, eager to run, filled with blood-soaked energy.

The bastard wouldn't let them out. Not any more. Not since Max had been killed. The dogs had nowhere to run, and like animals in the zoo, they were going mad.

She blew smoke rings at the ceiling, unable to keep from straining to hear him downstairs. The zombie, doing his own pacing, from room to room, his boots scraping and clumping, rye in his veins, groping inside his own coffin. He'd kept himself half drunk the past two weeks, while his wife lay in the hospital bed, jaw wired shut, fevered and fighting infection. Half drunk, some kind of purgatory, Jennifer supposed.

Her mother's fever had broken two days ago. Jennifer had walked into the room to find a thin, pale old woman. Sipping dinner through a straw, her eyes watery and puffy from the drugs. And the same question in them as she looked at her daughter.

'No,' Jennifer had said. 'No different.'

Are you surprised?

What had she expected? That he'd collapse under the guilt, that he'd pick himself up and become a man again? That didn't happen, not here in the real world. He was on the run – he'd always be on the run. All the while going nowhere.

Fuck that. Not me.

She lit another cigarette, pulling hard, swelling her chest as she drew the smoke down and held it there. *And that fucking doctor. Why doesn't he mind his own business? Fucking phone calls, the threats of sending a social worker. In my face with so-called offers of help – 'the school's been informed of the situation, Jennifer. You'll still have to repeat sixth grade, of course, because of your marks. But at least Principal Thompson understands the situation now, understands the reasons for your many absences. It'll be different this time around, Jennifer . . .'*

She released her breath. Nothing but air.

Down the hallway, steps shuffled into the bathroom. The door creaked as it swung shut.

Different this time around. Yeah, right. White knight Roulston, healing everything he touches. This wasn't the kind of infection someone could just cure. No, it had to be cut out. Cut away what's dead. And the man's dead, Roulston. He just doesn't know it yet.

She took another drag. The only way Roulston could help was by putting a bullet in her father's head.

'Your father has to admit that he's sick, Jennifer.

That's the first step. Nothing can be done to help him until he does that.'

Fucking idiot. Her father knew damn well he was sick. He's a drunk, not stupid. He doesn't pretend he can control it. In fact, he's surrendered. Completely. Hell, Roulston, he likes being sick. Can't you see that?

'He has to hit rock bottom, and he has to understand it when it happens. He has to ask for help, put aside his pride and ego . . .'

The toilet flushed. The door opened with another creak.

Rock bottom. There is no rock bottom, Roulston. Just mushy mud. You sink for ever. Once you admit to that, Doctor, then we can help you. It's the first step, Dr Roulston.

Her head was spinning. She'd smoked the damn cigarette like a joint. Tonight, she was going to fly. A hit in the dark womb of her room. Pink Floyd, Jefferson Airplane and the Velvet Underground. She'd circle under the ceiling, a giant bluebottle orbiting the lamp, and then it'd be time for David Bowie and Patti Smith, the only geniuses left who weren't burnt out.

Music inside and out, no skin in between. Catching her would be like trying to catch notes in the air, like trying to climb the scales with your hands and feet.

And then there's Owen. Owen Brand.

She wanted him. It had started out simple, a way to get to his sister. Remove the threat. But when she'd thought about it, the reasoning fell apart. For all Jennifer knew, Debbie might hate her brother. Telling Debbie that she'd fucked her kid brother, that she'd turned him on and then messed him up – what difference would that make?

The plan was flawed, but it didn't matter any more. Owen had proved elusive, and that was enough to make her want him, to make her all the more determined to pull him in.

She'd grown tired of the scene with Mark and Dave anyway. All she needed from them was the drugs, now that her visits out to Riverview had provided her with a new market, kids with rich parents, richer even than Barb's old man – who'd already told his precious daughter that he'd buy her a car on her sixteenth birthday. *What a laugh. Barb can't even walk straight these days, loading up on everything I bring around. And Sandy's gone for speed – could see that one coming.*

Speed was something Jennifer stayed away from. *Speed kills, or worse, it fries your brain and you end up finding God or Jesus or some dumb-fuck guru with all the answers.* But Sandy was eager, and it was *her* brain she was frying, after all.

Owen was only twelve. She wondered if he'd woken up yet with come on his sheets. She wondered if when she took his cock in her hands it'd come alive. Was he there yet? Did it matter? She'd take him there, eventually. He liked her tits – a good sign. Kids who just piss out of their cocks don't even notice things like that.

Jennifer reached under the pillow and found the tab of windowpane. She held it up for a moment, admiring how simple and harmless it looked, then opened her mouth and slid it on to her tongue.

She left the bed and kneeled in front of the record player. *Floyd to start, then 'White Rabbit' – just 'White*

*Rabbit', Grace Slick can't sing worth shit – then back
to Floyd—*

The door behind her opened. Jennifer swung around,
still on her knees. 'Get out,' she said.

Sten stared at her from the threshold. He hadn't
shaved in days. His undershirt was stained yellow under the arms. 'You fuckin' bitch,' he drawled.

The veins on his bare arms bulged suddenly. Jennifer's eyes widened. *Shit, no, not with him.* The veins
swelled fiercely, radiating purple and red waves of
heat. His eyes had fallen away, completely away, leaving just sockets.

'Got the fuckin' principal breathing down my neck,'
he said. 'Threatening me 'cause you never hardly
showed up last year and he says if that happens this
time he's calling the cops. What the fuck's the matter
with you?'

'Get out of my womb.'

'Huh? You're fucking stoned, aren't you? Fucking
taking drugs here in my house. What if Roulston
shows up right now? The shit thinks he can drop by
any time, just because she's in the hospital under his
care. I don't give a shit if your jaw's wired shut. Maybe
I'll just bust it again – you can have so many wires I'll
just stand on the roof and jerk you around your fucking precious garden. Think you can hide in your bed?
Well, fuck you, it's my bed too and I want to crawl in
and nail you right here and now, I'll do it 'cause I'm
your husband. You weak little bitch. I'd like to see you
hit back, I really would. I'd really like it if you just
took my head right off. He'll come by and sew it on
but it'll be too late and good fucking riddance. You

think you can do whatever you want in this house? I never wanted you anyway. Just one more fuckin' complication. I should've taken a coat hanger to you right away. Now get in that bed, the principal says you need a lesson and that's what I'm here for like a good daddy.'

He moved towards her, still standing, his legs motionless, his clothes burning away. She found herself flat on her back on the bed, and laughed because her hands were now knives.

'Touch me and I'll cut you to pieces. I fucking will, Daddy, and all the king's dogs and all the doctors in the world won't put you together again 'cause I'll tell them everything, Daddy. I will.'

'You're stoned, girl. What's the point of talking. Get out of my house. The kennel's full and no one's going anywhere, so you just run, little hamster. Run on your wheel and when I stick my cock in you you moan like you like it. You used to like it, remember? So let's go back to how it was. Okay?'

The door closed, rippling in its frame. Dog claws scraped on the stairs, going down, down into the bottomless mud.

Jennifer studied the wicked long, curved blades of her hands. 'Look at this. I can cut myself to pieces, and all the king's horses . . .' A part of her watched in amused horror as she began slicing open her flesh, starting at the breasts. *Too big*. She hated them. She hated everything, this new body, its new rules and hungers.

Cut it all away. I want to be pushed higher, higher on the swing, Daddy. Higher and higher.

III

The day had passed as if in a dream, in which I only half lived the hours waiting for its end. Miss Shevrin seemed physically to slow as the hours in the classroom passed, her bulk solidifying, turning to stone. There was expectancy in the air, but it was only anticipation for the end to come.

We scrubbed our desks, took drawings down from the wall, struggled to return the classroom to its sterile condition in which we'd found it on the first day. It seemed a pointless effort, and it seemed that Miss Shevrin knew it. She anchored herself behind her desk and left the last two hours for reading.

I finished *Jason and the Argonauts* and then started on *Tarzan of the Apes*. Written in 1914, its story felt strangely older than Jason and his world. My thoughts quickly filled with half-man/half-ape beasts, the images blurring into that of the body lying on its bed of sticks, images shedding coarse hair and becoming smooth-skinned, shiny. The story's solitude and loss spanned both scenes in my mind, shifting from the imagined to the real and back again, until I felt my life was a story, and that of Tarzan was as real as the desk's wooden seat under me.

The day ended with me feeling shorn and disturbed, trapped in a pale world. My final goodbye to Miss Shevrin a mumble, I departed from the classroom and the school at something close to a run. It was done. I'd never go back, but the act hadn't had the drama I'd anticipated. It had felt like flight.

I continued reading on the bus trip home. The world

beyond the windows rolled past unnoticed, powerless to capture my attention. Instead, I was witness to a child switched in a crib, and a human life launched on a strange, pathetic and wonderful journey. I longed for jungles embracing me. I longed for a simpler existence and discovery and revelation neatly packaged and bitterly satisfying.

When I stepped down from the bus the cool wind washed over me, and it was like awakening for the first time that day. The last day. School over, the city surgically removed from my body, summer begun.

My friends were nowhere to be seen. I stood on the side of the highway, feeling vaguely resentful but also relieved. There'd been nothing but arguments since we'd found the body. The secret was hard to bear, it felt heavy and dangerous, but none of us was willing to let go of it. Though we hadn't revisited it, the body rotted in our minds, the flesh swarmed in our heads, the face hid under the skins of our own faces. I knew the others felt the same. The body made us feel too old.

I walked along the highway's edge, not wanting to cross Fisk's field alone. Lord Greystoke's and Lady Alice's corpses lay forgotten in a small cabin at the primeval jungle's edge. The bones of a child ape rested in the crib. A man, a giant hairless, faceless man, lay on a beaver lodge, his flesh punctured by gnawed sticks, the crayfish working hungry tunnels inside his body. And Fisk sat in the shadows of his porch, covered in frost with dead flowers at his feet. They all felt real. They all felt more than real, they clung like tastes in my mouth, hinted their truths with each breath I took, were fed deep in my bones by racing blood.

I was glad to be alone. We'd argued, my friends and I, over anything, everything. Lynk had been the most savage of us all. Summer was coming, and he'd come alive, showing his sneer at each of us in turn. I'd thought I'd been mean to Carl, but I was nothing compared to Lynk. Carl's dad beat on him, and Lynk poked and jabbed at Carl's fear as if it were an open wound. Roland had been missing school, either taking care of his kid brother – who'd broken an arm – or visiting the doctor. He'd been falling behind in his homework. Lynk knew more about it than I did, and he worked on Roland, too. Hints, veiled attacks, working around the truth without ever touching it. And Roland seemed unwilling to defend himself.

The only person between Lynk and the throne of summer was me. I wasn't about to let him pass, and though he showed me his spite he didn't seem ready to try me yet.

All because of the body, all because we felt lost and scared.

I approached the wooden bus shack at the top of the 'U' road, and saw the jean-clad legs of someone sitting on the bench. As I came opposite I saw it was Jennifer, smoking a cigarette. Her eyes were huge as she looked up at me and smiled lazily.

'Owen Brand. Growin' Owen, want to sit down? We all got out of school early. Your friends are over at the candle factory. Lynk called you a fucking asshole, but he's scared of you. Why?'

I found myself sitting beside her, not sure why I'd accepted the invitation. A *disarming* smile – I remembered the description from a book I'd read once. *Disarming* – I'd looked up the word. Removing weapons, putting at ease. Opposite meanings, my favourite kind of word. Her smile was beautiful and left me with a delicious twisting and fluttering in my stomach.

'Someone cut out your tongue?'

I watched the cars roll by, smelling her smoke, and something sweeter, like burned rope, filling the air inside the shack. 'Nope,' I answered, thinking of the body's open mouth, lipless, the tongue – birds had pulled bits from it, leaving it white and stubby.

'I can't see why Lynk's scared of you.'

'No?'

She sat back, pulling hard on the cigarette. Twin streams of smoke shot down from her nose. 'Want some?'

'Some what?'

'The butt. Want some of the butt?'

'No.'

'Chicken shit. You'd probably cough to death.'

'Probably.'

'You like your sister?'

'Who? Debbie? Well, she's my sister, right?'

'So?'

'So you don't ever think about stuff like that. She's a sister, that's all. Don't you have any sisters or brothers?'

'No. Thank fucking God. I feel sorry for Debbie, having to look after you all the time.'

'She doesn't. All she does is listen to her records and talk on the phone with Dave, or Mark, or John or some other guy.'

'She doesn't care what you do?'

'No, why should she?' I scowled. 'Why are we talking about Debbie, anyway?'

Jennifer flicked her butt out on to the highway. We

watched it roll in the wind of the passing cars. 'So,' she said, 'you haven't got any friends any more. What's wrong with you? Are you a fruit or something? Or a suck? Are you a crybaby suck?'

'If I was, Lynk wouldn't be scared of me, would he?' I liked the thought of Lynk being scared of me. Maybe it was true.

She tapped her foot, her knee jumping. 'Fuck this,' she said, looking at me. 'You want to go behind the school?'

'What for?'

'What do you think? To neck. Never necked before, huh? Don't worry, I'll show you what to do. Come on.'

We left the bus shack. My heart was pounding hard in my chest. Jennifer's arm brushed mine, and even through our jackets the touch felt electric. We came to the crosswalk. I studied the school across from us. Its smoky glass reflected the houses behind us on the other side of the ditch. We looked small at this distance.

'If you like,' Jennifer said as we waited for a gap in the traffic, 'we can go together this summer.'

I glanced over at the candle factory. The side facing the highway had a huge geared wheel painted on the limestone. 'All right. Listen, Lynk and the others might still be around.'

'Oh yeah. Fuck. Well, there's an old farmhouse on the other side of the tracks.'

'Is that close to Roland's?'

'It's Fraser land, yeah, but they live down at the end of the section road.'

'Okay.'

We crossed the highway a minute later and went around the school. The chain-link fence dividing the playground from the railroad property was high, but without barbed wire at the top. We climbed it, and then crossed the raised train tracks. Beyond stretched rows of stubby, yellow winter wheat, the mud in between already spotted and patched green with weeds. The old farmhouse stood about a quarter-mile away. A gravel road led to it from the section road, which was off to our right, on the other side of the candle factory.

Jennifer led the way on to the muddy field. 'Are you going to miss supper?'

'No. Maybe. We don't eat till seven, sometimes eight. You want to eat at my place?'

She looked at me sharply over her shoulder. 'You sure? Aren't you supposed to phone first or something?'

'Nah. Debbie does it all the time. You can phone your mom and dad from my place.'

'Don't have to. Mom's still in the hospital. I cook my own meals.'

'Oh yeah, I forgot.'

'She's coming home soon.'

'Oh yeah.'

The land spread out here, north and westward for as far as I could see. A few clumps of trees sheltered farms, a few raised roads ribboned the fields, but mostly it was just cleared land. It wasn't crowded in the way the land edging the river was – no forest, no bracken.

I said, 'Anybody who looked would see us.'

'Don't worry about it. We're almost there. The ground's still too wet to plough up. Besides, this field's fallow.'

'Really? I thought this was winter wheat.'

'No, just wild oats and alfalfa.'

'How come you know so much about farming?'

'My mom's sister was married to a farmer near Beausejour. But she died. Cancer. When I was a kid we used to go out there a lot. I had a horse there.'

'That's what I want to learn. To ride a horse.'

'My uncle got married again. We don't go out there any more. He sold the horses, anyway.'

We arrived. The farmhouse was one storey, its windows broken. Tall yellow grasses crowded its sides. The bare mud and gravel around the front and back glittered with broken glass. A weathered grey outhouse leaned against a pile of planks near a collapsed chicken coop.

Jennifer walked up to the door, which was jammed half open.

'Who lived here?' I asked.

'The Frasers. Before they built the new place.'

'Before Roland was born?'

'Way before. Come on.'

I followed her inside. A narrow entrance-way opened out to a living room that made up the house's centre. The kitchen and bedrooms led off from it. Shattered glass littered the wrinkled tiles on the floor. A stack of rotting newspapers sat next to a raised brick section on the floor, where a wood stove once stood.

The air smelled damp and musty, though not as bad as I thought it would be. The broken windows let the wind through, chilly enough to make me shiver.

Jennifer crossed the living room and stopped outside one of the bedrooms. She eyed me until I looked away. 'Come on,' she said. There's an old mattress in here. Just think, Roland's mom and dad probably fucked on it for years. It won't mind.'

'How could a mattress mind?' I ambled slowly,

haphazardly, across the room, glancing around. There were swallow nests above the windows, the mud and twig lumps tucked at the join between the wall and the ceiling. The floor directly below was thick with bird droppings.

Jennifer waited until I came close then took me by the arm and pulled me into the room. The wide mattress lay on the floor – the only object left in the room. I stared at it. *She's been here before.*

'I want a smoke first,' Jennifer said, sitting down on the mattress and pulling out her cigarettes. 'Sit down beside me.'

The mattress felt damp, but not wet. I felt its chill seep through my jeans.

'You lived in the city?'

'Yeah.'

'So why'd you move out here?'

'My dad borrowed some money and bought a gas station on the highway.'

'Which one?'

'The Gulf station just this side of the perimeter.'

'That one's always getting new owners. Ever since the perimeter was built. But just because your dad now owns it, it doesn't mean you had to move out of the city. I mean, why come out here to this hell-hole?'

'Hell-hole?'

'Sure. Middlecross is a dump. It's boring. Stupid and boring.'

'I don't think so. Anyway, houses are cheaper out here.'

'No kidding. You want to try some?'

'No.'

'Ever smoked a joint?'

'No.'

'Want to?'

'Not really.'

'You're sounding like a suck.'

'I don't care.'

'Really? No, I mean, *really*?'

'Really. I don't care. I've never cared. Aren't you done yet?'

Jennifer laughed, throaty and low, and it made me tighten up inside. She said, 'Going with you this summer is going to be fun.' She took a last drag then stamped out the cigarette.

'The way you say that makes me nervous.'

'It should.'

She leaned close and pushed her mouth against mine. Her lips were soft, her tongue hot and leaving a bitter taste everywhere it probed. She put a hand behind my head and pushed her mouth harder against mine. The taste of her spit was a shock and I tried to decide if I liked it, then told myself that I'd learn to no matter what.

Jennifer finally pulled back. Our eyes met and she smiled. 'Not bad,' she said in a way that was both a question and an opinion.

I nodded.

'You hard, Owen?'

I nodded.

'Feel my tits.'

As I pressed my hands against her breasts she pulled me down so that we lay side by side on the bed. She unbuttoned her jean jacket, revealing the t-shirt underneath, and I reached inside, setting my palms against her nipples.

'Play with them. The nipples. You can pinch and pull, they won't break.'

I did this carefully, listening to her breathing, sensitive to how she moved. It was easy now since I'd already come in my pants, so quietly that she'd never even noticed; and though I was getting hard again it didn't seem so urgent this time.

We kissed and played for a few minutes longer, then Jennifer sat up, her face flushed as she stared down at me. 'Let's have a joint.'

'No. Maybe next time.'

'How come?'

'Because. Because I'm fine right now. I like how it is right now.'

Her immediate response was a scowl, then the expression faded and became thoughtful. I studied her face, knowing that I'd never forget how it was at this moment. The skin was smooth, clear, though the faintest lines bracketed her wide mouth and I remembered Mother warning Debbie about how smoking made wrinkles. Even so, I thought those lines were beautiful.

Her breath had quickened as I studied her, her cheeks bright red. She hadn't panted as hard when I'd played with her breasts. 'What are you doing?' she demanded in a harsh whisper.

'Looking.'

'Are you finished?'

I sighed. 'For now.'

She was silent as I sat up on the edge of the mattress. Suddenly I wasn't sure what her question had meant, and as a long minute passed, I concluded that she'd been asking about the necking. It seemed we'd stopped.

'Let's make this our special place,' she said as she stood and buttoned up her jacket.

'Sure.'

She rounded on me. 'That's it? That's all you can say?'

I grinned. 'This was great, Jennifer. I don't show my excitement much. My dad says he'll die of old age before he ever sees me excited.'

She lit another cigarette and blew out a stream of smoke. She smiled and studied me with half-closed eyes. 'I felt you excited, Owen,' she said quietly.

'Huh?'

'Never mind.'

We left the bedroom.

Outside, the air felt crisp, fresh. Clouds hid the dying sun. Jennifer laughed. 'So now I bet you'll run and tell your friends you got a girlfriend.'

'Do I have to?'

'Why not? Are you embarrassed or something?'

'No, just selfish.'

We started walking back to the highway. 'Well,' Jennifer said, 'I'll tell my friends.'

Hearing that made me feel good, so I thought for a moment then said, 'I'll tell them.'

We held hands as we made our way across the field.

'I got another secret place we can go,' I said as we neared the train tracks. 'One of the boats at the Yacht Club. It's in the yards. Abandoned. Me and Lynk and Roland broke into it. We were working on it, fixing it up, but they don't like going there any more. Too many people hanging around. But during the week the yard's as empty as it ever was.'

'My God, that's the most you've ever said to me!'

'Well, we're going together now, aren't we?'

We climbed the steep bank and paused on the tracks. Jennifer said, 'Looks like we won't have to tell our friends anything.'

Roland, Carl and Lynk stood behind the school, and that girl, Barb, was there as well. They had seen us.

We were still holding hands. 'Well?' Jennifer asked.

I frowned, unsure, then I put my arms around her. We kissed. A moment later we made our way down to the chain-link fence, climbed it, then approached the others. We weren't holding hands any more, but I knew that it didn't matter.

The girl, Barb, had a wild look in her eyes as she stared at us. Roland, Lynk and Carl said nothing, and none of them would meet my gaze.

'There's worms in his skull,' Barb said to Jennifer. 'My old man's head is full of worms, and the flowers have sharp teeth when we throw them and they drag him down, you sewing more threads, Jen? Sandy's a bitch, a blur, know who – what – I mean?'

I looked a question at Roland, who just shrugged.

Lynk said, 'She's been talking weird since we found her.' He glared at me. 'She never saw no worms in the skull.'

I slowly nodded.

'She's just ripped,' Jennifer said, laughing. 'Acid.' She walked up to Barb. 'How many hits?'

'None. He just strokes. Under the sheets. That's why I'm getting a car. But the highway's full of trees and the roots are ropes – I'm tied down now. Two hits, Jen, I can't come back, it's been weeks—'

Jennifer embraced Barb and held her close. 'Like hell, Barb. It's just been hours. Just hours. We're friends here. We'll take care of you while you come down.'

'I see scared's face. Like the moon and it's getting bigger. Closer. Closer comes scared's face, Jen.'

'Send it away, Barb. I'll help.' Jennifer led her friend to an alcove set into the wall.

'Holy fuck,' Lynk said. 'LSD. Holy fuck.'

Roland stepped close to me. 'You ain't said anything, have you?'

I stared at him blankly.

'To Jennifer. You ain't said anything, have you?'

'Oh. Of course not. Don't worry.'

He sighed, looking away. 'You two were at our old place, weren't you?'

I felt a sudden jolt inside. *Roland! He copped a feel with Jennifer. They'd necked.*

'My parents' place, right?'

'Oh. Yeah. Sorry.'

Roland smiled. 'What for? It's all right with me. Use it all you want, just don't burn it down or anything.'

'We won't.'

Lynk made a show of punching me. 'You fucker,' he said, grinning to take the edge off. 'You and her, eh? Fucker. I was going to go with Barb . . .'

I laughed, meeting his eyes. 'But you can't find her.'

He glared for a moment, then laughed as well. 'Fuckin' no kidding, Owen. Holy fuck, eh? LSD.'

It seemed all right between us right then, and I felt a weight slip from my shoulders. I was still wary, but it felt all right, then. Roland sighed again, as if to say things were okay with him, too. And I felt close to them now. Finally.

'Let's get out of here,' Carl said, his tone belligerent and with enough force to make me turn in surprise.

'What's eating you?'

He looked away. 'Nothing.'

Jennifer still held Barb, both of them leaning against the wall. Jennifer was singing to her friend, softly. I was startled to hear how beautiful her voice sounded. I headed over. 'What should we do?'

Jennifer's expression was worried. She paused in her singing and said, 'It should be okay, I think. I'm not sure. A real bad trip. She's done too much. You better go. She's spooked with all you guys staring at her. I'll see you tomorrow.'

'What about supper at my place?'

'Tomorrow.'

'Okay. See you, then.'

'Hey, give me a kiss first.'

I did. All the smells of her, the perfume, the cigarettes, now seemed familiar, welcoming. I whispered in her ear. She smiled, but it seemed uncertain, almost frightened. 'Me too,' she said.

We left them, and I found I was leading the way, Roland behind me, Lynk ranging out to the left but following all the same, and then Carl, of course, his hands jammed into the pockets of his blue corduroy pants, his eyes on the ground.

'Summer's begun,' I said. 'It's about fucking time.'

IV

The truck dripped wet mud into silver puddles. Overhead the sky was clear, on fire with the morning sun. Fisk felt heat stir in the air.

The health inspector, Bill, emerged from behind the

house, writing something down on his clipboard. 'Christ, Hodgson,' he said, 'how can you stand it?'

'Stand what? You going to cite me or something?'

'No.' He stretched out the word, pausing to remove his baseball cap and wipe his forehead. 'Man, summer's come early and come hard, eh? No,' he continued, 'it's within regs, though a part of me says we got to change those regs.'

'An official part?'

Bill laughed. 'Don't worry. Trying to get things through council's pure hell. It'll be years, though if the city rezones us all hell will break loose. Mink farms ain't popular any more, you know.'

'Doubt they ever were,' Fisk said, probing the bandage on his nose. *Walked into a door, Bill, can you believe something so stupid? Cold sober, too. Must be getting old, eh?*

They entered the house and Fisk led Bill into the kitchen, where he poured two cups of coffee. The inspector sat down and sipped. 'Of course, the market's still strong, eh?'

'Yep.'

'And what with all the ruckus about leg-hold traps, farming the animals makes sense. Even so, Hodgson, I don't envy you. Those aren't wild animals any more. I don't know what they are, but the way they look at you gives a man the creeps.'

'You get used to it.'

'No thank you.' Bill looked up at Fisk. 'Now, about that mound under the pole . . .'

'Household garbage.'

'You swear that's true, Hodgson?'

'On my wife's grave.'

'All right.' Bill drained his coffee and rose. 'There's a move to restrict burning to Sundays. Probably won't pass, but I'll let you know.'

'Sure thing.'

'Man, I don't envy you.'

They walked to the back porch. Bill slipped his pen into his shirt pocket. 'How come you never drop by the Legion? We'd welcome you, you know. Man, the stories *you'd* tell . . . I've seen your service record, you know.'

Fisk shrugged. 'What's the point of telling stories? Especially these days. The only people listening were there themselves. You see the way those hippies act on Remembrance Days? Bloody little shits.'

'No argument there, Hodgson. Even so, no matter what's being said these days, some of us know what's still important. You're a goddamned hero, Hodgson—'

'No I'm not. I had the bad luck of being in one nightmare after another, and the good luck of coming through alive.'

'We think it's important to keep alive the memories of those who weren't so lucky.'

Fisk scowled. He didn't like the way the conversation was going, and the tension and brittle anger behind Bill's words made him nervous. 'I remember them, Bill. Believe me. I don't forget, ever, and I'll defend those memories for ever, in my own way. Can't you leave it at that? I don't mean to be disrespectful—'

'I'd never think that, Hodgson. Not you. Anyway' – Bill sighed as he stepped down from the porch – 'we'd like your company, no strings attached.'

'I'll think about it.'

Bill climbed into his truck. Fisk waved once as the man started it up and drove around the maypole, then back down the driveway. He stayed on the porch and watched until the truck rolled out of sight.

'In my own way,' he said again.

The cellar was quiet. Bruise's death looked to have taken the fire out of the others. Fisk flicked on the lamp and activated the cattle prod. Bruise's body still lay in its cage, starting to smell, but Fisk didn't mind. He wanted the others to stay . . . mindful.

'Moon's turn, I think. Always following, like some sick puppy. Not too tough, eh? Probably die first time around. Let's see.' He inserted the prod. Moon backed to the wall and cowered in the shadows. 'Can't escape destiny, son. Take it from me.'

Moon screamed, but didn't die. Frustrated, Fisk went back upstairs. He masturbated on the sofa, re-membering Bruise's death and coming quickly. Some-thing was wrong. He felt incomplete, dissatisfied. The excitement of torturing Moon seemed pale compared to killing Bruise.

'I'll have to kill them, then. You finish torture with murder, right?' He rose and made his way back to the porch. 'That's what that Vichy bastard tried on me. Him and his Arab buddies. Should never have changed their minds. Should never have surrendered when the Yanks showed. Should've done me, so I wouldn't be standing here, remembering, keeping the memories alive.'

People don't have to know how I cried. How I begged him. Fuck that. 'The Legion can go to hell. So can the hippies and that's guaranteed. Vietnam's done them in, sure as I'm standing here.' *The boys got to die. Moon, then Rat, then Gold. They got to cry and beg for it. I'm sorry, my love, it's what I was all along. It's what I came back as. No soul. No heart. How was I supposed to love, Dorry? I loved my friends over there. And they all died. I tried loving you, and you died. I loved Bruise, too. It's not give and take. Never was. Just take. Stop reminding me. I remember how it was.*

The sun took the chill from him. The field wasn't black any more. Bright green weeds covered it.

'Summer's begun. Hallelujah.'

V

Going together. I'm not sure what I'd imagined that to be like. From what I'd seen of Debbie's various boyfriends, it had seemed to me mostly made up of tense negotiations, endless misunderstandings and phone calls that lasted hours where hardly anything was said. Every now and then something else happened, a kind of secret language, and with its locked gazes and small smiles it was a language of hidden awareness, as if an invisible tether linked Debbie with her boyfriend of the moment. Of course, with her lately, she was cutting them loose almost every week, and from what I'd overheard hiding by the stairs when she was on the phone, the most repeated phrase of her life was *I'm sorry but I just don't feel that way any more, so can't we just be friends, now?*

Going together. For Debbie it was a temporary, momentary state punctuated by going somewhere else.

It wasn't like that at all with Jennifer. The past week

I'd seen more of her than I had of my friends. There were things we talked about, and things we didn't. For the most part we necked, and with that, my world changed. Small things, mostly. Like, I'd never before considered blue jeans to be an object of frustration; and I'd never known how a person could close his eyes and disappear inside a girl's mouth, not like a cartoon, but in the way the senses closed in and left everything else behind.

I lay on the bed in my room, the window open to the morning's warm breeze. Somewhere way off a dog barked endlessly, and someone worked a rotor tiller in a garden. The model bomber hanging from the light fixture rocked and swung in wobbling arcs. Downstairs, Mother vacuumed the living room. For the first time, my private thoughts actually contained private things. Not private in the way the secret of the body was, but things all my own – this new way of looking at my own body, and at the bodies of women. I'd even caught myself casting a measuring eye at Mother, trying to see her the way Father would. She'd been standing in the kitchen, lighting one cigarette from another while Father dismantled the lawnmower in the garage. My glance had been short-lived; a wave of horror swept through me as soon as I realised what I'd been thinking.

Better to hide in my room, and in doing this – hiding in my room – I suddenly understood Debbie's touchiness when it came to her own room. Now, my closed door meant something more than it ever had before. It had come to be the first physical barrier between me and everything else.

My hours at home this last week had passed almost

unnoticed. My chores had seemed effortless. Debbie had played her records for me and I'd smiled and nodded, looking hard at her when she wouldn't notice. She was in summer school because of her grades and was now being followed around by a new herd of boys, all drooling and thick as planks to boot. I think even she was dismayed by how dumb some of them were.

In the driveway, the machine slowly disintegrated as piece by piece it was taken apart. The machine had come from a factory, I'd finally concluded, and had once driven conveyor belts or a press. Now only its innermost bones remained, smeared with grease to keep the rust away. My father took the bigger parts with him to the gas station, where they sat in buckets of gasoline for days before he got around to cleaning them and bringing them back. The parts filled the workbenches in the garage.

Mother spent her days in the kitchen or watching TV in the living room. The twins were in day camp, some kind of extended programme offered by the school. They'd been taken out of classes when we'd moved, and the day camp was designed to help them catch up. It was in Riverview, and there was bussing provided. They hated it, but came home exhausted every night.

At nights Mother read and reread pocket-books. James Bond, by Ian Fleming, and *I, the Jury,* by Mickey Spillane. Erle Stanley Gardner's Perry Mason and characters like Matt Helm lived in her mind every night. Sly and suave, a match for my Tarzan and John Carter of Mars. I think boredom had driven her back to those books. She didn't seem inclined to make any friends in the neighbourhood – one of the things that hadn't changed with our move.

With the weather warm and the trees budding new leaves, I spent most of my days out of the house. I'd meet up with Jennifer on the road beyond my driveway, arrangements we made the time before – we never phoned each other. She hadn't come for supper after all, running through a list of excuses until I took the hint. Her mother was still in the hospital. A relapse – into what I wasn't sure. She never mentioned her father, getting evasive and then short-tempered the few times I'd asked about him.

I wasn't that curious, in truth. Jennifer existed for me like an isolated island, a secret one. It had already occurred to me that my parents wouldn't approve of her. She smoked, took and sold drugs, didn't wear a bra, wore miniskirts sometimes and too much makeup. Clearly what Mother'd call *a bad influence*.

It would have been pointless to argue. I'd shared a joint and it did nothing for me. The only thing I liked about cigarettes was the taste they gave her mouth, the rich bite of her breath – and I knew that was a perverse thing, which made me like it all the more. But I didn't plan on starting smoking. The truth was, I had stronger role models than Jennifer. Every heroic character in the books I read each night became my aspiration, and they were all I needed to balance things out.

I listened to the rotor tiller churning up dirt, thinking about the last time Jennifer and I had met. The farmhouse had warmed up – she'd taken off her t-shirt, slipped her hand into my pants while I played with her breasts. We went at it for what seemed like hours.

I came so many times my crotch ached and by the end I felt completely used up. After a long while, it suddenly struck me that the whole thing had been incomplete. I wanted to even things out, do more for her, but I didn't know where to start and she wouldn't tell me. *'It's perfect right now, Owen,'* she'd told me.

Jennifer was visiting her mother today, then selling drugs to the high-schoolers behind the community centre in Riverview. Roland's day was being spent helping his father plough up a quarter section. Lynk and his family had gone into the city to buy him a new minibike for his birthday.

There'd been too much going on at the Yacht Club the past couple of weeks, even during the weekdays. The parking lot seemed for ever full.

And beyond its ground, deep in the greening wood, the body waited, and waited. I wondered what it looked like now. The memory, while sharp, had slipped into a kind of dream world, where spring's nasty thaw never ended, where the leaves never sprouted, where the beavers slept on and the crayfish never stopped feeding. A world of the past, and yet I knew it was out there still, a man lost to everyone but us.

In a way that made me feel responsible to him. He'd had a name once, and a life. He'd had dreams, fears, maybe even loves. Now, all that had been wiped away as completely as his own face. A man, a giant, a nobody. We owed him something – I wanted to give him back his face, his name, his history. I wanted to put him back in his rightful place. At the same time, he had come to exist only for us, and that made us more than what we'd been. He'd come to open our eyes, but they hadn't been opened enough. Not yet. He had more to give us.

Even as I thought those thoughts, I felt uncertain, uneasy. We'd made a pact with a dead man – he could only speak to us with what he had left, and he now existed in each of us and like an infection he spread his silence through us, until we hardly ever spoke about him any more. And yet, I sensed that we all felt the words piling up behind that silence. One day the dam would break, I suspected.

I thought about working on my models, just to kill time. I looked at the ones I'd already completed, trying to work up some enthusiasm, but instead my eyes found the attic's trapdoor.

The traps in the basement had killed two rats, but that had been all. Father told Mother that there'd probably been only those two, but of course I knew otherwise. There were more in the secret room above me.

You a suck, Owen?

I left my room, went downstairs to find a flashlight, the spare traps and a hammer. The war I'd promised weeks ago was finally going to begin.

I removed the nails in the panel, working slowly, methodically, making enough noise to let them know I was coming. I wanted them hiding while I set the traps.

The panel came away and I moved it to one side. The room beyond was lit by the two windows – as it was still morning most of the light streamed through the window facing the river. I saw no rats. I saw much more.

A desk sat against the half-circle window to my left, all in its own alcove. It was large, the wood dark, and on its dusty surface sat a pen-stand and a kerosene lamp. There was no chair. On the wall opposite me rose bookcases, crowded with books and chewed-up nests of paper.

More than I'd expected, less than I'd hoped. I stepped into the room. The floor under my sneakers – thick with dust and the leavings of rats – consisted of stained planks running lengthways, seeming to stretch the distance between the windows. The light coming in was diffuse, tinted by stained glass and a yellowy layer of dust. I forgot all about my war on the rats.

I approached the desk. The pen-stand was an old-fashioned one, its smooth wood black and unadorned, its inkwell empty. The fountain pen felt heavy in my hand. Its nib was dull gold-coloured and looked worn with use.

The lamp was about half full, I discovered once I wiped the dust from the globe. I checked the desk's drawers, but the only thing in them was a few sheets of yellowed stationery with the words *ex libris* on them.

The air felt close and hot. I checked to see if the windows opened. They didn't.

In here, I told myself as I looked around, a man might write *Tarzan of the Apes,* or *Treasure Island.*

I went to the bookcases. *A Short History of the World,* by H. G. Wells. I'd read his science fiction books, of course, but I had no idea he'd written other stuff. The pages were mostly gone, but the leather binding, chewed at the corners, still held what was left of them. I scanned the other titles. *Decline and Fall of the Roman Empire,* Volumes I, II and III. *The Golden Bough, The Elder Edda, Aeschylus in Translation, The Oresteia,* Plutarch's *Histories,* the Koran – at least that was what I concluded after pulling it down and studying it. The pages were made with the same kind of paper as the Bible, thin as onion peel, edged in gold. And the writing was Arabic.

I need pen and paper. I need to make a list.

Only when those thoughts raced through my mind did I realise that I was planning on reading copies of every book in here. There were about twenty in all, and the titles, as I pulled one out after another, left me breathless, my imagination conjuring up adventure and discovery. *The Prophet, The Art of War, Kubla Khan* – a poem, and the same for the next one – *Gilgamesh, from the Sumerian and Urdite tablets,* Bulfinch's *Mythology, The Once and Future King, Lord of the Flies, Nostromo, The Man Who Was Thursday, We the Living.*

I needed pen and paper.

Someone had left me a gift of their life. Reading these books, I believed, would tell me about who that person had been. For reasons I couldn't at first understand, I wanted to cry.

Another secret place, but not one I needed to pretend was secret. This place had been so for someone else, too. Here on the top floor, with a river passing ceaselessly below, someone's mind had walked the world. I vowed to do the same. I vowed it with all my heart.

One book was untouched by the rats, hidden as it'd been under the others. It was small, leather-bound, its title inlaid in gold. I carried it over to the south window and sat down in the warm, dusty sunlight.

Before opening it, I looked out of the window, rubbed the dust away to reveal the river's brown surface. *Here, everything but the body. Downstream, nothing but the body. Will you take this life, this one I'm about to discover? Maybe you won't have to stay faceless after all.*

The book felt warm in my hands. I brushed it off and read the title on the binding. *Les Misérables,* by Victor Hugo, translated from the French.

Will this do?

I began to read.

CHAPTER ELEVEN

I

'CHRIST, MOM, WHY don't we just go.' Jennifer fidgeted, walking around the bed to the window.

Elouise watched her dully. She'd been given a painkiller this morning. It left things hazy and blunted, but since they'd lowered the dosage she didn't feel tired or dizzy. She looked down at the clothes Jennifer had brought her. They hung loose, too big for what she'd become.

'Why don't we just take the bus?' Jennifer asked. 'This is stupid. He's waiting at home. What do you *think* is going to happen?'

Elouise wasn't sure. Dr Roulston had insisted on driving them home. He wanted to make sure of the situation there. Sten was sober, Jennifer had said – at least when she'd left the house that morning. Sober and looking scared.

'I wish you could talk,' her daughter continued. 'This is the shits. Who does Roulston think he is, anyway? He should be keeping you here.'

Elouise shook her head, but Jennifer still stood at the window, her gaze on the parking lot below. The girl looked older, and Elouise felt she had missed something these past five weeks, as if in that time Jennifer had unfolded in some way. *Still, so young. She shouldn't have to be this way. Not yet. She should have her freedom a while longer.*

The door opened and Dr Roulston entered. 'Are you two ready?' he asked brightly.

'Oh, Christ,' Jennifer breathed.

Roulston's tone hardened. 'I intend to make sure your mother is not entering a situation that endangers her health.'

'What do you plan to do, live in our basement?'

'If your mother had consented to criminal charges against her husband, we wouldn't be in this predicament.'

'Predicament?' Jennifer's face was red. 'Is that what you call it? Christ.' She walked over to the suitcase beside the bed and picked it up, glaring at Roulston. 'Fine, let's go.'

Roulston started the car. 'The charge is assault, and it's a serious one. He'll be arrested and thrown in jail.'

Elouise, sitting in the back seat, shook her head, but again neither the doctor nor Jennifer – who was in the front seat – saw her. *Not in jail. People will hear.*

They pulled out of the parking lot. 'Yeah, right,' Jennifer snapped. 'What's a little more humiliation for the Louper family, eh? Why don't you just brand our foreheads while you're at it? Fucking doctors.'

'That's quite a mouth you have there, Jennifer. I understand you're feeling vulnerable right now, but I have my patient to consider—'

'My *mother*,' Jennifer said, looking out of the window.

They turned on to the highway. The car picked up speed.

Roulston sighed. 'We share the same concerns, then, Jennifer.'

'We don't share a fuckin' thing, Doctor.'

'I don't understand what you expect me to do!'

Jennifer's laugh was harsh. 'You idiot. There's nothing you can do. That's the whole point.'

Roulston slowed the car and turned it on to their road. 'He needs help. He has to be convinced of that.'

'Put a gun to his head and he'll agree with anything.'

'I won't do that.'

'You already are, asshole. He's very smooth when he has to be.'

'I'm not easily fooled.'

They turned into the driveway. Feeling a need to escape, Elouise was the first to open the door and climb out. The garden, she saw immediately, was in bad shape, choked with weeds, the earth unturned. The dogs barked in their kennel. Roulston and Jennifer got out of the car, her daughter pulling the suitcase away from the doctor and walking towards the front door.

It opened before she got there and Sten stepped outside, dressed in his Sunday best, his hair slicked back. He looked pale, shaky, and his eyes shied from Elouise's after the briefest contact.

'Thank you, Doctor,' he said, taking a few steps and reaching for the suitcase in Jennifer's hand.

'Yeah, right,' she said, pushing past him and heading inside.

Sten smiled, shrugged. 'She's that age, isn't she?' he said to Roulston.

'When did you last have a drink?' the doctor asked coolly.

'Eight days ago,' Sten replied proudly.

'That's a start,' Roulston said. 'Shall we go inside?'

'Good idea.' Sten approached Elouise. He smiled timidly. 'Hello, dear. I'm so sorry for all of this. Can you talk? No, I guess not.' He made a move as if to hug her, then shrugged. 'I've made tea. I stocked up on soups, too. You've lost weight. Looks good. Come on.'

She followed him inside, Roulston at her elbow.

The house had been cleaned. Except for the worn fabric of the rugs and the upholstery, it could have been featured in some country cottage magazine. Elouise could smell the cleaner, and something else, faint, something deeper – sweet, cloying, as if slightly off. She'd never smelled it before, and it disturbed her.

Jennifer was already in the living room, sitting in the easy chair and smoking a cigarette. Sten gestured Elouise and Roulston towards the sofa.

'I'll get the tea,' he said, heading into the kitchen.

Dr Roulston looked searchingly at Elouise. 'How does this feel?' he asked.

She shrugged.

'Hopeful?'

'Give me a break,' said Jennifer.

Roulston's blue eyes fixed on her. 'Has he been drinking lately?' he asked.

'What do you think? What's your *informed* opinion, Mr Expert?'

'He seems sincere. He's trying his best. The last few days must have been very difficult. The body's need for alcohol is devastating once deprived. You've been here all this time, Jennifer. Has he been sick? Shaking?'

'DTs? He's always sick. What do you think I've been doing, following him around?'

Sten returned from the kitchen, carrying a tray. 'Everyone settled? Good.' He set the tray down and poured the tea. After a moment he collected his own cup, dumped in three spoons of sugar, then sat down in the chair opposite the sofa. 'Help yourselves.' He smiled at Roulston. 'I'm beating this, Doctor. I really am.'

'Have you attended an AA meeting?'

'I can do it all on my own. I'm doing it right now, right? Don't worry. All that's over with. Never again, I swear it. I get scared just thinking back on how it was for me. For all of us, that is. It's not the way to live, is it? No, there's not a drop left in the house. You can look if you want.'

Elouise saw her husband and the doctor studying each other. Sten's eyes were bright, almost challenging. A hint of a smile played at the corners of his mouth.

'Well,' said Roulston, 'that won't be necessary. Your wife and daughter have been given clear instructions. If you start drinking again they're to call me – day or night.'

Sten smiled tightly. 'That sounds more than professional interest, Doctor. Is this level of involvement approved by your medical association?'

Roulston's eyes widened slightly. 'Pardon me?'

'Well,' Sten continued, 'I mean, my wife's been discharged from your care, hasn't she? I don't mean anything by it. I mean, there's nothing you have to worry about. But I'm curious. Is this a new programme backed by the hospital?'

'No, Mr Louper. To put the record straight, while your wife has been discharged from the hospital, she's still in my care. She's my patient, and I take my responsibility to her very seriously. Are we understood?'

'So long as she decides to keep you as her doctor, you'll continue to feel responsible. That makes sense, I suppose. Part of the job description, huh? I'm sure you've got loyal patients – exceptional service and all that, so long as the file's still open, eh?' He smiled again. 'Your tea's getting cold.'

Roulston stood. 'Your wife will need a straw to drink hers,' he said.

'Crack!' Jennifer said. 'So much for perfection, eh, Daddy?'

'I'll be coming by periodically,' the doctor said to Elouise, 'to check on your progress. Remember to come by the office every Wednesday morning, nine a.m., for adjustment. If you feel the wires have stretched, or a screw seems loose, have your daughter phone right away. The same if the fever returns, or any burning sensation, numbness or sharp pain.' He glanced at Jennifer. 'That's not an easy addiction to get rid of, Jennifer. You're smoking a lot and very hard for someone so young. You'll pay for it later.'

'Go stuff yourself. You're not my doctor, Doctor.'

'She's that age, isn't she?' Sten said.

Roulston ignored him, still looking at Jennifer. 'No,

you're not my patient. But you might be, someday soon.'

Jennifer paled. 'Hear that, Daddy? He wasn't fooled.'

Roulston turned bright red.

Elouise looked away. She felt very tired, and that faint smell frightened her. It seemed to be coming from the floor.

'I was speaking of your addiction, not his,' Roulston said stiffly. 'Now, I'll be on my way.' He turned and gripped Elouise's shoulder, his hand firm and strong. He opened his mouth to say something, then changed his mind and just smiled. He straightened. 'I'll make my own way out.'

Sten rose and followed anyway.

Jennifer lit another cigarette. Her hands were shaking.

They listened to the car drive off. Sten went from the front door into the kitchen. A minute later he entered the living room and bent down over Elouise's cup of tea, which still sat on the tray. 'Have a drink, dear,' he said, placing a straw into the cup and handing it to her.

Elouise took it, studying her husband's face. He'd cut himself shaving at least a dozen times.

Sten sat back down in his chair. He sighed loudly. 'That wasn't so bad now, was it? I trust that's the last we'll ever see of him.'

Jennifer's head snapped around. 'She's his patient, you prick.'

Sten smiled. 'For now. I expect that won't last.' He looked at Elouise. 'Once he's no longer legally responsible, all that concern's out the window. It's how they all are. All that caring's just for show – he's paid to reassure, right? My wife knows all that. She's not stupid.'

'Don't you dare, Mom.'

Sten raised his eyebrows. 'Jennifer, dear. I could've sworn you wanted that man out of our lives. What if he finds out you're selling drugs to other kids? Kids in Riverview at that. How soon before one of them overdoses and ends up in Emergency? The cops'll show up and start asking questions. Who sold the drugs? You think Roulston wouldn't tell them if he knew, or even just suspected? Hell, he's the type to call the cops all on his own. He's not like me, or your mother. He's an outsider. He doesn't give a shit about us.'

'Go to hell,' Jennifer said. 'I'll be in my room, Mom. Then I'll fix lunch and stuff.'

'Going to shoot up?' Sten asked. 'That's the answer, eh?'

Elouise watched her daughter hurry from the room.

Her husband shrugged and said, 'I'll call his secretary tomorrow, then. Glad that's settled. It was good between us once, wasn't it? I'd like that again. Like at the beginning. Let's just forget all this. Well—' He rose. 'I'm gonna check on the dogs. They're probably thirsty as hell.'

Elouise sat alone, sipping her cold tea. Then she stood, listening. Sten remained outside. Not a sound came from Jennifer's room upstairs. *Shooting up? My God, please no.*

She went to the cellar. As she approached the door the smell was overpowering. She opened it and turned on the light, and recoiled. Her jam and pickling jars lined the shelves, each packed with a reddish-brown paste. The smell was rotting flesh, and it came from the meat grinder. Her jam and preserves were gone.

Elouise sat down on the floor. She felt the pain as

her mouth opened and at the first moan that came out
her strength collapsed. She cried, her body racked, her
jaw on fire as the animal sounds pushed out from
deep inside, terrible, bleating sounds.

It's okay, she tried to tell herself between gasps. But
it wasn't okay. Something horrible had happened.

Sten's house, it's Sten's house . . .

II

Heavy thunderheads scudded by to the south. Gribbs
added another splash of water to the putty. The bowl
in his lap, he sat in his chair outside the shack. As he
mixed with the spoon in his left hand, he tested the
putty's consistency with his right hand, rolling the mix
between his fingers.

He could smell the rain, hear the thunder, but the
sky above him remained clear. The days of summer
rolled on. The yachts sat moored to the docks. A few
were taken out every now and then, but mostly they
were there for parties and barbecues on the weekends.
The club had a new manager, who'd brought a motor
home which he had set up near the double garage. Some
trees had gone down for that. The manager, bald and
red-faced, his body round and bobbing like a buoy
when he talked, introduced himself the first day he'd
arrived. *'Reginald Bell, call me Reggie. You ready for
the overhaul? Yep, we're overhauling the entire opera-
tion. We'll be doing things Reggie's way. Great meeting you, Wally – I can call you Wally, hey? A delight.'*

That had been three weeks ago. They hadn't spoken
since. Gribbs didn't like the man. Of course, no one

had asked his opinion, and no one was likely to any time soon. But he'd met enough crooks in his day to know one when it bobbed up and shook his hand. *Call me Reggie.* Sure, Reggie's an easy name to call. Reginald's not easy. It makes a person pause, makes them look a second time at the smiling face, the booze-blistered nose, the evasive button-eyes.

He'd made the putty too wet, so he set the bowl aside and rose from his chair. The storms rolled past, not once swinging around, still only a promise. She rumbled out there, wandered, spat at shadows. *I ain't moved, dear. Still here in one place, one time, a piece of the bank watching the river flow by.*

Exhaustion had driven his dreams – his nightmares – from his waking memory. That had seemed to shake things up inside. A calm had come to his nights, a settled silence that he welcomed but didn't trust.

He collected his new walking stick, reassured by its solid feel in his hands. He'd made it himself, retrieving it from the tree-cutters when they'd come to cord the felled oaks. The magnificent hundred-year-old trees now sat stripped, sectioned, and seasoning in neat stacks at the far end of the parking lot. But he'd saved a piece of one of them, he'd laboured over it with his knife and with linseed oil, and now it walked with him as he made his rounds. The best he could do, although he amused himself with an image of using the stick to beat Reginald Bell into a small, quivering pile of spent affability. *Doing Reggie Reggie's way. A delight, a delight. The bell's sounded, gentlemen. And see, it's cracked crooked. A delight, a delight.*

Gribbs let the stick lead him down to the docks. The clubhouse's bar had its usual collection of members – he could see them lolling on the veranda. Always the same three. The retired doctor who drank himself senseless every day and passed out sitting in his chair, drink in hand. The businessman wanted for embezzlement in Florida. The rich wife of a man indulging a membership he never used. Gribbs liked the doctor, with his soused smile – the man didn't even own a yacht and didn't want one besides – a man without subterfuge, placidly embracing a pickled death. The woman was loud and flirty, quick with innuendo and broad winks, so bored and lost it could make a man cry just looking at her. The businessman professed his innocence to all who would hear, but refused to snowbird it south to face the music.

The three of them whiled the hours away each day, a blending of escape and forgetfulness, loneliness and pathos. He listened to the woman laughing loudly as he descended the slope and stepped on to the fixed dock running parallel to the bank.

Most of the club's members held themselves more upright, genial and lively and relaxed. They were generous with kindness and concern, though sometimes the deep-rooted insincerity showed through – not with all of them, but with too many for Gribbs to ignore.

The stick thumped steadily as he walked along the dock. The yachts looked good, clean and cared for, but to Gribbs's senses they were restless, their engines and screws impatient with the endless inactivity.

'Hey, Wally, how ya doin'?'

Reggie stood on the sloped bank in front of the raised veranda.

Gribbs nodded and waved in the man's direction as he continued down the dock's length.

'Hold up there, fella!' Reggie called. 'I'll join you!'

Gribbs sighed and waited, his eyes on the blurred sweep of water. Reggie's bulk registered in the creak of boards under Gribbs's feet. He listened as the manager clumped to his side. A meaty hand fell on Gribbs's shoulder, then slid off.

'Good to see you out'n about. I guess you've seen a lot of water roll by, eh?'

'And under. How are you, Reginald?'

'Reggie. I'm doing great.'

Gribbs smelled booze on the man. Bad for a manager to be dipping into his own stock. 'I'm relieved to hear it. Anything you want?'

'Just taking a walk with you, that's all. Having any trouble with trespassers?'

'No. Why?'

'Well, I've seen some kids around in the yards. Not members. Locals. We got to clamp down on that. I don't want punks thinking they can just walk through this place. We've been vandalised before, I'm told.'

Gribbs laughed. 'Dr Taft's grandkids, playing with matches behind a boathouse, damn near set the woods on fire. That was, what, ten years ago? Maybe longer.'

'Well, it pays to enforce the rules. That's Reggie's way. Always has been, always will be.'

Gribbs was silent for a moment. They'd come to the end of the fixed dock. He stepped on to the floating dock that projected out into the river. 'If you piss off the local residents, you'll get your vandalism, Reginald, and there won't be any way of controlling it.'

'Can't agree with you there, old feller. You come down hard, full prosecution, and the shit stops just like that. Of course,' he added, 'the problem may be something else. You still feel up to keeping an eye on things all by yourself? The grounds are a handful even for a young man. And like I told you, call me Reggie.'

Gribbs stopped and faced the new manager. 'Things have been running just fine, Mr Bell. There's been no complaints.'

'Well, yes there has. Your shack, for one. Quite an eyesore. We'll have to do something there. A new coat of paint, or even replace it entirely. It's on the agenda next board meeting.'

Gribbs laughed again and resumed walking. 'You can take it down at summer's end, Mr Bell.'

'Reggie.'

'I'll call you however I want. It's my job to take care of the yards. It's your job to manage the clubhouse. I don't answer to you, son.'

'Not the best of attitudes, Wally. I'd rather we get along.'

'Not much chance of that, sir. This club's going to regret hiring you, but I'll leave them to it. You do what you think you can get away with, they'll catch on before too long. There's not a fool among them and when it comes down to it, you're just a goldfish in a tank of sharks.'

'Where the fuck do you get off talking to me like that, old man? I can get you thrown out of here just like that. And that's exactly what I'm going to do, you goddamned bastard.'

'Go inventory or something, Reginald. I'm done talking.'

'You're out of here,' Reggie said, swinging around and marching back down the dock.

Gribbs came to the end and gazed at the sky above

the trees lining the opposite bank. The thunderheads had pivoted and now fled southward. The smell of rain was gone, the heat building once again.

Wait till he finds out I'm an honorary member on the board, and that I've been given a lifetime membership. Wait till he finds out I got a hundred and sixteen grand in an account in my name. He sighed. He'd have to actually attend the meeting. A first time for everything. *Hell, might be fun.*

The putty felt right between his fingers. He collected the tools he'd need and entered the yards.

The boy he'd met before was sitting on one of the rails, eating crab-apples and looking out at the river. Gribbs approached.

'Good afternoon, Owen.'

The boy turned and smiled. He looked older than the last time Gribbs had seen him. 'Afternoon, Mr Gribbs. What're you up to?'

'Was going to ask you the same thing. Since you don't look too busy, maybe you could give me a hand. Got an old yacht here, needs some filling on its hull.'

Owen climbed to his feet. 'Sure.'

Gribbs led him into the yards. 'Her owner's in jail. Has been for years. Racketeering. The boat's had a lien slapped on it, but that's about as far as it'll ever go. Enjoying the summer so far?'

'Seems to be going by awful fast. Right now I got a stomachache.'

'Bung you up, those,' Gribbs said.

'Crab-apples? Well, mostly I've been eating cherries and raspberries.'

'Good for you. What are gardens for, eh?'

They came to *Mistress Flight*. Owen stopped. Gribbs grinned at him. 'Anything wrong, son?'

'Uh, no. Nothing.'

'Good. Let's get to work, then.' He had the boy start on the wood rot, digging it out, leaving only sound wood. Gribbs then ran his fingers on the wound to get the feel of it, and when satisfied he applied the putty. 'She's in pretty good shape,' he said. 'Overall.'

'Mhmmm,' Owen replied.

'Might even be ready for the water in a month or so.'

'Really? But I thought the owner was in jail.'

'The lien's held by the Yacht Club. Past dues. Technically, the boat belongs to the club. I've been feeling inspired lately. Thought she'd like one more run.'

'Wow.'

'So where are your friends?'

'Roland's working on the farm, and Lynk's family went on vacation. Banff.'

'Wasn't there another one?'

'Carl? I haven't seen him around.'

'How come?'

Owen kept his eyes on the hull, frowning as he dug out rotted wood. 'Well, I got a girlfriend.'

'Ahh. Starting early. That's the spirit.'

Owen laughed. 'If my mom and dad knew, they'd have fits.'

'You sure about that?'

'Yep. She's got a reputation, I guess.'

'Any girl who's got one has at least something going for her.'

'Huh?'

'Sure. Means she's living, not hiding.'

Owen was silent for a while, then he shook his head and said, 'No . . . she hides a lot.'

'Ahh, a thinking man. Your type always made me nervous.'

'Sure,' Owen laughed. 'I heard you chewing out that fat guy. You didn't seem nervous then, so I figure nothing gets to you.'

'Sound carries, don't it? So I'm just a tough old coot, am I?'

'Yeah.'

'Well, maybe I am. Listen, this girl here needs at least two hands working on her. That's if you can drag yourself away from your reputable girlfriend, that is. Interested?'

'Reputable? But that means—'

'I know it does. Funny how words can turn around like that.'

'Yeah, I wonder why.' Owen stepped back and ran his gaze over *Mistress Flight*. 'It's the least we can do, isn't it?'

'You got that right, Owen, my friend.'

III

The dogs slept. Sten stood in the darkness between the kennel and the porch, watching them. Shane was dreaming, his limbs twitching, his teeth showing dull white as his lip curled back.

Probably ripping me apart. There in his head. Ripping me open, and the voices come tumbling out. 'Is this what it is to be free?' they ask. Yes it is, I answer.

Free as death. While Kaja and Shane and Caesar chase them down like rats, crushing their bones in their jaws.

He lifted the bottle to his lips, tipped in a mouthful of beer. The house behind him was quiet – his daughter off somewhere, his wife . . . *silent.* No words now. Just that look in her eyes, and the silence. They'd wired her shut, and now she stalked the house like a ghost. Whatever she said never made its way out. The words seeped into the bones of her jaw, or bled out in the swirling wake of her passage from one room to the next, settling into the walls, the floor. A spectral bitch, oozing nothing but hate for her husband. *For me.*

And Roulston giving him shit on the phone. The only person who could dismiss Elouise as his patient was Elouise herself. *Fancy trick, that. She can't talk. Ergo. Hah hah, you meddling bastard. First round's to you, but I'm not done yet. I'll bury you yet. You won't be coming back, that's a promise.*

Kaja moaned in her sleep. *Oh yes, Max is dead, dear.* Overhead the leaves flapped in the warm wind. Stars glittered, and two planets in the sky stood silent, one of them slowly slipping down the curtain.

Castor and Pollux, Cassiopeia and Ursa Major. Zodiac projections and it's written up there, read the signs, it's all there, oh yeah, my love.

There was nothing she could say. Venus plunging from the sky, Mars ascendant. She'd missed spring, and this new season was his.

Alcohol on the brain. New theories. Predisposition, lack of an enzyme, a protein, a lipid. Liver function. Modified inhibitors, synaptic suppression. Cycles of dependency. New cures. Invasive surgery was the latest, and one day all cars will run on hydrogen and then they'll be gone completely and the roads will just roll. New hope for the Great Barrier Reef, an ape-man in Olduvai Gorge, untethered and walking in space. Mars ascendant and Agent Orange – this is the modern world, dear. We don't play to no mutes any more. The modern world, Doctor, we have new treatments for your kind.

Roulston thinks he's the only one with brains.

Even so, Sten knew it wouldn't be easy. But he had one thing over the good doctor. Sten was fighting for his life. Everything was at stake.

He couldn't stand to be in the house with her. He couldn't stand having her back at all. *Nothing personal, dear. It's just the silence, dear, that's making me ready to explode.*

Of course, beer wasn't the same as rye. It was slow. It eased him along. It didn't shoot him up, white-hot into the sky like a giant, the way rye did.

The bottle's in the truck. The cashier smiled as she bagged it. She took my money and thanked me. I thanked her back. I thanked her for honouring this social contract, for recognising the necessities of civilisation. I thanked her for confirming my God-given right to drink, to drink hard and fast until I see clearly just how this world has fucked me over. And since the old man's dead and so is the spineless, unloving woman he married, I'll take it out on my loved ones. On the spineless woman I married. On the slut from my loins. So I thanked her for the smile that makes me legal. Oh, you might think otherwise, Doctor. You might take the position that I rescinded my rights as soon as I swung my fist. But come on now, Doctor, let's not be naïve. The world winks and nods and smiles, and not because it's trusting – it knows better by now – no, only because it's pretending to be trusting. The wink's for the game, the nod says 'your move', and the smile tells you everything will be all right in the end. A wink, a nod and a smile.

These are my rights, Doctor. These are civilisation's civil gifts, the sanctions people like me hide behind, with your blessing.

And I've got property rights, too. My house with its locks on the doors, the curtains to draw tight, and the bloody turf where I'm the tyrant – all so carefully, deliberately hidden from view. Out of sight, out of mind.

The new social contract. Fuck the huts with no doors to lock. Fuck the eyes of my neighbours – my uncles and aunts and cousins with their upstanding ethical regard to keep me in line. Fuck the threat of ridicule, the weapon of shame. Fuck the old unwritten tribal laws and the banishment that's a death sentence by any other name.

The new society doesn't need all that. I've read Psychology Today, *I've read* Popular Mechanix. *I've studied the stars, read the signs, and behold I proclaim the nuclear age of the nuclear family – boom! Amen to that, Doctor. Now, there are no eyes on us any more. We are sanctioned . . . private. The family's scattered and absorbed in their own privacy, their own miserable tyrannies. It's time for the monsters to come out. Time to play.*

Sten smiled as he watched Shane dream. The spurt of blood in the mouth, the quarry run to ground at last.

Someone approached from the road. Sten slipped into deeper shadows. His smile broadened as he saw Jennifer. She was stoned, staggering as she navigated her way to the back porch. She pulled her smokes from her jean jacket and sat down on the step, bending low over the cigarette, the flame of the Zippo wavering about as she tried to join the two.

Sten moved towards her, struggling to control his breathing. A moment later he stood in front of her. She hadn't noticed. She was still trying to light the cigarette.

Sten dropped his beer bottle and drove against her, one hand clapping over her mouth, the other pushing hard on her left breast. His weight flattened her on the porch. She tried to bite his hand and get her knees between his legs, but her efforts were weak, and she moved as if in slow motion. Sten stared down at her face, at the wide, terrified pools of her eyes.

He realised suddenly that he didn't want those eyes watching him. He reached up and grabbed her hair, twisting her head around, then her shoulders. Moments later he had her lying on her stomach.

The breath through his nose whistled as he pulled down her jeans. *Thank God for buttons.* 'Wouldn't want you getting pregnant, would we?' he whispered.

She tried to scratch him, but he pushed her hands away.

'Lie still and it won't hurt. Much.'

Behind them the dogs were awake. He could hear them pacing, panting. Kaja whined softly. A car rolled past on the road.

Sten pulled down his own pants, fumbled with his penis, then pushed it between her buttocks. She cried out.

A heavy hand gripped Sten's collar and pulled him upright in a single, powerful surge. Sten swore, spinning in time to see a fist flashing at his face. Colour exploded, the shock rippling through his head. Bones crunched, teeth broke. Sten staggered back a step, tottering for balance.

The big figure closed in again. Sten's head snapped back as the fist connected with his cheekbone. He heard more bones break.

Dad? Daddy?

He was hit a third time, but his face was already numb. Like so many other times, years ago, he somehow stayed on his feet. The man in front of him, hidden by the blur swimming in Sten's gaze, swung again, then again.

Someone was screaming. The dogs flung themselves against the kennel wall. The back door opened and someone rushed out, crossing the porch – not to him, but to the screaming girl. The neighbour's door banged open. A beam of light arced across the yard.

The man didn't stop. His fists rocked Sten's head steadily, evenly, with great deliberation. Sten did nothing, trying above all to stay on his feet, to not shame his father by falling down, or trying to protect himself. He wouldn't shame him. Ever.

The girl still screamed. The dogs were in a frenzy. The neighbour had shown up, yelling at his own wife to call the police, then rushing towards the man beating at Sten. The neighbour came up behind the man and wrapped his arms around him, yelling and pulling him back.

Sten stared. The ringing in his ears made everything faint, far away. The dimming, blurred vision cleared slightly, although only one eye could still see past the puffed, mangled flesh. The neighbour, Will Peters, who sold insurance and never once complained about the dogs, still held the man back, still yelled at him.

'For Godsakes, Hodgson! That's enough! That's enough, dammit!'

Fisk slowly slumped in Will's arms, his battered hands forgotten at his sides. His face was white, his dark eyes fixed on Sten.

Elouise came slowly to Sten's side. He blinked at her. She crouched down and pulled up his pants, fumbling with the belt buckle.

Jennifer sat curled up on the porch, her head buried between her arms. A broken cigarette lay white and unlit on the floorboards.

'That's fuckin' it for the dog food,' Fisk said. 'I come here and you're buggering your daughter.'

'Jesus!' Peters said, his eyes wide.

Sirens sounded on the highway. Other dogs in the neighbourhood had set up a cacophony of barking.

Sten tried to smile, but nothing moved right on his face. The ringing in his head got louder, almost a shriek. Drunk, he wanted to explain. I was drunk, Officers. Can't remember a thing. Not a damn thing. Firewater, Officers. Bad medicine. Will you help me now? Help me understand what's happening?

IV

She sat on the swing, the tips of her sneakers in the dirt. The taut chains in her hands felt warm, solid. Clouds scudded across the blue of the sky, and the grass of the playing field looked parched. The day felt old already, although it was barely past noon.

She'd never wanted to be the one in her family left to explain things. Explaining was a waste of time, especially when it came to what had happened the night before. *You don't explain things. Ever. You just try to forget.*

But everyone had wanted to know, and that big man, Mr Fisk, had made it plain what he thought he saw.

'The bastard was raping his daughter. What was I supposed to do, just stand there?'

Yes.

She saw her father before they took him to the hospital – irony of ironies. He was unrecognisable except for something in the mutilated twist of his lips. A smile. *His smile.*

Mr Fisk would have killed him, if not for Mr Peters. The realisation triggered nothing in Jennifer. She hadn't thought that what she'd say would get Mr Fisk in trouble. She hadn't been able to take things that far in her mind. Too stoned. Too numbed by the feel of her father's penis pushing into her. *Virginity intact, what a relief.* And now there was nothing but bitterness inside. *We slipped out of it, leaving Fisk looking like a homicidal maniac.*

Sten had been drunk. He'd been taking a piss. He'd fallen on to his daughter, there on the porch. That was all. *I swear.* Then all of a sudden some guy started beating him to a pulp. *I don't care what he said he saw. It wasn't like that. It was dark. No, my pants were up, what the fuck are you talking about?*

Sten and his smile. He'd shaken his head when the cops asked if he wanted to make a statement in writing, but then he shook his head 'no' to everything they asked him. 'Lie down on the stretcher, sir.' No. 'Were you under the influence of alcohol?' No. 'Were you sexually assaulting your daughter?' No. 'Do you understand what's happened here tonight?' No. 'Did you have an argument with Mr Fisk about something? Are you pressing charges?' No.

Mother hadn't seen a thing. She'd been watching television in the living room, then all of a sudden – screams from the porch. She'd had to write it out, then sign the statement.

She didn't see. Thank God.

The ground looked so parched. Where was the rain, the storms? Everything was drying up, dying.

Roulston came by that morning. He said he'd come to check Elouise. He'd seen Sten being stitched up in Emergency. He'd talked to the ambulance attendants, to the nurses, to the attending physician, to the police.

'Mother didn't see,' Jennifer told him. The three stood in the living room, awkward in the gloom cast by the drawn curtains. After a tense moment, Elouise sat down on the sofa, her back straight and her hands clasped in her lap. Jennifer smoked, her eyes on a game show on the television. People were applauding.

'Something happened last night,' Roulston said. 'That much is obvious. But you've raised the draw-bridges, haven't you? You should know that your responses are textbook perfect. I'd thought there were some smart people in this family.' He turned to Jennifer. 'I didn't think you'd be so predictable. It's rather disappointing.'

'Up yours,' Jennifer said. 'So her wires aren't stretched. You can go now.'

'Well, no. Not yet.' Roulston sat down opposite Elouise. 'I've consulted with Sten's physician. Do you want to know your husband's condition?'

Mother nodded.

'Eighty-seven stitches. The man who hit him must have had concrete fists. A fractured cheekbone, broken nose, damaged ligature in his left eye. Fractured maxilla – uh, upper jaw. Three broken molars and damage to the palate. And, finally, eighty to ninety per cent loss of hearing in his left ear, which is likely temporary.'

Elouise had nodded through all of this. Roulston fell silent, staring at her.

Someone lost a car on the game show. Wrong answer. 'So what're you expecting?' Jennifer asked. 'Violins?'

'Is that all you have to say?'

'No. How long?'

Roulston seemed startled. 'Pardon me?'

'How long will he be in the hospital?'

The doctor blinked. 'He's being released this afternoon. We've recommended he stay longer, but since he's not concussed – that is, he's displayed to his doctor's satisfaction that he's functionally aware – well, he's within his rights to discharge himself. There's nothing we can do.'

Jennifer felt her mother's gaze on her. She focused on the game show, crossing her arms.

Roulston asked, 'Do either of you fear for your lives?'

'No,' Jennifer said, turning to glare at her mother. Elouise shook her head. *Our lives? Wrong question, Doctor. Nothing behind that curtain.* 'Okay, fine. You can go now.'

'I have some questions for your mother.'

Jennifer sighed.

Roulston cleared his throat. 'Elouise. The X-rays – Sten's – revealed multiple past . . . incidents.' He pulled out a notepad. 'Dr Weins, his attending physician, did a detailed examination at my request.' He flipped the pad open, found the right page. 'Four distinct fractures of the left supraorbital ridge, a shatter pattern is evident on the right zygoma. Blockage of the nasal cavity due to a collapsed septum. Fractures on the mandible and on two molars – wisdom teeth unaffected. Probable eruption post-injury.' He looked up. 'In other words, he received those particular injuries when still an adolescent. We've made a request for any hospital records related to these injuries.' His blue eyes fixed on Elouise. 'Are we likely to find anything?'

She shook her head.

'It was certainly Dr Weins's professional opinion that none of the injuries was treated at the time of their occurrence.' He paused. 'Sten was beaten as a child. Severely beaten.'

Her mother nodded.

'His father?'

Yes.

Jennifer's full attention was on the two of them now. *No one tells me a fucking thing around here.*

'Was Sten's father an alcoholic?'

Yes.

Roulston sat back, his expression satisfied. 'The pattern repeats each generation. Be glad you have a daughter, not a son.'

Jennifer sneered. 'That makes a difference?' *Oh yes, he wouldn't rape a son.* Just beat the shit out of him.

'Well, I don't think he'll beat you – not if he hasn't up to this point, that is. Has he? I didn't think so. But the trauma – the psychological damage – will manifest itself in you. Differently, of course. It's my opinion that it already has, Jennifer. You're abusing yourself, completing the cycle – doing Sten's job for him. It's *his* situation, after all, *his* making. Now, none of this is my area of expertise, but I have consulted with the hospital's resident psychologist.' Roulston leaned towards Jennifer's mother. 'For your daughter's sake, it's important that we intervene. Now. I've contacted Family Services. A social worker will be coming out. She's on her way, in fact. If you'd like, I can remain here and be with you during the assessment and interview.' He swung to Jennifer. 'It's important that you be here as well.'

'Fuck that, Doctor. I'm not talking to anybody, and you can't make me.'

'If you don't co-operate, the worker will likely assume that you're fearful for your life under the present situation, or if not for your own life, then for your mother's. Jennifer, listen. You're better off being reasonable. The three of you need help, you lose nothing by asking for it. We can get this situation under control, keep the family together – each of you supporting the other. Counselling, therapy – they can be very successful once you acknowledge the need for help.'

'Nobody's taking me away,' Jennifer said.

'Well, it shouldn't have to come to that—'

'You swear it won't? Swear it.'

'Very well. I swear. But conditionally. You have to co-operate, you have to genuinely want to find a solution, to work through things. Promise, Jennifer.'

She turned away. 'Sure,' she said. 'I'm going outside. I'll be in the playground. Call me when the bitch from hell arrives.'

Jennifer twisted on the swing. *Co-operate. Sure thing, Doctor. I'm gonna lie like hell, and Mother's gonna nod her head at everything I say. Watch.* Roulston's promise had been a surprise. She'd almost fallen for it, but then she realised he was going to fuck them over. He'd say anything – he knew damn well it was the social worker's call, that she'd probably tell him to get lost. He'd made an empty promise. Maybe he was just stupid. More likely he knew. *And so, just like him, I'll say anything. No, ma'am, my father's the pathetic kind of drunk. He'd been aiming at a door when he'd hit Mother. He only beats up the house. He didn't mean to hit her, and he didn't mean to shove his cock up my ass. He didn't mean it, really. You didn't mean it, did you?*

She saw Debbie Brand riding a bike on the road. The girl approached, riding down and across the shallow ditch. The bike looked strange. It was a Mustang, lime green, with high handlebars and a banana seat. But it had an extra gear sprocket, and the slick on the back wheel was thinner than usual.

Debbie rolled up and stopped in front of Jennifer.

'Hi,' she said, smiling.

'Hi.'

'Got a cigarette?'

She took out her pack and handed it over. 'There's matches inside.'

'Had to get out of the house,' Debbie said.

'Oh yeah, I know what you mean. What kind of bike is that?'

'It's Owen's. Our dad fixed it up. Man, it's fast now. It's like a racing bike. It's got ten gears.'

'Huh. So how come he's not using it?'

Debbie returned the cigarette pack then got off the bike and sat in the swing next to Jennifer. They stared at the bike lying on the grass in front of them. 'All his friends are on vacation and stuff. He goes out in the

mornings and doesn't even come back for lunch, sometimes. Don't know what he's up to. I saw Carl yesterday – you know him?'

'I see him around.'

Debbie nodded. She tipped ash from her cigarette
on to her jeans above one knee, then rubbed it in.
'Carl says you and Owen are going together. Don't
worry about it if you are. I've got no problem.'

'We've only been together a few times the last couple
of weeks.'

'You breaking up?'

'No. But my mom was in the hospital, and now
she's home and I got to take care of her.'

'Oh.' Debbie frowned. 'So where does he go?'

'I don't know.'

'Weird.' She looked over at Jennifer. 'You turned
him on? Is he tripping every day?'

Jennifer laughed. 'Owen? No, he won't do anything.'

'Good. I mean, I don't mind, really. I'm sure he will
in a couple of years, once the revolution's won and
everything's legal and stuff.'

'You must be kidding.'

'What?'

'Nothing.'

They were silent for a minute, then Debbie said,
'Dave's such a jerk.'

'Yeah, a real prick.'

'I thought Mark was okay, but all he wants is to
fuck. They're all assholes.'

'I know.'

'I'm going to get my grades up. I'm going to go to
university.'

'Oh yeah. Going to change the world, eh?'

'Anything's better than this.'

'Going to burn your bra?'

'You don't have to be mean about it. Can I have another butt?'

'Sorry. Sure, take a few if you like.'

'Thanks.'

'So, does Owen's – I mean, do your parents know about me and Owen?'

'No. Lucky you. I hear Owen jerking off at night. His bed creaks.'

'He must be really going at it.'

'Yeah, you got him going, all right.'

'He's okay.'

'Yeah, for a brother.'

A car rolled into the driveway behind them. 'Got to go,' Jennifer said. 'See ya around?'

'Yeah.' Debbie's smile was pretty. 'Summer school's over. I got time now.'

'Great.' A car door slammed.

'See you.'

'Bye.' Jennifer hurried back to the house. *Mark told me once about social workers. Busting up families just for the hell of it. Sending kids to juvie homes. Roulston, she's gonna eat you alive. Say what you like to her. I'll make it obvious that you've jumped to the wrong conclusions. I'm good at this stuff. Watch me.*

CHAPTER TWELVE

I

I WASN'T TO hear what had happened at the Loupers' until almost a week later. Days passed without seeing Jennifer and it didn't bother me at all. In fact, as much as I enjoyed our times together, my mind was often drawn away, unscrolling in strange directions. The days seemed all too short, summer racing past all too quickly, and it made me feel uneasy as every word I devoured seemed to be pushing inside, forcing some kind of change.

The first book I'd chosen to read, *Les Misérables*, was a handful. The writing was dense, the story in some ways simple but in other ways anything but. My mind dwelt in a country far away, in a history I knew nothing about. Too late, I realised I should have tackled the history books first. I kept reading, determined to finish the book before I went on to the next one.

The stranger with his gifts had been older than me, a lifetime gathered behind him. Or her – *Les Misérables* sometimes felt like a romance. And under everything, there was something else, a kind of faith. Not in God, but in some kind of mysterious force that lived in the land, that made people the way they were without them even knowing it. It felt like the faith mothers should have – whatever it was that made them decide to be mothers. In any case, I wasn't sure whether the stranger was a fairy godmother, or a tyrant. The question felt important, because I felt that stranger's hands, shaping my future.

My unease spread its murky tide across my days and nights as the dry, unyielding summer stretched on. Momentary relief came with Jennifer, of course – I thirsted for the taste of her, the breath that was anything but innocent, the body that knew what it wanted. She'd made me insatiable, with or without her, and what I needed and explored twisted into itself, a thick knot closing off a secret place.

I didn't know if my new knowledge was a good thing. I didn't know if the path I was taking was inevitable, if everyone took it, but the way the knot fed on its own tension struck me as too desperate to be normal.

Even in going together, Jennifer wasn't the constant I'd imagined her to be. So far, our time together unfolded in a single dimension. Each and every time, we'd look into each other's eyes and become animal. Wordless and drifting through the other senses with nothing more than instinct guiding us. At least it felt that way with me, and at least it seemed to be the same with

Jennifer. She indulged herself with me the same way she indulged herself with cigarettes. Animal pleasure, something she could pull inside her body and hold there for as long as she wanted. She exhaled us both with the same look in her eyes. It was more than enough for me – it made me feel privileged to be possessed. But, even with all that, I knew my life was unfolding in other directions as well.

A new adventure was under way, and like the river it flowed between the worlds, from what I'd come to know, to what lay outside. *Mistress Flight* flowered, slowly, guided with deliberation and care. The old man and his unexpected friendship had drawn me into a place filled with possibilities, each dusted off and shown with pride. A life on the sea, ancient ports that had seen imperial triremes of Rome, a war conducted only on bitter cold nights when ice tumbled in the North Sea troughs and the hounds hunted shadowy wolves down below . . .

Every story, every poem, seemed to roll like waves, and when I looked at *Mistress Flight,* watching Walter nurturing her back into bloom, I felt the tug of adventure, the wandering pull. Of course, she had only the river, through lands where only the shallowest surface showed man's hand, but like Walter often said: you walk across the world one step at a time.

Gribbs had a way of opening worlds in my mind. New words, new ways for old words. He showed me that things could mean more than one thing – that important things always did. It made reading the books even harder.

* * *

We were getting close – *Mistress Flight* was almost ready. Walter said that today was the day he'd winch her over to the rails.

The morning was bright, clear and hot. I left the house, seeing only Debbie – riding off on my bike, which she'd asked to borrow so it was okay. Mother had taken to sunning herself down by the riverbank. Father said she already looked like an Amazon, but she said she wanted the tan to last, and that meant at least three hours a day, usually in the morning before the bus brought William and Tanya back.

I walked down the driveway and emerged on to the road.

'Owen!'

Lynk, Roland and Carl were down by the bend, near the end of the playground. They jogged my way. Lynk looked different, taller maybe. More likely it was just because I hadn't seen him in a while. Roland looked the same – for some reason, that seemed natural. He would never change.

'Got back yesterday,' Lynk said.

I shrugged.

Roland asked, 'What have you been up to? Apart from feeling up Jennifer, that is.'

'Not much.'

'Roland wants to go for a look,' Lynk said, pushing the hair from his eyes. 'I say fuck that. It's either washed away or rotted to nothing. Who the fuck cares? I want to take my minibike out.'

'There'd be bones,' Roland said, his eyes on me.

'I can't,' I said. 'Not today. What about tomorrow? Or Friday?'

'All right,' Roland said.

'Forget it,' Lynk said. 'I got better things to do.'

I ignored him. 'I think it's time to see, to see what's happened.'

'Who the fuck made you boss? Sometimes you act like it's yours. Like you fucking own it or something.'

'It's all of ours,' I insisted. 'What's got into you, Lynk? Too scared or something? Go play on your minibike, then, what the fuck do I care.'

'You ain't got one.'

I looked at Roland. We both laughed.

Lynk took a step towards me, then stopped as I swung around to face him. He hesitated, then shrugged. 'Let's go, Carl. I'll double you.'

'Nah, I'm heading home.'

'Forget that. Let's go.'

'I don't want to.'

Lynk rushed Carl, getting him into a headlock, then throwing him down on to the asphalt. 'Come on,' he said, standing over him. 'Let's go.'

Carl stayed down, his face red and his eyes filling with tears. He sat up and wiped his nose, leaving a wide smear on his tanned forearm. 'No. Fuck you.'

Lynk kicked him in the face. Carl folded up, rolling on to his side. Bright blood glistened on the black road surface.

Without another word, Lynk stalked down the road. He spun and walked backwards for a few steps, looking at Carl, whose nose gushed blood, then he turned and picked up his pace.

Roland's face had darkened. He stared at Lynk. 'I wish we'd never found it,' he said.

'Me too.'

Carl slowly climbed to his feet. His t-shirt was red,

as was the hand he held up to his nose, pinching the nostrils. He breathed loudly through his mouth. 'I'm going home,' he said thickly.

He looked small, broken, as he cut across a yard and disappeared behind a house.

His blood was bright on the road between me and Roland.

'Friday?' he asked.

'Okay.'

'See you.'

'Yeah.'

When I arrived at the yards, *Mistress Flight* sat on the rails. Walter crouched beside the main winch, reeling out an arm-length of cable. A bucket of grease sat beside him. 'Walk this to her bow,' he said, not looking up. 'You'll see where to attach it on the cradle. We need to firm up on this end before we release the side cables and remove the brakes. How're you doing this fine morning, Owen?'

'All right, I guess.' I picked up the heavy, greased cable and carried it to *Mistress Flight*. A ring had been bolted into the wooden cradle between the blocks. I opened the cable's clasp and locked it over the ring. 'Ready over here,' I said.

Walter straightened, one hand on the cable as he approached. 'Feels right,' he said as his hand reached and tested the clasp. He went back to the winch and started it up. The motor sounded loud. I watched the cable tighten. Walter disengaged the pull but left the motor running as he walked to the first of the side cable winches, which were hand-cranked.

'Unclip the first one there,' he directed.

I did so, and leaned back as Walter turned the

handle, keeping the cable straight as he walked me to him. We repeated the procedure with the second side cable.

'Time to knock out the brakes,' Walter said, grinning. He wore blue coveralls, grease-stained and threadbare. He squinted at me. 'Is that a frown you're wearing there?'

'Sorry.'

'Nervous?'

'I guess.'

'I packed us a lunch.'

'Sea rations?'

'God, no! A feast, my friend. Only the best for our inaugural voyage. You ready?'

'Yep.'

His face bright, Walter took out a rag and wiped his hands. He tossed it to me and I did the same, though mostly the rag just spread the grease evenly over my hands. I tossed the rag back. He reached for it, missed, then bent down and picked it up.

He went to the tool-shed and returned with a mallet. 'Good thing Reginald Bell's on a supply run today.'

'Are you going to get into trouble?'

'Don't worry. I'm not.'

The brakes were just wooden blocks set against the cradle's steel wheels, each held in place with a steel pin. Walter pulled the pins out, then with an expert swing he knocked each brake out cleanly. The cable creaked with the third and then the fourth ones. 'By the numbers, eh?'

I nodded.

'We'll need to fuel up. When she's down at the waterline, take the line looped over the prow and secure it to the gas dock. Once she's afloat, we can pull her alongside.'

'Okay.'

Until this moment I don't think I'd believed we'd actually get this far. Sometimes I'd suspected Walter was just humouring me, making all this into one of his tall tales. My heart pounded as I walked alongside *Mistress Flight* as she slowly backed down the rails to the river.

Walter stopped its progress when the muddy water lapped the base of the cradle. I clambered on to the frame and retrieved the line. The gas dock was to my left when facing the river. I carefully played the line out as I walked over to it. I secured it, then straightened and waved at Walter who still waited beside the main winch. He didn't move. I waved again, both arms, but he still seemed to be waiting.

'Okay!' I called. 'All secure!'

He gestured and then *Mistress Flight* edged into the water. Her stern settled alarmingly to my eyes, but finally rose just before her newly repainted name disappeared in the brown swirl. She rose free of the cradle, swung out into the current. I scrambled to make sure the line would hold, and watched as the woven rope lifted out of the water, pulling tight and shedding droplets as the current embraced the old yacht.

Walter reversed the winch, drawing the cradle back out of the water. He'd said he was going to leave it on the rails up top, moving it aside tomorrow. We wanted as much daylight as possible.

I stood on the gas dock, studying how she rode the water. She was beautiful, her new trim gleaming, sit-

ting even and high. It was a few minutes before I realised that Walter stood beside me.

I sighed. 'Yeah.'

'You said it. Let's haul her in and secure the stern
line. Nice knot you managed there. Just like I showed
you. We'll fill the tanks and then see what the old Sea
Horse can do, eh?'

II

'As the crow flies, it's about sixteen miles to the locks.
Of course, we'll be doing some twists and turns.' Gribbs
cocked his head. 'See any company?'

'Nope.'

'Feel ready to take the wheel?'

'Sure.' The boy moved up beside him. 'Stick to the
middle, right?'

'As simple as that.'

Owen set both hands on the chrome-plated wheel,
spreading his legs wide. Gribbs stepped back to give
him room.

'Let's play a game,' he said.

'What kind of game?'

'Stay at this speed. Stay in the middle. The game's
called *What can you see?* Pretend I got a blindfold on.
All I can feel is the wind through the ports. All I can hear
is the Sea Horse. I've got a blank space in my head and
it needs filling. It's up to you to fill it. What you choose
to tell me is all I'll have to go by. What you choose to
tell me shapes my picture. But so does what you choose
not to tell me. If you tell me everything, I might get

confused. If you don't tell me enough, I might misunderstand. Same for if you tell me the wrong things.'

'How do I know if I'm doing it right? How can some things be wrong?'

'Because you paint my picture before I do. But it's more than just a picture. You'll see after we've been playing for a while.'

The boy was silent for a few minutes. Gribbs sat back, reaching into the backpack and removing his Thermos. He poured a cup. 'Want some Coke?'

'Sure.'

Gribbs pulled a can from the bag and handed it over. Owen pulled the ring off with a snap and a hiss. He swallowed a mouthful, then set the can down on the teak surface on the other side of the wheel.

'The water's red and brown,' he said slowly. 'It's not flat, even though there's no real wind. It's, uh, it's spreading out around us, bulging in places, rising up from underneath. It twists on itself, too. You can see it because of the sunlight. The sunlight shows you the shape of the water. Its surface. But you can't see into the water. It's too muddy, and the sunlight only lives on the surface. Am I doing it right?'

Gribbs smiled. 'You tell me, son.'

'I'm doing it right. I started in the right place. It starts with the river—'

'It's a river?'

'The sunlight follows the current. The water spreads out from under us, but it follows its own path, and we're being carried along. But it doesn't care about us. It's chosen its path all on its own. It doesn't need to be seen to be there.'

'You sure about that?'

'Yes. It carries stuff all the time. Dead stuff, lost stuff. It carries . . . uh . . .'

'What?'

'Uh, history, I guess.' He drank some more Coke. 'A river. The river. Over it, over us, is the sky. Blue and no clouds at all. Just blue and the sun. It's got nothing to tell us. It's background, it's what's behind everything else. It doesn't tell us anything, it just shows us what we need to see.'

'Excellent. Go on.'

There was a growing excitement in the boy's voice, and an undercurrent of tension. 'I keep seeing too much. I have to keep closing it down. I have to decide what's important.'

'What's important? Remember, you're not just giving me the gift of your eyes, you're also giving me the gift of your mind.'

'Are you going to take your turn?'

'When you're done. Now, I see a brown river, and a blue, cloudless sky.'

'You must see more than that! After all I've described!'

Gribbs smiled and sipped his tea. 'Oh yes, but you're not done yet. I want to hear your voice, not mine.'

'The river spreads out to its banks. It was higher a while ago. But now it's pulled back, shrunken. You can see what it once covered. The clay is brown – no, grey. Sometimes the sunlight shows it blue. The clay looks smooth, but scarred. Cracked, maybe. Too far away to be sure.'

'Use your mind and take me there.'

'It's cracked, drying up, but that's just the top layer. Like a skin. And you can also see that the skin was once wet. There's bird tracks in it.'

'Birds?'

'Birds.' Owen fell silent.

Gribbs cocked his head. *Something important here.*

'Birds,' Owen said again. 'They're everywhere. They talk for the world. They talk with their voices for every tree they find. They talk the distance between trees, with their voices and with their wings. They scream when against the blue background. But when they're on the river, they're silent.'

'Birds,' Gribbs said, nodding.

'Gulls. White and blue and grey, but mostly white. With hooked yellow beaks. They say nothing on the river. They just ride the current, and watch. Their heads never stop turning. The birds in the trees are different, smaller. They're just shadows, like they're showing the meaning of something – of movement! Not in words, not in talking aloud, just in what they are. Birds. They map the world, I think.'

'You think?'

'No. I'm sure. But the river just carries them, and they stay silent – not always, but mostly. And the others stay on the banks, in the trees. They mark the river's flow, but stay in one place. So that's how your world is mapped. How your picture is painted.'

'Why?'

'I don't know.'

'You don't?'

'No. There's some things we don't have to know about. We don't always have to know why. Noticing's enough. Sometimes it's too much.'

'Is it too much this time?'

'They're silent on the river. The river says enough, because it's there and doesn't care if we're here or not. The birds know it, and that's all they need to know.'

'Do the birds care if we're here or not?'

'I think so. I think they watch us for the river.'

'Is my picture complete?'

'No. I have to talk about the trees. They're small, starting partway up the bank. Bushy, lots of twigs, lots of leaves, as if they're in a hurry. The bigger trees are inland a ways, past the bushes, the thickets, the bracken.'

'Bracken?'

'Sure. That's a word.'

'I know. Go on.'

'It's all dying.'

Gribbs sat up. 'What?'

'You can't see it, but you know it.'

'Owen—'

'No. There's people. Right now there's none in sight. But their current rides under the river. Hidden, the water black and poison. And the roots of the trees – their hold is desperate, but hopeless. The people are here, and they won't be stopped. They come with fire, and steel. The sunlight never shines on them – it just blinds them. They're burning out the roots, pulling down the trees. The birds scream against the blue backdrop. None of it is here, in front of your eyes. It's behind. It's underneath, in between.'

'Jesus, son—'

'But the river stays silent. The people can't hear it. They refuse to believe it doesn't care about them. To it, we're not giants, and maybe one man can become bigger. Maybe one man can come to mean more than he ever realised, but it's only so in the heads of others. We're smaller than we think, smaller than we'd dare admit—'

'What the hell have you been reading?'

'It doesn't matter. We're on the river, that's all we need to know. There's docks now. Wood. Grey. And parts of the bank are clear, grass lawns. There's porches and houses, and sheds, and boats pulled up on the clay, or tied to docks. There's a road, and two cars, one behind the other. The river feels wrong under us. It knows where it's heading. People have thrown a wall across it, and it's about to roar.'

'In anger?'

'Oh no. Just talking for the world. We never listen. We never really listen.'

'Can you see the locks?'

'Yeah.'

'Throttle up and swing us around. I'll drop the anchor and we can have lunch.'

'Is the game over?'

'Is it?'

'I'm not sure.'

Gribbs shrugged. 'Me neither.'

'I realised something,' Owen said.

'What?'

'You're going blind, aren't you?'

Gribbs smiled.

'And that's why I'm here.'

'Oh, more than just that, my friend. After lunch, it's my turn.'

'I didn't think I'd get scared playing that game.'

'Same here.'

III

'The taste of smoked salmon is exactly the same as its colour,' I said.

'Never thought of it that way,' Walter said around a mouthful. 'You might be right.'

We didn't say anything for a few minutes, too busy eating. Smoked salmon, cream cheese, bagels, French bread, Stilton cheese, prosciutto ham and watered red Portuguese wine. I'd never tasted any of it before, and it made me realise just how boring my family's own fare was. *Taste should be a surprise,* Walter had explained. *Each bite should cut across the palate, go in a different direction. Texture's highly underrated in this country's cuisine.* The wine was so heavily watered I barely felt it, but it swept everything clean between each bite of food. My head swam with the newness of it all.

'You know,' I said after a while, 'I don't know if I really see the world that way.'

'Oh?'

'I mean, I was painting you a picture, right? Just one kind of picture. I could've painted others.'

Walter nodded. 'I believe you. Even so, it pulled you in, didn't it? Hell, it pulled me in, that's for sure.'

'Summer's almost over. I can't believe how fast it went. The way my friends talked about it before school ended, I sort of pictured . . . something different, I guess. A wildness, as if the world was going to go back in time, as if the forests were going to fill with old, cold-eyed gods. And the ground under us moving ever so slightly, because the dwarves and demons were restless. Ever read *Beowulf*?'

'What?'

'It's a poem.'

'I know. You want to hear some of it? In Anglo-Saxon?'

I nodded, then said, 'Yes.'

'I've only heard it, mind you. Spoken. There was a man, once, a sea dog with his head full of old North Sea shanties and a whole lot more besides. Every time we ended up working alongside each other, he'd start. Reeling off lines, whole poems. Sometimes in Old French, or in High German, or Gaelic. Sometimes I didn't recognise the language at all. It took me a long time to realise he was handing them down to me, passing them on, the same way someone had done to him when he was young. The man couldn't read, couldn't write, but he was an artist. In the old way.'

'A bard.'

Walter grinned, then he cleared his throat and said,

> Þanon untȳdras   ealle onwōcon,
> eotenas ond ylfe   ond orcnēas,
> swylce gīgantas,   þā wið Gode wunnon
> lange þrāge;   hē him ðæs lēan forgeald.

I couldn't understand a word, of course, but the language was the clash of steel, the guttural clacking of oars in rowlocks, the heavy thundering flap of sail cloth and savage north winds. The words pulled me away. They pulled me too far. I found myself in a darker place, a place that heated my blood as if my body were being shaped on a forge; the hammer of my heart felt like iron, its taste biting my tongue. I took another mouthful of wine, savouring its bitterness.

Slowly, my eyes opened. Walter sat facing me.

'Yeah,' he said. 'Words spoken aloud can call you out. We each hold in us our own language, Owen. It can be brutal, like the language of *Beowulf*. Or rounded, humming with romance, like *The Song of Roland*. When you hear yours spoken for the first time . . . everything changes, doesn't it?'

'Yes. What's happening?'

'You've drunk too much wine, my boy, even though it's barely coloured water. You started guzzling it when you listened to your language.'

'Blood and iron,' I said. 'Wine tastes like blood and iron. Those words, what did they mean?'

'I don't know,' Walter said.

'What?'

'How could I? That's how I learned them, word for word, the sea dog thumping his scarred fist on the table in the ship's galley. Thumping in time, like swords beating on shields, I guess. He drove that poem right into my bones, his eyes on fire and a quick clout if I got it wrong.'

'So you've done the same to someone else? You passed it on like you were supposed to do?'

Walter looked away, squinting against the sunlight coming in through the front window. 'Here and there. I spread it out, you see. Maybe that was a mistake, but it seemed the safer thing to do. That one, *Beowulf*, well, I ain't passed that one on yet.'

'I'm going to learn it,' I said. 'In Anglo-Saxon and in English. I found an old book. Most of the pages are gone, eaten by rats, but it's about European folklore, and in the table of contents it starts with *Beowulf*. I plan on finding copies of all the stories. I plan on learning them.'

'That's quite a task you've set for yourself there, my friend. Your parents must be proud of you.'

I shrugged, picking at the ham. 'They don't do much. My dad fixes cars. My mom reads spy novels. She'd like to get a job somewhere but it never seems to happen. She used to know lots. She was at university. My dad wanted to be an engineer. But then Mom got pregnant so she quit school and Dad couldn't afford the night school any more and so he got a job at a garage. That was years ago. They don't do much these days. We moved around lots. Things happened, I guess. But then Dad got the loan and bought the Gulf station on the highway and they used that to get the mortgage, so now we got land and that's good. It's an investment, and that's good.'

'How's his business coming along?'

'Great. He's making tons. I don't think we'll have to move any more.'

Walter began packing away what little food we'd left uneaten, his expression thoughtful. 'Let's talk about land,' he said.

I nodded. 'Okay. It's your turn, after all.'

'So it is. Well. Land's not something we just live on. We're all from someplace else, if you go back far enough. We carry with us the stories of where we came from, what we left behind. Those stories put words and meaning to how we lived on the old land, the first lands. When we took to the seas – the first times – it wasn't a simple, easy journey. No vacations back then.

No. When people moved, it was because they had to. Driven from their homes and hearths on winds of smoke and blood. For some of them, they heard voices pulling them onward. Refugees, all of us, and pilgrims, some of us – pilgrims looking for an old holiness in a new place.

'We moved from one dark land to the next dark land, and the sea that carried us – it was the darkest road of them all. What lived in its deep wasn't for human eyes to see, so madness was always close by, a spectre ever ready to show us what we didn't understand, what we couldn't understand. A spectre of unreason – after all, it's senselessness that frightens us the most.'

He paused for a long moment. Under us, *Mistress Flight* swung on her anchor line, an easy rhythm that matched the swaying of his words. I heard gulls screaming.

'That old sea dog I told you about. When he was done, when he'd emptied himself into me, he made landfall back in his homeland. Denmark. Then he left all his life's possessions – a single leather sack – on a roadside and he walked into the bog and was never seen again. When I heard what he'd done, it left me cold. Scared. You know why?'

'Yes,' I said. 'He made himself into his last story. The last one to give to you. And you knew your future, then.'

'Clear and bright like a full-moon night.' Walter's eyes reflected something intense, almost wary. 'What's made you so old, Owen?'

I closed my eyes. *I made a promise, didn't I?* 'I've found a giant,' I said. 'He's my world, now. I think I live inside him. Lost, deep inside him. I need to climb out, up, through the top of his skull. But I don't know how, and it might be too late. I just don't know.'

Walter was silent a moment longer, then he climbed to his feet. 'Let's get a move on. Heading back's gonna be harder.'

Ten minutes later the Sea Horse worked us steadily forward, our path slicing the river in half, the screws under the stern churning the water into brown foam in our wake. I held the wheel, Walter standing beside me.

'Your picture,' he finally said. 'It painted a world where people are like ants, crawling on the surface, remixing the thinnest layer of earth. It was a true picture, for this place. This land's still raw. Human history is barely skin-deep here, like bird tracks on clay. It's what you were born to, it's what your eyes have seen all your young life. But there's other lands. Places where human history runs deep, almost down to the land's bones, and the land's muscle is of our own making. Life on life on life, generation on generation, century after century.'

'Europe,' I said, nodding. 'And Africa and Asia.'

'Visit those places, son. They'll open you out. People in this country are lonely. Some of them spend their time trying to talk to the land, trying to connect to it and find a spirit there. They're missing the point. They're jumping the gun. Put yourself on a hilltop in the Old World, and make yourself understand that the hill's man-made. It's tombs, barrows, hill-forts, villages, towns, even cities, right there under you. Look around and realise that the pretty view is a gift from a hundred thousand hands, building their lives brick by brick, stone by stone. Then you won't feel lonely any more. And you'll find a new perspective on things. What's come will go, and will come again, and go again, and so on. That's a comfort, a comfort deep in your soul, and it keeps you from desperate acts, desperate thoughts. Don't bother looking to identify with your land before you learn to identify with your species. Sorry if I'm sounding like a teacher, Owen.'

I shook my head. 'No. I know that what you're saying will stay with me. It'll all come back someday, when I need it to.'

Walter turned away. He left my side, walking around the small cabin, his hand tracking the teak trimming, the brass fixtures.

'Something wrong?' I asked.

He shook his head, keeping his back to me, then cleared his throat and said, 'I met an old woman in Istanbul, which used to be called Constantinople, after the first Christian Emperor of Rome.'

'Constantine.'

'She had gypsy blood, this old woman. I went to her to hear stories. I was young and still making my world. She lived in the old Greek quarter, her small house leaning against the city's inside wall, always in shadows at the end of an alley that showed cobbles under the garbage and dirt.

'A young boy led me to her door, and I saw that the door was a kite shield – you know, a warrior's shield, from long ago. It was hinged on one side, with spaces above and below it. The paint had mostly chipped off, but some flakes remained, showing white and red. A red cross on a white field.

'The boy wouldn't go inside,' Walter continued, completing his circle and coming around to my side again. He had his eyes closed as he spoke. 'The boy wouldn't go inside, and I admit I didn't blame him. The foulest smoke was pouring out from under and over the shield. I had to tie a cloth over my mouth before I went into that dark gloom.

'That old woman – she might have been the sea dog's sister, or mother. Not by how she looked, but by what I read there in her eyes. She was nearing her own end, rotting with leprosy, and she sat in front of a fire, a hearth there on the earth floor, ringed in ancient bricks. The walls were white with ash, and the ceiling was black – black as a starless night.

'Inside, the smell was fierce. You see, she had her hands in the fire. A leper with dead nerves, she was burning herself away. Nudge the throttle up a tad, we're losing headway.

'She was naked, and she opened her mouth and showed me the stub of her tongue. I asked myself: *How will this poor creature tell me her stories?* But she beckoned me closer, and I tell you, Owen, it wasn't an easy task to do her bidding, but somehow I managed. She laughed. Without sound. And when I got close enough I saw that, in the hidden places – places normally covered by clothes and modesty – her skin was tattooed. Dots, bar shapes, squiggles. And that's when I understood. Some stories are older than words, some stories live on in the oldest language of all, the language that is our own bodies.'

'Did you copy down the tattoos? Did you get them done on yourself? Did you decipher them? What did they say?'

Walter's smile looked sad. 'I was too late. So much

had rotted away. So much had burned away. The woman wasn't laughing. She was crying.

'Compared to the mountains and forests, compared to this river, we're not very old. Even so, Owen, we're older than we ourselves can comprehend. So much has already been lost. For her, I have only the story of her last days, and in my mind the memories. When her legs and arms were gone, she wriggled like a snake on to the fire. The boy brought me more wood, and it was me who piled it around her, making sure the flames caught and held, but at the same time keeping the house from burning down – keeping the fire wardens from finding out. So I had to stay till the end. The only thing I could give her was what my eyes saw. Sometimes, the price is too high. Some things you should never have to see, but it happens anyway, and you come away from it changed inside. A little colder, a little sadder. Maybe wiser, maybe a little madder. Beware that kind of madness, Owen. It'll take you like demon teeth from the deep, fast and when you're not looking.'

I was trembling, sensing the old man beside me with senses I couldn't even identify. 'Is that it?' I asked in a whisper. 'Is that your darkest corner?'

'Soon,' he said, 'I'll tell you about the Ship of Nails.'

I hesitated, then said, 'Could you tell me *Beowulf* again? What you can remember?'

Walter sighed, rubbing at his face as if his story had burned tattoos there. 'Let me rest a while.'

'Sure.' I scanned the river in front of us, squinted at the thick banks ceaselessly rustling past. Crows played in the sky above the trees, black like tatters of night.

Up ahead the oil refinery loomed into view. Our journey was nearing its end.

The beaver lodge passed by on my right. Unchanged, its woven cloak of normalcy complete – I could see nothing of what I knew was still there. The sunlight showed only the surface. Walter's words had sunk into me, crowding the giant's bones. Rotting flesh rose around me like quicksand. I wanted to struggle, to scream, but I knew it was hopeless. I'd seen something I shouldn't have had to see, making me colder, sadder. I'd already heard the maddening call, but I'd rejected it. I wondered if it had claimed one of the others, and I felt fear.

The river spread out from under us. It churned, the secrets tossing and boiling beneath the surface. I felt cursed to follow its path, both of us silent, birds speaking what we didn't dare say. *What ends is what was begun. We begin again. It begins with the river, and so shall it end.*

Walter cleared his throat, the first words rolling out, and somewhere a crows' chorus sounded as if in answer.

PART THREE

The Sacred Crib

CHAPTER THIRTEEN

I

THE DROUGHT HAD burned the land into a pathetic state. Dust muted all the colours, covering the windshield in grit. Joanne Rhide held the steering wheel in both hands. Ten to two, the positioning a perfect match with the illustration in the driver's manual. She scanned all the mirrors. The tank was full, the oil checked and the tyre pressure exact.

It wasn't a long drive to the school, but she'd never liked highways. And even though the start of classes was still a week away, and not a single leaf had turned from its uniform green, she dreaded the thought of the coming winter.

She'd done what she'd set out to do. She'd become what she'd set out to be. She had a right to be proud of her accomplishments. At twenty-three she'd be West St John's youngest teacher, one of the Education

Department's finest graduates, honed by a year of practical training in the inner city. And unlike most of the other teachers at West St John's, she knew the new programme intimately. The open-room philosophy lay at the heart of her education, its spirit fed by all that she had learned in her undergraduate years in sociology. There was no room for doubt, no reason for a crisis of confidence.

The car's air vents did little to cool the interior, but she wouldn't open the windows. The wind had a way of pulling her hair loose from the barrettes. Makes you look like a haystack, her mother always said.

Today was the first staff meeting. Joanne knew that she'd receive a lot of attention. Primed in the new methods as she was, they'd have questions. Some of them, she knew, would feel threatened. She was ready for that. She'd only offer an opinion if asked, she wouldn't be critical, she'd keep her enthusiasm and hope that it would prove infectious.

And in a week's time, there were the children. Her charges. They mattered more than anything else. No problem with enthusiasm there, she was certain. The new philosophy of education had finally taken them into account. At last they were part of the equation.

'In many ways,' Principal Barry Thompson had said at the interview, 'we view the sixth grade as the most vital year for the children.'

'Oh yes,' she'd replied, nodding vigorously. 'The pupils need to be prepared for Junior High, after all. It's a transitional year, both socially and, for some of them, biologically. At that age they need an environment that's safe and nurturing. They're finding their identities, exercising their egos, while at the same time they're very unsure of themselves, open to all kinds of new and sometimes troubling influences—'

'They're little hellions,' Barry had cut in, grinning.

'Oh, I don't see them like that at all,' Joanne said, watching his grin fade as she continued, 'They're exploring, and that's a natural process. It needs to be carefully guided, made constructive, not destructive. I'll be entirely sensitive to what they're undergoing. They deserve no less.'

The principal sighed. 'Well,' he said, 'we definitely need someone on board who knows the new programme.' He paused to jot something down on his notepad. Joanne thought him to be about forty-five, maybe slightly younger. Balding, tall, wearing a rumpled grey suit and a wide, short tie, burgundy with a gold pin. His face looked too small for the rest of him, at odds with his bony, lanky build. He finished writing and looked up. 'As far as my staff is concerned, they're a good group. They've been together a long time. I'd like you to make a presentation at the first staff meeting, should you be selected among the candidates, of course. The presentation would outline the new philosophy, giving an overview of the theories and their practical application. It will be a couple of weeks before our decision, which would leave you less than a week to prepare. Would that prove a problem, Miss Rhide?'

'Oh no, not at all. I still have my notes from university, as well as condensed outlines, which I prepared myself. In fact, I could probably make that presentation without any formal preparation at all. I know it that well.'

'Impressive,' Barry said. He hesitated, then continued,

'Earlier you said you'd be "entirely sensitive" to the needs of the children. I'd like to give you a word of advice.' He leaned forward on his desk, his calm blue eyes holding Joanne's attention. 'Don't be too sensitive, Miss Rhide. If you put your heart on the table for those kids, by year's end you'll find twenty pencils stuck in it. That's my experience talking, the kind of stuff you won't find in any textbook.' He leaned back, rocked in his chair. 'Oh, certainly there's one or two who are exceptional. With them, you could be the lousiest teacher on earth and it won't matter. As for the rest, well, most of them are spoiled, indifferent, or complacent, and more than a few are complete bastards – if you'll pardon my language.'

Blinking, Joanne cleared her throat and said, 'It's been found that positive reinforcement is far superior to the traditional forms of discipline. I believe that every child has the right to be respected for how and what they are, and that it's my task to show them their potential.'

'No doubt,' Barry said. He rose and held out a long-fingered hand.

Joanne took it tentatively. She'd always disliked shaking hands, and had always tried to make the act as short and lifeless as possible. Her mother refused to shake hands entirely. Joanne sometimes wished that she had that kind of courage and confidence.

Soon. Not long now.

'Thank you for coming out,' Barry had said, releasing her hand. 'You'll be informed in writing of our decision. Did you have any concerns with the Division interview? That board's made up of some real sharks.' He smiled.

'I believe it went very well,' she said. 'They mostly listened, which I took to be a good sign.'

Barry grunted. 'The new directives have everyone feeling a tad intimidated. We've all been hitting the books this summer, and for some of us, it's been a long time since we had to do anything like that.'

He walked her to the door.

Joanne thought about what he'd just said. 'I make it a practice to study right through each and every summer. I even sit in on classes at the university. Things are changing so quickly. We're discovering new methods all the time.'

'Of course, it all depends on how the rats perform,' he said.

'Pardon?'

'The rats in the new maze. Your students, Miss Rhide.'

She'd thought the interview went well, except for that last comment from Principal Thompson, which she found disturbing enough to lose sleep over for the next few nights.

Barry Thompson was clearly a product of the old system. Hard-handed and contemptuous of the children for whom he was ultimately responsible. He thought teaching was a matter of personality. He didn't see the social context, the collective imperatives. He didn't see the school – its teachers, its students – as an organism, an organic whole.

The future had arrived. There was a new way of doing things. A better, more reasoned way. The conventions were outmoded fossils from a culture long gone. The children had new needs – the result of the changing society around them.

Joanne knew she'd have to lead by example. She had twenty children to nurture, to save and to prepare. They would be her proof.

The turn-off was up ahead. She clicked on the turn signal and slowed, checking the mirrors. She came to a stop even though the opposite lanes were empty. Then she slowly swung the car on to the driveway and pulled into the parking lot.

There were only a few cars in the lot. She was early, but better that than late. The job was hers, and this presentation would show the others why she'd gotten it. She had good reason to be proud. Confident, relaxed and self-assured. She'd worked on the presentation from the first night after the interview with Barry Thompson.

Joanne collected her briefcase and opened the door. She stepped out, the wind hot against her long, pale face, pulling at her hair. She closed and locked the door, making sure the windows were up. As she turned to face the school a slight flutter caught her eyes, up at the front of the car. Frowning, Joanne went around for a better look.

A dead crow, crushed into the grille, its feathers splayed out and trembling in the breeze. The plastic grille was broken. Blood spattered the passenger-side headlamp and the bumper.

She remembered. Just this side of the cloverleaf. She'd thought it had made it off the road. But no, she'd heard the thump – it just hadn't registered. The Toyota Corolla was bumpy and loud enough on its own – one more sound wouldn't have been that noticeable. Besides, she'd had her mind on other things. Important things.

Joanne continued staring at the mangled creature. Her dress felt rumpled, wrinkled and damp. Wisps of hair had escaped the barrettes and now stung her face.

She'd overprepared. The presentation was too long, too detailed. The tone might sound strident if she tried hurrying through it. She knew she had a tendency to sound strident. Like her mother. It'd be a hostile audience, too. Rigid minds, inflexible and defensive.

She'd need to get the car washed right away. On the way home. *I thought crows were smart. Ugly birds, though. Never really liked them. They eat rotten meat. Dead rabbits on the roadside, squirrels and cats. Oh, I hope it didn't have a mate. I hope it isn't looking for its lover. It was an accident. I didn't mean it. Oh, why today of all days?*

Joanne pulled her dress where it stuck to her back. The staff-room would be air-conditioned. She'd get chilled, and when she got chilled her fingers turned bluish. She'd always been too skinny. Mother had told her so.

Two more cars rolled into the parking lot. Joanne didn't want to talk now. She didn't want to say hello, pleased to meet you, I look forward to working with you, and it's a hot one, isn't it? So she pretended not to notice, checking the flap of her briefcase, then walking purposefully towards the school entrance.

It was like exam time. She felt an anxiety attack coming on. It'd pass once she started her presentation, she knew. But tonight . . . *Tonight I'll get a migraine. I've gotten overexcited. Overexerted, Mother'd say. Oh, you stupid crow!*

II

Like clockwork. Idiots. So predictable it's pathetic.

The overgrown lot felt like an oven, only moments from bursting into flame. She tossed her butt and watched it bounce against the foundation wall. Owen would be here soon. Her body felt like a sponge, waiting to soak him up.

We'll soak each other up. A university professor in the city had brought back some peyote from New Mexico. He'd given half to a friend of his who lived in the North End. The friend pushed. Six buttons made their way into Jennifer's hands. She planned on surprising Owen. The buttons had arrived inside individual caramel squares.

They'd eat their candy, then neck, wrapping themselves around each other, and when it started, she'd tell him. It'd be too late. He'd be in her arms. She'd carry him through.

Poor Debbie and her revolution. I've cut myself loose and your brother's mine, dear. Don't you get it? The world's never changing. The shit just keeps piling up. You can either drown, or swim like you was made for it.

Maybe they'd fuck. Maybe it'd finally happen, both flying like apes with wings, laughing and grunting. They'd merge completely. She'd give him her breath. He'd give her his. She'd make him come deep inside her, then she'd roll over and make him come again from behind, like dogs. Maybe this time, it'd happen.

The world's never changing. Never, ever. Don't you get it yet?

The social worker, Anne, in her forties, wide-boned and low to the ground, expressionless but with eyes that never stopped moving behind thick glasses. She'd come dressed in a navy blue polyester sack that was reluctant to copy the movements of the body underneath. She'd come in, clipboard tucked under one arm, the glasses framing a nose like a rudder, wearing on her feet blue leather shoes with spring-loaded knife blades in the toes.

Jennifer grinned, stretching her legs out in front of her. The leaves snapped in the hot wind. Beyond them was the blue sky, which had forgotten its season of thunder and rain, becoming remote and changeless.

Anne the social worker, bat-winged with tyrannical power, eager to exercise her world-view, stepping to one side with Roulston and delivering three short, succinct sentences that made the good doctor's face turn bright red.

He'd come to them then and said, 'It seems that the assessment process does not allow for my presence in the room—'

'The house,' the social worker corrected.

'The house. The assessment must be independently conducted.'

Jennifer laughed. 'On your way, angel,' she said.

Anne shot her a look, sizing up the enemy. Jennifer made her answering smile innocent. *Anne. Anne Boleyn, Anne of Green Stables, Annie get your gun, Queen Anne kitchenware. Anne, slaying ogres with one look from her aquarium eyes. Swim in these waters, those eyes said, at your peril.*

'Dr Roulston,' Jennifer explained calmly to Anne, 'is our guardian angel. We don't really need one, but that's how it is with guardian angels.'

Roulston turned at the door. 'Jennifer,' he said sharply.

She ducked, just enough. 'Sorry, Doctor,' she said. 'I'm sorry for what I said.'

The good doctor actually slammed the door. *Finally got to him. Hah.* 'Please sit down, Anne,' she said. 'As you know, my mother had an accident. Her jaw is wired. She can't speak.'

'I've received Dr Roulston's detailed report, including his professional observations and opinions.'

'He's very diligent, and earnest, isn't he?'

Anne sat down opposite her mother – who sat on the couch as usual. For Anne, then, the seat of judgement. Occupied in its time by policemen, doctors, snake-headed witches. The woman named Anne swung her gaze from her mother. 'I also have your school records . . . Jennifer, is it? Yes, Jennifer. I'm not good with names.' Disarming smile there one moment, gone the next. Back to business. 'Now, I have a set list of questions. About your family life, your income sources and how you manage your finances, some medical history and the like. Mrs Louper, your husband resides here as well?'

Her mother nodded.

'But he's being treated at Riverview Hospital. I have the police report. Some of the statements are contradictory. As the investigation is on-going, we'll have to leave that alone for the time being. Now, Jennifer, you'll have to answer the questions on your mother's behalf, when you can. Otherwise, I have here a notepad and a pen. Mrs Louper?'

Her mother nodded again and accepted the writing material.

'Good,' Anne said, flashing the smile once more, this time for her mother.

Like a machine. A lie detector like the ones in dear Daddy's magazines, but with a built-in paranoia gewgaw. Working her questions like traps, coming around from different directions, testing for inconsistencies in Jennifer's answers. Querying more details on her mother's written replies. Jennifer found herself concentrating with all her power, all the while affecting a casual, relaxed pose. It was a game worthy of her, and it sharpened her as it went on, the minutes piling up into one hour, then two. Page after page, pause after pause as Anne wrote detailed notes, made private observations, skyrocketed the tension level with her choppy jottings, page after page.

Food groups. Hours watching TV, time set aside for homework, chores. Records of utility statements. Sten's disability income. Questions of alcohol abuse, wife abuse, child abuse.

Jennifer dropped her tone when talking about those last few subjects. She tried to sound duly embarrassed. The performance of her life, always on truth's edge – giving her words the needed authority. Jennifer wove her answers. With grace. *'Yes, ma'am. My father has a problem with drinking. We're all sticking together, working through it, as best we can. We need support. I understand that. My father has agreed he has a problem. He'll be attending his first AA meeting this Sunday morning. Violent? Only the dishes, sometimes, or a wall or two. Because he's been drinking, he can get a little wild – just look at Mom. It was an accident. Blackouts? No. My father remembers everything. He gets so full of guilt. That probably makes it harder to stop, doesn't it? We thought so. We've talked about it. We're trying to talk more, though Mom has to write things down for now. Yes, I'm doing the household chores. Cooking, the dishes. Well, Father's one love . . . did I say Father? But Mom, yes. I guess I'm getting pretty formal. Dad loves his dogs. Pure-bred. Show quality. He dotes on them. One got out and was killed by a car. That's what made him start again. Grief, I guess. He's getting over it, I think, but it still makes him sad.'*

On and on. Hours. Her father's arrival capped the whole thing. Perfect timing. Exquisite effect. Bandaged face. Sober and smooth and calm from the painkillers. Humbled, looking suitably pathetic in a homey, teddy-bear way. Harmless. He couldn't talk either. No wires, just cotton. A temporary condition.

Jennifer pictured supper-time, her and two Frankensteins at the table. She'd almost laughed aloud and went quickly to the bathroom to work the grin off her face.

A virtuoso performance. The encore in a week's time with Annie's follow-up visit. A week to keep everything in place – no problem. Her father understood. Her mother understood. Everything was understood.

A wasp buzzed in front of her face. She smiled at it. It hovered, then whirred off. There was no wind here inside this ring of trees. No movement at all. The air waited to unfold like a flower in front of their eyes – her and Owen, once they were on their way.

'You look dead,' Owen said, his shadow falling over her.

Jennifer smiled up at him. 'You look horny as hell. Undo your pants. I want your cock in my hands.'

'Why don't we just sit and talk this time?' He sat down beside her.

'What for? We both know what we want. C'mon, feel how wet I am. Go on, reach in.'

'Later. I haven't seen you in over a week. Are we still going together?'

Jennifer sighed. She sat up, resting her back against the foundation wall. 'You didn't hear?'

'What? No.'

'Y'know Old Man Fisk? He showed up a couple nights ago. He beat the shit out of my dad. The neighbours called the cops. They arrested him, took him away. Dad got forty-eight stitches. Or forty-seven. Something like that. All in the face.'

'Holy fuck. What – why did Fisk do that?'

'You'd better ask him. I haven't got a clue. Even the cops couldn't figure it out. Fisk had a deal with Dad, for dog food or something. Maybe they argued over the price.'

'Dog food? You mean, he feeds his mink dog food?'

'Probably. Buys it wholesale, I guess.'

'Holy fuck.'

Jennifer lit a cigarette, felt Owen's eyes on her. 'You like watching, don't you?'

'Yeah.'

'You're always watching me when I smoke.'

'I watch you other times, too.'

'Oh yeah? Well, I only notice it when I smoke. Ready to try it?'

'No.'

'You're like a robot with that word. What exactly are you watching?'

'When it's between your lips. The way your cheeks . . . bunch – the muscles – when you take a drag. And the muscles under your chin, too, when you pull the drag inside. Then I watch the smoke. You know, I've been noticing. People who smoke got bigger muscles around their mouths. You have to look carefully to see them.'

Jennifer laughed. 'I can picture you doing it. Looking, I mean. Studying. I can see the way your eyes narrow, like you're taking pictures in your head and you keep adjusting the focus. What do you do with all those pictures, Owen?'

He shrugged. 'Nothing. I just notice things. It's neat. It's like learning to look at things different from the way you normally look at things.'

'What for?'

He hesitated. 'You'll laugh.'

'No. Promise.'

'Okay. Well, when I look at something differently, and closely, I see how beautiful it is. It doesn't seem to matter what. Like the muscles around your mouth, and your lips wrapping around that filter. Or the way one of your tits has rolled down one side and it's pulled the t-shirt with it. Or even on the road out there. The tar makes bubbles that shine when you rub the dust off them. Or this place, the old walls. There was once a floor under us, and the ones who walked on it lived right here, and the mother probably put flowers in the kitchen window, and the father could step outside and look at the trees his own father had planted, and there'd be tears in his eyes, or something.'

'They're gone now,' Jennifer said, her eyes on the cigarette between the fingers of her right hand.

'Well, nothing lasts for ever.'

'And nothing changes.'

'I know.'

'I've got a couple of caramel candies.' She pulled them out, handed him one, and watched as he unwrapped the plastic covering and popped it into his mouth. 'They might be a little stale.'

Owen shrugged. He chewed, then swallowed. 'A little? Yuck.'

'Well,' Jennifer said, grinning, 'I'm no coward.' She put hers into her mouth, tasted first the sweet caramel, then something bitter, tacky. She quickly swallowed. 'Boy, did that leave a bad taste, eh?'

He nodded.

Jennifer took a drag, exhaled slowly. 'Come and kiss me. I'll give you a taste you like. And a whole lot more, maybe.'

He leaned over her. She reached up and pulled him down, kissing him hard and deep. He responded as if it made him thirsty, as if he wanted to drink her. His hand slid along her body and found the tit he'd talked about, pulling it back up and around. She slid her free hand into his pants and found him ready. She pulled her mouth away for another drag from the cigarette, barely getting it done in time before he closed in again.

She held the back of his head and pushed the smoke into his lungs. He reared back, his eyes wide.

'I feel sick.'

She laughed. 'It's just the smoke—'

'No. Before that. I'm feeling sick. In my stomach. Really sick. That caramel was bad, I think—'

Abruptly he rolled to one side, leaned over the foundation wall, and threw up.

Jennifer sat up and felt a dizzying wave roll through her. Then she gagged, her stomach spasming, and found herself on her hands and knees, everything down inside coming back out of her mouth. With each helpless retch, she felt pee squirt into her underwear. The ground in front of her, fouled with fluids and bits of food, contorted wildly, spun until she lost her balance and rolled to one side, coming up against the foundation wall.

Owen had stopped vomiting. His eyes were wide as he stared at her. 'What's happening? What was in that?'

Jennifer shook her head. This wasn't the same as acid. It wasn't the same at all. It wasn't in the head, it felt in the bones, in every cell of her body, spreading out from her stomach like long curling fingers. The head struggled to catch up.

'I don't think Fisk buys dog food,' Owen said, still leaning on the wall. 'I think he uses mink. Dead, chopped-up mink. He's rotting from the inside out, a bonfire in his gut, cold as ice at the tips of his fingers. You don't understand, do you? I'm the same as him. I'm inside, too, burning my way out, and the birds hang in the sky like crosses.'

'Fuck me,' Jennifer pleaded. 'Please. Up the ass. Your cock. Get rid of the way his still feels. Get rid of it, please.'

'Fuck you? I can't even find you.'

Then Owen was gone, and the ruins had changed around her. The foundation stones were wet, slimy under her hands. Water streamed down through the branches, poured from black leaves, rushed down the boles of the trees, but there was no rain. It was dark, impossibly dark.

'Owen?'

She jumped as a massive, snarling shape lunged at her. Chains pulled tight, spraying water against her face. A huge dog crouched in front of her, straining on the chain, which was attached to a steel collar on its neck, the other end running down into the earth. Jennifer stared, gasping. The dog's eyes burned into her. Its bared teeth, slick with blood, were huge and less than a yard away.

It wanted her, promising pain and death.

Max? Back from the dead, transformed by the journey – the unmapped forests, the depthless chasms and fissures between the worlds. Max. He's come back.

Jennifer couldn't move. She wanted to run, but there were chains beneath her flesh, wrapped around her bones and holding her to the earth. Down they went, unlit silver sunk through mud and clay and gravel, down into the ancient, stained bedrock. There'd be no escape.

Max lunged again. She saw how his flesh had rotted. Shreds of green garbage bag remained, twisted around his legs. Blood streamed from his mouth. The car's bumper had shattered ribs, pushing them into his lungs. The tyre had crushed his hips, parted his spine. But Max lived, returning huge, hungry, filled with madness.

I want wings. I need wings. I need to get away. Dying's driven him insane. He doesn't recognise me. I know who he wants, but the man isn't here. No one's here but me.

She heard music now, hard-tipped fingers on a piano. Desperate music, a Pied Piper call coming from the dark wood. Slowly, the music drifted into her body, calming and cool as raindrops. Max stopped his snapping and growling, settled back, his brown eyes softening, half closing. He knew her now. He wasn't afraid any more.

Jennifer stood. The chains rose up through the earth between her and Max, and she saw that it was the same chain. The imprisoning bedrock that she'd seen in her mind and had believed to be real, wasn't – a truth only in her mind, proved a lie by what she now saw.

Max rose as well. The music beckoned. Side by side, they entered the wood.

The trees marched away, leaving me alone in an open place. Jennifer's kiss had sent me on my way. I remained on my knees in the dirt, and yet I moved. The oaks and ash trees had stepped back, drifted away. The foundation and cellar depression settled into the dry earth. I felt thirsty, the need for water becoming a savage thing, burning like fire in my throat.

She'd sent me away. I'd have to go there before I could come back. The crows that had become crosses swung wide, silent arcs across the grey sky. I jumped as a rabbit darted past. *Jack-rabbit, look at him go.* An owl followed ghostly in its wake.

Prairie spread out on all sides. Rolling dun hills, black rock outcroppings, a wide river valley. I didn't belong here yet, but it was where I'd come from. There was no sense in that thought, but I knew it was true. The scene before me resided in my future, years away. Years and years.

I climbed to my feet, staggered a step before finding my balance. It was cold now. Snow dusted the hills. On my left a highway tracked the slopes of the valley,

glistening with frost and blacker streaks where cars
had passed. Not a soul on that highway, though. I was
alone. I looked to my right, where the valley stepped
down, hill by hill, to its floor. A creek or river belonged
there, but it had dried up long ago.

The flat top of a nearby hill had rings of boulders
on it, each rock in a nest of wiry yellow grass. My gaze
travelled over them, then beyond, to a larger humped
hill. There, a rock outcropping ran a twisted, serrated
line along the summit. *That's mine. My place. I need
to do something there, so that it's ready for me when I
come here again. Something. What?*

The stubble, moss and lichen crunched underfoot
as I walked towards the hill. My muscles felt tired, as
if I'd already walked miles and miles. There were hundreds of crows in the sky now. *I'm at the place where
the bird-souls pause in their journey. The Sunday school
teacher forgot to mention this place, because it wasn't
heaven. It was too old, this island in a dried-up sea,
between the worlds and beneath notice. Angels have
forgotten this place, and if I can, I'll make sure it stays
forgotten for ever. That teacher, heron-gaunt and ancient, she'd known. She'd known and forgotten on
purpose.*

I came to the hill's base. The ground rose in front of
me, steep and studded with cacti. The hill was massive, oblong. Tucked low into the side was a wooden
door. A single iron handle hung in its middle, encrusted
with lichen.

This door wouldn't be here next time. I would be
living in a grown-up world, then. Frightened of magic,
steeped in a predictable, ordered existence, and the
voices calling me up into the sky would be heard only

in my dreams. The invitation was doomed to fade on my awakening, the joy an illusion. I needed to do something. This was my chance, my reason for being here.

A voice spoke beside me. 'He's in there, you know.'

I didn't turn, but the voice continued.

'One day you'll stand here, and I'll stand beside you and we'll be talking hockey, then we'll go quiet. And I'll make a sound, because all of a sudden this hill shows me what's inside, this hill tells me it's for you. Your totem, Owen.'

I wanted to turn, to see this man with his dark, prairie voice, but my power to move had vanished.

'A dragon. Things like that don't happen, not even to a shaman. Especially not to some white boy. A dragon, Owen, do you believe me? Will you, when the day comes? Will you run? What will you do?'

Silence returned, and I knew I was alone again.

The door was never meant to be opened. Not from the outside. I pressed myself against its frosty surface and closed my eyes.

Trees, so thick and tightly packed, there was barely room to move. Dark and wet, the air close and clammy. The music filtered through, coming in from all sides. Jennifer had a hand on Max's shoulder, clutching his fur – a shoulder that brushed against her ribcage. The fur was cold, and not once did Max pant, not a single gust of white breath escaping him.

He's come back. To protect me.

Jennifer gasped. The music had stopped. Now only silence. The trees closed in on themselves, became figures, spectral, robed. Women, all facing her, motionless, their eyes hooded, veiled in shadow.

All at once she stood in a kitchen. Max was gone. Pickling jars lined the shelves, filled the open cupboards. In each jar, stuffed inside, entombed in liquid, a baby. Eyes open, staring, following Jennifer as she took a step back. The ghostly women brought more jars, moving around her to the counter where they began stacking them. The stream was unending.

Mothers and mothers and mothers and mothers and mothers and mothers . . . these are the days ahead, the years to come, for ever and ever. No point in screaming. No point in anger. Suffer silently, be the grey cloth covering everything, muting every struggle, every wrung-out cry. Learn to be . . . not yourself, but others. Always others.

Through the kitchen window she saw churches, one on every hill, the hills marching on for ever. Churches, and bonfires. Latin words on vellum unscrolled across the sky. And bridges and bars and flats and sharps rose like rainbows. From beyond the rumpled horizon came a faint howl. *Max.*

Rough hands grabbed her from behind and threw her down. The breath was knocked from her lungs. A penis drove into her from behind, splitting her down the middle. Something small and lumpy moved under her chest, inside her body. It crawled under her heart and curled up there.

Another one for the jars. Who's done me? Who is that lying on top of me? Please, I have to know.

The kennel was in tatters. The dogs had shunted their skins. Naked, they delivered mayhem outside. Church windows shattered, lightning flashed, ashes fell like rain.

The child unravels me. Turns me inside out. I'll crawl

on this floor for months, maybe years. Lost. Where am I? Where am I?

'Never mind. Just feed the damn thing.'

Too late.

Jars crashed, exploded, contents flopping purplebrown on to the floor. The dogs had arrived. Kaja, Shane, Caesar, their tethers dangling.

The unknown man still fucked her. *Unknown. Any man, every man.* Even as the dogs closed in and ate him alive. He screamed and shuddered with every tearing, ripping bite. But still he kept on, pumping, driving what was left of his body against her, now desperate, now crying.

'That's the world for you, right, friend? No one wins. We all have our demons.'

Jennifer turned her head, the floor cold on her cheek. Her father sat leaning against the cupboard, his mouth stained as he calmly devoured a pickled baby.

'My son,' he croaked. 'I've got no choice. None of us have. That's the joke. There's only one throne, and it's mine. I killed Father. I was his bile, deep in his liver. I turned him yellow and he died.' He took another bite, pulled an arm away – but it wasn't an arm. It was a wing. *Angel.* 'I broke into his house, you see. At the very end. Him or me. Us or them. I'd turned him inside out, just like you did with Elouise. How she crawled. Exhausted, alone. She didn't know anything. Neither did I. You sprang out of my head, a girl, my darling one. The world should never have stained you, my sweet. It had no right. But you saw what was ahead. Too soon you saw your future. You ran out of your mother's shadow, left us with nothing but envy. We're looking for you still. We'll look for ever, if we have to. You turned her inside out, but I want her back. What can you show us, Jennifer, to free us from worry? To free yourself from us? If you go forward, will that let us go back?' He held up the baby's head. 'It's not personal. I drink for revenge.' He bit into it.

Some time later the dogs devoured him, whoever he was. The weight left her. Jennifer rolled on to her back, feeling sticks, broken masonry and roots underneath.

She drew a deep breath. She didn't want to open her eyes. Not now. Not ever. She'd seen the future time, and it was the same as the past time.

Max was a shadow in her mind. He'd never leave her now. She'd always liked his playfulness, but he would never play again. She remembered how she'd cried in her room, how her father had cried downstairs. A dreadful, dulled night. Impervious, her mother had hummed while making salad.

Jennifer moaned. She raised her hands, and gasped as someone gripped them. Her eyes opened.

'Owen.'

'Never take candy from strangers,' he said, then smiled. 'Hello, stranger.'

III

They'd been thrilled with the refitting of *Mistress Flight*. Her value greatly enhanced, an auction was being planned. Other things had thrilled them far less.

'The boy isn't a member,' Bill Smith had said. 'He wasn't signed in as a guest. If something had happened to him, the Yacht Club would've been held legally responsible. Dammit, Walter, you can't see ten feet past your nose! That much became obvious with the launchings in June. Why do you think we brought Reggie on board? He'll take over management of the grounds come season's end.'

A watchman who couldn't see. A manager who couldn't manage. And a sky that wouldn't rain.

Gribbs sat in his shack, staring at the calendars on the wall. They were all a dim blur, but he had his memory to keep them sharp. It'd been the same with the river, its curves, its bends. The map he'd studied while on the train in 1962 remained perfectly etched in his mind. He didn't need a lifetime of cruises behind him, and when they'd been on the river, its currents, eddies and flows told him all he needed to know; the rebound of the Sea Horse's growl off the banks, between the pylons under the bridges – a map he built as they went, as sure as the ground under his feet.

But the machine's purpose had been taken away. No maintenance to maintain, no tasks to complete anywhere beyond these four walls. The muscles of his limbs had been relieved of duty, the edge of his mind and the backing of experience had been reduced to the aimless mutterings of an old man.

'You've earned your retirement, Walter. Sit back, feel the wind on your face. Drinks are on the house, from now on.' *C'mon, Walter, tumbling into the dark's as good a way as any. Put the body to rest, the mind's sure to follow.*

He knew he was feeling sorry for himself. It'd been a long life. He'd done some good with it. It just shouldn't have to end with a whimper, with the lights slowly going down.

*Who am I kidding? I'm wishing it could be that sim-
ple. Maybe it never is, unless you've gone senile, and
even then it looks to be more confusion than peace.
No, the dreams are back. I don't know why I still call
them dreams. They're visions. Promises. Nothing gentle and nothing good going into this night.*

*I never really expected it to be otherwise. All the
stories in my head, in my bones, all of them make one
thing clear. It's a hard world, always has been, and its
trueness is there under the songs, timed by the number
of words a human breath can hold, and by how slow
and how fast a human heart can pump. Our limits are
the only things giving order to the world. And as we
get older, each of us by ourselves and all of us together –
those limits get ever narrower. We look around but it's
all too fast now, too much, we can't make sense of it
any more.*

But I know what I see.

*Serpents roll in the dark mud, slip slipping through
the deep's pressures, gnawing at our beliefs and hoarding
our treasures – all that we've lost. And I can see, coming
out of the mist, that disordered host, cloaked in frost
and the lap of flames on their arms. Armoured with
uncertainty, shielded by doubt. Come to claim reason's
light – I think she's on her way, my lover of old, coming with company on the rainbow road . . .*

He wouldn't tell the boy. Final stories had a way of
wounding terribly, leaving scars that disfigure. No, the
Ship of Nails and the shining prince at her bow – they'd
remain his personal terror.

Owen had his own demons, in any case. Gribbs
knew he hadn't helped the boy there. He'd failed.
Having done as much as he could, his efforts had proved

inadequate. Too old, too many years between them. *He's already been wounded. A stranger's struck the blow – I see the blood in Owen's eyes, hear the pain in his words. And yet, what a gift he gave me. All that he saw, a picture of relentless erosion told by a sky full of messengers. The moment of apocalypse slowed down, stretched out, as certain as any tide. And yet, nowhere was there surrender. After all, a vision of wings offers the chance of escape.*

He's not a gentle boy. Not at all. That'll be his saving grace, I think. A hard child for a hard world.

There must be beauty somewhere, son. I'll tell you that, when we talk for the last time. My gift in exchange. Not enough to balance what you've given me, but it's all I've got left that's worth giving.

Ancient poems in cold-hammered tongues. Maybe the time's come again for sword-on-shield words, for cursing the heavens and the old men on their sagging thrones.

Schooners, sloops and ketches rocked wildly in the waves. His memory was that sharp.

IV

My head rested on her stomach, the soft folds under me warm and damp beneath the t-shirt. 'I can't trust you any more,' I said. My mouth tasted like ashes, each breath I drew felt harsh in my throat.

'Never again,' she said. 'Promise.'

She wouldn't tell me what had happened to her. She'd never trusted me with that much of herself, something that hadn't bothered me before but did now.

Whatever she'd experienced had frightened her. '*A bad trip. I panicked, Owen. You can't panic. One minute you were there beside me, then next you were gone.*' Were you alone? '*No, but you were gone.*'

I went away, my lungs still on fire with your smoke. It'd felt like thirst. Not for water, but for more fire. I went far away. I went home.

'We lost hours,' Jennifer said. 'But it only felt like minutes. Only look, the sun's almost down.'

I closed my eyes. 'Hours. I felt them.' *A long way, and you'd poured yourself into me and you're inside me now, a slow, steady burn.* I turned my head and looked up at her. The cigarette in her hand was near her face. She looked like a model, or a movie star. 'You wanted me to fuck you,' I said.

'I know. I, uh, I thought you did.'

I sat up. 'Did I?'

'No. It wasn't you. It wasn't anyone. Come here and kiss me. Lie beside me, I want your face against mine. Close.'

I rolled over and around. There were ants in the grass under us, but the numbness that started in our stomachs and spread out in slow waves kept everything away. I kissed her, then lay down on my side with my face alongside hers, our mouths within easy reach of each other.

'I found a word in my dictionary,' I said. 'Vicarious. As in vicarious pleasure.'

'So?'

'Nothing. Just a word.'

'I wish there was a drug that'd make us merge together. Like, completely. And we could both feel everything, both of us together.'

'We'd spend all day masturbating.'

She fell silent. Smoked. I remained, vicarious.

'Never again, Owen. I wanted to turn you on. But I don't want you like Barb, or Sandy. I hardly see them any more, except when they want to buy. One of them will OD soon. One of them will crash, and then talk, and I'll be in shit. I'm not selling to them any more. They can get it from somewhere else.'

I felt the muscles of her mouth move when she talked. Her words buzzed in my bones. Her voice was beautiful, low, rough at the edges. 'Glue me here,' I said.

She laughed, then said, 'I won't do it again. All my trips are going bad. I can't get away. I'm quitting everything.'

'Smoking?'

'No, and you don't want me to, either.'

'Do you believe in dragons?'

'You mean, like, dinosaurs?'

'No. Like in St George and the Dragon.'

'Who's St George?'

'Okay, like in Chinese paintings.'

She took a drag, pulled it into her lungs, then turned her head slightly and probed her tongue into the corner of my mouth. Then she settled back again, exhaled. 'They're just stories. Fairytales.'

'I guess.'

'You battled dragons, Owen?'

I frowned. 'No. No battles.'

'Fire-breathing?'

'Maybe. There's one right beside me now.'

'Roar!'

'Ow, my ear!'

Her laugh sounded liquid and delicious. I wondered if I was in love.

'I'm honing the fatuous,' I said.

'What?'

'Something told me, I think. Not aloud. "Stop honing the fatuous," it said.'

'What does it mean?'

'Don't know. But it felt like what my dad calls a kick in the pants.' I sat up. 'I'm hungry. Want to come over for dinner?'

'Feeling brave, are you?'

'I guess. I feel like shocking them.'

Jennifer sat up and said, 'I don't think that's a good idea.'

'So?'

'Well, would they kick me out? Swear at me? Maybe you'll get canned. Maybe they'll say you can't see me any more.'

'They won't kick you out. They won't swear. And they can't can me for ever. We'll be at school together, right? And if they say we can't go together, I won't listen. We just go back to doing it in secret again. You can't just go home now. Not after all this.'

'That's the last place I want to go. Anyway, Mom's started cooking and stuff again.' She hesitated, then shrugged. 'Fuck it. Let's go, then.'

Neither of us felt steady on our feet. We held hands as we left the overgrown lot and emerged on to the road. Across from us a lamp sitting on a pole had been turned on. Moths danced wildly around it. A mosquito buzzed in my ear – there weren't many around, because of the drought – and I lazily waved at it. 'We might be a bit late, but Mom always leaves some for me.'

'I'm only a little hungry. It's okay if you don't have enough.'

'Oh, we have enough. It just may not be cooked. We've got lots of food, in the fridge, in the cupboards.'

Jennifer gave me a strange look.

We continued on. As we came opposite Carl's house we heard an argument going on inside. Or, rather, Carl's dad yelling something about his torn jacket and it still wasn't fixed.

'Lynk beat up Carl,' I said.

'Big surprise. Carl gets beat up all the time. At school. Guys from Riverview. Gary and Dennis and those guys – you haven't met them yet. They're shits, little shits.'

'Well, Lynk's being a real asshole these days.'

'He's always been an asshole. Why do you hang out with him?'

I shrugged. 'It's me, Roland, Lynk and Carl. Has been since I first met them.'

'Want me to hide my smokes?'

'No. Mom smokes. Debbie does, too, in secret up in her room. She opens the window and it comes into my room because our windows are right next to each other. Mom knows, I think. She's always leaving her pack out – like rat-traps or something.'

'Maybe she's just being generous.'

'I hadn't thought of it that way.'

We cut across the ditch at the bend, approached the dark entrance to the driveway. We still held hands. I expected it to work the same way it had for Roland and Lynk and Carl, so there wouldn't be any of those awkward unspoken questions – the funny looks and stuff.

'What's that?'

'A factory engine. My dad's rebuilding it.'

Father sat on the steps, cradling a mug of coffee in his big hands. He grinned at me. 'Lots of leftovers. I'm sure your mother will manage, Owen.'

'This is Jennifer.'

He nodded. 'G'evening.'

'Hi.'

Father set his cup down on the step. 'Um, I suggest you two brush yourselves off before you head inside.'

I looked over at Jennifer. In the porch light's bright glow I saw that her t-shirt and hair were covered in twigs, dried-up leaves and moss. I looked down at myself and saw the same. 'Oh,' I said.

'Take a few minutes,' Dad said, straightening. 'I'll be inside.'

'Uh, yeah.'

He closed the screen door behind him. I started brushing the stuff from Jennifer's back. 'I gotta get to the bathroom right away,' she said.

'Sure.'

'That's your dad, huh?'

'Yeah.'

'He's all right.'

'Yeah, he's a mechanic.'

They ate alone in the dining room. Sort of, Jennifer corrected herself. His mother kept finding reasons to come into the room. *More bread? Would you two like another glass of milk?* Jennifer thought she was pretty, in a drawn-out kind of way.

All the usual questions had been asked. *Do you live close by? Have you two been friends long?* Jennifer was surprised at herself for feeling shy – she usually reacted to any grown-up giving her attention with nasty sarcasm, and contempt. But with Owen's mother, she felt vulnerable, lost.

The twins, Tanya and William, briefly showed up to giggle, then went back to the living room where they'd set up a train set on the rug, William driving the trains and Tanya being a mother living in a farmhouse near the station. Jennifer could hear them arguing over turf, there on the living-room rug.

Debbie had said hello, then went up to her room to play records. Owen's father had gone back outside to work in his garage, which left Owen's mother. She cleared the dishes away then came back in and sat down, cigarettes and ashtray in hand.

Jennifer thought to relieve one concern right away. She took her own cigarettes out from where the pack sat tucked in her jeans just behind the clasp. 'Owen's not one for peer pressure,' she said. 'Which is good, since he's surrounded right now.'

'What she means—'

'I know what Jennifer means, Owen,' his mother cut in lightly.

'I'm almost a year older than Owen,' Jennifer said. 'I'll be repeating Grade Six because my attendance last year wasn't good. My mother's been sick.'

'I'm sorry to hear that. Is she better now?'

'Getting. She's not going to die or anything.'

William crashed the train in the living room. Tanya screamed.

Owen's mother said, 'Debbie almost had to repeat this year.'

'She went to summer school, didn't she?'

'You've met.'

'There's not many kids around here. We met a couple of times in the playground. I live right beside it.'

'The house with the dogs?'

Jennifer nodded. Owen sat in his chair, his head turning from his girlfriend to his mother as the conversation went along. His face was expressionless, but his eyes moved sharply, as if comparing them. *Taking pictures like he always does.* Jennifer cleared her throat. 'I'm hoping Owen can help me with homework and stuff. He's pretty smart. He knows lots of words, reads lots of books.'

His mother was nodding. 'I'd been worrying that that was all he did. Books, books and more books. He came back from the library yesterday with a whole armful.'

'Owen can do lots more than just read,' Jennifer said. The words hung there and she felt a blush rise to her face.

Owen jumped off his seat. 'Sounds like trouble in the living room. I'll go calm them down.'

Jennifer glared at him, but the look was lost as he hurried out.

'I never thought Owen would have a girlfriend so soon,' his mother said. 'Debbie didn't show any real interest in boys until she was, oh, at least fifteen. Of course, Owen always was precocious.'

Precocious. So that's who he gets it from. 'It's different out of the city, I guess,' Jennifer said. 'Like, Roland drives a tractor all by himself. That's one of Owen's friends.'

'Yes, we've met. And Lynk, and Carl. Would you like some tea?'

'Do you have coffee?'

She rose, smiling. 'Coming right up.' She paused. 'Why don't you hunt down my son. He'll hide for ever if he can.' She turned and entered the kitchen.

Jennifer stared after her a moment, then laughed. Her amusement fell away as she stubbed out her cigarette and pushed back the chair. *Why them and not us? Is it because there's more kids? Is it because they wanted them in the first place?* She drew a deep breath. Tanya and William yelled at each other, moments away from a scrap. Jennifer pictured Owen sitting there, saying nothing, watching them, his eyes missing nothing.

CHAPTER FOURTEEN

I

THE RINGING PHONE woke him up. He climbed out of bed, wearing nothing, and made his way through the sultry air. It was 8 a.m.

'Hello?' he croaked, the day's first word.

'Hodgson? It's Bill. You awake?'

Fisk sat down in the easy chair, the fabric feeling like sandpaper under him. 'What's up?'

'Well, I heard what happened, eh?'

'Maybe you did and maybe you didn't.'

'Huh?'

'There's more than one version, you know.' Fisk looked down the length of his body. He'd begun to sag, he noticed.

'Yeah,' Bill said, 'well, which one do you think I believe? Louper's a drunk. He's capable of anything.

Peters couldn't be sure enough to swear it, but he thinks the girl's pants were down.'

'But he didn't want to get involved. I know. So who pulled the strings, Bill? I figured the police had enough to charge me on their own, and all they did was give me the riot act – as if I'll show up there again.'

'So they saw your service record. So they know enough to know what to respect. Besides, they've had run-ins with Sten before. He's got a half-dozen drunk driving charges as it is. Nobody wanted trouble, not in this day and age – the wrong kind of trouble, if you know what I mean. Sten got what he deserved for trying to do what he tried to do, eh? The Hodgson Fisk I know wouldn't just stand by and let that happen. And he wouldn't jump the gun, either.'

Fisk scratched a thigh. The damn chair was agony. A thousand biting ants. *The Hodgson Fisk you know, eh, Bill?* 'Thanks, Bill. For everything.'

'No problem. Listen, no money changed hands with that dog food deal, did it?'

'No.'

'Well, there's probably violations of the code, but I'm not going to bother looking them up. I'm just amazed the dogs actually eat that stuff.'

'It's ground up. Cut with regular food.'

'That what he told you?'

'Yeah. Why?'

'He's got jars of the stuff. It isn't cut with anything.'

Fisk sighed. 'Christ, that's one nasty nest he's keeping. Look, that girl's in trouble living there. The wife, too. They're scared. That's why they lied. Can't you do something?'

'There's a doctor in there now. He's intervened, I

think they call it. And Family Services is involved now, too. I guess things are in the works. Listen, Hodgson, I just want you to know, you come by the Legion and a lot of people will come up and shake your hand.'

'Kind of you. I'll think about it.'

'Great. Okay, see you, then. Go have breakfast, eh?'

Once he had hung up the phone, Fisk got out of the chair as fast as he could. A part of his mind had become convinced it'd turned into an ant-hill under him. He went back into the bedroom and dressed, thinking about what Bill had said.

He wasn't looking for handshakes. He didn't need them to justify what he'd done. But he appreciated that strings had been pulled on his behalf. Maybe it was time to . . . wake up again, step back outside. A shave, a bath, clean clothes. Not the Legion Hall, though. He wasn't the kind of man who needed to tell stories to stay alive inside and out. The past was done, dead and over with. None of it made any difference, and it was stupid and pathetic to pretend otherwise, to keep going back to the sandbox, which once seemed so big but was now tiny, overcrowded with old men in ill-fitting clothes.

He entered the kitchen and put water on for coffee, then stood, motionless, waiting for it to boil.

Three boys in the basement. School's started. Maybe I'll let them go. Clean things up. Maybe I'll do it one thing at a time. Make the slow walk back, step, then step, then step. The boys coming last of all. That Louper bastard – what happened that night – it's shaken me. Not a weakness, admitting that. There's a world out there. I'd forgotten. It's ugly and mean, and there's people who need help.

The war was about that. But nothing's really changed. The shit's flying all over the place. Never again, we all said. We'd felt like giants when we said it, because we meant it, because we'd seen enough. But it wasn't up to us. They fooled us, made us think we were important, made us think we'd done something, changed things for the better. Then, slow and sure, they resumed business as usual. The promise got compromised, just a little at first, then more and more. And all we did was get into our outdated uniforms once a year and tell each other stories over beers all the other days.

An ugly world. Old men with the scars fucked right over. Fool us and the rest are just puppies. No problem getting them to cower.

The kettle whistled. He found the instant coffee and a cup that was more or less clean.

People out there needed help. Of course, there were others, ready to step in, to intervene. They'd do the job, clean things up. Hell, who am I to think I'm important to anyone? Shouldn't be all worried like this. They'll get the girl out. She'll stop being afraid and she'll tell the truth then, and that'll be that. Sten will do time and what he did will mean he won't get out alive. Everybody's got rules, and some of those people are meaner than others when it comes time for punishing the ones that break them. Good enough. Here I thought I'd be useful again. No need. None at all. The boys below can rot a while longer. Bill and his buddies are raising me a toast. Good enough. I wish I'd killed that bastard. Christ, he wouldn't fall down. I've never seen anything like it.

His feet were getting tired, standing there. Fisk rubbed the bristle on his jaw. He'd shave, get cleaned up. *Nothing wrong with that. No special meaning. None at all.* He swallowed a mouthful of coffee.

The cage rows wavered in the heat beyond the kitchen window. He'd have to hose them down again. He'd lost six already to the heat, and too many still-borns. If the weather didn't break soon it'd be a tight winter. Might even go in the hole.

Maybe I'll shave tomorrow.

II

Elouise remembered a rabbit. It had probably been someone's pet, tentative as it made its way into her garden. Jennifer had been a child then. Though Elouise knew the rabbit would eat into her vegetables, she didn't have the heart to let Sten loose his dogs on it. And Jennifer had been so excited, crouching on the lawn in her frilly summer dress, her white socks pulled right up to her knees. The rabbit knew she was there. It heard the girl cooing, calling it forward with a celery stick in one hand.

The rabbit had escaped from somewhere, and now the world opened to it. It was both frightened and bold, far too confident for what was waiting out there. Dogs, cats, an owl, a hawk. Its fur was white, and it looked fat and slow – one day soon it would meet its end.

The little girl, had she known, would have cried her heart out.

Elouise decided that there were some things it was better for a child never to learn about, at least until she had to. Life was hard enough.

The rabbit ate its fill among the lettuces and endives. One of the dogs in the kennel saw it then and started barking, which set off the others. The rabbit cocked an ear, then padded away.

They never saw it again.

Elouise had found the memory alive in her mind as soon as she woke. It haunted her, as if the rabbit had calmly jumped out of a nightmare into her waking life.

But the garden was dead. For this summer at least. Whatever had seeded itself from last season had withered in the drought. There'd be no rabbits this year. They remained in their cages, unable to escape, unable to see what lay beyond the wire mesh. They didn't know it, but they were safe in there. Cared for and protected. As much as they might claw at the latch, they lived in a perfect world.

She stood silent and motionless at the kitchen window and watched Jennifer head up the road. The first day of school. The house behind her was quiet. Sleeping, sleeping all through the long days.

Poor rabbit. Elouise wanted to cry. *Poor thing.*

III

Jennifer left a quiet house. Her father had taken to lying in bed most of each day, venturing out when the sun set, when he'd feed the dogs and wander in the darkness through the yard, drinking the beer he'd hidden in the car – beer that had spent the day heating up and must have tasted hot as piss.

Her mother puttered around in the house, voiceless, something less than a ghost. The garden was a

weed-twisted mess. The crab-apples had fallen uncol-
lected from the trees, rotting on the ground and filling
the air with a sickly smell that would have been worse
if there'd been rain. Her mother seemed to have shriv-
elled up and died inside. She looked old, walked old,
lived old.

When Jennifer was home – as little as possible – she
stayed in her room playing records continuously to
keep the silence away, and to keep herself from straining to hear anything that might break that silence. She
was sick of being tense, coiled tight inside, sick of that
kind of exhaustion. Better just to shut it out.

Though the morning was warm, promising a swel-
tering day, she wore her jean jacket. It had an inside
pocket, where she kept her cigarettes. She'd broken
the rule of no smoking on school grounds enough times
to make getting caught a tried, familiar and harmless
ritual. Principal Thompson hadn't even bothered calling her into his office towards the end of last year.

But there was a new teacher, Miss Rhide, who'd already sent a letter to their house – expressing concern
over Jennifer's difficult circumstances at home, promising support and understanding and that things would
be different now, because she took her class very seriously, and felt very responsible to them, to their needs
and to their individual circumstances. She was so very
looking forward to the coming school year. She and
her class were embarking on a wonderful and challenging journey together, and she was very pleased to
have Jennifer joining in that journey.

*Very this, very that. Very very very. Christ. So very . . .
breathless!*

She approached the highway. The morning traffic

was a steady stream. She watched a school bus go by. Most of the students came in that way. She thought of the class that would meet poor Miss Rhide. Barb had been caught outside the Riverview Community Centre with a baggie of grass. A local scandal. Her supplier got busted an hour later. *Big surprise.* Sandy had tried running away from home. She'd made it into the city, then had panicked, phoning her father from a lobby in a seedy Main Street hotel. And then there was Jennifer herself, with a thick file folder with her name on it. *Poor, poor Miss Rhide.*

She neared the traffic lights. Lynk and Roland had their bright orange patrol belts on, herding the local little kids into a tight knot on the highway's gravel shoulder. Carl manned the button that would change the lights. Jennifer looked for Owen but didn't see him. She came to the group but stood slightly away from it, scanning over the heads of the kids, trying to see Owen on the playground on the other side of the highway.

Lynk ignored her, but Roland nodded in greeting.

'Seen Owen?' Jennifer asked.

He shook his head.

'Tell him I'm behind the school.'

'You going to be there until the bell rings?'

'Yeah.'

Lynk was the first to march out when the lights changed. He stood wide-stanced in the middle of the highway. Roland directed the group across, then ran back to where Carl waited. Lynk followed once all the kids had crossed.

Jennifer entered the school grounds with the usual sense of dread and disgust. Off to her right the seventh-, eighth- and ninth-graders stood outside the smudged

entrance of the Old Building, their drab, cool clothes a
perfect match with the pitted limestone walls flanking
the doors. Some of them looked her way, a couple
nodded, a few laughed.

She'd be over there next year, and it'd be like crossing a chasm. In a way, she dreaded that as much as
another year in the Sixth Grade. But at least they had
regular classrooms.

Miss Obell was the morning's playground moni-
tor. That meant Jennifer would be safe enough sneak-
ing a smoke behind the school. 'Oh-Hell Obell' rarely
bothered leaving the front grounds, keeping herself
stationary like a planet orbited by a dozen chattering, vying moons – little kids all wanting to hold her
hand.

Jennifer felt Obell's gaze on her as she headed around
the school's side. *Yes, Miss Obell. Another year. Thought
I'd be gone by now, I bet. Fat chance. Any words of
advice for Miss Rhide? Didn't think so.*

Barb and Sandy were already there, hanging out
with Gary from Riverview.

'Got a smoke?' Barb asked, her face flushed.

'Who, me?' Jennifer reached for them. 'Imagine,' she
said, looking up at the featureless wall, 'building a
school with no windows.'

'You mean a fucking jail,' Gary said. His stringy
brown hair was longer than the last time she'd seen
him, down past his bony shoulders. Bright shiny pimples pocked his broad, flat face.

'You flunked too, eh?'

He shrugged, turning to spit against the wall. 'Fuck
school. As soon as I'm sixteen I'm out. Work for my
dad at his plant.'

His plant. Says it all. Who needs brains when you got a rich old man?

Gary grinned, showing his chipped teeth. 'Hear you got a boyfriend. Some new kid, some fucker from the city.'

'You should stop eating all those chocolate bars,' Jennifer said.

Gary turned bright red. 'Fuck you. Fuck him. Fucking slut.'

'Go jerk off in a corner,' Jennifer said. 'That's all you'll ever get.'

Barb's laugh pierced the air.

Gary walked away, jamming his hands into his jean pockets, hunching his shoulders.

'I saw our new teacher,' Barb said, pulling fiercely on her cigarette. 'She's a horse. All freckles and hair. A beanpole.'

'That's not fair,' Sandy said quickly. 'She might be all right, how do you know? You don't know anything. You just saw her once, didn't you?'

Jennifer and Barb stared at her.

Sandy continued, her eyes darting from one friend to the other. 'I'm supposed to be nice. I've been canned for six months. So I'm gonna be nice to her. Get good grades. Top grades.'

'So?' Barb scowled. 'You'll still be canned for six months.'

'Maybe, maybe not. I'm gonna be top of the class. Watch me. I'll put my hand up every time. I'll be first in line. I'll do all my homework and I'll bring in assignments days early. I can read a book a day, easy. One a day.' She stopped to draw breath.

Jennifer stepped close, studying Sandy's pinpoint eyes. 'You're on speed, aren't you? Christ, it's the first day, Sandy!'

'You just watch me. My old man – when he sees my report card, he'll shit himself and I won't be canned any more. He'll say do what you want, whatever you fucking want—'

Jennifer and Barb looked at each other and burst out laughing. A moment later, after staring with wide eyes, Sandy joined in.

Jennifer laughed harder as Sandy doubled over in a giggling fit.

The bell rang. Kids started making their way towards the front of the school. Jennifer and her friends remained where they were. Sandy was laughing so hard Jennifer wondered if she was going to pee her pants.

Miss Obell appeared around the corner. She saw them and approached. 'Bell's rung, girls. Jennifer, are things going to be better this year? I see butts on the ground. Not a good start.'

'Not us,' Jennifer said, wiping tears from her cheeks. 'Could've been here for days.'

'Of course. Sandy and Barb now, too. Satisfied that your friends are as hooked as you? I'd have thought Barb here would have learned her lesson. As for you, Jennifer, something tells me you'll never learn.'

'That's the spirit,' Jennifer said.

Miss Obell's thin lips straightened into a tight line, the usual flush on her round face deepening a shade. 'Well, you've got a point there, Jennifer. You're smart, no question about that. I guess that's what makes it such a shame. Come along now. You don't want to be late.'

Sandy had recovered but now looked jittery. Paranoid. Jennifer felt herself getting nervous in response. Sandy wasn't in any shape to handle anything. *Oh, Miss Rhide . . .*

They followed Oh-Hell Obell into the school.

Owen wasn't there. Miss Rhide's long, pale face wrinkled into a frown at the silence following her reading his name on the roll-call. She looked up and scanned the faces staring back at her. 'Does anyone know Owen Brand? I understand he's a new student.'

Jennifer saw Roland raise his hand.

'I know him.'

Rhide checked the sheet of paper in her reddish hands. 'And your name is . . .'

'Roland Fraser.'

'Oh yes, of course. Well, do you have any idea why Owen isn't here today?'

'No, ma'am.'

Others giggled at the *ma'am*. *He's so sweet. Not my type, but sweet.* Jennifer leaned back in her chair – fibreglass, blue-grey and new, as were the desks, triangular with three kids to each one, with plastic drawers suspended in a metal cage under them. The carpet was also new, in the same blue-grey tones. Movable dividers separated the 'rooms'. The air seemed to shiver with all the noise, buzzing, washing like waves, a noise that seeped into the head and stayed there. The room itself was bigger than a gymnasium. At least fifteen separate classes, maybe more. Jennifer felt like a bee in a hive that someone had just kicked.

Rhide finished the roll-call. 'Now then,' she said, smiling as she rose from the stool she'd been sitting on, which was planted in front of her desk. 'I would like everyone to gather around, here, cross-legged on the carpet.'

Jennifer rolled her eyes. *Unbelievable.*

The kids began rising uncertainly from their seats, then, seeing Principal Thompson approaching with Owen, they hesitated. The man gestured and Rhide joined him. He said something, bending close and whispering. Rhide nodded, smiled down at Owen, who ignored her completely as he scanned the class until he found Jennifer.

She grinned. He grinned back.

Rhide returned to the front of the class. Principal Thompson left, and Owen found a seat.

'Okay, everyone come and sit down now,' Rhide said. She waited while the twenty or so kids moved to the floor, some jostling for position at the very front, others hunting around as if to find a place to hide. Jennifer placed herself at the back, closest to the desks, farthest from Rhide's beaming face. Owen made his way over and sat down, cross-legged, his knee touching Jennifer's.

Rhide perched herself back on the stool. Her knees looked bony under the mauve nylons as she rested her clasped hands on them. 'Now then, everyone comfortable? Since we have a student new to the school, I think it would be nice for everyone if he would tell us something about himself. Owen?'

Yeah, Owen, tell them how I taught you to lick between my legs.

His expression revealed nothing. 'I've been here in Middlecross since last spring.' He gave his shoulders a loose toss. 'That's about it.'

Rhide blinked. 'Well, what are your interests? Hobbies, sports?'

Owen's face assumed a scowl that Jennifer found wonderfully familiar. 'No,' he said.

'No?'

'No. Nothing special. Middlecross doesn't have a baseball team, doesn't have a hockey team, or a football team. The nearest ones are in Riverview. Why would I go out there? Middlecross is in between everything . . . uh, I forget your name – the principal, I forget his name, too, but he told me yours, only I forget.'

'Miss Rhide,' Jennifer informed him.

Owen nodded, then continued. 'Miss Rhide. As for hobbies, I have the usual ones. I don't hide in the basement with them. I don't have fish or model trains. I don't collect stamps or coins or bubblegum cards. So,' he finished, 'nothing special.'

Rhide said, 'I do recall from your file some comments from your last teacher, saying that you read a lot – some very advanced books, in fact.'

Owen's scowl deepened and the teacher seemed almost to flinch from it. 'That's not a hobby,' he said.

'No. That's true. Can you tell us what book you're reading now?'

'*Goldfinger,* by Ian Fleming. It's a spy novel. James Bond and Blofeld and Pussy Galore.'

'What?'

His face was innocent as he said, 'That's her name, Miss Rhide.' But Jennifer saw the laughter hiding behind it – he was pleased, delighted to have shocked her so.

'Um, I don't know if those kinds of books are worth reading.'

Owen shrugged. 'Then don't read them. What do you read?'

She looked taken aback, rattled. 'Well, textbooks, mostly.'

'Oh,' Owen said. Somehow he managed to pack a lot into that single word, and Jennifer saw Rhide's face redden. Her long fingers looked blue at the tips where they fidgeted on her knee. Her watery eyes were wide. She clasped her hands more tightly together and smiled at the class.

'Well, thank you, Owen. Now let's move on, shall we? I know this will be a very special year, and I hope you're as excited as I am. You'll be having classes in a number of different subjects, and just like in Junior High, you'll have different teachers for some of them.'

She went on, the sixth-graders cross-legged on the carpet, getting numb and their brains racing with fear. It was new. They didn't want new. Their teacher tried to make it sound exciting and that was like a klaxon, sounding the alarm. It was complicated, this new programme. Confusing. Jennifer could sense the unease around her, and she understood why. This changing rooms, changing teachers, it was all supposed to happen next year. They'd be in a different building. They'd be expecting changes. This, this wasn't the way it was supposed to be. It was unfair.

Jennifer wanted to laugh. It was also a mess. Taking your desk drawers with you, crowding the aisles between the dividers as you went from one area to the next. A giant game of musical chairs.

Mr Lyle would teach the maths and science. Miss Obell taught French and music. Rhide herself handled social studies and English.

What a circus.

Jennifer had been casually edging closer to Owen during Rhide's breathless speech, which seemed like it was never going to end, as if as soon as she began running down someone would come around and wind her back up so she could go on and on and on. Jennifer slid her hand under Owen's bum, probed with her fingers.

He shot her a surprised look, then returned his attention to worrying a loose flap of rubber on his sneakers.

His breath quickened, though, and the colour rose on his cheeks.

Directly in front of Jennifer sat Barb, playing with her stringy curls. Near by, Sandy looked to have buzzed right out of the picture. Roland was falling asleep, while Lynk seemed all ears, his eyes bright. Gary, sitting behind Carl, was doing something that made Carl uncomfortable – she could guess, but she leaned back slightly to confirm that Gary had pulled Carl's underwear up and was giving it sharp tugs every time Rhide's attention was elsewhere.

Jennifer reached farther under Owen, her fingertips finding his crotch.

He leaned over. 'Cut it out,' he whispered.

'Why were you late?' she hissed back.

He scowled. 'School starts at nine in the city. Not eight-thirty.'

'Excuse me,' Rhide said sharply, her eyes on them, the endless ramble interrupted. 'Jennifer Louper and Owen Brand—'

'Sittin' in the tree!' Sandy yelled. 'K-I-S-S-I-N-G!'

The whole class erupted into peals of laughter. The

surrounding hum from the other areas fell away as
people turned to look.

Rhide's face went white. 'Quiet, please! I won't tolerate this!'

Everyone settled down, except for Sandy, who
couldn't stop laughing. As soon as she seemed to gain
control of herself, she'd look up at Rhide and explode
into a new, helpless fit, doubling over, arms wrapped
around her stomach.

Rhide's voice was brittle. 'Very well,' she said, rising
from the stool. 'I think you'd better come with me.'

The students parted as she walked through the group
and collected Sandy, who had managed to climb to
her feet, her face beet-red and the tears streaming from
her eyes. She jerked as Rhide laid a hand on her shoulder. It was hard to tell whether she was laughing now
or crying. Jennifer saw a look of fear in her eyes – not
of getting into trouble, but of how she was feeling inside.

Rhide escorted Sandy from the area.

'Shit,' Jennifer said softly.

Owen looked at her. 'What?'

'She's on speed. If they find out she'll be expelled.
It's like drinking a hundred cups of coffee. If they take
her to the nurse . . .'

'What a stupid thing to do. The first day!'

Jennifer shrugged. 'Speed freaks don't think right.'

Owen looked around. The other kids were all talking, but quietly, because they could see Mr Lyle keeping an eye on them from the area nearest to theirs.
'What kind of school is this?' Owen asked in disbelief.
'Look at these desks, and what are we doing here on
the floor?'

'Singalong,' Jennifer said, then, seeing Owen's widening eyes, 'Just joking, Owen! At least I think I am.'

Rhide had reappeared, alone, and the class fell silent as she returned to stand in front of the stool. She was silent for a moment, scanning the students as if hunting for the next source of trouble. 'Clearly,' she finally said, 'it's necessary to talk a bit about discipline. I've told you what you can expect from me. Now it seems I have to discuss what it is that I expect from you.' She paused, sighing heavily through her nose. 'Very well. I will not tolerate any outburst like the one we've just seen. Just because someone acts out of turn, it does not mean that everyone else has to respond, giving them the attention they desire. Is that understood?'

Heads nodded.

'While it's important for you to feel able to express yourselves, it's equally important for you to respect each other – everyone must have an opportunity to learn. Of course, we'll be sure to have fun, because learning is fun, after all. I trust, then, that there'll be no more outbursts . . .' She scanned the faces again, then smiled brightly. 'Well! I'm glad that's cleared up. Now we can get on with the day – our first day!'

Jennifer and Barb sat inside the concrete tube near the monkey-bars. Owen and Roland stood at the opening facing the school, blocking the girls from view while they shared a smoke.

'Shit,' Jennifer heard Roland say. 'Carl's getting beaten up.'

'They're just wrestling,' Owen said.

'No. That's just how Gary does it. He laughs, pretending it's a game in case Obell sees them.'

'Oh. Nice trick. All he's doing is throwing Carl to the ground. Can't hurt much.'

'That's not the point,' Roland said slowly.

Jennifer handed the cigarette to Barb. 'You can finish it.'

'Wonder what happened to Sandy,' Barb said.

'What do you think? Guys, I'm getting out.'

They moved aside as she climbed from the tube.

Both Roland and Owen had their eyes on Gary, who was coming their way with three Riverview friends in tow. Jennifer scowled. 'Ignore him, guys. He's a dipshit.' But she could see both boys tensing up. She looked for Obell – nowhere in sight. *Typical*.

'Here, pussy pussy pussy!' Gary called, eyes on Owen.

'Get lost,' Jennifer said.

Gary was gearing up. His friends kept a lookout while he strutted closer, a sneer on his face. A year older, Gary outweighed Owen by at least ten pounds and was a few inches taller, too.

'Go somewhere and fuck yourself,' Jennifer said.

Ignoring her, Gary moved closer to Owen, who stood unmoving, his hands hanging at his sides. Gary's grin was tight. 'Fucking city kid,' he said. 'Fucking James Bond.' He took another step then widened his stance. 'Come on, then.'

Owen raised both hands, then kicked Gary as hard as he could between the legs. The sound was shocking, a crunching pop. Gary's eyes bulged as he folded over and fell down.

Owen stepped back, eyeing the Riverview boys. A crowd had gathered, and Jennifer saw Miss Obell rushing towards them.

'Anyone else?' Owen asked.

No one moved, except for Gary, who looked like he was trying to crawl into himself on the gravel. His face had gone from red to white, his eyes squeezed shut, face twisted in pain.

Owen looked calm, almost relieved.

Fuck, he's done it. No one will touch him now. Serves you right, Gary, fucking A.

Obell arrived, took the scene in at a glance. Her gaze settled on Owen. 'You,' she said, 'will be coming with me.'

'He didn't start it,' Jennifer said.

Roland nodded. 'That's right, he didn't. Gary was looking to start a fight with the new kid.' His face was flushed. 'He got it, Miss Obell.'

Barb giggled beside Jennifer. Her eyes on Gary, she giggled again. 'Boy, did he ever.'

Obell's frown made her look old. She went to Gary and slowly bent over him. 'Do you need the nurse?' she asked quietly. He shook his head. 'Can you get up, son?' He shook his head again. Obell straightened. She searched the crowd until she found one of her favourites. 'Get the nurse, Alice. Quickly.'

Gary was crying now, heaving and gasping. He still writhed around, kicking patterns in the gravel, his long hair a tangled, dusty mess. Slowly, he got on to his knees, keeping his forehead pressed to the gravel, still shaking with sobs.

The recess bell rang. Obell looked around. 'Everyone back to class!' She gripped Owen's arm. 'Except for you, and whoever else saw what happened.'

Jennifer remained, as did Roland and – to Jennifer's surprise – Lynk. She hadn't seen him there when the

fight started. He stood now, a strange expression on
his thin face – Jennifer couldn't read it at all, but something there disturbed her, as did what happened next.
Lynk waited until Obell noticed him, then he quickly
left, catching up with the other kids before they reached
the corner of the building.

'Detention,' Owen said in the lunch room. 'I used to
get out at four in the city. School ends at three here.
So it makes no difference to me.' He shrugged. 'What
do you do, clean brushes?'

Jennifer shook her head. 'No. You get maths tests,
from Mr Lyle. If you get a hundred per cent he lets
you go fifteen minutes early.'

'I'm lousy at maths,' Owen said glumly.

They were sitting with Barb and Roland at one end
of the long table. The lunch room was filled with
sound, voices rising and falling like waves.

'Hurry up and finish,' Jennifer said to Owen. 'I
want to go outside.' She mimed smoking a cigarette.

Owen nodded, biting into his tuna sandwich. Beside him, Roland had paused in his eating and was
looking carefully around.

'What?' Barb asked him.

He shrugged. 'I saw Lynk talking to Obell, then
they left. They haven't come back yet.' He looked at
Owen.

'What's his problem?' Owen demanded.

Jennifer saw the two boys study each other, and she
realised all at once that there was a secret between
them – and Lynk, the three of them. She felt instantly
jealous, even though she knew she had her own secrets
which she'd kept from Owen – from everyone, in fact.

Even so, she had good reasons – a matter of degree, anyway, of seriousness. Stung by their tense silence, she glared at Owen and said, 'What the fuck?'

He looked at her blankly.

Jennifer rounded on his friend. 'Roland! What's going on?'

'Nothing,' he said. 'Only Lynk's lying. He's going to get Owen in shit.'

'Why?'

'He won't fight me,' Owen said. 'Not now. But he'll do other things.'

'Yes, but why?'

Owen and Roland exchanged another glance, then Owen filled his mouth with the last of his sandwich. Roland sighed. 'It's just Lynk,' he said. 'It's just the way he is, the way he's always been, I guess.'

'You apologising for him?' Jennifer demanded.

'Well, no. But I've known him a long time. Since kindergarten.'

Jennifer sat back. She looked over to where Gary sat with one of his friends, Dennis. Gary wasn't sitting comfortably, and he wasn't saying a word. He looked broken, smaller. 'He's fucked,' she said. The others followed her gaze. 'The whole year, maybe every year to come. That's the first fight he ever lost, you know.'

'He wasn't hurt so bad,' Owen said. 'I once ripped a guy's ear – they had to take him to Emergency and sew it up or it would've fallen off.'

'Yuck.'

Roland said, 'Tell Gary to leave Carl alone, Owen.'

Owen slouched down in the chair, a look of distaste on his face. 'All right,' he said. 'If you want. All he does is push him down, you know.'

'I know.'

'All right, all right.'

Barb leaned close. 'Uh oh,' she hissed. 'Here come Thompson and Rhide.'

Owen took a deep breath. 'That little shit,' he said.

IV

Joanne Rhide had never imagined such a disastrous first day. It wasn't even the afternoon yet and she felt exhausted. She'd been called from the smoky staffroom by Barry's secretary, Mrs Reynolds, and moments later found herself in the conference room with the principal, Marianne Obell and Lynk Bescher, one of her students.

There'd been a fight – she already knew that – but the version given by Jennifer and Roland, which had indicated that Owen Brand wasn't entirely to blame, that version had just been challenged.

'Owen and Jennifer are going together,' Lynk explained again for her benefit. 'And Roland will do anything Jennifer asks him to do. I saw the fight. Gary wasn't doing nothing, Miss Rhide, and Owen just kicked him in the n— between the legs.'

Lynk clearly wanted to set the record straight. He'd been attentive all morning, his bright eyes seeming to mirror Joanne's own enthusiasm. She sensed already that he would be one of her special students.

It was wrong to make snap judgements, she knew. No doubt Owen felt a little lost, a little insecure, despite his spending the summer here in Middlecross. School was always a shock, and it'd been her task to cushion the blow, to ease that panic over into enthusiastic optimism. She'd done poorly despite her self-confidence, and that left her with a sickly feeling in her stomach.

Still, it was good to define problems early on, before things got out of hand. Owen was subject to a very negative, very dominant influence in Jennifer Louper – something that needed counteracting. Jennifer was the common denominator.

They sent Lynk out to eat his lunch in the secretary's office. Once the door had closed behind him, Barry swung in his chair and grinned at Joanne. 'You've landed yourself one hell of a class, eh?'

Joanne blinked. 'Well, I am very pleased with the majority of the pupils . . .'

Marianne shifted heavily in her seat, reaching out to pull the ashtray closer to her. 'Jennifer's a very intelligent girl,' she said. 'Given the conditions at home, she's had to grow up quickly. Prematurely, I suppose you could say.' She fixed Joanne with a heavy-lidded gaze. 'I teach music, as you know. Jennifer rarely focuses herself. She affects complete indifference. But when I challenge her, she performs effortlessly. She can read sheet music at a glance, as if it was instinctual with her. She can play circles around me on the piano, and her improvisations are nothing short of brilliant.'

'Clearly, then,' Joanne said, 'it's a matter of motivation.'

Barry and Marianne exchanged glances, then he cleared his throat. 'I think that's understood,' he said. 'We have to acknowledge, however, that Jennifer's influence on the new boy will be substantial.' He held up a hand as Marianne was about to interject. 'Granted, the new boy may be predisposed – they may have found each other. Joanne, you're the most familiar with his file from School Division One. Does Owen have a history?'

'He's been in a new school almost each year since kindergarten. The potential for trauma is indicated, the pattern suggesting – to me at least – an unstable situation at home.'

Marianne blew out a gust of smoke that rolled across the table and rose up around Joanne. 'Did he get into fights?' she drawled.

'Well, the incidents seem to occur at the beginning of the year, each year. Afterwards, there's no indication of problems in that area.'

'Is he a bully?' Marianne asked. 'Beat someone up at the beginning and terrorise for the rest of the year?'

Rhide shook her head. 'Nothing written down. No complaints, I mean. He's noted as a loner, usually with only one or two friends. His grades are just average. Again and again a teacher's commented that he has to try harder, which as we now know is a euphemism that could mean anything – is he a slow learner, does he have a learning defect, is the teacher showing any interest in him whatsoever?'

Marianne's tone was distinctly dry. 'Usually means the kid lacks motivation.'

'Yes, but why? That's the question we should concern ourselves with. His Fifth Grade teacher had included a comment about Owen's extracurricular reading activities. She indicated that some of the material was quite advanced. Now, I asked Owen about that in class this morning—'

Barry cut in. 'His first day?'

'Well, I asked him to introduce himself. Anyway, he said he was reading a book by James Bond – I mean to say, a book about James Bond. I can't recall who writes those. I admit, if that's what the teacher called advanced material . . .'

'Certainly educational,' Barry said, then laughed. 'Has it occurred to you that he just made that up on the spot?'

'Pardon?'

'If you nail down a kid who's new, hardly knows anyone, is feeling vulnerable and exposed, and if he's reading, say, Tolstoy – do you actually think he'll say so?'

'Well, he knew all the characters—'

'So he's seen the movie. And as for the fighting, that's a pecking-order thing. Kids aren't angels. More like little apes. Hierarchy is everything. I'd guess he's learned his lessons the hard way. I'd guess the local tough in each and every school has taken him on. Hell, he's learned to fight dirty – that should tell you just how desperate these things are. Gary – well, poor dear Gary's been this school's bully since the Fourth Grade, Joanne. As for Lynk, he's lying. Don't forget, he and Owen already know each other. Who knows how *that* hierarchy got worked out.'

Joanne felt her face reddening as Barry spoke. 'But how can you tolerate all this? You see them as if, as if they're all animals—'

'That's exactly what they are,' Barry replied. 'We all are, Joanne.'

'But we have brains. That means nothing? My goodness, I had no idea educators even existed who were so . . . deterministic—'

'Realistic,' Barry said. 'We're social animals, after all. Equality's just an ideal. Something to be strived towards, a modern Holy Grail. That doesn't lessen its value or its importance. But we still have to live in the real world, and it's full of grit and dirt and messy truths.'

He'd left her breathless with rage, and Marianne's patronising cynicism was as thick and as foul as the smoke with which she filled the conference room.

Barry walked with her to the lunch room. It had been decided to maintain the detention for Owen, to turn it into an opportunity for Joanne to talk with him one-on-one. Besides, George Lyle didn't even have a detention test prepared yet.

'You needn't be so dismayed,' Barry told her as they approached the lunch-room doors. 'It's only the first day. No one's settled. All the old familiar routines have been dismantled with this new programme getting into position. Give it some time, Joanne.'

'Yes, of course I will, Barry.' But in her mind, Joanne told herself something entirely different. *They're not little apes. And I believe Lynk Bescher's story. Jennifer and Owen deserve my utmost attention and understanding, of course. I intend to make them blossom under my guidance. There're always ones who are late bloomers, just like Mother said about me. They need nurturing, that's all. And I can begin today, with Owen. Just him and me, out of Jennifer's domineering influences.*

'What are your favourite subjects, Owen?'

He sat facing her in his chair, looking both nervous and bored. At the far end of the open room, a janitor was vacuuming, the distant drone the only other sound they could hear.

'I don't really have a favourite,' Owen said, looking around.

Joanne sighed. She sat in a chair like his, the student desk between them. 'I'd prefer it, Owen, if you looked at me while we're talking, rather than at everything else.' When he turned his hard blue eyes on her she almost regretted her request. 'You needn't be so angry.'

'I'm not,' he said. 'This is how I always look.'

'I can't believe that.'

He shrugged.

Joanne sat back, crossing her legs and resting her hands on the desktop. 'What about English? Do you like that?'

'Not much.'

'Why?'

He frowned.

Well, at least I've got him thinking.

'I don't like,' he said slowly, 'people telling me what books to read.'

'Hmmm. Don't you think some books are more important than others?'

His frown changed into a belligerent scowl. 'No.'

'Well, I'd have to disagree with you there, Owen.'

'Sure.'

'Can I explain why I disagree with you?'

'If you want.'

'Some books – wonderful, beautifully written books – they show us a part of ourselves. They show us things about, well, about life.'

She was startled as he rounded on her. 'Ever read

Tarzan of the Apes? War of the Worlds? Father Brown,
or *The Lost World?* I have. They're a part of me.'

'But they're not real life, are they?'

He sat back, looking away. 'What's real life?' he
muttered, then snapped her a harsh challenge. 'Ever
read them? Any of them?'

'That's not the point—'

'The first book I ever read was *Before Adam,* by
Jack London. How can you talk about books when
you haven't read anything?'

'But I have. I've read many books.'

He looked unconvinced. Joanne sighed. 'Well, let's
talk about something else. Can you suggest a topic?
Something you'd like to talk about?'

'Atavisms.'

'Pardon?'

'Throwbacks. Some people are less human than
others. They see a world in red. Like hungry animals,
plain and simple. And that's how they live, too, and
everyone else is scared to death of him, of that throwback. He's a monster, because he's what we all were,
once upon a time. Sometimes he's just a big black
shadow, right on our heels no matter how fast we run.
Sometimes he's all covered in fur, and he goes around
killing people, but sometimes he doesn't do that, he
doesn't do anything at all. He just lies there, and you
try and go around him but you can't because he's too
big. Even when he disappears, his shadow stays behind, and it like whispers in your head. That's what
Gary thinks he is, but he isn't. Lynk's afraid. That's
why he lied, plain and simple.'

'Where on earth did you get all this?'

Owen leaned back, gloating. 'Jack London's *Before Adam*.'

V

The huge geared wheel painted on the candle factory's yellow wall seemed to be turning, ever so slowly, in minute increments like a giant clock. I stared up at it as I approached the building, my conversation with Miss Rhide running through my mind.

She'd run out of things to say to me, questions to ask, not long after I'd talked about the throwback. While *Before Adam* had shown me the bestial character named Red-Eyes, and had taught me the word atavism, I realised, even as I spoke, that Red-Eyes was no different from Grendel, the monster in *Beowulf*. And that, like the body that had come down the river, they were all part of something else, all imperfect reflections of something primal and yet still alive.

Already – after my very first day – I saw Rhide walking among them. I didn't know why she belonged in that company, but she did. And for me, there was no escaping her. I felt that she would haunt me all my life, the same way the body haunted me, the same way Red-Eyes sometimes stalked my dreams.

The factory's door was padlocked, the front windows barred. Around the side facing the school, the high grasses and thistles hid a basement window. We'd worked the latch loose once, early in the summer, and it was the factory's cavernous basement that Roland had suggested as the place to meet.

I pushed through the grasses, paused to look around, then quickly crawled through the opening.

I heard Roland's voice. 'He's here.'

The drop from the window was about seven feet, down along a gritty, damp wall of large cut stone. An inner wall had been bolted to it once, but only the rust-smeared fittings remained. The floor felt gritty under me as I turned to face the others.

Lynk had lit candles, dozens of them, all over the floor, throwing out knee-high yellow light that revealed an ordered forest of wood postings, rising up to a tin ceiling stamped with ornamental patterns. At the far end of the room – which reached across the entire building – rose a steel staircase, powdered with rust where the black paint had flaked off.

Lynk paced, not meeting my eye as I entered the shadow-webbed light. Carl sat with his back against one of the posts, holding a lit candle and letting the wax drip on to his other hand.

I felt myself getting tense. 'Okay,' I said, eyeing Roland who stood opposite me. 'Not so bad. Not even an hour. Rhide talked and talked. Big deal.'

'What is this?' Lynk demanded. 'We've got nothing to meet about. For fuck sake.'

'That's not true,' Roland said. 'We've got to decide.'

'Decide what?' I asked.

'What to do. About the body. I think we should tell the cops.'

Lynk walked up to Roland. 'What body?' He pushed Roland back a step with a straight arm to his chest. 'It's fucking gone,' he said, pushing again.

'We don't know that,' I said, watching Roland. 'We

haven't been back. We haven't checked.' Roland had been needed on the farm that day we'd agreed to go, and I think we were both relieved. At any rate, we didn't talk about it again.

Lynk pushed Roland again. 'No fucking body. Probably wasn't real in the first place.'

'Oh, come off it, Lynk. Me and Roland took a good long look. He's real, and he's still there.'

'How the fuck do you know?'

'Where else would it be? The water level stayed down. That beaver lodge is high and dry. It's still there.'

'Have you looked, Owen?' Roland asked.

'No. Don't have to.'

Lynk shoved Roland hard with both hands. Roland staggered, his foot rolling on a candle. He fell heavily.

I waited for him to get up, to beat the shit out of Lynk. Instead, he slowly climbed to his feet and brushed the dust from his pants.

Lynk approached Carl. 'What about you, Carlie?'

Carl dropped his gaze. 'Nothing,' he mumbled.

Lynk pushed his palm against Carl's forehead. The back of the boy's head thumped loudly on the wood post. Carl rolled away.

Lynk laughed. 'Hear that sound? Hah, fucking great – Carlie's got a hollow head.'

I sighed, leaned against a post. 'Well, you've had a fun day, Lynk. Lying to Thompson, kissing Rhide's ass, trying to get me and Jennifer into shit. So what's got you so scared?'

'I ain't. I ain't fucking scared, not of you. Gonna kick me in the balls? Come and try it.'

'I was thinking about it,' I said.

He went still, facing me for the first time. His thin

face twisted into a sneer. 'Me and Gary and Dennis –
we're gonna beat the fuck out of you.'

'Three against one?' I laughed, though my heart
was hammering. 'Real tough, you guys.'

'You fight dirty. That's what we do to pricks like
you.'

I wondered if my expression showed my fear. I gave
him a grin. 'I'll take you on. Any time. Gary and Dennis can pound away – I'll go for you, Lynk. Just you.
You'll find out how dirty I am. Guaranteed. You know
how easy it is to dig an eye out with a finger? It just
pops out, just like that.'

'Fuck you.'

Roland's punch caught Lynk – and me – completely
off guard. The knuckles cracked hard against Lynk's
cheek. He reeled back, hands thrown up to his face,
then bent over and leaned on the wall.

Roland sounded apologetic as he said, 'I don't like
being pushed.'

I smiled when he turned to me, but there was no
response, the eyes flat. 'I think we should go back and
look. To make sure. Then call the cops. What do you
want to do?'

'Don't know,' I said, watching Lynk slowly straightening, tears running down his face, probing the split
cheek under his right eye. He was going to have a shiner,
a nice dark one. 'We can go look, sure. But I don't know
about the cops.'

'How come?'

I shrugged. 'Not sure. They'll probably tear up the
beaver lodge. The beavers never did anything. And
muskrats live there, too.'

Roland studied me. I knew my reason sounded lame,

but it was the truth. It was autumn already. The beavers needed a place before winter arrived. Same for the muskrats.

'Didn't think of that,' Roland said. 'It's like the bear, isn't it? Like when my dad wouldn't shoot it. It's like that, I think.'

'How?'

'Don't know. But it feels the same.'

'You're all fucking shits,' Lynk rasped. 'Fighting dirty, like a buncha fags. You're all fags. The body's gone, you won't find nothing. I took it. All the bones. I hid them, so fuck you.'

Carl jumped to his feet. He opened his mouth to say something, then shut it.

I felt something cold seep through me. 'Where the fuck is it?' I asked, my voice sounding brittle. 'Come on, you piece of turd, Lynk.' I stepped closer. 'Where the fuck is it?'

Carl moved back, his eyes flicking from me to Lynk and back again, something eager in his face.

'He's lying,' Roland said. 'We'll go look. He just doesn't want us to go look. Lynk's a liar.'

'Go ahead!' he shouted, one hand to his cheek. 'You won't find it! It's mine, now.'

I took another step in his direction. Lynk flinched back, then went to the window. He pulled up the wood crate we used as a step. 'You're all fucking losers.'

I moved to stop him. I wanted to pull him down, fling him to the floor. I wanted to beat on him until the truth came out. My thoughts all seemed natural, cool and logical. Lynk was lying. I'd beat the truth out, so he'd learn what lying meant. No more uncertainty, about anything.

'Let him go,' Roland said.

I wheeled around. 'Why?'

'He's lying.'

'I know!' I shouted.

'Well,' Roland drew the word out, 'it won't work. All we have to do to prove it is go there, to the body. Let him go.'

Lynk pulled himself up through the opening, his feet kicking as he squirmed through. A moment later he was gone.

Carl reached down for a candle. 'He's lying,' he said.

'Let's go look,' I said.

'Tomorrow,' Roland said. 'It's supper-time.'

'All right. I'll try not to get detention.'

'Good luck,' Roland said. 'Rhide's picked you out. You and Jennifer. Jennifer always gets picked. She grew up too fast.'

It was an odd thing to say, but as soon as he said it, I knew it was true. 'I'm meeting her after supper,' I said. 'We should get going. Fuck, what a day.'

He'd been reassembling it. Piece by piece, it grew each evening, gleaming and perfect. The machine looked bigger than ever, there in front of the garage. There was still enough light from the dying day to make its ancient lines and shapes visible, a machine that belonged to this hour, to the gloom and the quiet evening air, as if it were made to manufacture twilight.

I circled it, my footfalls as quiet as I could make them on the oil-soaked asphalt. My breaths came slow and deep, inhaling its steel scent, pulling it far into me.

My old Sunday school teacher once told me how I

was supposed to feel when going into a church. What she'd described had just been words – for me, churches had always felt emptied out, like a husk of something long dead. But those words, of awe and quiet wonder, returned to me now, as if they were what I was feeling, here in front of the machine in our yard's treed cathedral.

Father emerged from the garage. 'Long day, eh?' he said, studying me a moment before continuing, 'Got a call from your teacher.'

I rested a hand on the machine. 'Miss Rhide.'

'Yeah. Your mother took the call. We were expecting you a half-hour ago.'

'Sorry.'

He hesitated, his hands on his hips, his face looking chalky and gaunt in the failing light. 'Seems there's a pattern here, Owen.'

I nodded, running my hand along the cowling. 'Patterns, lots of them.'

'What do you mean?'

'Well, it's always a new school, isn't it? Every year. What am I supposed to do, get beaten up?'

He sighed. 'I figured it was some kind of warning to the other kids. Do you bully them around for the rest of the year?'

'No. I leave them alone, so long as they leave me alone. I don't keep fighting all year. You know that.'

'Where'd you learn to kick between the legs?'

'I don't know.' I frowned. 'No, wait. *Butch Cassidy and the Sundance Kid*. Butch does it to this big guy with a knife. Anyway, the only important thing is winning. Winning the fight.'

He leaned against the engine, crossing his arms. 'How do you do it, exactly?'

I fidgeted. 'Well, uh, I keep my hands down until he's close enough. Then I lift them and that's what he looks at, so that's when I kick him. My leg's longer than my arms, so he's not expecting it.'

He studied me a while longer. 'Got that from the movie?'

'No.'

'Figured it out for yourself.'

'I've had to think about it a lot.'

'Because it's a new school every year.'

'Yeah.'

'Makes life hard for a kid, eh?'

'Well,' I said, shrugging, 'it's just a pattern, like you said.'

Father turned around, leaned on the machine's engine, his arms resting on its top, his chin on his hands. He stared out at the dark yard. 'Sorry about that, son.'

'What? It's not your fault! Don't say that – I don't want you to, 'cause it's not right.'

'I know you know,' he said. 'That we're doing our best. You have to believe you can get out of a rut, that you're not doomed to spend all your life in it. It's a hard climb, sometimes, and, well, sometimes you wish someone could just give you a push. That's all it'd take. Up and out, eh?' He fell silent again, while the darkness seeped in around us, then he sighed. 'Your mother's better at this than I am. If words were tools . . .'

'You'd fix the world,' I finished, grinning. 'I'm, uh, sorry about the fight.'

'No. You do what you have to do. No apologies, you said. Let's make that go both ways.'

'Really?'

'Yeah. Let me go in and talk to your mom first, though.'

'I guess she's pretty mad, huh?'

He clapped a hand on my shoulder. 'It's not as bad as you think. Oh, she's mad, but not at you.'

I didn't want him to leave just yet. 'So, when are you going to start this up?'

He paused on the steps. 'Tried. Wouldn't go. Needs some fine-tuning, I guess.'

I let out a long breath. He couldn't know, but what he'd just told me, so casual and unmindful, had left me feeling crushed. I didn't know why – it was just some old machine, after all. He'd get it started soon, I was sure. But I felt myself trembling.

Father climbed the steps, then stopped at the door. 'Oh yeah,' he said, 'your mother's entertaining tonight, so be on your best behaviour.'

I stared at his dim form, realising that my mouth was open. 'Entertaining? Who?'

'Jennifer. She came by earlier, told us her version of what happened. Told us about this Gary boy. Her and your mom have been having a long talk, about lots of things.'

'Oh my God,' I said.

He laughed. 'Throw a tarp over that thing then come inside.'

They sat in the living room like old friends. William had planted himself on Jennifer's lap and looked like a king on his throne, his face flushed with glory.

I don't blame him.

'Hungry, Owen?' Mother asked from her chair. Her eyes glittered, as if she were seeing me for the first time. In a new way, a terrible, enlightened and bold new way. 'There's banana bread in the kitchen,' she said. 'You can eat in here, if you like.'

God, I don't have any choice, do I? Look at them, the cups of coffee on the table, the full ashtray, the crumpled napkins and the plates with crumbs on them, the stockinged feet. Jennifer had gone home to change. She was wearing a dress, looking beautiful and . . . *appalling.* 'Um, sure,' I managed. 'I'll be right back.'

In the kitchen I stood by the sink, staring at the oven and wishing I could crawl inside it. Instead, I cut a slice of banana bread, mixed up a glass of chocolate milk, found a napkin in a drawer, and returned to the living room. Father had disappeared, of course. *Probably in the oven.*

'Where's Debbie and Tanya?' I asked, not really interested in knowing, but needing something harmless to say.

'Debbie's giving her a bath,' Mother said. 'Come and sit down, Owen. No, on the sofa, beside your girlfriend. Not on the other end, beside her. There, now. So tell us what happened during your detention. Did you pass the maths test?'

'No test,' I said. 'Miss Rhide just asked me lots of questions.'

Mother raised an eyebrow. She reached for her cigarettes. 'About . . . *Goldfinger?*'

I glared at Jennifer. 'Yeah, sorta.'

'No, no, Owen. I want to get an idea of who Miss

Rhide is. You're saying she criticised your choice of reading material?'

'Well, I haven't really read *Goldfinger*—'

Mother laughed. 'Heaven forbid! In fact, you're reading a translation of some Greek historian right now, aren't you?'

She'd been in my room, obviously. I knew I was scowling. 'Plutarch,' I said. 'I finished that one.'

Jennifer turned to me. 'Why didn't you tell that to Rhide? Her hair would've fallen out! Owen!'

Chastised by my girlfriend, teased by my mother. I was in hell.

'I know why,' Mother said, smiling at Jennifer. 'One thing it's important to understand about Owen here. He likes not to be noticed. He's not shy. He just doesn't like being the centre of attention.'

'Pussy Galore?' Jennifer laughed.

'Oh my,' Mother said, sighing.

'But I know what you mean,' Jennifer continued. 'He can't take pictures if he's the centre of attention, can he?'

'Exactly. You're very sharp, Jennifer.'

'Common interest, I guess.'

They both looked at me. 'Cut it out,' I snapped, my face burning. 'Look, you're making Willie squirm – he doesn't like being ignored.'

Mother's expression changed sharply, now serious. 'Read whatever you want, Owen.'

'I will. She's just a teacher.'

'Exactly.'

'More coffee, Jennifer?'

I settled in for a long night.

* * *

'Where's Lynk?' I asked.

Roland shrugged.

I hesitated, feeling the hot sun on my shoulders through the t-shirt. Insects buzzed in the dry air, low over the tar- and oil-spattered ground. Behind us rose the boat-shed wall, its fresh tar glistening and dotted with dead and dying butterflies.

'So,' Roland said, shrugging again, 'are we going?'

'Lynk should be here. He'll just say we're lying.'

'But we'll know,' Roland said, his eyes strangely flat.

'All right,' I said.

We headed into the brush. I found myself in the lead, taking the trail that angled towards the river. The way was harder this time. Bushes and weeds snagged the path. I clawed strands of spider's web from my face. The midday light broke through when we neared the river.

The current matched our pace. Individual swirls spun with us, bits of wood, puffs of seeds from flowers. Watching it made me dizzy, as if the forest were doing the marching, away, away from the place we sought.

The clay underfoot was cracked, geometric, the fissures sprouting bright green blades of grass.

'Owen.'

I stopped, turned.

Roland slid his hands into the pockets of his jeans, looked inland. For a moment he reminded me of Carl.

'What?'

'I don't know. What do you think we'll find?'

'Bones.'

'Just bones,' he nodded, taking a deep breath, puffing his cheeks as he let the air out. 'Big ones, I guess, eh?'

'Maybe. I guess. Do you think we should've brought Carl, at least?'

He gave me an odd look. 'Couldn't find him.'

'Let's go,' I said.

We came to the thicket, now impenetrable with leaves, vines and thorns. Just beyond it was the lodge. I angled us inland, around the barrier. There was no wind, just the lap of water, the whine of insects. Mosquitoes spun around me, slow in the heat. I slapped one on my arm.

Something crashed through the bushes on the other side of the beaver lodge.

I stopped.

'What was that?' Roland's voice was harsh and close.

I shook my head. 'Don't know. A deer, maybe.' I listened. 'Anyway, it's gone.'

I'd thought there'd be darkness in the air, magic and ghostly. The sound of something running away should have filled me with terror – the giant's spirit, haunting, heavy-footed with remembered weight. But even this image triggered nothing. It was as if the world's wonder had died.

We came to the beaver lodge.

'Shit,' Roland said.

There was nothing. The body was gone.

'Lynk,' I said.

'He was lying. He's never come back here. No way, Owen.' He took a couple of steps closer, bent down and studied the tangle of gnawed sticks where the body had been. 'But maybe somebody else found it.'

'We'd have heard,' I said. 'Wouldn't we?'

'Yeah, I guess. It might have fallen back into the river.'

I laughed. 'Maybe it never existed at all. Just a trick of the light. A dead beaver, all its fur gone. A deer, a bear.'

'Well,' Roland said, straightening, 'a skinned bear looks a lot like a person, except for the head and the paws, but if you cut those off . . . it's close.' He paused, squinting, then shook his head. 'No, it was a body. A man.'

'I know,' I said.

He sat down on a log. I sat as well, leaning against a stump.

'It feels all wrong,' Roland said.

'What does?'

He shrugged. 'The whole thing. It's been in my brain, you know. Always there, and I go around and around it, all the time. It's like . . .' He shook his head, eyes on the ground, falling silent.

'It's like he's in a phone booth,' I said. 'Taking up all the space, but you're in there with him, moving around between him and the sides, looking for the door only there isn't one.'

'Shit, yeah. That's it. My head's a phone booth—'

'With a dead man inside it.'

He paled, looked out over the river.

'You're thinking we should've called the cops,' I said.

'No. Well, only when I, uh . . .'

'Get scared.'

'Yeah. But it's ours. Or it was, anyway.'

'Still is,' I said. 'We saw it. He's still there, like you said, in our heads. You, me, and Lynk.'

'Carl.'

'Yeah, Carl, too.' I picked up a stick, flung it into the river, watched it twist away. 'So, in a way, he's not dead any more.'

Roland's head snapped around, his eyes wide.

I met his gaze for a long moment, then found another stick.

'So which one is he?' Roland asked.

Which? 'All of us, maybe. In different ways.' I thought about what I'd said, wondered where the idea had come from. I thought about Lynk – he was going wild, like I always knew he would, only more than I'd ever imagined. As if the dead man was in him, fighting to get out, fighting to be anything but dead. A man drowning, endlessly drowning. Something cold touched me, the thought of eternal panic.

'That's what happened to it,' Roland said in a strange, tight voice.

I looked at him. 'What?'

'Why the body's gone. It came with us, Owen.'

I broke the stick in my hands. 'That's impossible, Roland.'

'I know.' He hesitated, then said, 'Your folks got money? You rich?'

I shook my head. 'No.'

'You poor? We're poor, even with the farm. We've always been poor.'

I nodded. 'Us, too.'

'It's like there's something wrong with us.'

I kept nodding.

'Is there? Owen?'

'Yes,' I said.

'What? What's wrong with us?'

'What's outside,' I said, 'doesn't match what's inside. That's what's wrong with us. We're always acting like everything's all right. Like everything's going to be fine, but it never happens. We never get there, to where everything's fine. But we keep pretending. What else can we do?' I threw both sticks into the river. 'It's all around us, all those people who've got money. They don't seem so different, but they are – you can see it when they look at you.'

Roland sighed. 'It makes me tired all the time.'

'It makes everyone tired all the time,' I said. 'My parents – they're always tired, because they're always trying so hard to make things seem normal. Now that Jennifer's there . . .'

'What do you mean?'

'It's almost desperate, how everything's focused on her. You see, she's got it worse, back home, I mean—'

'I know.'

'She told you? What did she tell you? When?'

'I just know.'

'She doesn't tell me anything!'

'You just said—'

'I was guessing,' I snapped.

'What should we tell Lynk?' Roland asked.

'About what?'

'The body, Owen. If we tell him it's gone, like he said—'

'What'll he do?'

'I don't know, really. He'll think he's won, I guess.'

'Won what?'

'I don't know.'

'Well, he's *your* friend, Roland.'

He scowled. 'I can't help it. We grew up together. I got used to explaining. For him, for the stuff he did. I held him back, too. Used to be we were always together, and I could talk him out of things. We broke into the school once, then he wanted to burn it down. I talked him out of it.'

'Burn it down? It's his favourite place!'

'He's always been like that. He's good at pretending. People don't like believing he's done stuff, and I used to lie for him, too, so he always got away with it. He's good at doing stuff then getting away. And Rhide's stupider than most—'

'She's not stupid. She *wants* to believe Lynk. There's a difference.'

'Maybe. Anyway, you got to watch out for him. He gets people.'

'Why?'

'Because that's what he does.'

'But not to you.'

'Maybe,' Roland said, stretching a leg out and plucking at the threads around a hole in his jeans. 'It's changed. He doesn't need me any more. Not to explain, or lie, or anything.'

Roland sounded sad. He'd lost a friend, I realised. 'He was using you,' I said.

He nodded.

I stood. 'I wonder where the beavers went?'

Roland climbed to his feet. 'Hiding, maybe, or out on the river.'

'It looks bigger.'

'Yeah.'

'Let's go. We don't tell Lynk. Not anything.'

'Yeah. Okay.'

CHAPTER FIFTEEN

I

THE RAINS FINALLY came, in sheets the colour of lead, in torrents that made the earth run blind. The rains came, making the world sightless for a time, and Gribbs no longer felt alone.

'Pour the water on to the tea,' Owen recited. 'Right?'

'That's culture you're learning, my boy,' Gribbs said. The chair creaked under him as he settled back, his eyes closing. 'There's ways to do things. Ignorance is no excuse.'

'That's what my teacher keeps saying. Of course, she doesn't know anything.'

Gribbs laughed quietly. 'You're too damn sharp for me. But you've got an appreciative audience here.'

Owen brought him his tea, then sat down on the wooden crate.

Water leaked through the roof in a dozen places,

splashing lightly into the pots and pans Owen had placed. Like the buzz of a million wasps, the rain surrounded the shack with an insistent, overwhelming noise. The air had cooled, but not enough. There was thunder and lightning on the way, a monstrous front raised up in the middle of the continent, on the prairie that had once been a sea. Above it, the sky swelled, swirled and rumbled with the memory of those ancient waves. She was on her way.

'The river's gonna flood, do you think?'

Gribbs shrugged. 'Might. Depends on how fast and how much. Mind you, it was awfully low.'

'I was wondering about that beaver lodge. We were out there a few days ago. It's huge, bigger than ever. But we didn't see any beavers or muskrats.' He paused. 'We didn't see anything at all.'

'Wouldn't worry. It's not going to float away or anything.'

'They'll be hibernating soon, I guess.'

'Beavers don't hibernate,' Gribbs said, sipping his tea.

'Really? Oh. Then they just swim under the ice and stuff?'

'Yep.'

Owen didn't speak for a time. The pouring rain continued to hammer on the roof, the sound filling the void of words. Gribbs massaged his left arm, kneading the muscles to work out the dull ache that had settled there over the past month or so. 'You're a bit down, aren't you?' he finally said. 'School's that bad, is it?'

'Nothing I can make out, but something about it, something about my teacher, I guess.'

'Don't get along, huh?'

'No. I don't know why. She's nice enough, I suppose. It's only been a month. Maybe I just haven't got used to things there. Maybe that's it.'

'What are you reading these days?'

'Not much. Rhide wants us to write instead. After Christmas we'll be reading a book called *The Steven Truscott Story* – I think that's what it's called.'

'How can you write when you don't read?' Gribbs demanded. 'Bloody ass backwards, if you ask me. What about the stuff you read on your own?'

'Not much. I've got all this homework every night. Maths. I don't get maths at all. It's pretty frustrating.'

'Can't help you there,' Gribbs laughed, trying hard to dismiss the unease that answered Owen's words. Something was wrong; something was happening.

'Jennifer helps,' Owen said. 'It's easy for her.'

'She sounds like quite a girl. I'd like to meet her some time.'

'Sure. She doesn't get along with most grown-ups, except for my mom. But I know she'd like you, and you'd like her.'

'I do already, from what you've told me. You've fallen hard, eh?'

'Well, Rhide hates her, picks on her all the time. She gets detention for the littlest things, but never the same days as me. We don't get to see much of each other after school. Except for weekends, of course. What do you know about her parents? Anything?'

Gribbs leaned his head back, his eyes still closed. 'A story there,' he said. 'A sad, sad story. Sometimes Sig Fraser comes by – or used to, been a couple years since

I last saw him. Sig told me what he'd heard about Sten—'

'Sig, that's Roland's dad.'

'Right.'

'Well, what's the story?'

Gribbs hesitated. 'Jennifer's said nothing?'

'No. I haven't even met them. I've never even been in the house. Rhide acts like she knows something – she uses it, too.'

'Christ,' Gribbs said. 'Well, I've got to respect Jennifer's desire for privacy, Owen. Though she really should talk. She may think she knows everything, but she probably doesn't.'

'Wait,' Owen said. 'I changed my mind. I don't want to know anything more.'

'Good choice. Knowing's not always the same as understanding, anyway. And understanding doesn't always come easy, and even when you come to it, it doesn't always mean you can just excuse things. We each have to take responsibility sooner or later.'

'Rhide says she's responsible for how we behave. She says we share that. Not just her, but everyone – all the grown-ups in all the world. That's why it's not good to misbehave, because it hurts the grown-ups.'

'You believe her?' Gribbs asked softly.

'It's not an opinion. It's just the way it is. That's what we've got to learn, so things will be better when we're all grown up. It'll be our job to make things better.'

'Any tea left, Owen?'

'Sure. Hold your cup out.'

The pot's neck clinked on Gribbs's cup. He listened to Owen's soft breathing as the tea was poured, reached out and found Owen's other arm. He stared up at the blur of the boy's face. 'Please, son,' he whispered, his voice ragged. 'There's something inside you – it's what you look at when you look inside yourself. I know – it's drowning, I can hear it in your voice. But please, don't let it die. Please, Owen, don't.' He released his grip, fell back, exhausted, ignoring the sudden welling of tears. 'Everything's opinion,' he said, 'when it comes to how you should live. Everything. For God's sake, make up your own mind – why won't they let you do that? Why?'

Owen's voice was gentle – all the more painful to hear. 'I don't know,' he said. 'Um, I'll try. What you said. I'll try, Walter.'

Was it just his own private darkening world, or was the boy in front of him fading away? *Too old, too tired. What can I do? How can I get him out of here, out of that school? What am I trying to do anyway? I can't fight his battles. I shouldn't try, either. But there must be something.*

'I'm sorry,' Owen said, 'if I upset you.'

'No, no.' Gribbs shook his head, wincing at the worsening pain in his arm. 'It's me, Owen. Don't worry about it. Go and sit yourself down, or you can go if you like, if I've frightened you.'

The wooden crate creaked. 'I'll stay a while longer, if you want me to.'

Gribbs wiped at his cheeks. 'I'd like that. I guess nobody else knows just how generous you can be.'

'Jennifer,' Owen said.

Gribbs felt his humour return. He smiled. 'Most

men find *that* the hardest thing to be generous with, son. Don't ever get cold. Stay warm. Always.'

'I've got no choice. She's in charge.'

He couldn't help but laugh. The pain in his arm fell away. 'Son, you've just discovered the secret of the world. Of course they're in charge. They all are.'

'I don't mind,' Owen said. 'It's fun.'

'Hah! Well, that's the other secret, isn't it?'

They were silent for a long while, while the rain whispered down outside. Walter felt his thoughts spiralling inward, was unable to stop their dark plummet. *I can see the ship. Coming closer. Fear. Is this the boy? Will he be there, at the door, at the damned prow? Oh God, not him, not this one.*

He'll see my face – that boy burning bright. It'll break him, send him over an edge. Whatever secret he's keeping behind his eyes – it'll come out. He'll see my face, I'll see his. No, please, not this boy.

'You've got a secret,' Walter said. 'Holding it a long time, since we met, I'd say.' He suddenly felt very tired. 'I wish you'd tell me, Owen. It might make it . . . easier.'

Owen said nothing for a half-dozen breaths; when he spoke there was a shrug in his tone. 'You said you were going to tell me, too.'

'What?'

'The Ship of Nails.'

Walter looked away, squinted at the wall – a greyish blur. 'Now, that wouldn't be fair of me. I thought about it, Owen. But . . . it's a story you'd better discover yourself. On your own. It'll come when it's time for it to come.'

'I can't,' Owen said. 'I promised.'

'But you're regretting that promise. Some secrets aren't safe to keep, aren't healthy, I mean. Is it that kind of secret?' A shaft of pain lanced through his arm, faded, left him trembling.

'I promised.'

Walter sighed. 'Fair enough.'

II

Jennifer was caught after lunch. Owen had been with her – not smoking too, just with her. They'd both looked flushed, as if there'd been more going on.

My God, he's only twelve! Joanne felt the smallness of his arm in her grip as she marched him to the conference room. She'd deal with Jennifer afterwards. Owen was far more important. *I'm effecting a change in him. He's coming around. Damn that girl!*

They strode into the room. Joanne shut the door, still holding Owen's arm. She regretted the roughness of her actions, but it was necessary to show him just how disappointed she was. She sat him down in a chair then positioned herself on the table edge, close to him, close enough that he couldn't raise his walls. She looked down at him. He had his eyes on the opposite wall. He scratched his nose.

'Look at me,' Joanne commanded.

He did, a nervous flitter in his eyes. *No longer the icy regard. No, he's learning. About consequences. About behaviour that will not be tolerated.*

She studied him a moment longer, then sighed. 'What are we going to do with you, Owen?'

He shrugged, but the old defensive gesture wouldn't work this time. She'd show him that.

'You insist on remaining friends with a very troubled girl. Not to help her, of course, but precisely because she's troubled. You've set her influence against mine, but let me tell you, it's an unequal battle. She has nothing good to offer you. She can't prepare you for the adult world. She doesn't nurture you – your strengths, your qualities, the many positive things that I can see in you. No, only the negative. That path, Owen, will lead you to ruin. Are you listening?'

'Yes.'

'Good. Look at your friend, Lynk – it wasn't you who gave him that black eye, was it?'

'No.'

'He *is* your friend, isn't he?'

'Sort of, I guess.'

'He's my finest student. He's excelling in every way. He's the one you should turn to as a positive example of how to behave.'

Owen's eyes flashed. 'Lynk's fooling you—'

'No–he–isn't!' Joanne almost shouted, punctuating each word with a palm on the table.

Owen jumped in alarm, his eyes widening.

She leaned close and spoke softly but firmly. 'No he isn't,' she repeated. 'Do you think I was born yesterday? I cannot, simply cannot, tell you how disappointed I am in you, Owen. I truly believed we were making progress. Is it back to square one with us, Owen? Is it?'

He looked down at the table. 'No,' he said.

'I'm glad to hear that. There'll be detention, of

course. Monday afternoon. Not today. And finally, I will have to call your parents. As you know, the parent-teacher interviews are coming soon. I'd like to be able to tell them just how much you've improved. I'd like to tell them what I'll be telling Lynk's parents – that you're one of my best students.'

'Yes, Miss Rhide.'

'Do you understand just how disappointed I am? Do you realise that we shouldn't have to be like this? Do you finally see that Jennifer is not the kind of companion for you? We don't want to lose you, Owen. It's not too late, but we're quickly running out of time, and patience.'

'Yes.'

'Very good. Now, return to the class and please inform Principal Thompson that I'll be there shortly, after I've dealt with Jennifer.'

'Yes, Miss Rhide.'

'Tell the secretary to send Jennifer in.'

She moved aside to let him rise from the chair, and watched as he quickly left the room. *So small, so young, so very important to us. They all are, of course. With one exception – I'm being realistic in this, aren't I? Just being realistic. She'll end up a druggie, an alcoholic. It happens. Some are beyond our reach.*

The door opened and Jennifer strolled in. *No bra. I'll comment on that when I call her mother – little good it'll do.*

'Sit down, Jennifer.' Joanne went to the far end of the table, sat in the swivel chair where Barry usually sat. 'Look at me, Jennifer.'

'Get real.'

'Very well, if that's how it's going to be. I am authorised to tell you that if you are caught smoking on school grounds again, you will be suspended for one week. If you persist after that, we will have to expel you.'

Jennifer looked over and slowly raised an eyebrow. 'It was the smoking?' she asked. 'I thought it was because I let Owen cop a feel. I thought it was against the rules to get wet on school grounds. Against the rules for Owen's prick to get hard. On school grounds. It's just the smoking? Oh, well, what a relief.'

Joanne stared, feeling the colour rise in her, feeling her fingertips getting cold. 'He's only twelve!' she said, almost pleading.

Jennifer grinned. 'It came early.'

'But this is corrup—' She stopped, bit back the word. *Corruption. Mother would say that. Her word. I'm not supposed to use it. Teachers don't use that word.* Jennifer was coolly eyeing her, as if trying to read her thoughts. That searching look made her furious. 'Now listen, Jennifer! Stop looking so superior. You're not. You're a bad, a disgusting influence in my class – in this school. Don't you dare look at me that way – don't you dare!' She realised she'd screamed those last words. In the office beyond the door the typewriter went silent. Joanne took a deep breath.

Jennifer seemed to have wilted under that last assault. *Good.*

'Clearly,' Joanne said in a quieter tone, 'you don't understand what it is to be a proper girl. I know, the influences on your life have been terrible – but you're old enough to choose new influences now. You don't have to choose to drink—'

'Drink? I don't—'

'Quiet! You don't have to choose to act like a . . . a slut – I don't like that word, but it fits, I'm afraid. You don't have to repeat your parents' mistakes, or their failures—'

'My mother's not a slut,' Jennifer said.

'Of course not. I didn't mean to imply—'

'Maybe not on purpose—'

'Stop interrupting me!'

'Is your period overdue or something?' Jennifer asked. 'Still a virgin, are you? That's too bad. Did your father cheat on your mother? Did—'

'How dare you talk to me like this?'

'The same way you just did, you fucking bitch. Didn't like it? Well, I didn't either. So now we're even. So either suspend me or can we go back to class? Barry Thompson's bound to be wringing their necks by now, and you'll be responsible if it happens. Oh my,' she sang shrilly. 'Whatever will we do?' She rose, her eyes narrowing. 'Aren't you just so very angry, Miss Rhide? So very, very angry. I know this doctor – he's perfect, a catch. He's so very, very caring. Should I call him, make introductions?'

Joanne also stood. 'One more word—'

'And what? You think Mrs Reynolds couldn't hear every word you said? You're a banshee, just like Owen said. What else did he call you? Well, never mind. Too obscure for you, anyway. You and me, Miss Rhide, don't you get it? You want me to be just like you – is that my future? Are you my future? Well, no offence, but fuck that. And you – you want to be just like me – a part of you does, anyway, the hungry part. Well, keep on dreaming, Rhide, it's all you've got and all you'll ever get.' She paused, trying to regain her breath.

Joanne could only watch, helpless, unable to defend herself. She remembered Marianne Obell's words: *Watch out, Joanne. She's exceptional. She's a razor, a goddamned razor.*

Jennifer continued, 'Ask the secretary out there. We're not the only angry ones. Ask my mother. Now show me something worth being. Hell, since you've made yourself God, show us all, Miss Rhide. Wave your hand and wipe the anger away, from everyone, for all time. If you can't, then shut the fuck up and stay out of my way.' She whirled and rushed from the room.

Joanne heard Mrs Reynolds call out, 'Jenny! Wait! Please—' Then the outer door slammed.

Joanne slowly sat down. She was shaking, trembling. She felt like she was going to vomit. Mrs Reynolds appeared at the door, her gaze like flint. 'I'll get you a glass of water,' she said.

'Thank you,' Joanne whispered. 'I'm sorry, Jill.'

The older woman stared down at her. 'It's a start,' she said, then left.

III

Jennifer made her way to her chair. Thompson stopped his bored lecture on the fur trade and watched as she sat down.

'And Miss Rhide?' he asked.

She shrugged. 'I didn't kill her, if that's what you're asking.'

There was a brief tug at the corner of his mouth, then he swung his back to the class and began wiping his notes from the blackboard.

Jennifer looked over at Owen. He mouthed the word *bitch,* jerking his head towards the office. She nodded, then sighed and looked down at her hands on the desktop. She'd almost cried, standing by the outer doors with the endless rain ripping down just a few feet away. *Got to me. Never again, Rhide. Go to hell, go to fucking hell.* She'd smoked a cigarette, and that had calmed her down. *Almost cried. Fuck you, Rhide.* Detention, phone calls, letters – she knew she was under attack. The year ahead stretched out in front of her mind's eye like a road of broken glass. *Still, just a year, a winter, one winter. She'll go away, like a rash of zits. A temporary torture.*

Barb leaned towards her. 'How'd it go?' she whispered.

'Piece of cake,' Jennifer hissed back.

Miss Rhide strode stiffly to the head of the class. Thompson handed her the chalk then leaned close as she whispered a few words. The man frowned, studied Rhide searchingly, then, looking troubled, left for his office.

'Well! Sorry for the delay.' She tried to smile enthusiastically, but it came out as a grimace. 'I believe you were learning about the fur trade . . .'

Detention over, Mr Lyle's expression revealed as he finished marking her test. He was a pale-skinned, dark-haired man, always wearing suits in shades of green. Tough as nails, but fair, never malicious.

'You know,' he said, rising from behind his desk, 'I'm having to write up special tests just for you, Jennifer.'

'Sorry for the extra work.'

'Oh no, it's becoming a real challenge. I haven't even taught you this algebra yet. It's really very impressive. You definitely have a talent.'

Jennifer scowled. 'Mr Lyle, you know you're not supposed to tell me things like that.'

He sat on his desk, looking tired after a long day. 'You don't get told often enough, I think.'

'Is that the problem, then?'

'You tell me.'

She fell silent.

'Well, then,' he said, standing. 'You can go. But Jennifer, if you ever want to talk to someone, I'll listen. No lectures, I mean. Just listen. You've got some people here pulling for you, you know.'

She couldn't meet his eyes. His words echoed inside, piling up, filling spaces that had been empty for so long. *Only Owen's done that. Only him.*

'Get your coat on,' he said, shrugging into his olive raincoat. 'I'll drop you off. No point in getting soaked.'

'Oh, that's okay. I can walk. It's not far.'

'How about the top of the road, then? Halfway, as it were.'

'All right. Thanks.'

'Don't know about you,' he said as he collected his leather briefcase, 'but I'm dying for a smoke.'

The drive to the turn-off was a short one. 'Are you sure you don't want me to take you the rest of the way?' Mr Lyle asked.

'That's all right,' Jennifer said, opening the door. 'I like rain, anyway.'

'See you Monday, then.'

'Bye.' She stepped outside, closed the door then

waved. The teacher pulled the car back on to the high-way.

She crossed to the other side, feeling the rain soak into her clothes and through her hair. It felt cleansing, life-giving. The day had left her shaken, wrung out. She would have liked to have met Owen right now – she hoped he'd held out against Rhide better than she'd done, that he'd gone away unscathed, not wounded and still bleeding. And the thought of going home, back into that shadow game, the smoke and mirrors still being played for Roulston and Queen Anne's ben-efit, filled her with dread. Her house ticked like a bomb, and the fuse smouldered behind her father's placid smile.

Someone was in the bus shack near the turn-off. She saw a boy's legs, the jeans wet, the sneakers cov-ered in mud. Thinking it might be Owen, she headed over. As she came around the side she saw that it was Lynk.

He had a chrome lighter in his hands. A pile of crumpled newspaper smoked under the bench in one corner. Startled, he looked up.

'What the fuck do you want?' he asked, flicking the lighter.

'Nothing.' Jennifer turned to go.

'Hey!' Lynk said.

His cheek was still blue under one eye, making him look like a sad dog.

She said, 'What?'

'Want to neck or something?'

'You're dreaming—'

He sat up, flicking the lighter back on. 'Why the fuck not? I won't tell.'

She turned away again.

'Come on, you slut! I'll feel you up. You like that, don't you?'

Slut. That's what I am, isn't it? What Rhide called me. I wouldn't have to go home. Not right away. He can play with my tits. That's what they're there for, anyway. Roland's played with them, too. And Owen. And Mark and Dave and Mark's kid brother – what was his name? He sucked on them like a baby, then he started crying when his brother and the others started teasing him. I'd been stoned. We'd got the kid stoned, too – what was his name? I kept putting my cigarette into his mouth – he was so out of it he didn't even cough. Mark said later his brother was hooked now – on everything. He was eight, or nine. Maybe even seven – can't even remember his name.

Slut. Slut slut slut. She pulled out her cigarettes. 'Give me a light,' she said, sitting down beside him.

His hand was shaking so she had to take it in both of hers to light the cigarette. 'You can't make it obvious,' she said. 'Some cars go by slow – I don't want anybody to see.'

'No way,' he laughed. 'With this rain, nobody can see anything.'

He reached over and cupped one of her breasts. The nipple was already hard, with the wet and chill, but she heard her own breath quicken. 'Twist it,' she said. 'The nipple. Twist it hard.'

Awkwardly, Lynk moved closer, then pushed his mouth against hers.

She punched at his chest, drove him away. His eyes were wide.

'What the fuck?' he said.

Jennifer felt like crying. 'No kissing,' she said.

'What the fuck's the matter?' he demanded. 'We're supposed to be necking, you bitch.' He set his hand against her breast again and pinched the nipple.

She pushed him away. 'Fuck off. I changed my mind.' She stood, started buttoning up her jean jacket.

'I can do it as good as Owen,' Lynk said, his face red. 'Better. You said we'd neck. I want to cop a feel. Come on, I'll put my finger in you – you like that, don't you? All girls like that.'

'How would you know?' Jennifer said with a harsh laugh. 'You don't know shit.'

He grabbed her, pulled her around.

She punched him in the face. He sat back down heavily, putting both hands against his nose as the blood streamed down.

'Bastard!' Jennifer hissed.

'I'm telling Owen,' he said, his voice muffled.

'You do that, and I'll tell everyone how a girl beat you up, gave you a new black eye.'

'Fuck off.'

She left him sitting there. She lifted her face to the sky and let the rain shower over it, the water running down her neck, down between her breasts.

Why did I let him do that? Just because that's how it always happens? Some shithead wants a handful of my tit. I let him, pretending I don't care, only thinking about the way it feels. Just wanting to feel good for a change. To close my eyes and listen to the guy's breathing, to his gasps and grunts as he loses control. Then a private smile. Took out another one, another one looking shamefaced and unable to meet the calm knowl-

edge in my eyes. But they all want me, and it's good feeling wanted.

And yet, Jennifer knew that what they wanted wasn't really her. Just parts of her. For so long, it had seemed like she wasn't supposed to expect anything more. Nothing else counted, nothing else mattered. She'd been unable to believe that there could be more to things. *Use me, and I'll use you back. We'll call it 'going together', until we get tired of each other, until you want someone else to use, and I want someone else to use. Like Owen.*

She felt dirty inside. She'd betrayed Owen, and punching Lynk in the nose wouldn't change that. *A slut.* Rhide was right.

But I don't like it any more. I can't be that way. I don't want to. Owen's mother said that Owen was lucky to have me as his girlfriend. She might have to change her mind, but I don't want her to, I want to be what she wants me to be. Never again. It's over. Lynk showed me that.

She decided to visit Owen later, come to the house. He'd squirm, but she liked his mother, and they had fun talking, teasing Owen, acting like sisters sometimes. And Debbie might come downstairs and they'd all smoke and gab away, until Owen managed to make his escape, then they'd talk about him, but more privately, and talk about other things, too. And she'd complain about Rhide.

If only Rhide left us alone. It's none of her business, the bitch. She acts like it's a love triangle or something. Weird, sick, the way she acts. She's the 'good' influence. I'm the 'bad'. It's that simple for her, but it isn't for me. Owen's smart. He should be doing good, he should like school – that's not my fault. It's like Rhide's draining him. Like a goddamned vampire. It's like he's shutting down inside – Christ, I think that's what scares me the most. Not me – I'm a lost cause. But Owen, what's happening to Owen. Something's wrong.

Maybe she'd talk about that.

Still, she felt dirty inside. She wasn't sure if she could face anyone tonight. She needed to be alone. She needed to think.

Jennifer walked up the muddy driveway. The dogs were lined up along the wire fence that was visible from the front yard, and started barking as soon as they saw her. They were soaked, the fur matted down, making them darker, more frightening.

They look like Max.

She hurried to the door and quickly went inside. As she closed the door she heard the rumble of thunder, and the dogs howled in answer.

IV

Silent, Gribbs lay in his cot. The lightning flashes blossomed in dull motes through the darkness that now shrouded his sight.

She'd pushed through, the only one left who could now. A last answer to his unseeing eyes. She was out there, she told him. She'd finally arrived.

He'd waited for so long, but now he was afraid. He wished he could strip the years away, be young again, with the world stretched out in front of him. He thought of the old woman in Istanbul, and saw clearly – for the first time – how they now reflected each other. A final night in a dilapidated shack, betrayed by the flesh that had carried them faithfully for so long. With the last story lost, still to be played out.

He wished he'd gone out like the Dane. Something as deliberate, something that was itself a statement, an heroic embrace. Instead, here he was, huddled under the blankets, cowering as she cracked through the black sky somewhere overhead.

Earth's own blanket. I should've heeded the Dane's decision, the boldly inscribed reasons that took him, step by step, so measured and certain, into that end. And the old woman, writ as she was in the flesh, both glory and decay, she made fire her final blanket, the smoke gathering under the roof, settling black over more ancient smears and smudges, her own layer, her own continuing of the story – I've seen caves just as dark, the walls an eternal folding of lives, one over the other, that spoke of ages and ages. She did the same, there in that house in a forgotten corner of an ancient city. The Dane and her – they'd made themselves part of their own history, gestures without choice, so very fated and seamless and inevitable, so . . . perfect.

But Gribbs had no such luxury. The tradition that called to him rolled unseen in depths thousands of miles away. *Pilgrimage. I'd forgotten, I've rejected my own temple, squandered all these years. Denying the signs. Ignoring the call. And now it's too late.*

Outside, the wind thrummed through branches, trees creaking and swaying. Howls, distant howls, sounded like horns, proclaiming the beginning of something. *What? Can I pretend to be that blind? Can I keep turning away as if, as if unmindful? Too old for that game. Still, the end of a life doesn't necessarily mean a final acceptance, a coming to terms. Dying doesn't insist on a last few minutes of peace. There's no rules, none, none at all.*

V

The smell of cooking filled the house. Jennifer paused just inside the entranceway. *Not porridge, not soup. Roast chicken.* She kicked off her sneakers, peeled the sodden socks from her feet, which were wrinkled and white.

The tap in the kitchen went on, water drumming into the sink. She hesitated, then walked towards the sounds. Her mother was making supper, the way she used to do. Potatoes, greens, chicken, bread rolls. Her father sat at the table, his forearms flat on the red Formica, a glass of beer positioned in the gap between the hands. He looked up blearily as Jennifer entered.

'Decided to talk, Mom?' she asked. 'Come on. The wires are out. Roulston says you can talk. Are you going to say something?'

Her mother shrugged.

The wind battered the sides of the house, the rain rattling like hail. Thunder rolled in from all sides, and the dogs kept howling.

'I'm getting changed,' Jennifer said.

Her father spoke as she turned to go. 'Got a goddamned nother call from your teacher. Goddamned calls us every other fucking day.'

'Should be used to it by now, Daddy.'

'Fuck that. You want us to get in trouble, again? Fucking smarten up, girl.'

Jennifer cocked her head, pretending to think. 'Hmmm,' she said, 'I think I'll call Roulston, or the witch. Daddy's drunk, I'll say. Right here in the kitchen, he's threatening me. Please help us. Please please please!'

'You ain't learned your lesson,' her father growled, his expression dark and ugly.

Her mother turned from the sink, a pot in her hand, her eyes on her husband.

'Your lessons, I mean. That's what the teacher said.'

Jennifer left the room. She headed up the stairs. *Even drunk, he thinks fast. Got to hand it to him. Mom should've brained him anyway. Self-defence, in anticipation of, or whatever. Splashed his brain all over the wall. Tile and Formica's easy to clean. Easy.*

In her room, she stripped out of her wet clothes and lay down naked on the bed. She'd lost her appetite. There was a hit of acid left from her cache. She'd be taking a risk – with the storm outside and the monster prowling motionless under her floor. But there was a lock on her door now. She'd put it there herself, a sliding bolt, and with it in place she felt secure. The flashes of lightning would add to things, provided she was in the right state of mind.

She thought of the hard crunch under her knuckles when she'd punched Lynk. *That felt good. Satisfying. Lynk won't tell. I won't either. I wish Owen would just beat him up and get it over with. Lynk won't start it, though. He'll keep finding other ways. He'll keep using Rhide, and anyone else he can think of. He's scared of Owen. They've got a secret. And he's jealous,* too. *Owen doesn't know that, but I do, now I do. I won't tell.*

She rose and put on an album, then returned to the bed. *Now for the acid.*

The wind broke down the walls, sweeping in not wet but dry and hot, lifting straw and ashes into the air, biting, tearing, stinging on the flesh.

Somewhere outside, beyond the smoke, beyond the trees that now stalked forward, slick and glistening with frost – beyond all this, a fire raged unseen. An inferno, a sea of flame rising higher, getting closer with every moment.

Ghosts swept through the smoke, their fingertips trailing thick threads of blood, their pale heads swept back as they wailed soundlessly at the sky.

The wind rattled the world, twisted the black clouds overhead, drove them down into columns that spun out vapours that clawed the throat, seared the lungs. Thunder pounded, a slow drum that shook the ground.

All at once, the flames were visible through the curtain of smoke, and new sounds, a faint creaking of spars and wind thudding sailcloth. From out of the smoke small, wiry black figures appeared, shedding moss and smouldering earth from their broad, gnarled shoulders. Some crawled on the broken ground. Some danced. Some wallowed and flopped about – every limb broken, their spines twisted.

Pain. Pain in the body now, so much pain, rockets firing inside, along each vein, each artery. A skull ready to burst, but the eyes kept seeing, the eyes couldn't turn away.

Someone was pounding on the door.

The creaking came nearer, a shape grey and silver cut a swath through the roiling smoke.

Lightning, the flashes coming quicker and ever quicker, matching the cavorting pain, the lightning exploding in sheets like a sail above the ship. The smoke parted, tumbled away to reveal a hull of bones, armoured in blood-smeared nails – so implausible, so ghastly. Nails, pared from the fingers of the dead.

Someone pounded on the door.

He stood at the ship's prow, glowing bright, framed there in the doorway. A boy. A man. His eyes were fire inside black circles, and he was smiling, his face streaming with rain. He held broken chains that dangled from his small hands. Wolves fanned out in his wake, furred black and oily, their eyes flashing in the incessant lightning.

The drums pounded on.

Pain everywhere, in each visible face, in each twisting, dancing body, pain in the tortured air and in the stalking, stumbling trees.

He stood in the doorway, shining so very bright. He reached out a hand, let the chain in it slip through, rattle heavily to the floor.

Gribbs screamed as the lightning cracked out, throwing the earth upward, driving the air down. The pain in him flashed in answer, then was gone, and he saw in the growing darkness a huge wheel all afire, geared, mechanistic, tumbling, rolling and bounding down a hill, down and away, its fire getting more distant, falling away, then winking out.

* * *

Someone pounded on the door. Jennifer spun on her bed. She remembered a devastating crash, a sound and feeling that shook everything, and now the world hummed in the aftermath, reverberating with the explosive shock.

'Come on, you bitch!' her father roared drunkenly through the door.

Naked, Jennifer curled up on the bed, her eyes on the sliding bolt that shook and rattled as her father hammered repeatedly with his fist on the door.

The rain spat lightly at the window. The wind falling off. From the highway came the wail of sirens.

Lightning strike. Something's been hit.

'Your mother and me!' her father yelled. 'Are you dead? What was that screaming, girl? Open this fucking door or I'll take a goddamned fucking sledgehammer to it!'

Imps clambered along the walls. Jennifer hissed, 'Go away!' *Max? Where are you? Please, help!* 'Go away!' she screamed.

The imps flung themselves into every crack and corner, disappeared back into the walls, under the floor, into the roof.

Her father fell silent. Another sound was out there, outside the door. Weeping. Her mother.

Jennifer giggled, then fought it down. 'I'm fine,' she said loudly. 'I had a bad, uh, a bad dream. That's all.'

'Open the door, girl,' her father said.

'No. I'll come down in a few minutes.'

'The fucking lock goes,' he growled.

'No,' she snapped. 'I'll tell Roulston! If it goes I'll tell him everything!'

She heard him move away, down the hall, his footsteps uneven.

'It's all right, Mom.'

A moment later Jennifer heard her leave as well.

Fuck!

The bed crackled under her as if the mattress was filled with straw. Her throat was as dry as dust. Things kept shifting in front of her, then settling back. She smelled clover, then cinnamon, then roast chicken.

More sirens on the highway reached her. She uncurled herself, reached for her cigarettes. *Poison in, poison out, that delicious numbing spike, down, down into the chest.*

'Oh, damn!' she hissed. She'd broken a nail.

VI

Saturday morning broke grey and cold. Roland called with the news. I ate a hurried breakfast, pulled on my jean jacket and quickly left the house.

On my way to the highway, I saw Carl up ahead. He'd run a few steps, then walk a few, then run again. I recalled how he'd been in gym class, hopeless at everything, running flat-footed, unable to handle a basketball, hit a volleyball, clumsy and pathetic, picked last on every team.

He got poor grades, too, but I didn't count that against him. Maybe, like me, he wasn't trying, didn't care, had better things to do – like dreaming about primeval jungles and lost cities, and growing up outside humankind, outside civilisation's dulling, ignoble prison. Maybe he too dreamed about freedom.

He had reached the highway by the time I came to the top of the hill. It started to rain again, a light spattering that felt cold against my face. As I passed opposite the overgrown lot I saw that a tree had blown down, its trunk and broken limbs crossing the old driveway. The dust from its rotted core was visible on the mud.

As soon as I reached the highway I could see the damage. Roland, Lynk, Barb and Carl were already there. The candle factory's top floor had been shattered near the front. A savage black streak traced a jagged path down the front of the building, cutting right across the giant geared wheel. Black timbers jutted from the broken corner, and soot stains from the smoke flared up above the second floor's broken windows.

I crossed the highway.

Roland grinned at me. 'Almost went up,' he said. 'But the firemen got here in time. And the rain kept it down, too.'

'Lightning,' Lynk said.

I saw that his shiner had spread to under both eyes now. *Boy, Roland must have hit him hard.* 'No kidding,' I replied.

Roland pointed. 'That's its scar – I heard the lightning turned the stone to glass.'

'Really? Holy shit.'

The fire trucks had rutted the ground in front of the building, leaving behind deep puddles that glistened with soot.

'Here comes Jennifer,' Barb said.

I turned, watched her approach. My heart always sped up whenever I studied her, the way she moved, the shifting of her hips. She had a much better body than my sister, and best of all, she knew just how good it looked.

She came up and wrapped her arms around me, surprising me with a long, deep kiss.

'Whoo!' Barb sang out behind us.

Jennifer pulled back slightly, smiled at me, then stepped to one side, pulling me around with one arm along the small of my back.

We faced the factory again.

Jennifer said, 'I almost hit the ceiling when I heard it.'

'We lost a whole set of china,' Roland said. 'We thought we'd been hit ourselves.'

Jennifer let go of me to take out her cigarettes. She pulled two out and handed one to Barb. After they got them lit, Jennifer settled back against me.

I felt wonderful. I felt owned.

'Wish the whole fucking thing burned,' Lynk said, spitting into a puddle.

Jennifer's laugh seemed to sting him, because he swung his back to us.

I looked up at the building. The lightning streak gleamed dully in the pale light.

CHAPTER SIXTEEN

I

STEN'S PRIDE.

The dogs needed to run. They needed open fields, the ground a blur under them. They needed to run the way a fire needs to burn.

Elouise studied them as she stood at the edge of her garden. The dogs eyed her in turn, tails wagging fitfully, ears cocked, waiting and – more than anything else – wanting.

Wanting to be free. Simple words that should carry more than they did, that shouldn't roll so lightly in her thoughts. The garden was lost. Nothing to harvest, and the air promised an early winter.

Roulston had come by earlier, his usual Sunday morning visit. *Too regular, too easy to plan for. Sten stayed in bed, anyway, pretending to be asleep.* Anne's follow-up report had been inconclusive – the social worker just wasn't sure. She was concerned, especially on Jennifer's behalf. Possible drug use, trouble at school – a deliberate bad influence on other children . . . *and she has a boyfriend. Her first real one – they've been together all summer. I've never even met him. Were they taking drugs together? Had he done that to her or was it the other way around? The school had an opinion.* Miss Rhide, who'd become a part of the family the same way Roulston and Anne had, had invaded them with phone calls, letters, notes sent home with Jennifer.

'There's no reason for this silence,' Roulston had said. 'Not physically, I mean. I understand that it's proved useful, that it's a way of avoiding things, of keeping yourself withdrawn. Tell me, how long will you let others speak for you, Elouise?'

For ever. You don't know my life, Doctor. You don't know anything about me. My grandfather died in the First World War. My father died of cancer when I was ten. My only brother, just a kid, died at Dieppe. My mother's grief killed her from the inside out, as if she'd taken into herself the world's nightmare. I was young and the future was laid out in front of me. Nobody talked about choices. Find a man, a hard-working, decent man. A veteran, if at all possible, one who wouldn't talk of what he'd been through, but one who'd know the difference between right and wrong. A solid, silent man. Then bring forth children. The world needs children, more now than ever. And a mother at home, and new dish soap and minor crises of cleanliness to cope with between the soap operas on television. The world needs women on diets, women with the morning coffee on a tray for their hard-working men. The woman needs to rely on him, just as he relies on her. A partnership in the producing and raising of children and bettering their future.

Money at hand, the struggles now over – together and independent, they would create the next generation, each in their modern homes, with their two cars and the endless highways of opportunity and adventure.

No choice. Expectation was everything. Even though the optimism rang false, the search for the ideal was desperate enough to achieve something like it. The false security of surfaces, of appearances, the pressure – *the horrible, driving pressure, to be as we seemed to be.*

The lie destroyed them. It was only natural for the young people today to reject everything they'd done. The hypocrisy was impossible to ignore.

Jennifer won't be fooled. She won't follow me in life. She's living for herself. She's learned to indulge, she's learned what being young is all about. But . . . but where can she go? The choices are narrowing down, the expectation pushing her from all sides. She's only thirteen. How can she withstand them, how can she keep from buckling?

'Jennifer is the main concern for Family Services,' Roulston had said. 'We have her future to think about. What's happening now will affect the rest of her life. She's in great danger of slipping into the abusive cycle. It's familiar to her, and familiarity is a magnet. She can cope with what she knows – she'll go looking for the same patterns in adult life.'

Elouise could see that. She could see the genuine concern in the young doctor's face. His words made her frightened for Jennifer, and yet a part of her answered him, bitter and sly. *From one cycle into an-*

other. The first one we can all agree is terrible, tragic. The second one – where she breaks away from her family's history – is where you want her. Where she can pretend to be happy, well adjusted to the perfect world of twenty years ago. A solid, dependable husband, a solid, dependable Hoover in hand in woman's war against dust-balls. The preferred cycle, keeping us at home and helpless. She doesn't deserve either, Doctor. What else can you offer?

I saw on the news. Women were burning bras. It was silly, but I cried.

The dogs pawed at the mud alongside the chain-link wall. Kaja – the mother who'd lost a son – *one step from showing just how savage she can be.* She dreamed of the chance to rewrite the past, to defeat the helpless despair of watching Max die under a wheel – with the cage wire wall between her and him. She was muscle and bone and teeth and in her body was the memory of pain – the fire's white-hot core.

Caesar strutted. He always did, these days. When his mother was in heat and penned up in the separate run, he wanted her desperately, but had to settle for Shane instead. The normal, natural horrors of living in a cage.

The back porch door opened and Sten stepped out. He went down the steps, moving loosely, sloppily, and tossed an empty beer bottle under the porch. He straightened and grinned at her.

'God's day of rest,' he said. 'And Hallowe'en's coming. The night of spirits, the worlds overlapping, the souls of the dead returning. Kaja will be . . . delighted, don't you think?'

He walked unsteadily towards her. 'Such a fine garden,' he said, still smiling. 'Nature wins in the end.

Don't you know that, dear? Nature wins and we all revert. The civil façade peels away, the masks and costumes meant to fool the dead, they all come off. It's the naked truth, *hee*, at last. Just the naked truth.'

He was hard, the bulge obvious under his brown work pants. He slipped his hands into the pockets. 'Jennifer's out,' he said. 'We have the house to ourselves. Why not . . . ?'

Elouise shook her head.

Sten scowled. 'Not good enough any more, am I?'

She shook her head again, trying to convey her fear, her doubts, trying to hide her revulsion.

'The dogs want to run,' he said after a moment, turning to them. 'All this . . . inaction. It's against their natures.'

Find a hole in a wall, Sten.

'I heard Roulston, you know.' He faced her again, his eyes hardening. 'He suspects, doesn't he? What did you do, slip him a note? "Help! I'm being held prisoner by an ogre!" Is he climbing into his armour even as we speak? You really think you can get away with it, don't you? Slipping him notes, setting me up. You don't scare me. Roulston doesn't scare me. I've faced worse. A lot worse.' A flash of pure horror racked his face. 'Come Hallowe'en, when the ghosts walk.'

Oh, Sten.

He turned away, shaking his shoulders loose – the way his dogs would do. 'That was my last beer,' he said, then walked back into the house.

Shane yelped. Caesar had him cornered. Their mother watched, just watched. *Sten's pride.*

II

I sat in my secret room. In a few nights it would be Hallowe'en, but I already felt him at my side.

I'd gone to the boat yards a few days after the first storm, to find *Mistress Flight* gone, and the manager, Reggie, overseeing two workmen as they pulled down Walter's shack. Reggie had finally noticed me standing there with my bag of sandwiches in hand.

'You must be Owen Brand,' he said, coming over, his walking stick thumping the ground. 'I'm sorry, son, to be the one with the bad news . . .'

'He's died,' I said.

'You've heard, then?'

I shook my head. I just knew it, a piece of my insides torn away, flung carelessly into the river. *Gone.*

'Heart attack,' Reggie said, watching the front wall coming down. 'The look on his face when I found him . . .' He shivered, the gesture looking exaggerated.

'What?'

'Must've been in a lot of pain before the end, that's all. Of course, he's at peace now. At rest, as they say. The last few months were difficult – you and I both know that. It was hard to watch the decline. Mental and physical, both failing together like that. Hard.'

Mental decline? What is he talking about?

'Generous of you to befriend him at the end, though,' Reggie went on. 'Guess he needed someone to ramble on with. He got pretty carried away with you, with your small gesture. All you had to do was wait, eh?'

'What? I don't—'

Reggie clapped me hard on the shoulder. 'Better get along, son. The club's private property, you know.'

'Where's *Mistress Flight?*'

'Sold. Moved on up the lake. Won't be coming back. Now, I don't want to cause you trouble, but these grounds are off limits, and I mean to enforce the rules. Reggie's rules.'

The chill wind rattled the trees in the yard, draughts gusting through the window joins. A library copy of *Beowulf* sat in front of me. Already a week overdue. The library had had to order it from the university. The book had a translation on one side and the original Anglo-Saxon version on the other. I struggled to read the old language, referring again and again to the pronunciation notes in the introduction. I needed to concentrate on the book and things like it – things that kept all of my mind occupied, distracted. I told myself that Walter was here beside me, as was the stranger who'd once been in this room. And the giant belonged here, as well. I kept telling myself I wasn't alone, but it wasn't a belief, it wasn't a faith. It felt like I was lying to myself, trying hard to make convincing the idea that the world worked that way – that spirits did indeed exist.

But the room was cold, empty except for me, the desk and the books. And the wind that made my hands icy and blue at the fingertips.

I studied that effect on my hands. I was learning to cope in school. Learning to evade, to slip notice, to keep quiet and anonymous. I was learning the right way to answer questions. Things were settling down.

But *Beowulf* delivered different lessons. There were monsters in the world. They lived on hate, survivors of the Flood, children of Lilith or the sons and daughters of Cain, or both. Giants and demons and dragons, each alone and lost in a new world that had no place for them. They were darkness, struggling to hold back the light.

Walter had said to take away the Christian stuff in the poem, because it was probably put there later. *Go back to the story's own world. You'll be able to read it right, once you do that. It's not what it seems . . .*

Well, I knew that *that* held for everything, but I couldn't manage that discovery in the poem. If not Cain's brood, then what? Where did the monsters come from? Why were they cursed, so full of spite and hunger? *Just atavisms, maybe, throwbacks to what we once were. But dragons?*

I'd met the creature. It still lived, despite Beowulf's final self-sacrifice. And what I knew of it from that meeting made the entire poem different. I'd rather the hero failed completely. I wanted to reject this version. It was like Beowulf had killed me.

Walter had believed in dragons, too. The ones that lived in the seas, in the depths where the light never reached. There, the monsters had won their war. I envied them, cheered them on, fervently hoped that they really did exist.

Sometimes, I wanted to believe, the light must fail.

Snowflakes sped down on the wind, melting as soon as they touched the earth. I could hear the steady flap of the machine's tarp. Father had tried a second time, had failed again.

All the mysteries were fading away. Rhide would call it *growing up.*

Somewhere, far to the north on the lake that looked

as big as a sea, *Mistress Flight* was being winched on to dry-dock. It had felt the hands of an old man and a young boy. It would never feel those hands again. The storyteller was gone, the final tales untold, and he'd been so frightened the last time I'd seen him. Frightened for me, I'd thought. But now, with Reggie's blunt words echoing through me, I believed otherwise. He knew he was going to die soon. He was blind, far from the sea, and alone. *Like the giant, dying all by himself, no one there to hold his hand, or keep him warm. No one to say goodbye, either. I didn't get the chance to say goodbye. I didn't come to visit often enough. I'm sorry, Walter.*

I felt I should cry, but it wouldn't come out. Everything was locked up tight inside, and seemed content to stay that way. I sighed, shivering in the cold draughts, and set my attention once again on the book in front of me.

III

Skeletons danced on the wall. Witches rode brooms above the blackboard and jack-o'-lanterns grimaced with gleeful menace from the support posts. The younger children had been so excited at recess. *They're the special ones, unsullied by life, not yet beyond reach.*

Joanne returned her thoughts to the tests. Her students were reading and learning about the war of 1812, when the Americans had been driven back, their invasion foiled by loyalists and English redcoats. She wanted to finish marking the tests, because she knew the night would be busy, the children coming to the door eager for treats, and she wanted to give them all her attention. She had a witch's costume and theatrical make-up – it had always been one of her favourite nights, ever since she'd been a little girl hand in hand with her mother, rushing from door to door all the way down the street. She'd then ration her candies, trying to make them last right up until Christmas, often succeeding.

The class was quiet. They'd learned the value of reading, and being conscientious. The test scores were indicative that she hadn't pushed them too far or too fast. It was up to her to make the subjects exciting, to make learning an adventure. That was her side of the partnership, and she took the responsibility seriously. In turn, the students behaved and participated with questions, answers, propelling the adventure ever onward with their enthusiasm.

Oh, my. The test she was marking was going to get a failing grade. Each answer seemed to be reaching in the right direction, then falling short. She flipped back to the front page. *Owen Brand. Well, at least he got his name right.* She felt the disappointment seep into her. He'd changed for the better, she'd thought, over the past few weeks. Jennifer was still a problem, of course, but manageable – different desks, different activities, keeping them apart while at school. Joanne believed it had been efficacious. Owen had ceased being a problem in class, or at recess. He didn't talk any more, didn't pass notes, didn't make scenes, didn't fight. He seemed genuinely to try when she asked him questions. *Although, come to think of it, he rarely gives the right answers.* She'd been paying too much attention to the disciplinary problems, forgetting the academic aspect. Of course, he'd always been just an average student. *But this, this is dreadful.*

Joanne looked up. Owen was writing notes in his booklet. There seemed to be a lot of papers slipped into that notebook, and it looked well used. *Even so . . .* She rose, made her way towards the desk where he sat, still writing. *Actually, not writing. Doodling. He's shading something in with his Bic pen.* He turned the page as she neared.

'Owen,' she said.

He looked up, expressionless.

'May I see your notebook?'

He handed it to her.

'Thank you. Have you finished reading chapter four?'

He nodded.

'Well, move on to chapter five, then.'

'Yes, Miss Rhide.'

She took the notebook with her back to her desk. Sitting down, Joanne set it in front of her and began examining the pages, starting at the beginning. Owen's Social Studies Notebook – *properly labelled, at least.* The first page began with decent note-taking, only a single doodle along the margin. *He has talent. Odd that no one's commented on it yet. I'll have to have a chat with Miss Stein. Definite talent.* The picture was a detailed pen sketch of a man riding a dinosaur. Cartoonish in style. It was a moment before she realised that the dinosaur wore high heels that matched her favourite pair. She flipped to the next pages.

The descent into chaos was rapid. Some pages had no notes at all, just drawings. *It doesn't matter how good they are. I've been teaching for two months. Two months of Canadian history. Where is it? Where are his notes?*

She realised that she had planted her elbows on the desk and was kneading her forehead, her fingers describing circles on her temples. *A migraine's coming. Tonight.* She also realised she'd begun to cry. The class was dead silent. Not a single page turned, not a single body shifted position.

Joanne pulled a wad of tissue from her sleeve, wiped her nose, then pressed the Kleenex against each eye. Her mascara was running.

Where are his notes? Where are all my handouts? What has he been doing?

Drawing. Men in medieval armour. Dragons, dozens of dragons. A barren treeless hill studded with dark rocks, filling two entire pages, worked over again and again, each blade of grass, hatching and cross-hatching – she stared at it, then saw all at once the dragon sleeping within the hill, present only in gradated tones, a ghostly apparition. He'd spent hours on these two pages, on this single scene. Hours, *while I've been talking, trying to teach. Day after day, after day.*

The tears wouldn't stop. Her nose dripped on to the pages, smearing the ink. She sensed someone at her side.

'Miss Rhide?' Lynk asked.

She tried to gather herself. 'Yes, Lynk?'

'Should I go get the principal?'

She shook her head. 'Uh, no. That's all right. Lynk, can you ask Mr Lyle to keep an eye on class. I'll be back in a minute.' She rose, patting her face with the sodden tissue.

As Joanne headed out, she saw Jennifer grinning at

her. *You . . . bitch! You think you've won. I'm going to see you out of here, out of this school. I swear it.*

She hurried out into the hallway and rushed into the girls' washroom.

Nothing but drawings. I've failed him completely. It's all my fault. I was complacent. It's my fault. We'll have to do something: we'll have to find a solution. Another talk, just the two of us. Remedial assignments, to get him caught up. We can fix this. Another call to his mother, a strongly worded statement – that should work. She's an intelligent woman, although a bit abrupt. She'll take my side on this. I'll bring up Jennifer, too. The bad influences – we'll work together on both fronts.

Lynk's my shining example. A dear, earnest boy. He was the only one to show any consideration, the only one who didn't just . . . watch.

She checked herself in the mirror. Puffy-eyed, but otherwise okay. The migraine was building, however. She'd have trouble tonight. She took a few deep breaths, gathering herself, then left the washroom.

Barry was waiting outside, genuine concern on his face.

Joanne smiled. 'It's all right,' she said.

They stood alone in the hallway.

'Jennifer again?' he asked.

'Yes. No, not directly.'

'Come to my office. George has things under control.'

'It's not fair on him,' she said. 'I know he can handle it – the students are, well, terrified of him, after all. But it's okay, Barry. I'm ready to go back. I can handle this.'

He took her gently by the arm and walked her towards the office. 'I feel very protective of you,' he said. 'It's only been a couple of months, after all . . .'

She let him lead her into his office. While she opposed his attitude towards the children, he was nevertheless a generous, caring man. He treated his staff with exceptional confidence.

Mrs Reynolds was out.

'Head on in,' Barry said. 'I'll get us some coffee.'

She entered the office and sat down in the chair facing Barry's desk.

He arrived with two cups, handed one to her then leaned against the desk.

'Owen Brand's not doing very well,' she explained. 'I thought there was improvement—'

'Well, behaviour is one thing, lack of intelligence is quite another. Listen, Joanne, would you like to join me for supper – not tonight, of course. But maybe next week?'

Joanne blinked. 'You mean, as professionals?'

He shook his head, his eyes holding hers. 'No. I am interested in you, Joanne – in every way, if I make myself clear.'

'But . . . you're married.'

'We have an understanding. We're together for the kids. Once they get a bit older . . . it's all right on that end, Joanne. I'm not the sordid type. I'm attracted to you. What do you say?'

Mother, you wouldn't approve. Is that what makes the idea so exciting? He's a handsome man, in his own way. Not your type, of course. But then, who was? He's ten years older, at least. But I've always had mature tastes. Well, Mother, it's time, isn't it? She smiled up at him. 'I'd like that very much, Barry.'

'Great! Now, better drink up.'

'Of course! George must have his hands full.'

'He's an understanding man in his own right,' Barry said. 'He's held the fort for me many times. Very reliable.'

'I don't intend to keep you long, Owen, but we have to get a few things worked out. About your notes, and the fact that you failed this last test. It's clear to me that we have a lot of work ahead of us. But if we work together, I think we can make some significant changes – for the better.'

He sat attentively at his desk, his gaze not once straying from hers.

'You understand,' Joanne continued, 'this will require that we work harder, that we complete extra assignments – an extra half-hour after school each day – until we're caught up. Starting tomorrow, we go back to page one in your book. We take notes. No doodling, but notes. Do you understand?'

He nodded.

'Very good. We don't want a repetition of what happened today, do we?'

'No.'

'All right.' She eyed him, not quite trusting his open, receptive expression. *We'll see, won't we?* 'You can go now, Owen.'

He collected his coat and quickly left. Joanne straightened, massaging the pain behind her forehead, then went to her own desk. She put everything in order for the next day, then left for the staff room. She wanted to talk to Mrs Brand before her son got home. *Both fronts, we'll make sure this time.*

IV

I entered the house to shouting. My mother, her back to me, was in the hallway, on the phone. A cigarette was in the hand she had on her hip. Her posture was stiff with anger.

'. . . keep your nose out of it,' she was saying, her voice loud and harsh. 'This isn't some Nazi version of the Dating Game, lady. Get that straight. It's none of your goddamned business who he's holding hands with . . . Of course I approve. She's a wonderful girl . . .'

I pulled off my boots. My heart was pounding. Looking in on the living room, I saw the twins sitting wide-eyed on the floor. Debbie – who looked to have just come home, her school having an in-service today – was grinning at me. She slowly waved one hand – *hot, real hot.*

Miss Rhide was on the other end of that phone line, and as I listened, I almost felt sorry for her.

'You've overstepped your bounds, miss,' Mom said. 'Keep this up and I'll register a complaint to the school board . . .' She fell silent then for a long minute while Rhide talked. I saw her shoulders hunch. 'Listen,' she cut in. 'Listen. I don't think you should be telling me this. That must be privileged information. I don't think you have the right to fling personal details around like that. Whatever the situation at home, that's surely confidential . . . no, stop right now! You called about Owen – or at least that should be the full extent of this conversation . . . Finally. Yes. I'll talk to him about it. I'll be very interested to hear his version – listen, his version is legitimate, dammit . . . So stop attacking it.

I'll make up my own mind, thank you very much . . . Yes, yes, fine. Is that it? Good. Goodbye.'

She slammed the receiver down. She lit another cigarette, then crossed her arms. 'Next time, Owen,' she said, her back to me, 'walk, don't run home.'

'Uh, sorry. I didn't know she'd call.'

'Count on it.' She faced me and stepped close, resting a hand on my head. 'With Miss Rhide, count on it every time.'

'Okay.'

'I need a coffee,' she said. 'Let's go into the kitchen.'

We sat on the stools at the counter. She sipped coffee, tossed out smoke rings, looking thoughtful. Finally, she sighed and said, 'Jennifer's having problems. How much do you know?'

'At school? Well—'

'No, I mean at home. Her parents. The situation there.'

'Nothing,' I said. 'She doesn't talk about it. Ever. I haven't even met them.'

'Well, that makes sense. Sort of. I've learned things I had no right to learn – about all that. The last time Jennifer and I sat down, I could see there was something she wanted to talk about, but I didn't push it. You can't push it. She'll run if you do that. Rhide's supposed to be there to help. Christ, she's just one more problem for Jennifer. Where's the support?'

'I don't know,' I said, completely lost. What was it about her parents? What was so terrible?

'Sorry,' Mom said, 'thinking out loud. So your teacher has put herself between you and Jennifer.'

'Oh, yeah. Since day one. It's a pain, but we're still going together, and that won't change.'

'Good for you. It's none of Rhide's business.'

'She thinks it is.'

'It isn't. She's out of line, Owen. That can happen to teachers as well as to anyone else. Don't let her intimidate you on that. If she tries, call me – just walk out of class and call me right away. I'll go straight to the school board.'

'Okay,' I said quietly. I'd never seen my mother so agitated, so fierce.

'Now,' she said, rounding on me. 'What's this about your grades? And your note-taking?'

I shrugged. 'She's teaching what I learned last year—'

'Not very well, it seems.'

'The test? Oh, that. She said it was a practice test.'

'A practice test?'

'Yeah, doesn't count on your grades. I pass all the real ones.'

'Then why did you get all the answers wrong?'

'Not wrong, exactly. Just incomplete. Like I said, it didn't count. I didn't study. Besides, I wanted every answer to be exactly ten words long. One sentence, ten words. It's hard to pack everything in. Harder than I thought, I guess.'

She closed her eyes and ran a hand through her hair. 'Oh, Owen,' she said, 'go get into your clown costume.'

I jumped down from the stool.

'From now on,' she added, 'just do the tests properly. Practice or not.'

'Okay. Do you think Rhide knows she's teaching Fifth Grade social studies?'

Her eyes squeezed shut, she shook her head. 'I have no idea, Owen.'

V

Snow like ashes. Sten smiled at the scene through the kitchen window. It was nearing midnight, and all the world's runts were snug in bed. No more knocks on the door. No more shrill proclamations – *Trick or treat!* Just the silent snow left, draping its meaningless whiteness on to everything.

With winter, our house gets smaller, and smaller and smaller. The walls are alive with chittering tongues, the floors heave with restless passings. Our shoulders brush the hallway's peeling walls, we hunch to keep our heads from scraping the ceiling. We grunt our thoughts like Neanderthals in a cave, and I want that hair in my fingers, my cock huge in my hand.

But it was almost midnight, and he was on his way. *The lich. The peach-skinned bastard walks tonight, with his drooling grin and the pits inside which I can see my own eyes, embryonic and blasted with venom. I'll hear him soon, in the clank of bottles, the shuffling feet, and I'll smell his stench – he's dripping with bile, spitting out pieces of his guts while crows cling and squabble in a black mess of feathers right there at the hole under his belly button. Ripping out slices of liver, heads jutting as they work the morsels down their narrow throats. And his fists are huge, onion skin wrapped over cracked, misshapen bones. There are bits of my face on them still, pieces of meat, shards of tooth, my spit and my blood – all still there because that's how I see his hands now, how I'll always see them. Those inexorable, relentless hands.*

'Fall. Fall down, you little shit! Show me just how

*goddamned spineless you really are! Stay up after this,
and this! And this andthisandthisandthis—'*

*I stayed up. I never went down. I won in the end. I
won.*

The house remained silent behind him. Elouise asleep.
Jennifer asleep or drugged out or maybe masturbating
upstairs. His smile broadened. Outside, the dogs padded restlessly. They'd barked themselves hoarse. All
those kids – they'd wanted soft throats in their jaws, so
bad, so bad, and the hunger, the desire remained, keeping them awake, still hopeful. *Still ready.*

The wind had picked up, swirling the snow, raising
itself to a low moan. *That's him, isn't it. Hallowe'en,
the night of the dead. The wind rips through the fabric,
it opens the way, and now he's coming. Closer, closer.*

Sten felt something warm dribble down his chin.
He wiped at it, saw blood on his hand. His welcoming
smile had set his gums bleeding. The memory of Fisk's
knuckles returned in a dull ache. *Better than you,
Dad. That old man, he knew how to punch. He knew
how to go for effect, to break something each time. He
wasn't drunk, Dad, that was the difference.*

Sten clawed at his face. The pain was unbearable,
the throbbing of cracked bones, all those flaws that
now answered the storm outside. There was blood
coming down from his nostrils. His ear was ringing, a
high-pitched pressurised scream.

He raised the rye bottle and tossed back three
mouthfuls.

*I need. I need protection. This time he won't get to
me. I know what I need. I know exactly.* Moaning
with pain, Sten staggered to the back door. He set his
bottle down and shrugged his way into his felt coat.

Cold out there, so cold, so cold. He collected the bottle and drank some more, then pushed the door open and stepped out on to the porch.

My dogs. They're watching me. They know he's coming. But they're mine. Mine, not his. Four savage, hungry beasts. Four – no, three. Oh, Christ. Max.

He wiped the blood from his face with a sleeve, the plumes of his breath streaming into the wind. The air was bitter cold. *Winter, my winter.*

Sten went down the steps. He took the wind on his face, feeling the stinging snow on his cheeks, willing the cold to seep in and numb the pain. His gut was on fire, churning like a maelstrom. Squinting, Sten stared at the sky. Pallid clouds, their western edges reflecting the city ten miles away – a lurid cast, coppery and sickly. Snow speeding down like stars tumbling from heaven, melting to nothing against his face. The wind shrieked in his head, and he could hear now – faintly, so faintly, the clang of bells. *Bells. Bottles. He's coming. I hear him.*

Kaja whined in the kennel. Ignoring her, Sten rushed for the work-shed. He pushed open the battered aluminium door, then paused at the entrance to drink another mouthful before plunging into the darkness.

The shovel slipped from its hook when he groped for it, falling in a loud clang. He hissed a curse, picked it up and headed back outside. *He's coming, I hear him.* He hefted the shovel, scanned the far edge of his wife's garden, now all snarled with snow-matted grasses.

Kaja let loose a howl. *She knows, the bitch knows. She's calling, listen to her joy!* The other two dogs picked up the chorus. Grinning, Sten stumbled over the garden's uneven ground. *I know you're coming. With your beasts all fanning out through the clouds. Still burning from hell's fires, you're coming back. And you want my blood. Again. You want it again. But I'll fight fire with fire. My hell against yours, Dad. It's Hallowe'en. Both ways, Dad. Boy, won't you be surprised.* He reached the uneven earthen mound, stabbed the shovel into the frozen dirt. *My favourite. Here to protect me again. One more time. You think your horns frighten me, don't you? But listen to my dogs answer you. Listen to them! They're going wild!* He flung away clumps of earth, his breath coming in gasps. *Dammit, what's with this rye anyway? Oh yeah, it's water. I'm clean. I'm dry. My stomach's killing me, 'cause I'm dry. It's been days. My God, days. Remember Christmas, Dad? All those festive occasions, when it all started going bad, when you fucked up and by the time dinner was served you were puking your guts out in the bathroom? Remember those times? My memories of Christmas, every Christmas, Dad. How my guts churn every Christmas, every year. But you're dead now. I've been walking in your footsteps. How could you do that to me? How?*

The tears froze on his cheeks, the blood from his nose hung thick and slimy, cold against his lips.

But Hallowe'en, now. Different. I'm all grown up. I can fight back. Watch me. Oh, I hear you, so close now. So close. You think you'll win again.

His shovel snagged on the garbage bag. He fell to his knees and clawed at the wet, cold mud. *Kaja's so happy. Listen to her. Yes, dear, I'm bringing him back. Your beloved son. Oh, Max, oh, Max, my friend. It's all right. Listen to your mother, your brothers – they're going mad with joy. Listen to them!* He pulled the bulky bag free. The smell caught him by surprise. He reeled back. *Max?* The body inside the garbage bag felt too soft in places, too hard in others. Max sounded wet, soaked, all curled up inside the bag, the tendons drawn tight around his rotting guts. Sten kneeled beside him. 'Oh, God,' he croaked. 'I'm sorry.' He pivoted and looked at the kennel. The dogs were in a frenzy, the chain-link wall shaking as they flung themselves against it. *Listen to them. Oh, what have I done? Kaja – I'm sorry. I should never have done this. I'm so sorry.*

He pushed the bag back into the hole, his fingers raking dirt over it. He picked up the shovel and quickly filled the hole. When he had finished packing down the earth, he paused, racked by shivering, the spit in his mouth foul with the taste of Max, his entire body a mass of pain.

I need a drink. I'm dry. I'm hallucinating. I thought I'd dug him up. I thought I'd called his soul, 'cause it's Hallowe'en. It's this storm, that wind, those clanging, clunking bottles, the shuffling footfalls coming up behind me.

Sten spun around. He screamed as the fists flashed out at him.

Trick or treat.

CHAPTER SEVENTEEN

I

ANNULMENT. MENTAL INCAPACITY. Reversion to the previous document, moneys to go to a charity for veterans, minus owing rent and interest, and funeral expenses. Reginald 'Reggie' Bell was deeply distressed by the decision. He'd hoped for the best – for the boy, of course. But that was for the judges to decide. The rent had been owing since '63, plus interest, of course. The old man should've taken better care of his affairs, all things considered.

A pot of gold had been shown to my father and mother. Shown, only to be swept away again. I couldn't make much sense of the details, but it seemed that Walter had tried to leave me some money, but there'd been legal hitches, and the money was going elsewhere.

It was hard to tell how my parents took the news. They'd seemed bewildered by the whole thing. It occurred to me that it would have been better if we'd never heard about any of it. Reggie had called his visit a courtesy, in case the boy – me – had been expecting different news in payment for befriending a rich old man. Reggie always fashioned himself a courteous man, but in the end he was responsible to the Yacht Club, and if he needed to challenge a will on the basis of debts incurred by Mr Gribbs while living on the grounds, well, then he was obliged to represent the club's interests. *Of course, you can call the lawyers if you wish to, Mr Brand. Unfortunately it won't change things. Besides, the charity's very grateful, very excited. That portion will go to good use, I'm sure you'll agree.*

Nothing was done. Something seemed to break after that, break deep inside my parents. There were more arguments, and long conversations reaching hours into the night. Dad's business wasn't doing well – the news was a shock to me, though it became obvious that my mother knew, and so did Debbie. I'd been kept in the dark, and it made me feel young and stupid, and I spent the weeks approaching Christmas under a brooding cloud.

There was hardly any money available. There'd be few presents, and just for the kids. I wasn't sure if I qualified as a kid in that equation. I didn't much care. I'd made a list, of course – mostly books, but they were all ones I could get out of the library in the city, which I continued doing. I'd wanted, more than anything else, a copy of *Beowulf* for myself. Now I dismissed the wish. It didn't matter.

Finding a spirit to match the season proved difficult. The days got shorter, the snows came and stayed,

school dragged on – dull and dulling – and we all felt
lost.

My only hope of reprieve came from Jennifer. Whatever was happening with her family had directed her
closer to me and my mother. She visited regularly, sometimes just showing up at the door, looking frightened
and embarrassed. But my mother insisted that there
was an open-door policy in place for her. Any time,
day or night. She could phone, she could visit. The evening when my mother told her all this, I thought Jennifer would cry. It was a close thing, but of course she
held it back.

I didn't know what to make of it all – I felt out of
my depth, but I could see that Jennifer needed my
mother as a friend, maybe more than she needed me.

It changed our going together. We still fooled around,
but not with the same abandoned greed that had marked
the summer. There was more caring in it, more quiet,
slow times. I began to miss the old ways, but I could
see that Jennifer wanted it the way it was now. Needed
it, maybe.

The first term was nearly over. I'd set up my hockey
net in front of the garage and practised shots and rushes,
using a tennis ball. No one played hockey around here,
except for the Riverview kids. There was a rink, set up
behind the school, but no nets. I desperately wanted a
real game. I couldn't understand the lack of interest.

It was Sunday afternoon, and I was waiting for Jennifer. Sunday dinners at our house had become a regular routine for her, and so Mom had made it a special
occasion for us as well. We'd never managed to maintain things like that before, with Dad often working,

but even he'd made allowances. It seemed that the
person pulling our family together wasn't even family,
but on Sundays, that was now the case. I wondered if,
with the news about Walter, we didn't need her as
much as she needed us.

I practised wrist shots, picking the corners. It felt
kind of ridiculous, since my usual position was as a
goalie.

Jennifer came down the driveway. 'Hey!' she shouted.
'It's Bobby Hull!'

'Ha ha.'

She wrapped me in a bear hug. 'Cheer up,' she said,
kissing my cheek. 'Only three days left, then no school,
no Rhide till January!'

I shrugged.

'I'm going inside,' she said, stepping back. 'Coming?'

'In a few minutes. Dad's not home yet.'

She threw me a pout.

'Tonight,' I said, 'I'll show you a secret.'

'Sorry, I've seen it,' she replied, grinning.

'Not that. Something else.'

'Okay.'

She headed in, her bell-bottoms frozen stiff at the
flares, her hips swaying beneath the down-filled parka.

I started on my backhand shots, the kind of shots
even Bobby Hull had trouble doing.

She was wearing two of my sweaters, and I could see
her breath as she looked around.

'The candles will warm things up a bit,' I said. 'But
it takes a while.'

Frost covered the stained-glass windows. I'd lit ten
candles, each in its own saucer, and the yellow light

glistened gold on the ice crystals. 'I'm reading all these books,' I said while Jennifer slowly walked around. 'Copies of them, that is. These ones are all rotten.'

'Rats,' she said. 'Seen any here?'

'Yeah. But not lately. We set traps.'

'Your parents know about this?'

'No. The traps went downstairs. In the basement and stuff.'

'You kept this a secret. From me.'

'Sorry.'

'Well, it's okay, I guess. I've never told you things. Like about my dad. He's a drunk, an alcoholic.'

'Oh.'

'Your mom knows, doesn't she?'

I nodded. 'I think so. Rhide called once. My mom was so mad. You wouldn't believe it. Rhide said stuff she shouldn't have said. Private stuff. Mom gave her shit.'

'I figured she'd heard something.' Jennifer perched herself on the desk and pulled out her cigarettes. 'She probably thinks we're necking right now.'

'Yeah. She sat me down, a while ago, and told me all about sex.'

'You're kidding.'

'Nope.'

'That must've been a real scream.'

'Yeah, we both started laughing. Finally she just told me to be careful, 'cause you might get pregnant.'

She took a drag, watched me. 'You want to do it? Fuck? You want to fuck, Owen? I won't get pregnant. Guaranteed.'

'Here? It's freezing.'

'In your room.'

'In my parents' house?'

'Why not? If your mom's already talked about it—'

'Forget it,' I said. 'Not here, I mean. Not with my parents downstairs. Let's find somewhere else.'

'Where? It's the middle of the winter. We'd freeze our butts off at the farmhouse.'

'I don't know. Somewhere.'

'Well, you think of somewhere and let me know. Only, we have to time it right, so I don't get pregnant. You're right, the candles are making it warmer.'

'Let's go back down,' I said.

Jennifer grinned. 'Got you going, eh?'

I went to the passageway. 'Can you blow out the candles? You know, my mom puts an ashtray in my room, for when you come over.'

'So?'

'So. It's weird, that's all. It just feels weird.'

Jennifer moved from one candle to the next. The room slowly dimmed.

It was then that we noticed the reddish glow from outside, from the window facing the front yard. I walked over. Something was burning, beyond the trees, lighting the skyline. Jennifer leaned beside me.

'That's the candle factory,' she said. 'It's going up.'

'Is it ever.'

There would be no saving it this time. Fire trucks lined the side of the highway. Traffic was backed up as policemen in buffalo hats and mitts directed the vehicles, one lane either way. Every car or truck that rolled past was bathed in a red glow. The black-and-grey smoke towered over the factory, swelling and bulging, climbing ever higher. The air was acrid, reminding me of the garbage heap at the Yacht Club.

We stood on the other side of the highway – as close as they'd let us get – watching the firemen running this way and that, watching the water rip out from the hoses, rise up and disappear into the second-floor windows. Water poured down the building's face, made a lake on the ground out in front. Smoke tumbled out of the main-floor windows and the open doorway. Things crashed down inside, sending out dazzling sparks that spun and whirled against the black sky.

Every now and then, the heat rolled up and swept over us, but for the most part the bitter cold air embraced us, making the scene in front of our eyes seem unreal, dislocated, as if we were watching a movie at a drive-in.

'Look,' said Jennifer. 'They're worried about the school. They're concentrating on that side.'

'There's no wind,' I said.

'I think they're just making sure. Too bad, eh?'

There was a flare beside me as Jennifer lit a cigarette. A sudden feeling struck me and I almost gasped – something about the flame from Jennifer's match, so close beside me. It had been as if the two fires had reached out across the distance between them, then touched, and all at once we were all connected, woven together.

The wheel turned, alight with that furious red, and I imagined the wall giving way around it, the wheel rolling as it came down, a roar of sparks like a thousand voices, the flames sweeping and spinning. A concussion, hammering through the earth, radiating out in waves until the world went still and listened, filled with terror and awe, waiting for the next shifting beneath their feet, the next trembling wave of uncertainty. *It's coming, it's coming.*

'Holy shit,' Jennifer said.

I saw the crack now, zigzagging its way down the building's ravaged face. Firemen were yelling, pulling back, splashing and sliding as they ran. The crack widened, one whole section tilting, separating as it shifted to one side.

I've seen all this. I just saw it.

'It's gonna come down,' Jennifer said.

Sirens wailed from the police cars. The traffic on the highway had been stopped at both ends, the cars trapped in the middle being frantically waved on, making a gap, a widening space.

We stood on the shoulder opposite that gap, unnoticed.

'There's Lynk,' Jennifer said, not sounding surprised.

In astonishing silence, the wall and part of the corner fell away. The wheel spun for real this time. Sparks billowed out from the exposed insides, followed by a gush of flame, roaring, that drove a wall of heat against us. The inside of the factory raged bright.

The wheel turned, as I knew it would.

It shattered when it hit the ground. Water and steam engulfed it for a moment, then slowly thinned to reveal a jumbled pile of cracked, blackened limestone. The firemen with the hoses trained the water on the new opening, but it was hopeless. Everything was crashing down inside. The second floor had already collapsed, and the factory was just a shell now, holding within it a firestorm.

'Hey, you kids!' A man's booming voice made us

look down to see a policeman jogging our way. In his buffalo hat and mitts and the long coat he looked monstrous, bestial.

'We're all right,' Jennifer said.

'Move back across the ditch,' he ordered. His face was bright red. 'Is that a cigarette?'

'Afraid so,' Jennifer said.

'Did you see the fire start?'

'From my house,' I said. 'Down by the river. We were having supper and we saw the glow.'

The man removed his mitts and pulled out a notebook. 'I'd better take down your names.'

'Did someone start it?' Jennifer asked.

The man didn't answer. He simply asked for our names, addresses and phone numbers. I pointed out that we'd been at my place since the afternoon. He just nodded.

I looked around, but Lynk had disappeared. I think Jennifer and I were both thinking the same thing – from the look she gave me after the cop walked off.

The flames were falling back. Nothing left to burn. I was chilled, and I stamped my feet, but they'd gone numb. 'Let's go,' I said.

'I'm sleeping over tonight.'

'What?'

She grinned. 'In the guest room. Don't worry, my mom knows. Your mom called her.'

'And it was okay?'

'She knows. She didn't say anything. She can't talk yet. They've just taken the wires off her jaw. She had a broken jaw.'

'Oh.'

A broken jaw. The words lodged in my mind.

II

Christmas morning broke clear and cold. Fisk drank down a hot cup of coffee, marvelling at the crispness of the scene outside the kitchen window, then he went into the bathroom and shaved.

The ritual calmed his churning stomach, freeing his thoughts to wander from the pain and sickly feeling that had plagued him the past few weeks. He resurrected the memories of other Christmas Days – with Dorry, the two of them closing together on that special day. Always a sadness, an undercurrent of regret that they freed themselves to share. No children, the house all too quiet. Never a celebration, but at least a kind of sharing, a kind of comforting. At least that.

He'd cut himself. Not surprising. It'd been a while. The blood turned the shaving foam under his jaw a frothy pink. He ignored the cut for now, began working under his scarred chin.

The sound of a truck coming down the driveway startled him. He worked a little faster, the razor tugging at the bristles.

Doors slammed outside, boots crunched on the snow covering the porch steps. The door thumped under a fist.

'Come on in!' Fisk yelled.

There were two of them, stamping snow from their boots. Bill's voice echoed through the house. 'Hodgson? Brought some Christmas cheer! Sig's with me. Sig Fraser.'

'Hello!' came another voice.

'Make yourselves comfortable,' Fisk answered.

Then get the hell out. 'I'm shaving. Be a couple of minutes. There's coffee.'

'Thanks! Where's the tree?'

Let's not get sentimental here, fellas. What am I supposed to be celebrating? He heard the two in the kitchen, talking in low tones, then footsteps heading back into the living room. The blood trickled down his neck. He grabbed a towel and wiped it away. *Almost done. Shit, another one. Goddamn it.* He finished up, then washed his face with cold water, until his cheeks went numb. The second cut only needed a dab of toilet paper, but the first one required a butterfly bandage as well. He sighed, studied his flushed, aged face in the mirror, then left the bathroom.

The two men sat on the sofa, cups of coffee on the low table in front of them. Sig looked as robust as ever, a big man, almost as big as Fisk himself, with a farmer's hands – Fisk had seen him before, but they'd never spoken. On his forehead ran the permanent line from his cap, everything beneath it grey and weathered, but still strong, and above the line, pale, freckled skin, greying hair slicked straight back, military cut around the sides and back, his left ear clipped along the top. *Bullet, or shrapnel, from the looks of it. What had he been? A pilot, maybe – the old bastard still doesn't need glasses, and he's got a bombardier's eyes, cool and sharp, quick to narrow down, each blink carefully timed.*

Fisk sat in his chair, his gaze on Sig. 'RCAF?' he asked.

Sig's grin displayed a mass of wrinkles only hinted at before. 'Nope.'

Bill laughed. 'Sniper. A killing machine, was old Sig here. A Kraut-killing machine.'

'All over with now,' Sig said, shrugging.

'Got that right.' Fisk leaned back.

'Hey!' Bill exclaimed. 'Merry Christmas!'

'Same to you both,' Fisk said. 'Can't complain about the weather.'

'You ain't been outside yet,' Bill said. 'Damned awful year, if you ask me. I'm sure Sig here'd agree, eh, Sig? Goddamned drought, then killer storms, finally an early snow and it's been dumping ever since. Sure hope next year's better, eh, Sig?'

'Yep.'

Bill swallowed a mouthful of coffee, then sighed, his eyes on the table. 'We lost one a while back,' he said quietly. 'Walter Gribbs. Sig knew him better than I did. He was like you, Hodgson. Never came down to the hall, never one to jaw much. Was in the navy, right, Sig?'

'Done his duty,' Sig said with a smile.

'That's too bad,' Fisk answered once he realised that Bill waited for one. 'Of course, we all got to go some time.'

'That's a fact,' Sig said.

Fisk understood Sig's smile. It was a sad one. *Fair enough. The man's settled with himself. One of the lucky ones. Fair enough.*

Bill pulled out a small wrapped present. 'We all tossed something in,' he said. 'From the boys, every damn one of them.' He handed the present to Fisk. 'Merry Christmas, Hodgson.'

'Thanks,' Fisk said, a tightness in his chest that he didn't want. 'That's kind of you. I, uh, I didn't expect any company today – if I'd known, I'd have got you something—'

'No problem,' Bill said, still leaning forward. 'Listen, Sig here's come with an invitation. Now, they eat ham, not turkey, but what the hell, eh? It's a feast. I've seen the layout. A feast.'

'Be glad to have you,' Sig said.

'That's a generous offer,' Fisk said, still holding the present, which looked tiny in his hands. 'You might not believe it, but today's a day I still spend with . . . with Dorry. I know, it sounds silly—'

'No it don't,' Sig said, his eyes bright.

'I'd feel like, well, like I was abandoning her – alone in this house. I couldn't do that. Your offer touches me, Sig, it really does.'

'No problem,' Sig said. 'I hear you.' He rose, reaching down to tap Bill on the shoulder.

Startled, Bill looked up, then slowly climbed to his feet. 'Sorry to intrude,' he said gruffly. Then he grinned. 'Of course, if we hadn't, you might've bled to death – that razor cut needs some ice and pressure, Hodgson.'

'Damn,' Fisk said, smiling. He reached up and felt the blood. 'Well,' he said, studying the stains on his finger. 'I've seen it before, right, Bill?'

'I bet you have. You take care of that now, okay?'

'Sure thing. Anyway, you didn't intrude.' Fisk rose. He wiped the blood from his hand, held it out. 'Merry Christmas,' he said as he shook hands with both men, in turn.

Sig zipped up his parka. 'Be all right if I dropped off some leftovers tomorrow?'

'That'd be nice, Sig.'

The man nodded. *I like him. He's not living in the past like Bill. He's not trapped in a war he won't let end.*

They pulled on their boots and headed out, Fisk smiling as he closed the door behind them. He stayed in the dim hallway, listening until the truck drove off, then he went back to the living room and sat down. He unwrapped the gift.

It was a watch. A Rolex. On the back was engraved Fisk's battalion and company, along with his name and all the medal acronyms, then the Legion number and the hall that had presented it.

A goddamned watch. A Rolex. Time unending, time going on for ever. Christ, Bill. Christ.

He stood, tossed the watch down into the chair where it bounced on the cushion. Blood dripped from his chin, dropped down to the faded carpet. Fisk rubbed at his eyes, then headed for the bathroom. *Some cotton. Then it's back to bed.* Christ.

He lay under the covers, shivering. Shaving had been a mistake, the ritual proving empty, a lie. There'd be no changes, nothing crossed over. All he had ahead of him was time, ticking away, round and round an implacable, meaningless face. He was bound for hell. He knew that. He'd welcome the change. But even that seemed a thousand years away.

He'd lied to Sig, and he regretted that. There was no Dorry for him, not on this day, not on any day. His dreams of her had become nightmares, racked with shame, all twisting up inside with guilt. He wasn't the man she married, wasn't the man she loved. Without her at his side, he'd gone the wrong way. The field out back told him that, every spring. No more flowers around the maypole, and it was just a pitted and scarred and wholly dead rod of metal. She was gone. He'd abandoned her, years ago. It was far too late.

This year, in the spring that was coming, he'd let the field take him. Anything was better than this.

He closed his eyes. The pain in his stomach was back. He took deep, controlled breaths – something he'd been taught to do in Recovery, when they'd weaned him off the morphine. *Control the pain, narrow it down then rub it out, like a smudge under an eraser. Feel each breath, follow it down, follow it out. Imagine it coming out darker than it went in, dark with all the pain. Let it loosen the knots, let it carry you away. I think I'll visit the cellar tonight.*

III

'He snatched me away,' Sten said as he stumbled down the hallway from the dining room to the living room. 'Snatched me away.'

Elouise sat in the kitchen, listening to her husband's endless mumbling. *He snatched me away. Hallowe'en night. He snatched me away. I screamed, but no one heard. No one heard.* He'd been saying things like that since the first day of November, and each time the words slipped out, he seemed to get duller, his skin losing a shade of life, becoming greyer, like wrinkled paper.

He spoke loudly, alone in the living room. 'Do you remember? The old Christmases? You'd tie me down on the log, there up on the pile of sticks. What a bonfire that was. I remember how my blood boiled, how my skin went red and split and smoked. Like a suckling pig. And you'd dance with all the other women. Wallflowers no more . . .' His voice fell away to muttering.

Elouise could hear Jennifer upstairs, the music loud, her occasional footsteps creaking through the kitchen ceiling.

'Christmas Day!' Sten laughed, the laugh turning into a hacking cough. 'I forgot the presents. I'll get some. I promise. Just a few days late, that's all. A few days.' He coughed again. 'It's beer, that's all. I'm not drunk. No, not any more. I don't need your goddamned pity!'

There was a loud crash and a thump. Elouise rose and went to the living room. Her husband was lying on the floor, the coffee table on its side, a pile of magazines splayed out over the carpet. His blurry eyes looked up at her. 'Merry Christmas,' he said. 'I'm sorry. I really am. I hate this day. It's torture. He's in my head, now. Since Hallowe'en, he's been in my head. I'm sick. I feel sick. I can't stop shaking.'

It's all him. He's the world, the entire world.

She heard Jennifer coming down the stairs. A moment later her daughter stood beside her.

'Christ,' she said, staring down at her father. She righted the table and set a present on it. 'This is for you, Dad. Open it when you can. Me and Mom are going out.'

Sten's eyes widened with fear. 'What?'

'We deserve better,' Jennifer said. 'We're visiting friends. We're going to have a real Christmas. Your version sucks. We don't want it any more.' She came up to Elouise and took one of her arms. 'Come on, get your coat on. It's not a long walk.'

Elouise shook her head.

Jennifer's face hardened. 'We're getting out of here.' She pulled her mother into the hallway, then hissed, 'We don't deserve this!'

Elouise tried to pull away. She didn't want to meet anyone, she didn't want to go anywhere. It'd be an awful intrusion. Worse, it'd be embarrassing, stinging her pride, to be the objects of pity. She kept shaking her head and trying to pull her arm free. But Jennifer wouldn't let go, wouldn't back down.

'We're going,' she said, pulling her coat on, then taking Elouise's coat and dressing her mother like a doll, like a child.

A shopping bag sat filled with presents beside the front door. More than had been under the tree, some in wrapping paper she didn't even recognise. Jennifer had planned this, but had given no warning. She hadn't let Elouise have the time to think about it, to find ways to tie herself here. No time for elaborate excuses. It was all too sudden, too overwhelming, and before she realised it, they were on the road outside the house, walking towards the river.

It was cold. They had to walk quickly to stay warm. Sundogs mimicked the sun in the crystal-laden blue sky. The air burned in the lungs, but it was all beautiful – so clear, so brilliantly *there*.

They came to a tree-lined driveway, to a lot that went down to the river. Many years ago, Elouise recalled, there'd been a family living there, very rich, treating the place as a summer home. It wasn't big, compared to the houses on either side, but that left more room for the yard. Majestic, frost-rimed trees relieved the monotony of the lawn, which was under a yard and a half of snow. Too much shade for a vegetable garden, of course. This was a place that had been stately once. Maybe forty years ago. Now it was quaint.

The door opened as they went up the steps. A woman in her late thirties stood there, smiling and welcoming.

'Merry Christmas!' she said. 'Come in, before you turn into icicles!'

Once inside, Jennifer made introductions. It seemed she didn't need to mention that her mother couldn't speak, and Elouise was quick to see the familiar ease that existed between her daughter and Owen's mother. She wondered if she should feel jealous, but as she watched her daughter – so comfortable in this house, smiling and laughing, and the genuine affection she wasn't hesitant to display with her boyfriend, Owen – Elouise instead felt a crumbling inside. She'd forgotten that her daughter had once always been like this – so free, unmarred by anger and the stains it left on the heart. Her daughter's flushed face and bright smile were, she realised, a gift, unexpected and worth more to her than anything else on this day.

The boy, Owen, was a serious-looking young man, but there was magic in his eyes – a dark kind, yet lively all the same. And whatever he and her daughter shared seemed honest and true. They seemed too young for a bond so deep.

Susan and Jim, who was a quiet man with eyes very much like his son's, led Elouise into the living room. She was already trembling with unexpected emotions, and the sight of the twins squealing with impatience in front of the Christmas tree, poking eagerly among the as yet unopened presents, made Elouise sag suddenly, her knees giving way. Jim was quickly at her side, and Elouise nodded her gratitude as he helped her to a chair. There was deep concern on all the faces surrounding her, but she could barely see them through a sudden welling of tears. A glass of water was carefully placed in her hand. Deeply embarrassed, Elouise smiled and shook her head.

Jennifer kneeled in front of her. 'Mom? Are you okay?'

She nodded, reaching for the box of Kleenex that had been placed on her lap.

'Are you happy?' Jennifer asked. 'Is this just happy?'

Elouise nodded again. *Happy, yes. In pieces. In pain. But happy.* She leaned forward and kissed her daughter on the forehead.

As she slowly regained her composure, she felt drawn into the excitement coming from the twins, Tanya and William.

'We usually open our presents Christmas Eve,' Susan explained. 'But this year is special. Needless to say, nobody slept a wink last night. Part of the fun.'

'Fun?' Owen scowled. 'It was exhausting.'

'But worth it, right, Owen?' Jennifer's expression was dangerous.

He seemed unintimidated, grinning as he said, 'Sure. I'm all for torturing little kids. What else is Christmas for, eh?'

'Owen,' his mother warned.

Elouise smiled at him. *No tiptoeing around for this boy, thank God. I'm so sick of thin ice.* She tried to think of a way to put everyone else at ease, to keep them from trying too hard, but Owen seemed determined to do it for her. He rose and came over.

'It's quieter in the kitchen. And there's food, some of it edible. Nobody's allowed to open anything till after you and Jennifer get something to eat. So let's torture the runts a while longer.' He held out his hand.

Elouise couldn't keep the smile off her face. She delicately placed her hand in his and stood.

He faced the others and spoke in a high tone. 'Like my teacher always says, the sound of kids having fun can be simply intolerable. We'll be back. Jennifer?'

A bewildered Jennifer trailed them as Elouise held Owen's hand all the way to the kitchen. *We'll survive this season, after all. My girl was right. We don't deserve Sten's version of things. I can make it to the spring, now. Maybe we all can.*

IV

It was the middle of February. Jennifer was shrugging into a second sweater when the doorbell rang. She opened it to find Dr Roulston, bundled up in an expensive parka, his car, still running, in the driveway.

Scowling, she let him in.

'Good morning,' he said, pulling off his leather gloves and untying his hood.

Jennifer pushed her feet into her sneakers. 'Mom's in the kitchen. Dad's asleep,' she said. 'I've got to go. Mustn't be late for school. Rhide might just skin me.'

'Actually,' Roulston said, 'I thought I'd take you. If you thought yesterday was cold . . .'

Jennifer pulled on her coat. 'Wasted trip. I'm walking.'

Her mother arrived. Roulston smiled. 'Good morning, Elouise. How are you doing?'

Elouise nodded, looking from Jennifer to the doctor and back again.

'I was offering Jennifer a lift,' Roulston said. 'It's the coldest day on record. Been a nasty month altogether, wouldn't you say?'

'You'll give up sooner or later,' Jennifer said. 'My mother the mute. Doesn't want to talk ever again. It's more convenient that way. For her, at least.'

'We need to talk, Jennifer. You and I. That's why I'm driving you to school. It's better if you don't make a fuss, don't you think?'

'"Wouldn't you say?" "Don't you think?" Do you need an opinion on everything, Doctor?' Jennifer stared at him, then her shoulders slumped. 'Oh, all right. What the fuck.'

'Goodbye for now,' Roulston said to her mother. 'If it's okay, I'll drop by later this morning.'

She nodded.

Jennifer followed Roulston out to the car. 'I like walking,' she said as she opened the passenger door and climbed in. 'It's the only fresh air there is. The whole fucking school stinks of hot metal and dust and oil. Everybody's climbing the walls in there.'

'Buckle up.'

'Christ.'

'It's become obvious,' Roulston said as he backed the car out, 'that your father is making no progress.'

'Really? But he hasn't hit anything in months. I figured the way he cleaned himself up for your surprise Sunday visits had you convinced.'

'Anne's a lot sharper at this than I am, Jennifer. She's seen it all.' He pulled out on to the road. 'We're still very concerned. For you and your mother.'

'We're fine. Daddy's trapped inside his own head. He doesn't come out any more.'

'He's hit bottom, then.'

Jennifer laughed. 'There is no bottom, Doctor.'

'How much is he drinking?'

'No idea.'

'Come on, Jennifer.'

She shrugged. Three, four beers a day. One gets him drunk – hell, sometimes all he has to do is just look at one and he's wasted. I'm having a smoke now.'

'Your idea of fresh air?'

'Beats the sanctimonious stench in here.'

Roulston pulled the car over at the mailboxes. Traffic rolled past on the highway in front of them. 'You're not expected until after morning services. Sanctimonious, that's a heavy word for a thirteen-year-old.'

'Fourteen next week. I know the word – I've been fed it for long enough. You got a point to all this?'

'With your mother's permission, we can have your father committed to a mental institution – I want you to convince her that it's for the best.'

'Fuck you, Doctor.'

'There's a treatment programme there—'

'You once said he has to choose, he has to decide to get help all on his own.'

'There're indications of mental illness here, Jennifer. I've finally acquired his medical records from the insurance company. Your father displays paranoid tendencies. He experienced a trauma years ago, and it's manifesting itself to this day. He needs therapy, and medication—'

'What trauma? Let me guess, the day I was born, right? Well, that's just too bad. Boo hoo.'

Roulston stared – Jennifer felt those blue eyes on her, searching, seeking something. She smoked, watched the traffic stream past.

'Your birth?' he asked softly. 'No, Jennifer. You're wrong. Your father was a crew foreman. He had an apprentice under him – just a kid, didn't know anything. Well, the young man was killed, crushed between two train cars. Your father blamed himself. He had a nervous breakdown. That's the trauma I'm talking about, Jennifer. You, you were a gift, you helped pull him back – not all the way, it appears, but even so. I thought you knew. Anne assumed you did. Why do you think you're so important, so vital to all this?'

'My father's a drunk, Doctor. Just like *his* father. He was probably drunk when the guy got killed. I don't give a shit what happened to him. You and Queen Anne – you're always looking for excuses, just like my dad, and even if you can't find them, you just make them up. You're all the fucking same. The guy tries to bugger his daughter – well, that's because she's so *special* to him—'

'Is that what happened? Did I hear you right?'

Jennifer rolled down the window and tossed out the cigarette butt. 'Hear what right, Doctor? Did I say something? Maybe I lied, just to get him into trouble. You can *excuse* that, can't you? I'm sure you can. Am I going to school or what?'

'I think that one just slipped out,' Roulston said. 'It wasn't calculated at all. After all, you don't want to give us just cause, do you?' He paused, then sighed. 'You're not going to help convince your mother – although you should know, she may not need convincing—'

'Get real. She likes things the way they are. That much should be obvious. Daddy likes the sound of his own voice. He doesn't like being interrupted, doesn't like having his version challenged. She says nothing. Daddy's happy talking. It's all perfect. No complaints.'

'It's an untenable situation—'

'No, it isn't. Now, are you going to drive or do I walk?'

He put the car in gear, then waited for a gap in the traffic. 'There're conflicting reports about you from your school,' he said.

'Conflict's my middle name.'

'Some teachers want you out. Others are just as determined to keep you in. You've divided the staff, Jennifer. And I hear – only now – that you have a boyfriend. What does he think about your situation at home?'

'None of your business, and I don't give a shit what the teachers think.'

A gap appeared and Roulston pulled the car on to the highway. 'Do you plan on continuing, through high school at least?'

Jennifer looked out of the side window. 'Does it matter?'

'I think it does. To me, it does.'

'I don't want to be your special project, Doctor.'

'Well, you know, I think I'm one of the good guys. I like you. You've cut into me on occasion' – he laughed – 'like a surgeon, but I can't help appreciating your intelligence. And some of your teachers say you have talents – music, especially. You used to play piano, didn't you?'

He swung the car into the parking lot. Jennifer leaned

back in the seat, closing her eyes. 'Doctor, I already have friends. I don't need any more. If people want to fight about me, that's their problem, not mine. I'm tired of being jerked around like a puppet – by you, by Rhide, by everyone. Everyone does it, except my friends. Do you see the difference, Doctor?' She opened the door and stepped out into the bitter cold.

'I'll keep trying, Jennifer!' Roulston called out as she closed the door.

'Brother,' she sighed, heading towards the entrance. She stopped halfway. Someone had spray-painted the glass doors, and down the entire length of the new building's front wall. Bright red paint, easily a whole can's worth.

NOT ME NOT ME NOT ME –the words repeated dozens of times, inside circles, wavy boxes, hearts, star shapes. *NOT ME NOT ME* and *FUCK OFF RHIDE* and *FUCK OFF THOMPSON, BITCH RHIDE, FUCKER THOMPSON, OWEN AND JENNIFER FOR EVER – LEAVE US ALONE, NOT ME NOT ME NOT ME . . .*

Roulston's car door slammed. Jennifer turned to him, watched his face harden as he read the graffiti. Then he looked at her.

'I'd be smarter,' Jennifer said.

'I believe you.'

'So would Owen. He can draw. He knows how to draw.'

'Let me park the car,' Roulston said. 'I'll come in with you.'

'Why?'

'I think you could do with an ally. Not a friend – I

got your meaning. I understood you, Jennifer. But an ally – will you accept that?'

Jennifer looked back at the school. 'I haven't got much choice. Again.'

'Wait there,' he said, jumping back into the car.

She walked up to the smoky glass doors and leaned against them. *Lynk. Rhide's darling. He got clean away with the candle factory. Now this. No way to prove it. We're fucked. We'll be expelled. Sorry, Owen. This isn't right.*

'Let's face the music,' the doctor said as he came to her side.

They entered the school. 'Never mind going to class,' Jennifer said, removing her coat. 'Straight to the office, I think.'

'You're the expert,' Roulston said, trying a grin.

Mrs Reynolds looked up as they entered the office, her expression grave. The conference room door was closed.

Roulston introduced himself.

Mrs Reynolds nodded, her eyes on Jennifer. 'Real trouble this time, Jenny. The police are on the way.' She rose. 'I'll inform Principal Thompson that you're here. He's presently speaking with Owen, awaiting the boy's mother.' She headed to the door, knocked, then stepped inside, closing it behind her.

'It's not fair,' Jennifer said. 'We're not stupid. We wouldn't sign our names, for Christ's sake.'

Roulston picked up the phone on Mrs Reynolds's desk.

'What are you doing?' Jennifer demanded.

'Calling the hospital. This may take the whole morning.'

'Thompson will say it's none of your business and kick you out.'

'We'll see. Don't worry, I won't call Anne. I suspect the police will do that if they deem it necessary.' He dialled, then began speaking to his nurse.

The conference room door opened. 'You can go in,' Mrs Reynolds said.

Owen was alone with Thompson, looking ashen, in shock. Jennifer sat down beside him while Roulston introduced himself.

Thompson was quick to the punch. 'I'm not sure I see your relevance here, Doctor. No offence, but this is a school matter, and a police matter.'

'Jennifer is in my care, Mr Thompson. With her situation at home, I've assumed the role of guardian. Her mother has agreed to this in writing – you should have that in your records, by the way. As I understand it, this boy's mother is on her way here. I will act for Jennifer in a similar capacity.'

Thompson's eyes narrowed. 'You'll assume financial responsibility as well?'

'I didn't realise you've already concluded their culpability. Have you wrung out a confession from this young man, then?'

Thompson was silent, his expression belligerent.

'Frankly,' Roulston went on, 'it seems to me rather naive to assume that these two are in any way responsible. They're the intended targets, obviously. That, of course, is my point. It's clumsily done, wouldn't you say? Do you actually think they'd write their own names on the wall?'

The two cops arrived then. *Constable this, Constable that.* They sat down and listened quietly while

Thompson talked – one of them listening, the other taking notes.

'There have been difficulties with these two,' Thompson said, indicating her and Owen, 'all year, specifically with myself and their homeroom teacher, Miss Rhide, who was so upset by this incident that I sent her home for the day. It's my belief that these two are the culprits.'

One of the cops faced Owen. 'Did you spray-paint the wall, son?'

'No.'

He then turned to Jennifer.

'No,' she said before he could even repeat the question. 'We're not stupid.'

The cop frowned, then he sat back and said to Thompson, 'Any evidence pointing to them?'

'Well, only what I've told you. Motive, I guess.'

Jennifer rolled her eyes. 'This isn't some crime show,' she said. 'It's pretty obvious someone wants to get me and Owen into trouble.'

'He can't draw,' Owen said.

The same cop turned to him. 'Who can't draw?'

'The one who painted the wall.'

'I think you know who that might be, don't you?'

Thompson cleared his throat. 'I remain convinced—'

Roulston rose and said to the other cop, 'Why don't the three of us talk in the principal's office. Mr Thompson?' He then laid a hand on Jennifer's shoulder and leaned down slightly. 'You'll be fine here on your own for a few minutes?'

'Yeah, no problem.'

The second cop, Thompson and Roulston left the room.

As soon as the door closed, Owen said, 'I'm guessing, sir, and there's no way to prove it.'

'Lynk Bescher,' Jennifer said, knowing her face was flushed with anger. 'The little shit. He hates Owen, and he's jealous 'cause we're going together.'

Owen's eyes were wide. 'Lynk?' he said. 'I was thinking Gary.'

'Who's Gary?' the cop asked, looking intrigued.

'I had a fight with him,' Owen explained. 'First day of school.'

'Owen kicked him in the balls. End of fight, end of Gary. Yeah, he hates Owen, too. But he's even stupider than Lynk. Maybe they did it together. But Lynk's the one, only he's Rhide's favourite—'

'Rhide,' the cop cut in. 'That's your teacher?'

'Yeah,' Jennifer nodded. 'Lynk's sucked her in. He'll deny it, and there won't be any proof.'

The cop sighed. He opened his mouth to say something but just then the door flew open and Owen's mother arrived, her face dark.

'Let's go, Owen. You too, Jennifer.'

'A moment please,' the cop said, rising.

'Sit down, sir!' Susan snapped. 'Take a minute to think things through—'

'Wait!' the cop said, holding up his hands. 'I agree with you! We were just trying to work out who has it in for these two. So please, relax. Join us. Calm down, Mrs—?'

'Brand. Owen's mother.' She unbuttoned her coat and sat down. 'I'm sorry, but Principal Thompson seemed convinced—'

'And clearly wrong. He's very angry, of course—'

'Not thinking straight, you mean.'

'He's with Constable Holmes right now, and the doctor.'

'Holmes?' Susan asked, a smile cracking through her fierce expression.

'This is Constable Watson,' Owen said.

The cop sighed. 'I get it all the time. Not from thirteen-year-old boys, though. No, my name is Rawlins.'

Susan turned to Owen. 'Who did it, then?'

'We're not sure. Maybe Lynk, maybe Gary.'

'More likely this Gary boy,' she said. 'There was a fight early in the first term—'

Rawlins nodded. 'So I hear. We'll be talking with both boys. We'll see how that goes.'

The door to Thompson's office opened and the three men entered. The principal was scowling, but the set of his shoulders made it clear he was beaten. Roulston introduced himself to Owen's mother – and Jennifer saw her raise her eyebrows when he told her he was acting on Jennifer's behalf.

'Well,' Thompson said. 'You two can go to your class now. If you'll excuse me a moment.' He went to the secretary's office.

Susan eyed both Jennifer and Owen. 'I'm taking you both to lunch,' she said. 'I'll be by at noon, in the car, out front.'

'We're not supposed to leave the school,' Owen said.

'They can try and stop us. You need an hour out of this place. And Jennifer, I'd like you and your mother over for supper tonight.'

Jennifer grinned. 'Usual time?'

'Yes.'

Roulston was looking at Susan with renewed interest. Jennifer watched him rearranging things in his mind, watched the effect on his face. *Hope, excitement. Another ally. Yes, Doctor, we have friends. Real friends, now.*

'May I speak with you?' he asked Susan.

'Go ahead.'

'Uh, privately. Just a minute or two.'

'All right.' She gave Jennifer and Owen quick, firm hugs, then followed Roulston out.

The PA announced that Lynk and Gary were to report to the office.

Jennifer took Owen's arm. 'Let's go.'

Owen held back and looked at Rawlins. 'Can't I watch? I have a right to face my accusers——'

Rawlins coughed into his hand, then said, 'Wrong right, son. Now, no loitering.'

Owen let his mother pull him from the room.

Mrs Reynolds studied them. Jennifer smiled. 'All's well,' she said.

'I gathered.' She looked at Owen. 'Like the Charge of the Light Brigade in here. They didn't stand a chance.'

'Well,' Owen said, frowning. 'The six hundred got massacred.'

Jennifer tightened her grip on his arm. 'That's because your mother wasn't there. Come on.' Out in the hall, she shook her head. 'She was only being nice, you know. You're so . . .'

'Pedantic?'

'Whatever.'

They passed Gary and Lynk on the way. While Gary looked scared, Lynk just grinned at them and mouthed *fuck you* as he walked by.

* * *

The substitute teacher provided a welcome, if slightly confused, change from Miss Rhide, and the morning passed without incident. It was clear to Jennifer that neither Lynk nor Gary had confessed to anything, leaving the whole thing at a standstill.

The cold-weather warning meant no recesses, forcing everyone to stay inside, their time spent on arts and crafts, and the walls seemed to close in. The air grew more stifling, and the teachers' fuses got short. By noon, the smell of chaos was in the air.

Jennifer realised that the spray-painting had weakened the school's authority, and somehow the students sensed it. No longer quite as docile as before, they started crossing lines. Detentions were being levelled on all sides. The substitute teacher looked completely bewildered.

Jennifer and Owen weren't intercepted when they left the school at lunch-time. Susan was waiting for them, as promised.

'We're off to Riverview,' she told them once they'd climbed into the car. 'There's a restaurant there—'

'I know it,' Jennifer said, lighting a cigarette. 'It's the only one.'

'What a morning,' Owen muttered.

'Idiots,' Susan said, pulling the car around.

Jennifer wondered what had passed between Roulston and Owen's mother. A few months ago, she would have been furious, she would have felt betrayed and threatened. But now, it seemed like a relief. Others would say what she couldn't say – no matter how much she might want to. Confessions didn't seem to be part of her nature. There'd been little peace in her life. Just war, the battle endless. No time for introspection, no time even to relax.

Susan had changed that, and though Jennifer could barely admit it to herself, Roulston had changed things, too. He was stubborn – a match for her in that. He refused to go away, and now she had almost come to accept his presence, his involvement in their lives. Even stranger, she'd come to recognise that the doctor felt – truly felt – that he had something at stake, that it mattered to him. So far beyond the call of duty that Jennifer still had trouble trusting it. A sudden thought came to her as they approached the community of Riverview. *Maybe the good doctor's got his own history, his own rattling skeletons. That would make everything make sense, wouldn't it?*

There were still secrets, and one in particular that she and Owen kept even from Susan. *Today,* Jennifer smiled to herself. *Owen's found a place. A perfect place. Perfect in so many ways. Today, Susan, this afternoon, your son's going to get laid.*

Beneath the stage in the gym was a crawlspace. One half was blocked by horizontal rows of folded chairs that sat on tracks which allowed for each row to be pulled out or pushed in. The other half was crowded but not filled with the vinyl-covered foam mats used during Phys-Ed. Fifteen wood panels sealed the crawlspace from the rest of the gym.

It was 3.30. The school was quiet. Jennifer waited in the darkness for Owen. He'd been given a regime of remedial work by Rhide and it added a half-hour to every day, whether Rhide was around or not. He'd expected to finish early.

A shaft of light appeared from down by the panels. Owen crawled in and pulled the slab of varnished wood back into place. Hunched low, he hurried to her side. 'Christ!' he hissed, fairly jumping with excitement.

'What?'

'I went to the office,' he said breathlessly. 'To drop off the assignment. Mrs Reynolds wasn't there.'

'So?'

'So, I heard Thompson in his office. He was on the phone. Talking to *Joanne*.' He paused, waited.

'Joanne? You mean Rhide?'

'Yeah.'

'Okay, so?'

Owen crouched down, looking around in the gloom. 'Barry wanted to know if he could come over. He said, "Margaret took the kids to their grandma's" . . .'

'They're having an affair?' Jennifer almost squealed with laughter. 'Ooh, Barry's landed another one, and it's Rhide! Holy fuck. It's her!'

'Another one?'

'She's not the first. When I was in Grade Four. Didn't hear much. Too young to really get it. But a teacher had to leave. A kindergarten teacher. Real pretty.'

'Wow.' Owen sat down on a mat. 'What an asshole.'

Jennifer giggled. 'This is great. Fucking great. We've got the bitch.'

'Huh?'

'It's called blackmail, Owen. She'll have no choice. She'll back off, leave us alone—'

'No,' Owen said, his voice hard. 'No way.'

'Why not?' she demanded. 'Has she played fair? No. She deserves it. I'm fucking going to use it, Owen.'

'Don't. Please, Jennifer.'

'Why shouldn't I?'

He shrugged. 'I don't know. It just doesn't feel right. She's not succeeding, anyway. She hasn't changed us—'

'Yes she has! She's changed you!'

'Stop shouting,' he hissed.

She took a deep breath. 'She's changed you, a lot. I can see it, and so can your mom. Rhide's made you . . . I don't know, it's hard to explain . . . she's made you smaller. Inside. Smaller inside. Like she's beating you down.'

He was silent.

'I remember,' Jennifer continued after a moment, 'when I saw you for the first time. I was coming down, from acid. I saw this thread, a glowing thread over you. Your thread. It was so bright, so pure. It took my breath away—'

'What thread?'

'A thread. I don't know. That's what I saw. A glowing thread. Anyway, since I'm not dropping acid any more, I've never seen it again. On you, or on anyone else—'

'Other people had these threads?'

'Yeah. A few. You each had a different colour. Anyway, what I'm saying is, I don't know but I think if I saw your thread again, it wouldn't be, uh, as bright, not as pure, either. It wouldn't be as strong – I don't know. It doesn't make sense, eh? But she's changed you. And I want it to stop. I don't want to lose you—'

'You won't.'

Jennifer threw up her hands. 'Fuck,' she sighed.

'You mad?'

'Frustrated. And scared, I guess.'

Owen moved closer and put his arms around her. She sagged against him, closing her eyes.

'Walter Gribbs,' he said, 'the watchman at the Yacht Club—'

'The one who died.'

She felt him nod. 'Walter. Well, he said the same thing, I think. About me. He told me to hold on to myself. I'd been telling him about school—'

'About Rhide.'

'I guess.' He was silent again for a few breaths. 'I wish,' he said quietly, 'you could have met him. He liked you, liked hearing about you. I wish, well . . .'

'Me too,' Jennifer said. 'He was right, Owen. What he said about you having to hold on.' She stopped when she saw Owen wipe a sleeve across his face. 'You okay? Owen?'

He nodded. 'Sorry. I guess I miss him.'

'Are you crying?'

'I'm all right.'

Jennifer held him against her. He shook, but no sound came from him, none at all. After a minute he wiped his face again and moved back slightly. *Damn, I'm no good with crying.*

'Rhide has to back off,' she said. 'I can make her do that, now. If I spilled things, she'd have to leave. She'd have to quit.'

'Why her? What about Thompson?'

She laughed harshly. 'Forget it. That's not how it works. Trust me, Barry's staying.'

'Because he's the principal?'

'No, Owen. Because he's a man.'

'What difference does that make?'

She laughed again. 'Oh, let's shut up and fuck. I'm tired of talking.'

'Promise me something first.'

'What?'

'That you won't use it right away. Hold off. Make it a last recourse.'

'A last recourse. I love the way you talk.' She hesitated, thinking, then sighed. 'All right. But I get to decide when it's time.'

'Okay. Look, I know about it now. That something's happening to me. That makes a difference.'

'Are you sure?'

'Uh. Well, it should, shouldn't it?'

She wasn't convinced. *Knowing doesn't help, not one fucking bit. It's like the flu. You know you're getting it, but you can't stop it from coming. You trust in knowing way too much, Owen.* She said nothing, pushing it out of her mind as she removed her sweater and her shirt.

Owen did the same. It was hot and dusty, and the sound of their breathing was loud.

'We start slow,' Jennifer said.

'Okay.'

'Like the usual stuff, I mean.' She pulled off her panties. 'Come over here.'

She'd been more nervous than she'd care to admit, and all the things that they always did with each other felt different, because they were all now leading to something else. And they both knew it.

Jennifer had expected . . . something other than what happened, but her imagination proved no match for the feelings that flooded her when he uncertainly, tenderly slipped inside. *All so easy, so natural. Why did we wait so long? I'm glad we did.* She thought she'd be the one feeling vulnerable, but it didn't feel like that at all. *He's helpless, pressed here against me, moving inside me – not fast and eager, but exploring, deliberately exploring. It's happening – I'm finally swallowing him up, and I'll make him safe, here, inside me. Safe, that's what it's all about. I . . . I didn't know.*

V

Midnight hours. Sten lay curled up on the sofa, shivering under the blankets. *One after another after another, endless midnight hours. Get out of my head. There's not enough room. Not for both of us, and I can't leave. I've got nowhere to go. Get out get out get out wherever you are!*

Water dripped steadily from the guttering above the living-room window. *A warm spell. So sudden, a shock to the system, to the ordered brilliance of the human body. I'm sick. Something broke, I feel it rattling inside me. You can't fix it. No one can. Rattle rattle rattle. I'm cold. I can't catch up. I'm permafrost. Mammoth steaks, that's me, surrounded by starving Russians.*

The dogs rubbed against the kennel's walls. *Rustle rustle, rattle rattle. Inside and out, we've all come loose. Escape is impossible. Life is what it is. Only Max has got away. I never beat any of you, but you hate me anyway. Why? You all stink of fear. So do I. What's the difference? We're all animals of the earth, chained to our natures, trapped inside our own fates. You were the first to walk with us, the first to share heat and food. We're in step with each other. We've always been. I don't understand.*

Water dripped. There was no wind, none at all. The world's fierce breath was held in check, and Sten's heart hammered with terror. Outside . . . *rustle rustle, the chain-link fence recording perfectly the restless beasts and their restless lives.*

Another beer? It's a warm spell. An early spring, maybe. The ice on the river has thinned, stripped of snow and showing its bruises. It's been a week. Or two. Makes no difference, but the snow's vanishing, shrinking down to blood-coloured pools. God, I'm thinking clearly. It's all clear now. I've drunk a dozen beers today – all in my head, nowhere else. I don't know, is anyone out there?

All so clear. The things I've done. My games, played to the edge of death. My winter, frozen in place for so long now. Thawing, and there I am, lying in a puddle, revealed at last.

Water dripped, sloshed muddily.

Rattle rattle. Here I am, sick and lucid, lucidly sick, the jester done his dancing, finally at rest. I've drunk a dozen beers. I'm blasted. I can't even get up. Why get up? I'll only fall down. She's cleaned up the bed. It's hers now, smelling of bleach and bath oil. She says nothing. I talk endlessly, here in my head. Drunk. The fantasy is real, in here. She's done the same. She talks inside, too. What's she saying?

Sleep. They can both sleep. Dreaming of freedom. It's not what I wanted, not what I ever wanted. I was a kid, once. I knew how to laugh, once. I didn't dream of this. I never guessed my fate. The boy never guessed his. He used to laugh at me and shake his head. I couldn't even walk straight, vodka in my Thermos, that stinking switchman with the cataracts I took my 'coffee breaks' with, both of us getting soused and laughing at the great joke we were playing. Fooling the bosses, kids behind the school with a bottle in a paper bag. The boy used to laugh.

Water dripped, the only sound from outside. The only sound. Sten went still, held his breath. Nothing. He sighed, wrapping the blanket tighter around himself.

There's no such thing as freedom. Just a blood-smeared joke. The couplings pushing into place, with a boy in between. Through his pelvis, crushing bone, his guts, front and back, driven together, seeking to join and caring nothing about his screaming and the gushing fluids. Just trying to come together, the way they were meant to.

Water dripping, and silence.

He climbed to his feet, holding the blanket around him. He walked into the hall, the floor cold through his socks. He came to the back door, opened it and stepped through on to the porch.

The kennel door was open. The dogs were gone.

VI

Fisk woke slowly, a kind of climbing struggle as his mind battled with a sense of urgency and the exhaustion that clung on, that told him it wasn't yet morning, that there were hours left to this night.

He groaned, rolled on to his back, and opened his eyes. The room was still, cast in greys and blacks. The luminescent numbers on the clock read 3 a.m. He tried to think of what had woken him.

The thaw had come. By morning, he knew, the field of mud would be clear, black and depthless and waiting for him once again. Another spring, another season for his torture. It would be his last – he'd let the field embrace him, drag him down into darkness.

The thaw. The river's ice would show its fissures, undermined by the too-warm water coming from the city, rotting and fraying beneath the sun. It had been a season without end, swinging around again and again, and all he could do was wait. *This is the last one.*

He rose from bed and went to the bathroom.

The little ones would be awake in the cellar, still tuned to the outer world's cycles. Rat would be chewing at the cage door. Moon and Gold would be pacing, that bobbing motion that carried them back and forth, up and around. They'd have heard his footsteps now, and his piss splashing into the toilet. They'd be nervous, twitching with fear. Rat was going wild, so frantic, so thoroughly insane.

His face in the mirror looked ancient, yellowed and cracked like a picture in a photo album from the last century. A face that didn't belong to the modern age, a face that was winter itself.

But the season has turned.

Fisk wasn't looking forward to the hours ahead, while he waited for dawn. He still felt a trembling urgency, and wondered at its source. *Heart attack? No. No pain. Nightmare? Can't remember one.*

He left the bathroom and went to the kitchen, still in only his underwear. The rows of cages outside waited in the darkness, blockish and black between the aisles of snow patches, mud and puddles.

Something was wrong. He leaned over the sink and rapped his knuckles on the window. He waited to see the glitter of eyes, waited to hear the rattles and the scraping claws. *Nothing. They're not there any more.*

He walked slowly into the hallway, threw on his winter parka and stepped into his boots. At the back door he flicked on the yard lamps, then went outside. The white light revealed each empty cage – its door back in place, and the thousands of mink tracks scattering everywhere, and among them, down each aisle, the tracks of a person – the boot imprints small, the steps short.

The cold air came up under his parka, making his legs shiver, his crotch tighten. He could feel panic, deep inside him, but he wouldn't let it out. No point in letting it out. And rage – but that too could wait.

One of those boys. I should call the cops. But what can they do? It's too late anyway. My beasts are free, racing away through the darkness, flowing across the night. They've escaped, each one insane, each one unleashed.

He walked down the first row. *My beasts are free. Out into the thaw. I'm ruined. Wiped out.* The tracks in their thousands were all that remained, claws pinching the mud, darting memories of escape. Not one left. So many would die. On the highway, to dogs and owls, but mostly the highway. They'd run. *Nothing will stop them, run until exhausted, run until dead of burst hearts.*

But I still have the ones in my cellar. Enough for me, for now. From now on. That's the place for my . . . my anger, my revenge. Nothing more to say, nothing more to do. He turned around and headed back inside. *My beasts are free. Thank God.*

CHAPTER EIGHTEEN

I

STEN WASN'T HOME and the car was gone. So were the dogs. *Maybe he's taken them for a run.*

Elouise began preparing to make breakfast for her and Jennifer. It was Sunday, and Dr Roulston would be by before noon. She wondered if she'd be the only one there to meet him, since Jennifer was sure to head out – the day was clear, bright and warm. She'd want to be with Owen. It had come slowly, but Elouise could now see the change that had come to her daughter. The anger was still there, of course, but Jennifer had found friends that mattered, and they'd given her a safe place, a refuge, where she found strength, maybe even faith.

Elouise remembered Sundays as a child. She remembered a church, where they sang hymns and listened to an old man reading from the Bible. The sun would come down through the windows, stained by the glass into rainbow streams. A cloth on the altar, candles throwing out wavering light, some of them flickering dangerously through the morning – she had watched those ones, holding her breath when it seemed they would go out. She'd lose track of the old man's words – only the candles mattered, and the fear that they'd go out. She couldn't recall if they ever did.

She stood in front of the sink. *I'll have to walk. At least a mile on the highway. I'll be able to make the eleven o'clock service. I'll wear the blue dress – it's the only one that still fits, which is funny, because it used to be the only one I couldn't wear any more. Not for years. I'll leave Jennifer a note, and another one for the doctor.*

She returned the egg carton to the refrigerator and went upstairs to the bedroom.

They'd stopped going to church after the war. With her brother's death, a candle had gone out in the family, the fragile illusion of faith had been shattered. The men who came back cussed, smoked and drank. Some of them had spilled blood in churches, after all, and they were all more in this world and less in the other. Most of them believed in one thing – chance, the unguessable twist of fate. There were those who tried to go back, to the old ways, and some seemed to succeed – at least to all outward appearances, but so many others stood stiffly at the pews, fidgeting, their eyes turned inward, bringing with them memories of hell.

Things changed. For everyone. It was harder to believe in God, and there were riches in the world now, so many temptations easily served.

She looked at herself in the mirror. The dress carried

her back ten, fifteen years, but the face that she saw looked old, pulled down by hard years.

The front door banged open downstairs and she heard Sten's boots clump into the living room. 'Elouise!' he called harshly. 'Where the hell are you?'

As she stepped into the hallway, she heard music from a record come on in Jennifer's room. Elouise hesitated, then went downstairs.

Sten had moved to the kitchen, tracking mud all over the floor. He looked sober, but exhausted and shaken. He was spooning ground coffee into the percolator. 'Someone sprung them,' he said, not turning. 'My dogs. They've run off.' He slammed the percolator down on an element and turned the heat on. Elouise went over and removed it, shaking it in answer to his glare – *no water*. He sighed and sat down as she went to the sink.

'Car's in the ditch,' he said, massaging his temples. 'Slid off a section road. I looked everywhere. Had to walk back. Think I broke the rad. And an axle. They've run off. I've got to call the farmers around here, tell them they can shoot if they have to.' He paused and looked over at her. 'That's nice,' he said sourly. 'Getting dressed up for Roulston, eh?'

She shook her head and took from her purse a pen and notepad. She wrote down *Church* and showed it to him.

His face twitched as he read it, then he sat back, looking away. 'A fuckin' waste of time. What are you going to do, walk?'

She nodded.

'Fuckin' waste of time. I'm heading out again. After some goddamned breakfast, which I see I'm going to

have to make on my own. This is what it's come to.
Well, you go pray, dear. Go sing your hymns. Go, get
out of my sight.'

Her path along the west side of the highway was rutted and muddy. There were dead animals everywhere,
at least a dozen within sight – on the highway itself,
flattened and smeared by tyres – and on the shoulders
and in the ditch on her right. All the same kind of animals, small, their bodies longer than a cat's, their fur a
thick, dark brown. Weasels, or mink – she didn't really
know the difference. She stepped over them, walked
around them, feeling fear, a growing sense of dread, as
if she were in some way gathering each one to her, collecting something from each tiny, motionless body, as-
suming a burden that she couldn't identify.

*Like the rabbit, they were so helpless to their fate.
Where did they all come from? Where were they going?*

The gravel was soft and greasy, yielding beneath
her boots. The sound of trickling water surrounded
her, punctuated by the wet hiss coming from the occasional car. The sun felt surprisingly warm, and there
was almost no wind. She could see the church spire
now, rising above a line of leafless trees. *Orthodox. I
should have remembered. I've never been inside, but
I've seen it from the car window. Orthodox. That
would have mattered once, it would have stopped me.
But now . . . now it's just what's built around the altar, just the walls holding it in. It doesn't matter what's
on them or how they're shaped, or that things are
done differently inside. It doesn't matter which face
they've put on God. Not any more.*

She knew why she'd come. She was tired of being

alone. She'd lost her beliefs; her solitary voice wasn't strong enough against everything else. There'd be people inside, all believing, all knowing the importance of coming together. That was all that mattered. She didn't need to ask for anything, didn't need God answering her prayers – she no longer had faith in that, anyway. God was the solid wood of the altar under her hand, the sun's heat out here as it filled the morning air, a hundred voices guiding a hymn. God was what couldn't be called into question.

I need to be reminded of that. That spire, the shiny chrome of the cars clustered out front, those crows hopping across the highway to feed on a dead animal, and the ones wheeling down from behind the spire, loud as they join all those others in the branches.

Elouise reached the driveway. Her legs trembled. She could feel the weight of what she'd gathered on her journey – it had settled into her bones, as heavy as mourning for a lost one. As she passed down the treed aisle, she looked up at the crows in the branches. They chattered, bickered, batted their wings and fidgeted on their perches. They all seemed to be waiting for something.

She crossed the parking lot and approached the front steps. An organ was playing inside. Beside the front door stood a poster-board, listing the day's sermon – in Ukrainian – but the word *Welcome* was written below it.

Elouise turned at the sudden cacophony coming from the twin rows of trees. The crows, cawing and laughing, had taken to the air, flapping out over the highway, off to their bounteous feasting.

They'll find only flesh. The thought came to her all

at once. *I've done that much. I hope I can light candles here. After the service. Will that be possible? Their deaths can't be questioned, after all. So, neither can their lives. The crows know that. They help the flesh disappear, and they don't question anything. Why doubt the taste on your tongue? I'd speak for them all, if I could. My hand touching the body of God. A moment of comfort, of connection, for us all. I can free us all.*

She opened one of the heavy doors and stepped inside to singing, but she knew now that God's music was behind her, filling the air.

II

The playground had turned into a lake. I saw Carl, in rubber boots, standing out in the middle. He had a sapling in his hands – at least seven feet long – which he used to push around pieces of ice.

I stopped on the roadside. 'Hey!'

He looked over.

'Where is everybody?' I asked.

Carl slowly sloshed towards me, making sure he didn't get a soaker. He stopped on the other side of the flooded ditch and leaned on the pole. 'What?'

'Where's Roland? I thought we were all meeting, heading down to the river?'

Carl shrugged, then wiped his runny nose on the sleeve of his blue-checked jack-shirt. 'Don't know. I haven't seen him. Or Lynk. Haven't seen anybody.' He glanced up at my face, then away. 'Well. Roland. This morning. He was looking for Mr Louper.'

'Louper? Jennifer's dad? Why?'

'Don't know.'

I looked up the road. 'What about Jennifer?'

He shook his head.

'What are you doing out there?'

'Nothing.'

I pointed at his arm. 'All that stuff come from just your nose, Carl? Is that all you do, make snot?'

He hefted the sapling, water running down to his gloved hands. 'Fuck off.'

I grinned. 'Gary beaten you up lately?'

'No. Fuck off, Owen.'

'How come, do you think? How come Gary doesn't beat you up any more?'

''Cause you kicked him in the balls, I guess.'

'Maybe because I told him not to,' I said, watching his face.

He looked at me sharply. 'Why? So you could?'

'I've never touched you,' I said. 'Not since that first time, on the boat. You're not worth it, Carl.'

'How come you hate me, Owen? I've never done nothing to you.'

All those Carls. In every school. You get nailed early, and that's it, you're stuck. 'Wipe your nose,' I said, turning away.

I thought about heading to Jennifer's house, or at least hanging around outside until she saw me. But my mood had gone dark. I'd wanted to talk and wander around with Roland, even if it meant Lynk being there, too – even though they hated each other, they still hung out together. They'd been doing it too long, and there really wasn't anyone else. I think they expected everything to settle down, even out, sooner or later. I think they were waiting for the return of how things used to be – a year ago, two years ago. Before the body. Before me.

I decided to head to the river alone.

Lynk didn't even believe the body ever existed. I couldn't understand him. He'd seen it along with the rest of us. We'd all talked about it, and he'd been the one to convince the rest of us not to call the cops. He'd talked about the guy being murdered, and the killer was out there and would go after us. Ridiculous, when I thought about it now. We'd been like . . . *kids*.

So much had changed. We'd since built our worlds anew, and each of us in a different way. Maybe Lynk's version couldn't accept what we'd found.

I went along the road that ran beside the bottom end of the playground. Carl had returned to the middle of the lake, but I could see him glance over at me every now and then. I left his line of sight, slipping through the windbreak and emerging on to the south edge of Fisk's land. I remembered a year ago, walking with my friends here, coming down from the highway. It seemed like centuries had passed since. In that time, I'd given up my claim to the city, just as it had done to me. It had become an *other* place, still familiar but not my own. This new world – no longer as new to me as it had once been – was now a part of my life. The mud under my boots, the crows specking the sky above the highway, the dark thickets edging the river – all mine, now. And yet, something told me it was all changing, getting older even as I did, and that the shaping of what I'd become had to do more with time than with place. And that, like the body, my life here and now would one day disappear, become tenuous and unreal – that

Lynk's world would win out in the end, would engulf and drown us all.

A bank of snow marked the line between Fisk's field and the ribbon of trees and bushes lining the river. The snow remained among the trees and the air felt colder as I stepped into their shadows.

There were tracks everywhere – tracks that might've come from squirrels, or weasels, and tracks from deer, and rabbit and dog. And, among them, the deep punching of a man's footsteps, winding a seemingly random path through the snow – I crossed them again and again as I approached the river.

The snow was gone, leaving only the ice and pools of water. The ice had cracked, making veins and dark blotches all across the pitted, uneven surface. I walked down to the bank's edge. Brown-stained snow crowded the waterline, about six feet below the embankment.

Walking its edge, I headed north. I'd come to houses soon, on my left, where I'd begin crossing back yards, eventually arriving at my own house. There were no fences to cross, just a few hedgerows to go around along the river's edge.

This section of the river ran straight, all the way to the Yacht Club. As I came clear of some bushes, I saw, out on the ice, a man and two dogs. And then I saw a third dog, wallowing helpless in a patch of open water, its front legs chopping the water as it struggled against the current.

The man had gone down to his hands and knees and was crawling through ten inches of water towards the drowning dog. The other two animals ran back and forth behind him, as if playing.

The scene was there in front of me, eerily silent.

The drowning dog saw the man and tried to swim to him, but there was broken ice in the way. The dog then tried to climb on to the rafts, but kept slipping back as they turned under its weight.

The man lay down. He squirmed to the edge of the open water. The ice pitched under him and he spread-eagled. The dog in the water had been pulled by the current to one edge, but it had gotten its front legs on to the ice and was pulling itself along, closer and closer to the man.

I jumped down the embankment, landing in deep snow. Clambering free, I hesitated, unsure of what to do. This side of the river was the most melted, since it faced south, but there were broken chunks of ice crowded on this side, most of them frozen into the mud bottom. Although water covered everything, there were places to cross over, on to the thicker surface beyond.

The ice the man lay on tilted and I stared as he slid head first into the water. The dog he'd been trying to reach at that moment scrambled its way on to solid ice.

The man broke surface weakly, the current forcing him against the jagged ice. He reached out and threw his arm over its edge. The river tugged at him, sweeping his legs until he was jackknifed, both arms and head above water, everything else beneath it.

I moved gingerly out on the frozen slabs, then jumped and landed, skidding, on firmer footing. Then I ran towards them.

The man was losing the struggle. He clawed at the ice, but I could see him weakening.

Then the dogs were there, biting into his arms and pulling him, worrying him with savage tugs. New

cracks appeared all around them. The man screamed –
the first sound I heard apart from the splashing under
my boots and my harsh breath as I ran.

One of the dogs got the man's parka hood in its
jaws. Pulling on it had driven the man's face against
the ice. Another scream came, this one muffled.

'Pull him!' I yelled. I was still about thirty feet away,
water spreading out between us. The ice the dogs were
on was going down – I knew that my added weight
would just hasten its plunge.

*They're all going to drown. All of them. He'll go
under the ice. His flesh will swell, go pale and sodden.
The fish will eat his eyes. And the crayfish will feast on
his insides. He'll drift along the bottom, for miles and
miles, until he snags, until the gases inside him lift him
up, carrying him to the surface. Maybe he'll be found,
then, or maybe he'll go through the dam or the locks.
Maybe he'll disappear for ever.*

But the dogs dragged him on to the ice. He couldn't
move, though his fingers still groped. The dogs dragged
him along, over ice that dipped and tilted and was
awash in churning brown water.

'Here!' I called. 'Over here!'

The man tried to look up, but the hood stopped
him. He twisted his head around, and I saw his eyes,
wide and encrusted, blood streaming down his face
from countless lacerations, his mouth open, his lower
lip a blotch of bright red.

Three dogs. I knew who he was. 'Mr Louper! Try
crawling! The ice is going down – too much weight.'

He gaped at me.

The tilt sharpened. They began sliding back. I

swore and jumped on to the raft. My weight, slight as it was, evened things out. They stopped sliding, and the dogs resumed dragging him closer to where I stood.

When the tilt reversed itself, I leapt off the floe. It helped, but they all slid towards me, towards the widening crack between us. I got down on my hands and knees. The water was numbing, sending a shock through me.

'Tell them to let go!' I said. 'I'll catch you. You're sliding right to me. They have to get off!'

Mr Louper twisted his head again. He blinked, looked around as much as he could. 'Away,' he croaked. 'Caesar, away!'

The dog gripping his left arm in its jaws ducked at the command.

'Caesar, away! Behind the boy! Away!' The dog let go and bounded across the crack, its paws leaving streaks of blood.

I heard it pacing behind me, coughing as it breathed.

'Kaja, away! To Caesar, damn you!'

The dog with the hood in its jaws jumped back, slipping on the tilting ice, its back end skewing around. I reached for its tail and managed to close my fingers around it. My grip was weak, numbed by the cold, but I pulled anyway. Kaja's back end went down into the water. I lost my grip but reached out again and found her collar. I needed both hands to pull her on to the ice beside me.

Mr Louper was calling off the third dog, Shane, but it paid no attention at all, still pulling on his right wrist even as they both slid into the water. Mr Louper went down on top of Shane. I saw him reach out with his left arm and I grabbed the wrist. I tried to pull him out, but he was too heavy. I felt myself sliding and lay flat.

'Climb!' I said. 'Just climb!'

Shane was nowhere in sight, and Mr Louper's whole right side was under water. He kicked and his left leg slashed upward. I let go of his arm with one hand and clutched him around the ankle – he'd lost his boot and sock, and the foot was blue and cold. I pulled his leg up and he got his knee on to the ice.

'Climb on me,' I said.

He pulled his arm free from my grip and I felt his hand clutch my parka. He kicked his other leg on to the ice and all at once the air was pushed from my lungs. He rolled on to me, his right arm stretched straight down into the water.

'I'm not losing you,' he gasped. 'I'm not. Not again.'

I squirmed my way clear, rolled back through the sloshing water.

Mr Louper reached for me with his left hand. I gripped it, still lying flat out. I felt him straining, then with a heave he raised his right arm and lifted Shane's limp body by the collar, out of the water.

'Come on,' I said. 'It's flooding – come on!'

Somehow, he got to his feet, Shane in his arms. Flanked by the other two dogs, he followed me back to shore.

'That's my house over there,' I said, teeth chattering uncontrollably. 'Let's go.'

Slowly, we made our way to my yard. Mr Louper held Shane with its head down by his knees. Water streamed from the dog's open mouth. The man was sobbing, clutching the animal against his chest.

THIS RIVER AWAKENS 507

We'd reached the lawn when I heard the dog cough. It kicked a hind leg, catching Mr Louper under the jaw. He grunted in pain and sagged to the ground. Shane squirmed free of his arms and fell on to his side, retching. The other dogs came up and each tried to lie down beside Shane, but he kicked them away when he felt their touch.

Mr Louper was bawling his eyes out.

I looked at them all a moment longer, then I went to get help.

III

She remembered him inside her, and his body against her. *It doesn't make me a slut. I won't do that with anyone else. Everything's changed now. I'm over with, I'm not the way I was, not any more.*

The house was silent, the only sound the melting snow outside. Her mother had gone somewhere in the morning, and her father had left a little while later. She'd stayed in her room, the door locked, listening to records until she was certain she was finally alone.

Jennifer lay on the bed, letting the quiet surround her with its peace. She wanted him again. Here in this bed with the door locked and no one else at home. They'd have hours together, as many as they wanted, with Rhide disposed of, Roulston back in his hospital, Queen Anne in someone else's cupboard, her father ... dead or gone – dead, so he'd never come back, never fuck her up the ass again – and her mother in a convent or something, where everyone else held the same vows of silence.

She heard the door open downstairs, heard her mother's boots, the steps careful, few as she stopped on the small, square rug intended for muddy shoes, where she unbuttoned her coat, placed her gloves on the shelf, then stepped out of the boots. Stockinged feet moved down the hall, into the kitchen. Water filled a kettle.

Sighing, Jennifer sat up. *Another record? No, I'm hungry.* She unlocked the door and went downstairs.

Her mother was wearing a blue dress — Jennifer thought for a moment that it was brand new, then she remembered it, a vague collection of scenes from years ago taking form in her mind. 'Well,' she said, entering the kitchen, 'I barely recognised you.'

Smiling, her mother started taking things out of the refrigerator.

Jennifer sat down at the table and lit a cigarette. She saw the note and angled it so that she could read it. She looked up. 'Church? You're kidding. Have you ever been to one before?'

'When I was a child,' her mother said, her voice rasping, her back to Jennifer as she broke eggs into a bowl and began whipping them.

'Oh.' Jennifer tapped ash on to the ashtray. 'You talked! Was there a faith healer there or something? Christ, you talked!'

'I'm out of practice,' she said slowly. 'I'm sorry. It hurts.'

'Don't tell me you've found God.'

Her mother set a frying pan on to the stove-top and flicked on the heat. She turned and smiled. 'I think,' she said, an odd light in her eyes, 'that it was the crows.'

'Huh?'

'On the road, yes,' she said, brushing at her greying hair. She turned and poured the egg into the pan. 'They were all talking. On the way home. I talked to them, and they talked back.'

Jennifer held her attention on her mother, following her every move. 'You didn't accidentally drop some acid, did you?'

'I don't think so. Is that what it's like, Jennifer? Do you talk with birds?'

'Well, you might. Like, a whole conversation.'

'Oh.' She shook her head. 'No, I couldn't understand them. There were dead animals on the road. The crows were eating them. They got angry when I came too close. I told them not to worry.'

Jennifer frowned. 'This is so strange. You're talking. I'd almost forgotten the sound of your voice. And here you are, talking about crows. Eating dead animals.'

Her mother removed the pan and dished scrambled eggs on to two plates. She brought them over, then moved behind Jennifer and rested her hands on her shoulders. 'You're growing up so fast,' she said. 'I'm sorry it's what you had to do—'

'Not a problem,' Jennifer said quickly. 'Really. It's better this way.'

'I know. What I meant to say . . . I'm proud of you.'

'Oh Christ,' Jennifer said. She laughed, then stood and faced her mother. 'You must be kidding, Mom. I'm a mess!'

'You're fine,' she said. 'You are. And I plan to say a few things to that teacher of yours.'

'You don't have to. Owen's mom chewed her out. So has Dr Roulston. She won't cause any more trouble—'

'That's not the point. I have things to say to her, that's all.'

'All right,' Jennifer said slowly.

The phone rang and she went over and answered it. Susan was on the other end.

'Jennifer? Your father's here.'

'What? Oh, I'm sorry—'

'No, no. He fell through the ice. He was trying to save one of his dogs, I think. Owen saw it. Owen helped him. So, your father needs some dry clothes – he's swimming in Jim's. And leashes for the dogs – they're in the garage right now.'

'All of them?'

'Well, three. Is that all of them? Your father mentioned one called Max—'

'No, that's all of them. We lost Max about a year ago.'

'One almost drowned, but he seems all right now.'

'Okay, I'll be right over.'

'Is your mother there?'

'Yes.'

'I'd like to talk to her, Jennifer.'

She handed the phone to her mother, who'd come to her side.

'Hello?' She listened for a moment, one hand going to her chest, then, seeing Jennifer, she waved her away.

Jennifer hesitated. Susan was doing all the talking. Her mother gestured a second time. 'All right.' She went upstairs and entered her parents' room. *He almost drowned. Unbelievable. His clothes. Yuck. Idiot, fucking drunk.* She found a travel bag, trying not to think about what she was doing as she quickly went through the drawers – underwear, socks, work pants, undershirt and shirt. She found a sweater in the closet, among the shoes, and a pair of scuffed work boots. With everything stuffed into the bag, she headed back downstairs.

Her mother was still on the phone, still listening, her face wet with tears. Jennifer set the bag down by the door. She went into the kitchen and found a box of Kleenex, which she brought back to her mother. She paused then, thinking.

Leashes. By the back door.

They hung on a peg, four sets of long, worn leather. She collected three of them and returned to the front door. It was too painful to watch her mother. She quickly threw on her jacket and pulled on her sneakers. Shouldering the bag, and with the leashes in one hand, she quietly left the house.

The asphalt road was bare, but wet. Water filled the ditches, and the playground had flooded. The sky overhead was a stunning, bright blue.

Jennifer had reached the bend down at the bottom of the playground when she saw Lynk, emerging from the windrow down the path to her right.

'Slut!' he yelled, approaching. 'You're all fucked. Don't blame me 'cause you're all fucked!'

'What's your problem?' she asked as she continued walking.

He came up beside her. 'Roland knows. I told him everything. You don't know shit. Neither does Owen. Just Roland.'

'You mean spray-painting the school? Burning down the candle factory? Get real. We know, Lynk. You're a fucked-up little shit. So what?'

'Hah, you don't know anything. But I'll tell you.

Only I want to neck. You and me. That's the deal. I can tell you something – you won't fucking believe it, Jennifer. But that's the deal.'

'Fuck you.'

The driveway was just ahead.

Lynk pushed her, grabbing for her tits. She twisted away, staggering, the bag dropping to the ground. She turned as he came close again, his face twisted with hate. She swung the leashes at that face. He shrieked in pain and jumped back.

Jennifer glared at him, the leashes held ready.

Lynk rubbed at the red marks on his cheek. 'Fuck,' he said. 'What's with my face anyway?'

She watched him walk off, then picked up the bag and headed down the driveway.

Her father looked shrunken, pitiful inside Jim's morning coat. He sat hunched over on the sofa, a cup of coffee in his hands. His eyes shifted briefly as Jennifer entered, then he resumed staring at his hands.

'Are you drunk?' she asked.

The Brands had left the room, were all in the kitchen. He shook his head, not looking up.

Jennifer dropped the bag beside him. 'Get dressed. I'll be in the kitchen.'

Owen was bundled under blankets, flushed from a hot bath. He grinned as she sat down and lit a cigarette. 'You should've seen it,' he said. 'The ice was breaking up everywhere.'

'You saved him?'

'Nah.'

Jennifer's gaze found Susan's as Owen continued, 'I couldn't get close enough. The dogs saved him.'

'The dogs?'

'They pulled him out. He's got the bite marks on his arms to prove it.'

Susan's expression was hard to read, intense, with something like fear and relief and a half-dozen other emotions all mixed up behind her eyes. After a moment, she went over to the stove. Jennifer looked back at Owen. 'What about the cuts on his face?'

'One of the dogs had his hood. He got scraped across the ice.'

Susan set a cup of coffee in front of Jennifer. 'Now you can sell the story to *Reader's Digest*. Man's best friend, as they say.'

They were trying to put her at ease, but it wasn't working. She felt so ashamed of the little man getting dressed in the other room. Her friends here couldn't help but see her differently now. They couldn't help but feel pity. Even Owen, because he'd seen everything, the stupid old man out on the ice, floundering helpless in the water. 'What was he doing out there?' she asked.

'One of the dogs fell in,' Owen said. 'He was trying to save it.'

Susan added, 'But it ended up the other way around.' She sat down beside Jennifer.

'I'm sorry about all this—'

'Don't be,' Susan cut in. 'It was an accident, but it turned out okay. That's all that counts. I think your father's all right. What's shaken him, got him thinking, isn't what you'd expect, Jennifer.'

'What do you mean?'

'Well, he said he couldn't believe that the dogs saved him. He thought they hated him, which was why they ran away.'

'You mean they escaped? I didn't know that.'

Susan looked at Owen, who shrugged and said, 'That's what he told me. Someone let them out. Last night.'

'Christ.'

'Hungry?' Susan asked.

IV

The sun was setting, bringing to a close God's day of rest. Fisk sat in his living room, the cattle prod on the table in front of him.

They're waiting down there. For me. The bastards think they can do anything. It's their season, after all. This sinking away, into the earth, the land's own darkness showing itself again. They think they can just walk up, set everything loose, and I'm not going to give a fuck. What did I fight for, all those years ago? For the little pricks to just walk all over me, like I didn't matter, like I was a piece of dirt? I took a chunk of shrapnel for them. What the hell for?

It's time to pay the piper, it's time they danced to my tune. I've been letting things slip. Lost my vigilance. I went soft, and they got to me. Never again. They'll pay the piper, with screams, with so much pain they'll age right in front of me – the light in their eyes will dim away to a dull flicker. They'll finally see things how I see things, all the tired, cracked refuse cluttering this modern age. I'll make them old. I'll twist every season around them. There on the maypole, drawing the ribbons tight.

He pushed himself upright, the cattle prod in his

hands. His crotch ached in anticipation. *No more waiting. I've been letting it slip away. No more. They've hurt me. Now it's my turn. And not just playing any more. The game's over with. It's for real this time, finally for real.*

He walked down the hallway, making his footfalls loud. *Let them know I'm coming.* The wallpaper on either side looked even more faded, less real and more just a tired, useless memory. He reached the top of the stairs and opened the door.

Listen to them. They finally understand what's coming.

Fisk turned on the cellar light and went down the stairs, his breathing loud, but tight in his chest. He felt his cock against his leg, rubbing with each step. *There'll be an accident if I'm not careful. An accident. How embarrassing.*

He reached the uneven concrete floor, came to the cages. He saw at once the hole in Rat's door, the wires chewed, the wood gnawed. Rat was free. Fisk turned quickly, expecting to see the creature scampering up the stairs. But the steps were unoccupied. So far. He backed to them, until one heel clumped against the bottom step. He scanned the floor, squinting at shadows in the dim light.

He thought he heard a faint call. Something like a voice, coming through the walls. *Dorry? Go away, dear. Not now. You don't want to see me now.*

Rat was hiding, somewhere – beneath the cages, or under the workbench. He'd gotten out of the cage, but he wasn't free. Not yet. Not ever. The other two mink paced in their prisons, watching, their eyes glistening. Fisk waited.

He'll be fast. He'll get by me. I'd better close the door. He began climbing the stairs, backwards, his eyes scanning the cellar, the steps below. He reached the top, the open door behind him. He activated the cattle prod and held it ready in his right hand, then groped backward with his free hand, hunting for the door-knob.

The floor creaked behind him. Gasping in alarm, Fisk spun around. The cattle prod pushed against something and discharged. Fisk staggered, halfway around, as he was pushed. He tottered, clutching for something to hold on to as the pushing continued. Then the weight slipped past him – a body, plunging, thumping hard on the stairs, rolling, tumbling down to lie motionless and small on the cellar floor.

Fisk stared down at the boy, unable to think, unable to register what had happened.

He's not moving. His eyes are wide open. One of the boys.

He went down the stairs, crouched beside the body. *He's dead. Dead outright – I know that look. He was dead before he hit the stairs, before he fell against me. He was dead instantly. That can't be. It was just a cattle prod. This doesn't make sense.*

Oh God, can you hear me? God? Let me go back, bring the sun back up into the sky. Do this for me, please.

Rat bolted past him, leapt for the stairs and vanished beyond the doorway.

Rat's free. Escaped. Rat's gone wild, unleashed. Rat's looking for the throne of summer, he is. It's his now, finally his. And all the blossoms come pelting down, and the ashes that hung in the air from the burning wheel, the rain will bring them down. Down to the earth. Rat's free, finally free.

Fisk stood. He went to the other cages. 'I'm sorry,' he said. 'Game's over.' He flipped open the cage doors. The mink jumped out, followed in Rat's path, clambering lightly over the boy's chest and hopping up the stairs.

He went back to the boy and picked him up. *Too light. Damn you, God. Damn you to hell.* His shoes thumped loudly on the stairs as he made his way upward.

I'm going to jail. The rest of my life. I'll lose everything – but not enough, not nearly enough. He had to make a phone call. They'd all come, car after car slewing down the track, crowding his driveway. And Bill would be there, on his face a helpless, confused look. He'd study Fisk's face. He'd ask, *Why, Hodgson? After all you've been through, why bring it back now? Like this, why like this?* And Fisk would shrug, eyes on the field of mud, eyes like broken windows and the mud swirling as it pulled his soul out, sucked it down into the dark. He'd gag, but only momentarily, as the mouse pushed its way clear of his throat, claws biting as it clambered over his swollen tongue, the fur damp and bitter-sweet. Flying out as he coughed, landing at a run, straight for the field, because that's where mice lived. *Why, Hodgson? Stupid question. We let it all go, Bill. I saw faith skewered by a bayonet, pinned writhing on the dusty ground. I saw it, and felt nothing. What was left? Ashes. You don't know how Dorry became my shadow, because mine had disappeared. You don't know how she held me at night. You don't know how much I wanted kids of my own, so I could tell my story, so I could relieve the . . . the pressure. Just once, that's all it would have taken, and I could've walked tall, upright for ever afterwards.*

You don't get it, Bill. You never did, you and your buddies down at that crypt you call the hall. We pissed our pants back then, struggling through the salty water up on to the beaches, coming face to face – for the first time – with what people could do to each other. I didn't want their blood. They didn't want mine. What the hell were we doing? You sit there night after night swapping tales, pretending what you did back then was worthwhile. A fucking cause. Freedom – oh, how Rat's laughing right now, but Rat's mistaken. Deeply mistaken. Freed into madness, don't you see? They proclaimed a war, and gave us the rules that freed us to become insane. The more insane you were, the more medals you got. I got a chestful, Bill. And once you've been there, there's no going back. Not for real, because you know what a fool you were, falling for war, falling for all the excuses they gave you to go mad.

I didn't want their blood, but I took it. They didn't want mine, but they took it. We were good little boys, because our dads gathered at the Legion and played on. They didn't explain how it'd been the first time – they didn't want to be lessened in their sons' eyes. What a joke.

It was an accident, Bill. That's all. This time, I wasn't given permission. This time, I didn't have any rules backing me. And I'll tell you something, Bill. Something I've learned, just now. God's up there and He sees no difference. Every cross they stuck in the ground above those faceless bodies in those flowering fields, it's like a stake in His heart, a piercing of His soul. He never meant it that way, Bill.

So look at my face, sir, and see what death has cost me. I'm what God looks at in the mirror, too numb to even cry. And you and the boys can mutter and shake your heads, but inside each of you I'll be there, cold and spinning like an unmelting chunk of ice in the river, caught in the currents for ever. Crusted and dirty, I'm your terror of knowing. Sorry, but that's how it is. That's how it will be for the rest of your lives.

He pictured himself, sitting in a cell, as the seasons went around, and around. Others would be set free in the night. Others would die. Guards would change, retire. But he would remain, unending, rocking back and forth in his chair, the blood swishing back and forth in time, there in his head, numbing his cheeks, numbing everything, until only his eyes felt alive. He'd be grinning at all the ghosts. 'It's all right,' he'd tell them. 'I'm going to live for ever.'

When the first of the police cars came down the road, Fisk waited for them beside the maypole, the boy in his arms.

CHAPTER NINETEEN

I

JOANNE STUDIED THE faces arrayed before her, the students cross-legged on the carpet. *Too young for this.* 'I have a very sad announcement to make,' she said slowly. She paused, her hands folded in front of her, standing with the desk's edge pressing against the back of her thighs. The news had come that morning, a call from the police. A tragic accident. An old man charged with manslaughter. There was no bringing the boy back, but she sensed in this many levels of justice, ending with, of course, God's own.

They had decided that there'd be no assembly, that each teacher would deal with his or her own class. Joanne knew that it was the students seated in front of her who would be the most affected.

'Roland Fraser died yesterday.' She looked at Owen, saw him go very still, the blood draining from his face. 'A tragic accident. And I share your sense of loss, and your pain. I think it's important to talk about it, to get your feelings out, to share in your grief. As you can imagine, each teacher is talking with their own class – this is something everyone in this school must deal with. Of course, this class is special, because it was Roland's. I know that he had very close friends among you, and it's important that those others of you – who perhaps didn't know Roland as well as they did – that you come together now, and offer support.'

'How did he die?' Owen asked bluntly.

Joanne moved to the stool and sat down. 'Well, that's one of the things that needs to be talked about.' She glanced at Jennifer, who for once looked shaken. 'It seems Roland was involved in . . . some activities . . . yesterday. No one can understand his reasons for doing what he did, but he'd chosen a path that was hurtful, and, I guess, mean. He went to a mink farm and freed the animals. The man who owned the farm caught him.' She scanned the faces again, and was surprised to find Owen's attention not on her, but on Lynk, who sat with his arms wrapped around his bent legs, his eyes dull, clearly in shock. 'Evidently, Roland had a heart condition, and it's believed to have contributed to his death. I realise how terrible this sounds, but we should all think about this. We should think about choosing the wrong paths in life. You have so many choices ahead of you, after all. And together, we can direct those choices, into positive, helpful directions.' She looked down at her hands. 'As Roland's teacher, I feel now that I failed him, in some way.' She looked up again, at Jennifer, Barb, Owen and Lynk, each in turn. 'Just as I'm sure some of you feel. Well, it's all right, it's perfectly understandable. But it's important to realise that we're not perfect, that sometimes we miss the signs—'

'What signs?' Owen asked.

'Owen, I don't see the value in your constantly interrupting me—'

'There weren't any signs.'

'Owen, please—'

He turned to Lynk. 'Why did he go to Fisk's, Lynk?'

Lynk seemed to shrink inside himself.

'Because he told Roland,' Jennifer said. 'He told me he told Roland. That's what you meant yesterday, wasn't it? You let the mink go. Didn't you?'

'Listen!' Joanne said, raising her voice. 'I expect you to control—'

'He was going to explain things,' Owen said, now on his feet. 'That's what he'd do—'

'Miss Rhide!' Lynk called shrilly. 'Get him away! Tell him to stop – can't blame me, it's not my fault! Send him to the office!' He scrambled to his feet and edged closer to Joanne, his eyes wide as he stared at Owen. 'You screwed everything up! It's not my fault – it's yours. I forgot about . . . about what my dad heard, about his sick heart – and he never said, did he? How were we supposed to guess?'

Joanne rose. 'Everyone, please!' Other classes were looking their way. Mr Lyle took a few steps in their direction. *I can control this. I don't know what's happening, but I can control this.* 'Quiet down, right now!'

Though she shouted, neither Owen nor Lynk seemed to hear. They simply kept staring at each other, in a way that sent a chill through her. She saw Jennifer watching, too, holding herself silent and motionless as if tethered down.

'You fucked everything up,' Lynk said.

There were gasps. Joanne stepped towards him. 'Lynk Bescher! What's . . . what's—'

'It's not my fault! You're lying, Owen! You're just one big fuck-in' liar! There's nothing there!'

'For God's sakes!' Joanne shouted. 'Be quiet!'

She saw George Lyle moving quickly towards the office, his pale face filled with alarm. 'It's all right,' she called to him, knowing how shrill she sounded and hating it. To her shock, he ignored her. *You can't do this! It's my class – you can't do this to me!*

'She's on my side,' Lynk said to Owen.

What?

'It's just you now, isn't it? I win. I win. No one believes you any more. I win—'

'Lynk?' Joanne asked softly. 'What on earth is going on?'

He grinned. 'Nothing. All he does is lie. About everything. It's not his fault, though. He can't help it. None of us can. You have to help him like you did me. I know what's real now. Nothing's wrong. You should take him away, though. He's gonna beat me up. Kick me in the balls. He's already beaten me up. Twice. And Jennifer hit me with a dog leash yesterday. They keep beating me up, the two of them, because I know everything – I copped her, Owen. You were going together, and I copped her tits. She begged for more—'

Jennifer rushed Lynk, but Joanne pushed the boy behind her and threw out a hand. It caught the girl high on her chest – Joanne's fingers jabbing her in the throat. The girl's feet went out from under her and she fell, landing on another student, who shouted in pain.

Joanne glared down at Jennifer. 'Don't you touch him,' she rasped.

She saw Barry hurrying towards her class. *Thank God.*

'Joanne!' he said. 'Step away from those kids. Right now!'

II

Jennifer sat up, still slightly winded and feeling the sting of the scrapes on her neck from Rhide's fingernails. She heard Principal Thompson's words, but her attention was now on Owen. He was staring down at her, not a single thing alive in his expression.

'He's lying,' Jennifer said.

Thompson took Rhide by the arm and escorted her to one side. Rhide started talking, fast, her tone defensive. Jennifer saw Thompson nod, his shoulders dropping. *Bitch. She's saving her own skin. Roland's dead. I wish I knew what Lynk and Owen were talking about. Something else. Something terrible.*

'Jennifer,' Thompson said. 'You'll come with me. And you too, Owen. Both of you—'

Owen bolted.

'Come back here right now!' Thompson's voice was a bellow. Everyone was watching, watching as Owen – ignoring the command – raced out of the open-room.

And then, to Jennifer's surprise, she saw someone

following him. *The four, the four of them. They know something. Shit, what's going on?*

'On your feet, Jennifer.' Thompson reached down and took her arm in a firm, painful grip. He pulled her upright. She saw Lynk, behind Rhide again, looking not triumphant, but more like an animal, cornered, nowhere to run.

'Call Dr Roulston,' Jennifer said.

'Let's go,' he growled, pulling her along.

'And my mother. I'm getting the fuck out of here.'

'This is a school matter. A problem in discipline. I'll decide who to call.'

They left the open-room.

Jennifer said, 'I'm leaving—'

'Like hell you are. I don't give a shit who you let feel your tits, but attacking another student – in class – I care about that—'

'So expel me. Kick me out.'

'Shut up.'

They reached the secretary's office. Thompson directed her inside. Mrs Reynolds and George Lyle stood by the desk. George looked a question at Thompson upon seeing Jennifer.

'You can go back to class now, George,' Thompson said. He released his grip on Jennifer's arm but put his other hand against her back, pushing her towards the conference room door.

'Is that necessary?' George asked.

Thompson stopped and faced the man. She could see the principal was shaking with rage, and felt frightened for the first time. 'Didn't you hear me?'

Lyle hesitated.

'Now,' Thompson said.

'Please,' Jennifer said to Lyle.

The teacher's eyes flicked to her, then back to Thompson. 'I'd like a word with you first. In private.'

'Later. I'm busy. Get along now, George, before something irrevocable happens.'

She saw the teacher's dark eyes harden. *Not just with us kids, Barry. He's lost his temper with you now. Look out.*

'Very well,' he said quietly, 'if that's how you want it. I don't give a shit what your lover's told you. In fact, I'm suggesting that you've lost your objectivity here. I heard enough out there to know there's a lot more going on than just a simple fight. So, before you judge and execute the wrong people, why don't we exercise some professional restraint here and get to the bottom of this.'

Thompson's face was white. His hand, where it pressed Jennifer's back, was hot and wet. 'Pack up, George,' the principal said, 'you're out.'

'This is going to come out,' Lyle said. 'Everything. You thought the last scandal was bad. I think your head will roll this time.'

Mrs Reynolds cleared her throat and Thompson looked at her. She said, 'I think we should let everything calm down. Emotions are a little high right now. A thirteen-year-old boy – one of our students – has just been killed. It seems we're quickly losing track of what's important here. Everyone's in shock, given the circumstance of Roland's death. We need to sit back and let things settle.'

Thompson drew a deep breath, removing his hand and leaving a palm-sized sweat stain on Jennifer's shirt.

'Wise counsel, Jill.' He turned to Lyle. 'I was hasty, George. Two of Joanne's students just left the school. We're responsible for them, and I don't know where the hell they've gone. It's a goddamned nightmare.'

'I can go look,' Lyle said. 'I'm sure Joanne could use your presence in the class beside hers. All the kids could.'

'Good idea.' He held out his hand.

Lyle shook it then turned to Jennifer. 'Can you promise not to cause a scene in class, Jennifer? It's important, no matter what Lynk might say to you, that you show restraint. It's important not just for Miss Rhide and the other students, but for you, as well. I think you can manage.' He smiled. 'I'm not convinced about Lynk, but that's Miss Rhide's concern—'

'He's a liar and a fake,' Jennifer said.

Lyle nodded. 'His "blossoming" is a little suspect, but that's neither here nor there, is it? Can you handle this?'

Jennifer shrugged. 'Sure. I guess.'

'I knew you could.'

'All right,' Thompson said to her. 'Let's head back.'

Mrs Reynolds said, 'She'd better see the nurse first – those scratches on her neck need tending to.'

III

'It doesn't make sense,' Sten kept saying, motionless on the sofa.

Elouise poured tea for herself, Sten and Dr Roulston, then sat down beside her husband. She noted the doctor raised his eyebrows at that.

Sten looked up. 'You see, Doctor, they hated me. They had to. Nothing else makes sense.'

'It's a remarkable story,' Roulston said. 'But not unique. There's clearly a powerful bond between you and your dogs, and there's precedent all through history for that kind of relationship.'

'The oldest partnership of all,' Sten said, nodding.

'You're probably right—'

'Of course I am. Unless you count fleas, but they're notoriously fickle.'

Roulston smiled. 'Has this changed you, Sten? Or am I witness to more games here?'

'You tell me. I'm sober. I've been sober for weeks. Even the dry drunks are gone.'

'Do you trust yourself?'

'Hell, no,' he said.

'And you, Elouise?' the doctor asked. 'How do you feel? Do you trust that your husband's on the road to recovery?'

'I'm not sure,' she said. 'I want to, of course. But, well, hope's a little slower to arrive these days. There's a group, meeting at the church. It's for people with alcoholics in their family. I'm thinking I might go. Maybe I can get Jennifer to come, too.'

Sten scowled. 'Why? I'm cured. I did it myself.'

'There's no cure,' Roulston said. 'Don't fool yourself. The sickness doesn't go away.'

'I don't want to drink any more,' Sten said.

'That's a start, Mr Louper. That's all it is.'

Roulston began talking about AA, and Sten seemed to be listening. Elouise closed her eyes and sipped tea. *It's almost time. The thaw's come so quickly. I'll have to get to work. All the weeding, digging air into the earth.* She'd need to buy fertiliser – they had no compost this year, but what had rotted in the garden would help. She'd have to rake up the old crab-apples as well, and check on last summer's growth. Some cutting back might be needed, something she should've done in the fall. It'd be like starting all over again, in her garden. *The thaw's come so quickly. So unexpected. May be a long growing season ahead. We'll see, I suppose.*

IV

I ran across the highway, my only thought being to get away, to escape. Old Man Fisk killed him. Lynk freed the mink – it had to be him, so that made him responsible. *He's won, like he said. He's won.*

I reached the road, then heard footsteps behind me. I wheeled, expecting to see Jennifer, but it was Carl. He stopped, ten feet back, his runners sinking into the mud of the shoulder. 'What do you want?' I demanded.

He shrugged. 'I'm going with you,' he said.

'Where?'

'Where you're going.'

'Where the hell's that?' I had no place in mind, nowhere I wanted to go. Just away. But Carl obviously thought otherwise.

'He says it never existed,' Carl said. 'He's lying.'

My laugh sounded harsh. 'What? The body? Who the fuck cares? Roland's dead, and Lynk and Jennifer—' I stopped.

'He lied,' Carl said.

'No he didn't.' I turned away. 'I saw it in her face.'

He came up beside me. 'It's all, uh, all about the body, Owen.'

'What is?'

'Everything. Don't you see?'

I grunted. 'No.'

'For Lynk it is.'

I continued walking, not wanting him beside me, wanting to be alone.

But Carl wouldn't leave, and he wouldn't shut up. 'He's been weird, nuts. Ever since we found it. He was always an asshole, but not like this—'

'That's because of me,' I said. 'I was the only one who didn't kiss his ass. Me and Roland. He could push you around all he wanted to. He still can, and you just take it. What's your problem, anyway?'

He shrugged, looking down at the ground, his hands in the pockets of those ugly navy blue corduroy pants.

We came opposite the overgrown lot. There was a new FOR SALE sign on it, and a placard reading SOLD had been pasted across it. *There'll be a house there. Soon. It's all disappearing. Lynk won.*

'Lynk,' Carl said, 'he's the same as Rhide. And Thompson, and all the others. You were different. So was Roland. But you're not the same any more. All you care about is Jennifer, and not being noticed in school. Remember Pussy Galore? When you said that, Rhide looked completely fucked. Do you remember?'

'Stop talking about me. You don't know shit about me.'

He fell silent.

I wanted him to leave. 'I'm not going,' I said.

'Yes you are. But you don't want me to come.'

'Fine. So get lost.'

'No. I was there, too. It's not just yours.'

'All you did was bawl your eyes out. Me and Roland, we looked.'

'It's mine, too. It's more mine than—' He shut up, looking away.

'What the fuck does that mean?'

'Nothing. It's mine, too.'

'I'm not going there!'

He said nothing, but there was a stubborn set to his mouth.

Why'd you let him do it, Jennifer? You hated him. Why did you do that to me?

We came to the bend in the road. To our left was the track leading into the Yacht Club. To the right, thirty paces along the bottom road, was my driveway. I stopped, glaring at Carl. He wouldn't meet my eyes, but I could see he was about to cry.

'You have to,' he said.

'Why?' I demanded, exasperated and confused. The possibility had long since occurred to me. The lodge had grown. Maybe the body didn't have to have moved to disappear.

I didn't want to go. It didn't make any difference. Roland was dead. Jennifer had betrayed me and we were over with. Everything had fallen apart. 'Why the fuck do I have to?'

'Because of Lynk, that's why. We got to show him – and everyone else.'

I stared at him. All the Carls of this world, in every class. Roland asked me to protect him. I didn't want to. *I still don't.* There were too many Carls. Way too many. They live, they grow up, they disappear, not

even shadows in people's memories. Just . . . gone.
Like the body. Like how Lynk wanted it.

*I'm a Carl. I was. I might be again. Rhide wants me
like that. She wants a world full of Carls – lost, silent,
needing to be cared for, spoken for, explained away
and described and defined until no one asks anything,
no one does anything. No one counts. Like the body,
faceless, unknown, no longer the beast, the giant living
inside me – inside all of us. Gone, vanished, forgotten.*

I thought I understood something then. About Carl,
about all of us, but about him the most. The man
who'd drowned – no one came looking for him. No
one cared. He was a nothing, in life and in death. He
was the boy standing in front of me.

'I don't care,' I said. 'Not about you.'

He seemed to collapse inside.

'For Roland,' I said, watching the hope creep back
into his eyes as I continued, 'and because of Lynk –
and everyone else – what you said about them. Come
on, then.'

We went in silence, cutting across the Yacht Club
grounds, heading into the snow-patched wood lining
the river. I tried to think of Carl as only a witness, of
no more value to me than that. I wasn't responsible
for him. I didn't want a pet.

We arrived. The pile of chewed sticks and saplings
and mud was still encrusted with ice. The lodge looked
huge, and of course the body was nowhere in sight –
as gone as it had been the last time we'd come here.
Vanished. I stared down at the mound, a helpless feeling sweeping over me. 'We could dig, I guess.'

Carl shook his head. 'No. He's under, on this side.'
He pointed. 'Right there.'

'How do you know?'

'I came back. I kept coming back. All summer. I saw him when he was just bones, and the beavers started building over him. He's there, right there.'

I went closer and crouched down. There was a runway of slick mud, leading from this side of the lodge down to the water. Webbed tracks marked its grey-brown surface. I got down on my hands and knees and looked into the narrow tunnel leading inside. 'Shit,' I said. It was dark in there, and would be a tight squeeze.

Despite what Carl had said, I still didn't think I'd find anything. *He kept coming back. Alone. Christ, he was right. It belongs more to him than to us. But I guess that's how it should be.*

I lay down on my stomach, trying to pierce the tunnel's gloom. Would I meet a beaver in there? What would it do? Attack, if I cornered it.

Carl seemed to read my mind. 'They have an escape route,' he said. 'Other side.'

Even so, I was scared. I hesitated a moment longer. *Having a witness is a pain in the ass.* Then I wormed my way into the tunnel.

The clay was cold, soft and slightly yielding under my hands. I could smell a musty presence – wet fur? – and the air was surprisingly chilly. I wished for some matches, a lighter, a flashlight. I couldn't see a thing after a few feet, the tunnel narrowing, branches closing in on all sides. I felt a moment of panic but pushed it down. My feet were still clear, still visible to Carl. I had to keep going.

Something moved in the darkness ahead. I stared, made out two eyes level with mine. They moved away. A muskrat, or a baby beaver.

Faint splashes sounded outside. I heard Carl swear, then felt his hand on my ankle.

'They're gone!' he said. 'Into the river!'

I resumed crawling, snaking forward. When I'd gone twice my length, I saw, a few feet ahead, a widening of the tunnel. Faint light seeped down – my eyes had adjusted, and I found I could make out vague shapes. I twisted my head, looking around. But nothing – no bones anywhere. No proof.

Carl spoke again, his voice muffled and sounding far away. 'In the clay,' he said. 'Check under you.'

I couldn't push myself up – there were branches jabbing down into my back – so I moved forward, towards the cave-like space ahead. The smell was very strong now, acrid and almost overwhelming. I clambered into the cave and slowly worked my way around. *Under me. In the clay. Fuck, I've crawled right over him.* I ran my fingertips back along the tunnel. All smooth, except for the tracks. My fingers probed further. They found something long and straight. I clawed at it, and wood splintered under my nails. *This is useless.*

Then my fingers brushed over a slight ridge, a ripple that felt harder than the surrounding clay. I followed it and found that it described a rough circle. There was another one right beside it, and an indentation in between and slightly below. I'd found the face.

I dug into the clay, scratching around the bone, working all sides, climbing closer in order to dig deeper. The clay was hard-packed, solid and ice-cold. My fingers went numb, but still I clawed.

'Owen?'

'I have it!' I shouted, wincing as my voice came back at me from all sides. I reached a level of entwined sticks, most of them breaking when I twisted them. I realised I could've used one of the sticks all around me to dig and swore at my own stupidity. With one of the ones I'd broken off, I resumed digging.

The face, the skull, the upper teeth, but no lower jaw. Near by I found a long bone which had lain flat in the tunnel, and was worn smooth by the passage of oiled, furred bodies. I dug it free. I kept looking, but found nothing else. It was time to go.

I had to push the skull in front of me as I snaked along. Ahead there was light, and the sight of Carl's muddy sneakers.

The day's light and warm air felt wonderful. I clambered clear, the skull tucked in one arm, the long bone in my other hand, drawing in deep breaths of fresh, clean air. I sat down on a log, wiping the clay from my face.

'Listen,' I said. 'You got to promise something.'

'What?'

'We say we found just these bones, from the very beginning. And in the brush, not here. That's all we say.' I turned the skull in my hands. There were fillings in all the back teeth that were still in place. The skull was filled with hard-packed clay.

'Okay,' Carl said, sitting down beside me.

'I don't want them tearing up the beaver lodge,' I explained.

He nodded.

'Fuck,' I sighed, looking out over the river. The ice had broken, piled up, and was jammed in place. Nothing moved, no sign of the water rolling past underneath.

'I think I know who he was,' Carl said.

'What?'

'A guy fell off a trestle bridge, in the city. Last spring. I read it. I checked the newspapers – we got a stack of them in the basement. I don't think they ever found the body.'

'We did,' I said slowly.

'Yeah. Maybe.'

'Now what?'

Carl grinned, showing his yellow, coated teeth. 'Show'n'tell?'

I wrapped the skull and the long bone inside my jean jacket. We didn't say anything all the way back to school. I thought about Roland, about when I'd last seen him. *He'll never change. Not from that time. Not for me, not for anyone.* I remembered him, solid, quiet, his slow, even voice. Like a piece of the earth. He'd seen his own face on the body. But he'd been wrong. I remembered Roland's face exactly. I knew I would always remember it.

We could now put names on things, we'd come to that time. All the faces. Fisk's – a wintry mask of hate for four boys. Walter Gribbs – old and frightened and full of stories, stories that went with him when he died. He'd always have them, there, in every wrinkled line.

I was waiting for Lynk's face, for what I'd see when everything collapsed, fell away. I thought of Carl, walking beside me. He seemed unchanged, in some ways more solid than Roland, but I still shied from thinking about him too hard, too deeply. I wanted to believe there was a difference between us.

We arrived at the doors. Carl looked at me. I shrugged. He reached up and pulled one of them open.

I saw myself in the dark glass, smeared with grey, drying mud, my jacket wrapped around something and pressed like a soccer ball against my stomach. And my own face. 'Christ,' I said, then stepped past the image, stepped inside, with Carl on my heels.

The hallway, with its rows of boot and coat racks, was otherwise empty. The heaters were on, blasting out hot, stale air. Carl moved ahead to the inner doors leading into the open-room. He looked back at me, an eager light in his eyes. 'Come on,' he said.

'You think this is going to be easy?' I asked him. My heart was pounding.

He shook his head. 'But you don't want Thompson showing up, do you?'

He was right. We heard a car's tyres outside and I turned.

'That's Lyle's,' Carl said.

'All right, all right. Let's get going.'

Carl opened the door. I marched in. No one really noticed us until we approached Rhide's class. She was perched on her stool and had everyone sitting on the carpet again. I saw Jennifer, red-eyed and looking dishevelled and with bandages on her neck, in her usual place at the back, Barb sitting close beside her. Lynk was sitting cross-legged almost at Rhide's feet, his head tilted up, watching her every move.

In the class beyond them was Principal Thompson. He was walking between the desks, while the kids sat writing on sheets of foolscap.

Rhide saw us first. Her eyes widened in alarm. Carl moved ahead of me and sat down behind Gary, who swung around to scowl at him. Gary looked up and met my eyes, then turned back to face Rhide.

I stopped beside Carl. 'Go ahead,' I told him. 'Pull his gotch right up over his fucking head.'

I don't think Rhide heard precisely what I said, because her surprised expression didn't change.

'Owen,' Jennifer said.

I looked over at her, still cradling my prize. I knew my eyes were cold and distant. I didn't want them that way, but I couldn't help it. I went to the front of the class.

'What is it, Owen?' Rhide asked, rising from the stool.

'Show and tell,' I said. 'Carl's idea.'

Lynk crabbed backwards as I approached, pushing against other kids, who parted for him uneasily.

Principal Thompson had finally noticed. He was on his way over, so I knew I had little time. I faced the class. 'Me and Roland and Carl,' I said. 'And Lynk. We found this last year—'

'He's lying!' Lynk shouted. 'Send him to the office. He's lying!'

I unwrapped the skull and set it down, on Rhide's stool. 'Carl maybe found out who he was. A guy from the city. Fell off a bridge and they never found the body. We did. It came down with the thaw last year. This is what's left.' I studied Jennifer's face. 'It was our secret. But Roland wanted to tell. He didn't want it to be a secret any more. And Lynk says it never existed. He's wrong. It's a man who drowned. And we found him. Me, Roland, Carl and Lynk.'

I turned to Rhide. 'I'm going. I'll be back tomorrow, but I'm going now.'

Principal Thompson was staring at the skull. 'I

think you'd better stay,' he said. 'The police will have questions.'

'Carl can answer them,' I said. 'I'm going.'

Jennifer got to her feet. 'Owen, please . . .'

I shrugged, retrieving my jean jacket. No one stopped me as I made my way out. Jennifer caught up at the doors. We went out into the hall, to find Mr Lyle standing there.

'Jennifer?' he asked.

'It's okay,' she said. 'Roland and Owen were best friends. He wants to go home.'

'All right, but—'

'I'll take him. All right?'

He hesitated, then nodded.

I turned to Jennifer, knowing how cold my eyes were, knowing, but unable to change them. 'I don't want you,' I said. 'I don't want anybody.'

I saw a change come over her face, I saw the colour leaving it like someone had pulled a plug under her heart. She opened her mouth to say something, then shut it again.

Lyle cleared his throat, laid a hand on Jennifer's shoulder. 'Come on,' he said quietly.

I pushed the doors aside and stepped out into the warm spring air.

V

The attic room still held winter's chill. My hands shook as I lit the candles on the desk and reached for my book. I tried to bury myself in the words I read, tried to sink down, away, out of sight, leaving not a ripple. But it was no good – the voice in my head wouldn't be silenced, no matter how much I hated it now, no matter how much I wanted to run from myself.

He was dead. He'd seemed as strong, as solid, as the earth itself.

The shaking spread up from my hands. I bent over in the chair, lowering myself down on to my thighs, my hands tucked under my chin. The trembling got worse, my teeth clacking, as I stared at the woodchip-snagged lumps of cotton on the floorboards under the desk.

I thought about the stranger, the one who'd once used this secret room, the one who'd sat here at this desk absorbing words and words and words, swelling, bloating and still devouring pieces of the world, until its face had become every face, and no face. The stranger, who was no more in anyone's mind but mine. And the stranger's secret, this room and all its books, nothing but food for the rats.

I'd tried so hard. Dragging the giant to the history in this room. Dragging this history to the giant on his bed of sticks. I'd thought it important, as if in remaking the world I'd find in my hands a gift. Of understanding, of feeling, of something other than this shivering solitude.

The skull had felt heavy in my hands, but that was only because of the river clay inside it. It hadn't seemed especially big. Just a man's skull, after all, and here, in this room, just a stranger's leavings – not enough clues to shape a history, to reshape a world. So much more was needed, and I didn't feel up to the task.

It's the histories that just vanish. Like that old woman's in Constantinople. Like Walter's, and Old Man Fisk's. It's the histories that stop almost before they've begun. Like Roland's, and the Boorman kid who'd died on the highway. They all sank away without a sound, reduced to a handful of words in some story.

I sat in the gloom of this secret room, like they now sat in my head. Each alone, as I was alone, each nothing more than a few rat-chewed pages in some tattered forgotten place where all the memories gathered dust. And I could do nothing for them. There wasn't enough left of me.

The phone was echoing through the floor. My lie of feeling sick was about to be revealed. There'd be footsteps on the stairs, a knock on my room's door. I didn't want the questions that would come, the soft looks of sympathy, the comfort of arms around me, the confusion in my mother's eyes – *something about a skull?*

I guess I wanted too much. All along. I wanted a normal life, a house and a yard, the same friends for more than just a single year at a time. I wanted a place where I belonged, a history that didn't always break. I wanted to stop being ashamed of a father who – no matter what he tried – couldn't earn enough money to keep his family in one place, and a mother who'd tried so hard making friends, only to leave them yet again, and again, until she'd stopped trying. I guess I just wanted to be sure – of something, anything. That's all. Just to be sure, just to feel that it was okay, just once, just one thing, one small thing.

Oh, Roland.

VI

It was the morning of the funeral. I woke to the sound of metal hammering, crashing, clanging on metal. One of the twins let out a wail from the front steps which quickly fell silent. Outside, the hammering continued, frenzied, wild.

I leapt out of bed and raced downstairs. I came to the porch, where Mother stood, smoking a cigarette, the twins flanking her. Their backs were to me. I stepped around them, to see my father with a two-handed wrench, in his t-shirt and jeans, wearing slippers. My father, almost unrecognisable as he swung the wrench at the machine, smashing pieces from it, huge dents in the cowling – which had mostly come away, revealing the insides.

Ignoring us, ignoring everything else, he swung the wrench into the machine, over and over again.

'Owen,' Mother said calmly. 'Take the twins inside.'

I saw the shock on their faces, the wonder and fear in their eyes. Heart thundering, I grabbed them by their shoulders, swung them around and propelled them through the doorway. I then turned back, to watch. A sickening memory washed over me. *The toaster.*

'Mom?'

She sighed, not looking down at me, eyes on her husband, on my father. 'It's been coming. For some time. Not the best of days today, Owen.'

'I know,' I said.

'Not enough. There's other news.'

'Oh.'

His hands were bright red, his hair hung in uncombed strands. He was impossibly thin and long-limbed, grunting and gasping as he destroyed his machine.

When he finally fell to his knees, the wrench clunking on the driveway, she took a step forward. But he shook his head and she stopped, her shoulders falling slightly. He looked up at me, his eyes red. 'I'm sorry, son.'

I shook my head.

'No, Owen. I'm sorry. It's the day for your . . . for you, I mean.'

Mother said, 'He means—'

'I know,' I said. *Today's for Roland. I know.*

'I'll get ready,' he said, climbing to his feet.

'Let's go inside,' Mother said, resting a hand on my shoulder. 'We'll talk.'

'Okay.'

The cemetery was old, a burial place for farmers. Trees boxed it in except for the gravel track that came down from the crossroads. Four section fields met here, all of them fallow, messy with yellow stubble and crusted slabs of ice. The fields reached out in every direction to distant trees, a raised rail track, farmhouses, barns and combines.

Crows crowded the leafless branches on all sides, all silent in the chill morning air. There was no wind and the grey sky seemed remote overhead. The air smelled of decaying leaves, a bitter taste of mud on the tongue.

The new gravestone with Roland's name on it was at the end of the family's row – another Fraser sunk into this earth. I stood, flanked by my parents, close enough to read the names and dates on the other stones. An older brother, an older sister, a baby girl. All the names, all the dates within the past ten years, left me confused, a little frightened. So many children had died.

The parson spoke on. I'd stopped listening to his words. God had no place here. The parson was just a stand-in, and it seemed as if the soft earth devoured his voice and everything attached to it. God wouldn't step into this scene for fear of sinking, leaving not a trace. God – if he existed at all – lived in a desert thousands of miles from here.

I looked around, at the barren trees, at the huddled black smears that were the silent crows. I looked over at the gravel track, and at all the cars and pickups lining the shoulders of the crossroads, their flanks splashed in mud. There was a graininess to every image my eyes found, as if I were looking out on the world through a thin layer of sand. It hurt to blink, it hurt as I jerked my head from one thing to the next.

The sky was like porcelain, and I had a sudden sense that everything was about to break overhead.

The people – all looking weighed down and tired – were huddled around the fresh mound. I looked down at the mud of the grave itself, the reddish clay that told me the river had once reached this far. I looked at the wreaths, then over at the black hearse, and finally at the man in black with the black-bound book in his white hands. I imagined he was holding a crow, wings spread out, reading nothing but unable to stop talking anyway, unable to let silence take over. The red wilted flower of his mouth moved to shape words. The sounds meant nothing to me, less than the whimpering of a lost dog.

There were so many familiar faces in the crowd, so many complete strangers. None looked very human. Teachers, kids from school, other farmers, lots of old people. And Roland's family – just the one boy left now, little Arnie, who looked so old he might have been a dwarf, with hands too big, a slowness to his gestures – moving the hair from his eyes, shifting weight from one leg to the other. *He's old enough. He's stood here before.*

Roland's father was squinting straight ahead, as if studying something beyond the line of trees, something on the western horizon, where bruised clouds squatted heavily against the flat line of the earth. Roland's mother – who had given Roland her hands and her solidity and her strength – stood straight-backed beside her tall, thin husband, one hand on Arnie's shoulder, her eyes holding on the parson with so much unblinking concentration I thought the droning man might burst into flame.

It was the wrong time for words but still the parson kept talking.

Roland liked it quiet. Everything quiet. He'd be scowling, a scowling face in the crowd. He'd rather listen to the water dripping from the cars. And then we'd talk about bears in the spring, coming down from the interlake, and we'd talk about how shooting them just broke the silence, shattered everything, ruined the whole season. Let the bears roam, leave them alone. Okay? Just leave them all alone.

And then we'd head through the woods, down to watch the river as its cold skin fell apart. We'd be on

the edge of summer, on the edge of our season of free-
dom, even though we knew it'd race past so swiftly –
almost unnoticed – until autumn reined us in. And the
bears sought caves to sleep in when the north winds
came down and browned the forest leaves. Not a shot
fired. Just free to live – it's all we ever asked, all we
ever wanted.

Jennifer and her parents stood across from me.
Sten still looked blue and shivering, as if he'd just
crawled out from the river. His hands made darting
motions, his hair hung in long greying strands over his
broad, lined forehead. His wife – Jennifer's mother –
stood with her eyes closed, as if straining to hear the
parson, her black-gloved hands folded around a small
black purse.

Jennifer was crying, quietly, just tears coming down
from her eyes in a steady stream, eyes that wouldn't
leave my face.

I wish you'd stop that now. You're embarrassing
him. We never cried. Except for Carl. There was noth-
ing that could make us cry. Not even the body. We
wouldn't have cried like your dad cried, there on the
ice. Or like Rhide, sitting there at her desk looking at
my notebook, looking at my dragons. Don't you see,
Jennifer? We never cry ourselves. We let others do that
for us. You should be like us, like how we were, like
how we still are, like how we'll always be. Me, Lynk
and Roland.

It doesn't matter that it's all over, Jennifer. So stop
crying now.

My eyes moved on, from one person to the next. I
saw Lynk, tucked in between his large, red-faced father
and his washed-out mother. The light that had once

glittered in his eyes had dimmed now, replaced by something dulled and knowing, and he wouldn't look my way, wouldn't look down at the grave, wouldn't look outside himself at all.

I showed him the skull. The way Roland would've done. Remember when he ran from Fisk? Remember that, Roland? I don't think he ever stopped, not from that point. Running, running wild, always running.

He was ready for summer's throne. He'd loosed the hounds. He'd scattered the mink and all Fisk could do was kill Roland. The wrong boy. *I get it now. That throne had been Roland's all along. But Lynk wanted it. And now it's his. No one standing in his way. Not even me. Lynk, the only one of us who didn't lose his way.*

Lynk looked stripped down, shrunken so far inside, his skin wrapped around the thinnest muscles, the frailest bones. His parents always bought him things, rewards for nothing, and I could sense it all around him, like barricades, behind which something inside Lynk starved and starved, and withered and would one day soon be gone.

I thought I sensed, then, how gauze-thin and fragile memories are, how they alone hold nothing up, not for long, not without fraying apart, not without letting everything fall, fly loose, race off into oblivion.

It was all I had left, and it wasn't – *will never be* – enough.

I felt you pass out of me, Roland. There in the secret room, where winter's air made the candles flicker. I felt your shaking passage, out and away from my life. You didn't even say goodbye.

The parson had finished. The crowd in its closeness

was fragmenting, drifting back. Men and women came, pulling children, to Roland's father and mother. They spoke quiet words, then, heads bowed, moved on, heading for their vehicles.

'Owen,' Dad murmured, his hand gripping my shoulder.

I nodded, and we joined the procession.

Standing in front of Roland's family, I found myself facing Arnie.

He gave a half-shrug that was Roland's. 'He liked you,' he said.

I nodded. 'You're just like him.'

'Have to be now, don't I?'

Our parents were saying things. I heard my mother say something about friendship. I didn't want to hear anything more.

I half reached out to Arnie, wanting to touch him, to give him – what? I had no idea. My hand fell back down. I saw Rhide in a gathering of teachers, her hands punctuating her words – too far away to hear. 'Watch out for Rhide, next year,' I said.

Arnie nodded.

'Watch out for all of them, Arnie. All the grown-ups. All of them.'

I was tapped on the shoulder. I nodded at Arnie again and then we were moving on, tugged on by the currents.

Jennifer stepped in front of me. She'd stopped crying, her hands buried deep in her coat pockets. 'Owen. Please?'

I felt something relent in me. 'Meet you outside my driveway?'

'When?'

'Half an hour?'

She sighed, looked down then up again. 'Okay.'

When the first car started up, one of the crows cawed sharply, and then the others joined in the chorus. I saw the parson glance over at the trees, his expression hard to read – maybe annoyed, maybe uncertain.

It was over. The sound of scolding followed us all back to where the vehicles waited. It was, I think, all we deserved.

VII

'I stopped him,' Jennifer said, watching Owen as he walked down the road. 'At first, well, it was like it used to be. Like with Roland and all the others. But then I realised I was different, that I wasn't the same any more. Because of you, and your mother, too, I guess. So I stopped it. I punched him in the nose. I'm sorry, I should've told you.'

Owen looked strange in his grey Sunday clothes. But there was a glow in his face, something like what she'd seen there a long time ago. It wasn't the same, though. It looked . . . harder, tempered, more resilient. She could see him thinking about what she'd said, but his words surprised her, took her breath away.

'We're moving,' he said. 'Back to the city. The gas station went bankrupt. I found out this morning.'

'Oh.' *Oh*. 'When?'

'At the end of school. We've found an apartment, near my old school.'

She wanted to cry, but smiled instead. 'I've got a good excuse for going into the city, then. Every weekend.

All summer. I can sleep over.' *Oh hell, who am I kidding?*

His answering smile broke something inside her. 'Sure,' he said. 'That sounds great. It'll be great.'

'Well . . . Forgive me, at least?'

He nodded. 'It's okay. I was just mad. It would've been better if you'd told me right away, that's all.'

'I know. I'm sorry.'

'Forget it.'

'Where are we going?'

He shrugged. 'I want to go down to the river. The Yacht Club. Where they launch the boats.'

'Okay. Hold up a sec.' She stopped and lit a cigarette. He watched her, of course, but with a sad expression on his face.

'You hooked me,' he said.

'Really?'

'Sort of. The word's vicarious.'

'Well, I didn't mean to.'

He laughed. 'Yes you did.'

They started walking again, and entered the club grounds, stepping past the newly posted NO TRESPASSING sign. There were no cars in the parking lot, no car in front of the mobile home.

'Reggie's not here,' Owen said, sounding relieved.

'Who's Reggie?'

'The new manager.'

They walked to the boat yards. All the yachts were still in dry-dock, covered in tarps. The concrete bed and the rail tracks were clear as they ran down to the water's edge, disappearing under the ice. They stood side by side.

'Do you believe in God, Owen?'

'No. I was sent to Sunday school a few years back. I only went once. That's how it was – is – with us. We try, every now and then. But that's all. Just *trying*.'

She wasn't sure what he meant. 'I hear Him sometimes,' she said. 'In music, and then I think, these days, He's angry. But then I realise, it's just me. He's not really there, it's just how I feel, how I am. And you know, sometimes it makes me feel *good*.'

He nodded.

'I don't want you to go. To leave me.'

He nodded again.

'I don't want to be alone again.'

'Me too.'

'What are we going to do, Owen?'

'I don't know.'

'Was I, was I good for you? You know, was I . . .' Her words fell away. She held her breath.

Owen's mouth quirked slightly. He looked at her, his eyes alive. 'The best thing in my life, Jennifer. The best.'

She slowly sighed.

'I keep expecting to see him.' His shoulders jumped in a helpless shrug.

'I know,' she said, pulling hard on the cigarette.

They resumed watching the broken river's endless grinding past.

Two crows stood at the very edge, dipping their beaks at something in the water. Jennifer gasped as Owen – seeing them – raised both hands into the air and charged down the slope.

Shrieking, the crows took to the air.

VIII

Two crows returning. The years sweep past under their wings. The clouds scud like motes before their eyes. Roll away these years. It is too late, too late to stop their driven flight.

Memory and thought, each a shadow of the other. Scatter them now, back into the present time, and let them descend like tears.

Once again I see the world beneath me, the brown worm of water, the forests and the cleared land. And the city beneath a mantle of steam and smoke, its air crowded with pigeons. But it's not the same. It's all changed, because it's the way of the world, the way of life itself. And wisdom itself is not the gift it seems. I fool no one in the end. No one.

The giant had a child's face. I knew that from the very beginning, I knew that from the moment I set him free. It's not the innocent who remake the world, after all.

So remember me in this season's quickening breath, when comes the thaw, the time for rebirth. Remember two crows, returning. Remember what they do to souls. The boy knows. He's always known.

Fly!

I wish to thank the many people without whose support (all those years ago) the writing of this novel would not have been possible, or would at the very least have been highly unlikely . . . From the Lundin family, my father and my brother; my wife, Clare Thomas, and our son Bowen, who together give meaning to my endeavours. I also wish to convey my gratitude to Susan Thomas and Peter Knowlson, David Thomas Sr, Harriet Thomas and David Thomas Jr, who each in turn took the wide-eyed Canuck in hand when it was most needed; friends new and old including Keith Addison, Pat Carroll and Mark Paxton-MacRae; for W. D. Valgardson and his advice of years ago that remains fresh in my mind to this day. I would also like to acknowledge my gratitude to the Manitoba Arts Council for their crucial support in the writing of this novel. And special thanks to my agent, Howard Morhaim, and to Simon Taylor and the great people at Transworld Publishers for giving this story new life. This was my first novel, and people said *'it's a bit long . . .'*